THE CASE AGAINST WILLIAM

Born and educated in Texas, Mark Gimenez attended law school at Notre Dame, Indiana, and practised with a large Dallas law firm. He has two sons.

MARK GIMENEZ

THE CASE AGAINST WILLIAM

SPHERE

First published in 2014 by Navarchus Press LLC
First published in Great Britain in 2016 by Sphere

2

Copyright © Mark Gimenez 2014

A CIP catalogue record for this book is available from the British Library.

ISBN 978-0-7515-6727-4

Typeset in Bembo MT by Hewer Text UK Ltd, Edinburgh
Printed and bound in Great Britain by Clays Ltd, St Ives plc

Papers used by Sphere are from well-managed forests and other responsible sources.

MIX
Paper from
responsible sources
FSC® C104740
www.fsc.org

Sphere
An imprint of
Little, Brown Book Group
Carmelite House
50 Victoria Embankment
London EC4Y 0DZ

An Hachette UK Company
www.hachette.co.uk

www.littlebrown.co.uk

'It's not whether you get knocked down;
it's whether you get up.'
– Vince Lombardi

Prologue

'Flex Right, X Right, three-twenty-four Train, Z Colorado on two hard—'

'Wait! What do I do?'

William looked at D'Quandrick Simmons, number eighty-eight, on the far side of the huddle staring back at his quarterback with wide eyes. D-Quan – his street name – stood six feet four inches tall, weighed two hundred fifteen pounds with 4 percent body fat, ran a 4.4-second forty-yard dash, and could go airborne to catch any ball thrown in his general vicinity. But he wasn't so good with the playbook. They were coming off a timeout, so William had time to explain the play to D-Quan. He pointed at the other receivers.

'Cowboy, he's lining up left and running a deep crossing route to freeze the free safety. Cuz is going in motion right – I'm hoping he takes the strong safety with him – then running a deep out. Outlaw's running a short out. You're slot left. I'm trying to iso you on the corner deep, so you're running a Train, hitch-and-go at fourteen—'

'Say *what*?'

William sighed. Every player – except him – suffered brain farts, moments in games when the pressure or the excitement or the exhaustion caused his brain to cease functioning for all intents and purposes. He just played on adrenaline and innate street skills. D-Quan was experiencing a brain fart. That, and he was a few fries short of a Happy Meal. William had learned that at times like this with D-Quan, it was best to keep it simple.

'Just run down the fucking field and catch the ball.'

D-Quan pounded his chest twice with his fist then fashioned goal posts with his thumbs and forefingers, his signature gesture.

'End zone, baby.'

They were huddled up on their own thirty-six-yard line in the center of the field of thick green turf in the bowl of the ninety-thousand-seat stadium. The tight space inside the huddle reeked with the scent of sweat and testosterone oozing from every pore on the eleven large male bodies. The five offensive linemen, white guys weighing in at over three hundred pounds each, stood bent over with their hands on their knees, panting like wild beasts, spitting saliva balls, and sucking oxygen, their massive bodies pushed to exhaustion from blocking equally massive defensive linemen for three hours in the ninety-degree heat of mid-October in Texas. Ty Walker, aka Cowboy, the tight end from Amarillo, spit tobacco juice through his facemask; he had grown up bull riding in rodeos, so a football game barely provided enough danger to get his blood pressure up. Ernie, the halfback from Houston, was cool and black and headed to the NFL; he just wanted to get out of his final college season with his knees intact. And the three wide receivers – Maurice Washington, aka Cuz, Demetrius Jones, aka Outlaw, and D-Quan – all tall and black and blazing fast with tattoos emblazoned down their long sinewy arms and dreadlocks hanging out the back of their helmets, stood with their hands on their hips and their 'hood expressions on their faces, as if questioning whether their white-boy quarterback could come through one more time.

He could.

William Tucker, number twelve, was the senior quarterback for the Texas Longhorns. He was six-five, two-thirty-five, and fast; he could throw, and he could run. He could have gone pro after his sophomore or junior years, but he wanted a national championship trophy sitting between the Heisman Trophy he had won last year as the top college football player in America and the one he would certainly win this year, the first back-to-back Heisman winner in forty years. They were undefeated, 8-0, and ranked number one in the nation. Oklahoma, their opponent that day, was also undefeated and ranked number two. The winner of this game – known as the Red River Rivalry and played in the Cotton Bowl in Dallas each year during the State Fair of Texas – would be the odds-on favorite to win the national championship. They were down four points with eight seconds left in the game. So far that season, they had won five times on dramatic fourth-quarter comebacks engineered by William Tucker. But his teammates still didn't believe in his destiny.

He did.

He was born to play football. Specifically, quarterback. He had the height to see over the defensive line, the hands to hold a pro-sized football as if it were a peewee league ball, and the arm to hurl the ball far downfield, a requirement in the pass-happy offensive schemes employed by the pros. And the pros were chomping at the bit for William Tucker. He was the prototype NFL quarterback: big enough to withstand the physical punishment pro quarterbacks suffered at the hands of three-hundred-pound defensive linemen, strong enough to stand in the pocket and make the throw, and fast enough to evade the rush when his protection broke down and turn a negative play into a positive play. He was big; he was strong; and he was fast. He was the best there ever was. He was on the cover of the current edition of *Sports Illustrated*.

In five months, he would go number one in the pro draft and sign a five-year, $100-million guaranteed contract with Dallas. Word was, the Cowboys were trading up to take him. William Tucker would be their franchise quarterback. He would make Big D forget Meredith, Staubach, and Aikman (the fans had already forgotten Romo). He was twenty-two years old; the dream that had first taken shape in his mind ten years before – 'I'm going to be the Cowboys quarterback,' he had said, as all twelve-year-old boys in Texas say – would come true. But he wanted a national championship to close out his college career, and Oklahoma stood in the way. He had to motivate his teammates for one more big play. Playing quarter-back was part athlete, part motivational speaker, part religious leader; he had to make them *believe*. He often felt like Moses – if Moses had played quarterback at the University of Texas at Austin. He stepped to the middle of the huddle and yelled over the crowd noise.

'Look around, guys. This is why we play game. This is why we play for the Texas Longhorns. Ninety thousand fans in those stands. Millions more watching on national TV. We win today, it's a straight shot to the national championship game. We lose, we're done. I don't know about you boys, but I didn't come up to Dallas to lose to a bunch of fucking Okies. And we're not going to lose. One play. One touchdown. We win. Now suck it up and kick some Okie ass!'

He stuck out a fist. The ten other players crowded close and placed their hands on top of his fist.

'On two hard. Ready – break!'

They broke the huddle and hurried to the line of scrimmage. The offensive linemen took their pass-blocking stances; a pass play was a given. William stayed back in the shotgun formation, flanked by Ernie on his left. He looked at the weak-side linebacker's feet – his left foot was forward; he was blitzing. William motioned Ernie over to his right side. He then focused on the middle of the defense; he stepped close to his center and slapped his wide butt.

'Fifty-five's the Mike!'

His offensive linemen had to account for the middle linebacker – the 'Mike' in football jargon – otherwise, the two-hundred-sixty-pound Mike would crash through the line and be all over William before the play had time to develop. Game over.

'Fifty-five's the Mike!'

The center called out the blocking scheme to each side of the line – 'Scram! Scram!' – and William bounced back to his position five yards behind the center. Cuz was spread left, D-Quan in the slot outside Cowboy, and Outlaw wide right. He scanned the defensive secondary. Who would cover D-Quan? He yelled the signals.

'Omaha!'

That meant they were going with the play he had called in the huddle.

'Set!'

Cuz took a step back and came in motion across the offensive formation. The strong safety paralleled him across the defensive formation. Which meant the strong-side linebacker would follow Cowboy on the deep crossing route. The corner stepped in closer to D-Quan, leaving the sideline open. He would cover man-to-man with free safety help over the top. The free safety took a step toward the sideline to protect deep, but Cowboy crossing in front of him would distract him. At the speed the game was played today, one split-second of distraction was all William needed.

'Green eighteen, green eighteen! Forty-three! Hut, *hut*!'

The center snapped the ball back to him. The receivers exploded off the line of scrimmage like sprinters at the Olympics. The offensive linemen dug their cleats into the turf, grunted like feral hogs, and held the defensive line's surge to a standstill. The Mike dropped back into coverage. The weak-side linebacker blitzed, but Ernie cut his legs out; he flipped head over heels. William darted around them and drifted over to the right sideline as if he didn't know what to do – as if he didn't know exactly what he was going to do. He was luring the defensive backs to his side of the field and buying time for D-Quan working on the far side.

His favorite receiver wasn't going to graduate Phi Beta Kappa – in fact, he wasn't going to graduate at all – but he could sure as hell play football.

William didn't so much as glance D-Quan's way because the free safety was playing his eyes to see where he was going with the ball, but he knew that D-Quan had just hit the four-teen-yard marker, the point where all down-the-field pass plays break . . . he was *hitching* – chopping his feet and turning his upper body back to his quarterback with his hands raised as if expecting a pass – and praying that the cornerback jumped the route to intercept – and then *going* – spinning around and exploding down the sideline, hitting his max speed at the twenty-four-yard marker, going vertical up the field like a fucking rocket ship into space . . . and William knew D-Quan had left the corner in his wake when the free safety turned his body hard, ducked his head, and broke into an all-out sprint to cut D-Quan off at the fifty-four-yard marker – the goal line. But he figured wrong. William wasn't going to throw to the fifty-four-yard marker; he was throwing to the sixty-four-yard marker – to the pylon at the back corner of the end zone.

An American football field is one hundred twenty yards long, including the two end zones, and fifty-three and one-third yards wide. The line of scrimmage was UT's own forty-six-yard line. William now arrived at the right sideline of his forty-yard line; D-Quan raced down the left sideline. A pass from William's position all the way across the field to the back pylon in the end zone would require the ball travel eighty-three yards in the air. A football is a pointed prolate spheroid eleven inches long with a twenty-two-inch circumference at its midpoint; it weighs almost one pound. But it's not like throwing a one-pound rock. A football is designed to spiral at approximately six hundred revolutions per minute when thrown, thus creating an aerodynamic reduction in air drag; you can throw a spiral farther, faster, and more accurately. To throw a football eighty-three yards accurately, you must release it at exactly a forty-five-degree angle to the ground and at a velocity of exactly sixty-five miles per hour. Perhaps three quarterbacks in the country – college or pro – could make that throw, and only one with the season on the line. William Tucker planted his right foot, gripped the leather with his right hand, and in one powerful yet fluid movement raised the ball to his right ear, stepped forward with his left foot, rotated his upper body hard, and flung the football with his textbook throwing motion. The ball came off his hand cleanly, and he knew instantly that he had made the perfect throw. The ball flew in a tight spiral on a high arc, rising into the blue sky until it seemed to soar above the stadium . . . the stadium fell silent as ninety thousand fans held their collective breath . . . William's eyes dropped to the field . . . D-Quan's long legs crossed the five-yard-line . . . the free safety looked back for the ball . . . and realized his mistake . . . as D-Quan blew past him into the end zone ... and extended his hands ... into which the ball dropped.

Touchdown.

All across the state of Texas, Longhorn fans jumped for joy, screaming and shouting and spewing beer before their seventy-inch Vizios with the vicarious thrill of victory; all across the state of Oklahoma, Sooner fans fell to the floor, crying like babies and groaning with the vicarious agony of defeat. They lived and died their teams' wins and losses. Football in America. There was nothing else like it in the world. Teammates and coaches and cheerleaders and UT students stormed onto the field and mobbed William Tucker and the other players, whooping and hollering with their heroes as if they were victorious gladiators. Perhaps they were. Heroes and gladiators. Romans had bet on gladiators and Americans bet on football games. In Vegas, winners tallied their winnings and losers their losses, just as the TV network tallied its Nielsen ratings and commercial revenue and the athletic directors of the two universities their respective takes from the game. There was much money to be made from college football. For everyone except the players. They had to play college ball for free for at least two years; if they proved that they could play at that level, they were invited – via the NFL draft – to play for pay at the next level. The highest level of competitive football in America. The National Football League.

William Tucker had proven himself again that day. He was ready for the next level. His days of playing for free would soon be over. He would be a very rich young man. All his dreams would come true.

But that day was still a few months away. So he did not think about it. He had learned to stay in the present, to execute this play and not worry about the last play or the next play, and to never look ahead to the next game. So he reveled in the present. He threw his arms into the air and screamed. He turned in a circle in the center of the field and soaked up the fans' adoration, as if he had just saved the planet from a zombie invasion like in that movie. But he had achieved something far more admirable in America: he had won a big college football game. He embraced the moment – and two buxom blonde cheerleaders sidling close. One on either side, he leaned down and reached under their firm bottoms and lifted them into the air as if they weighed nothing. They sat in his arms and kissed his cheeks. Photographers snapped their picture, which would make every newspaper, cable sports channel, and sports blog in America tomorrow. To the victor go the spoils – and the girls. Oh, the girls. So many girls and so little time.

The life of a college football hero.

The big bass drums of the Longhorn marching band pounded like artillery explosions and reverberated through his body; the two girls clung tight, and he inhaled their scent like a narcotic that ignited his manly senses. They were intoxicating. The noise was deafening. The moment was all about William. He started to carry the two cheerleaders off the field when the on-the-field television crew pushed close with a camera. He figured the two girls might distract from his hero shot on national television, so he lowered them to the turf then faced the camera. Two state troopers stood guard in case a disappointed Oklahoma fan decided to take out his frustrations on William on national television. The female reporter stuck a microphone in his face and yelled over the chaos.

'William, unbelievable game. You threw for four touchdowns and ran for two more. You're a lock for the Heisman and on your way to the national championship. How do you feel?'

How do I feel?

Like every star athlete, William Tucker had suffered many such stupid questions; it came with the territory. Sports reporters were the guys – and girls – who couldn't make it as weather reporters. But he had been coached well by his media consultant. He swept his curly blond hair from his sweaty face and flashed his white teeth. He had given TV interviews since he was sixteen. As they say in Texas, this wasn't his first rodeo.

'I feel blessed. But it's not about me. It's about my coaches, my teammates, and our fans. They deserve all the credit. And the Good Lord.'

He looked up and pointed his index fingers to the sky, as if to thank God. As if God had made that throw. As if God could give a shit about a football game, particularly a college game.

'He gave us this great victory.'

Straight out of Interviews 101. It was corny, it was dumb, and it was a lie, but it's what the fans wanted to hear, it's what the networks wanted the stars to say after the game, and most importantly, it's the image sponsors wanted their athletes to project when endorsing their products, like tearing up during the national anthem before the game when the cameras were on you. Wholesome. Clean-cut. God bless America. On the field, it's all about winning; off the field, it's all about image. So William Tucker sealed the deal with his country-boy (even though he had grown up in Houston) 'aw shucks' smile for all of America then turned away and threw his arms around the student body – or at least the bodies of the two cheerleaders; but he heard the reporter's final words to the game announcer up in the booth and her national audience across the U.S. of A.

'You know, Kenny, I've met and interviewed a lot of star college football players over the last five seasons. To be quite honest, all too many are the kind of prima donna, I'm-entitled-to-everything, I've-got-the-world-on-a-leash kind of athletes we hate. Who we secretly hope fail. Who all too often end up in trouble with the law because they think they're above the law. William Tucker is not that kind of athlete. Not only is William Tucker the best college football player in America today, he is also one of the finest young men in collegiate sports today. He's a role model for boys all across America. He's the kind of young man every father hopes his daughter brings home. He's almost too good to be true.'

'Get dressed and get out.'

'William, I'm sorry, I'm just not comfortable having sex this fast.'

'Get out.' He grabbed his cell phone and started scrolling through the photos. 'I can have a sub here in five minutes.'

'We could date a while, get to know each other, then maybe—'

He laughed. '*Date?* I don't think so. Come on, hit the road, honey.'

'Will you call me?'

He laughed again. 'What world are you living in? I'm William Tucker.'

The team had arrived back in Austin at nine, and he was in bed with one of the buxom cheerleaders by ten. It was that easy. If you were William Tucker.

'Okay. I'll do it.'

He tossed the phone onto the recliner.

'Roll over.'

'Aren't you going to put on a condom?'

'You got AIDS?'

'No.'

'Then I don't need a condom.'

'But I'm not on the pill. What if I get pregnant?'

'You never heard of abortions?'

11

Dumb cheerleaders. He climbed on top of what's-her-name and started to push into her when someone banged hard on his dorm door.

'William Tucker!'

'Go away. I'm busy.'

'Police! Open the door!'

'Go – away!'

'If you don't open the door, we're gonna break it down!'

'If you don't go away, I'm gonna—'

The door broke off its hinges and crashed into the room. Four cops in uniforms stood in the doorway. Two pointed guns at William. He stood naked and regarded the cops as if they were water boys.

'You know who the hell I am?'

'William Tucker, you're under arrest.'

'*For what?*'

'Rape—'

He pointed at what's-her-name scrambling to cover her naked body.

'She's eighteen. I checked her school ID.'

'—and murder.'

Handcuffs held his thick arms tight behind his back. He had been arrested before – three times – and each time he had been quickly released once they had discovered who the hell he was. The handcuffs had come off, he had signed a few autographs and taken a few photos with star-struck cops, and he was out the door and on his merry way.

That's how life worked for William Tucker.

He fully expected this arrest would be no different. But when the cops opened the back door of the police cruiser and pulled him out, it was different. Cameras flashed and loud voices shouted at him. He squinted against the bright lights and saw that a media gauntlet had formed on the sidewalk leading into the Travis County Jail in downtown Austin. Nothing the media liked more than capturing a star athlete being hauled into jail in the middle of the night. His prior arrests had been for public intoxication, DUI, and solicitation; in Austin, such offenses merited only a brief and humorous mention in the sports pages. Just athletes being athletes.

But rape and murder – this arrest would be front-page news and the lead story on every cable and network newscast. William Tucker, another felon in a football helmet. His first instinct was to duck his head from the lights and turn away from the loud voices; but he recalled all the other star athletes he had seen on television walking the media gauntlet after being arrested – the 'perp walk,' as it had become known. They had hidden their faces and looked like disgraced athletes. Like guilty criminals. His media consultant had even used those video clips as training tools; she had repeated over and over that when – not if – he found himself in that situation – even though guilty, a status she had assumed – he was not to hide his face. He was to hold his head high. He was to look directly into the cameras. His face was to show the shock and his voice to express the righteous indignation – the outrage – of an innocent man being wrongfully accused by the American criminal justice system. Prepping for the perp walk was now basic media training for American athletes. And so, like an athlete who falls back on his natural ability in a pressure-packed game situation, William Tucker fell back on his media training as the two cops grasped his arms and escorted him on the perp walk.

'William, did you rape her?' a reporter shouted. 'Did you kill her?'

He pulled the cops to an abrupt stop and stared directly into the bright lights of the cameras. He tried to infuse his strong

13

masculine voice with just the right amount of outrage and righteous indignation.

'No. I didn't rape anyone. I didn't kill anyone. They arrested the wrong man. I'm innocent.'

His media consultant would be proud. She had said he was a natural in front of the cameras, said he would make a fortune in endorsements. The cops yanked his arms hard and pulled him inside the jail. The doors shut out the bright lights and loud voices. It was suddenly quiet. Faces peeked up at him and a few cell phones clicked photos as the cops led him down a corridor and into an interview room then pushed him down into a chair in front of a table. The younger cop cuffed William's left ankle to a steel ring embedded in the concrete floor then removed the cuffs from his hands. William rubbed his wrists to restart the blood flow.

'Get me a Gatorade,' he said to the younger cop. 'Orange.'

The cop gave him a look then shook his head and left the room. Like most star athletes, he viewed the police more as personal bodyguards than peace officers sworn to uphold the law. Their job was to serve and protect *him*, not uphold the law *against* him.

'What's his problem?' he said to the older cop.

'You beat Oklahoma this afternoon and get arrested for rape and murder the same night,' the older cop said. 'That's a fast fall, stud. By the way, that was a hell of a throw. Say, would you autograph a football for my son? You're his hero.'

'Drop dead. You know how much a football signed by William Tucker is worth?'

'I promise not to put it on eBay.'

'Like I haven't heard that before.'

The cop wasn't pleased. He slammed a landline phone down on the table in front of William.

'You got one phone call, William Tucker.'

14

William stared at the phone. It had never gone this far before. He had never been cuffed to the floor ring or given one phone call. By now he should be taking photos with grinning cops. He felt the first twinge of nervousness. He decided that the game situation required a different play. So he smiled, as if he were endorsing sneakers.

'All right, I'll sign some autographs and take some photos, okay? Then I need to get back to the dorm and sleep, get some rest, see the trainer tomorrow. Knee's acting up. We got another big game Saturday. I could probably get you some tickets.'

The cop did not smile back. His nametag read 'Sgt. Murphy.' He had gray hair and a big belly. He sat on the edge of the table and crossed his arms. He regarded William. His face turned fatherly, and he sighed as if William had just wrecked the family station wagon.

'Son, this ain't no joke. The star card ain't gonna get you out of jail this time. You're not charged with being drunk and rowdy on Sixth Street. You're charged with rape and murder.'

The smile left William's face.

'I didn't rape or murder anyone. This is a big mistake.'

'I don't think so, stud. They found your DNA on the victim.'

'What DNA? What victim?'

'Texas Tech cheerleader. You raped and murdered her two years ago here in Austin, same day you played a game against Tech. With that DNA evidence, you could spend the rest of your life in prison.'

'*Prison?*'

Something was terribly wrong.

'I can't go to prison – I've got a game Saturday. I've got to win the Heisman Trophy and the national championship. I've got to go number one in the pro draft, play for the Cowboys, win the Super Bowl. I'm William Tucker, star quarterback.'

'Not anymore. From now on, you're William Tucker, accused killer.'

At that moment, reality hit William with the force of a blitzing linebacker: this arrest was different. The cops weren't grinning. They weren't joking. They weren't bringing him Gatorade and treating him special. They weren't begging for photographs with him. All of which meant one thing: he was in serious trouble. Rape. Murder. DNA. Prison. That twinge of nervousness had escalated into a full-body anxiety attack. His respiration ramped; sweat beads popped on his forehead. He didn't know what to do. What play to call. Who to call. His media consultant? His quarterback coach? His mom? He leaned forward, put his elbows on the table, closed his eyes, and covered his face with his massive hands. For the first time in his life, William felt small.

'Oh, shit.'

When he opened his eyes, he was staring at the phone. He looked up at the cop. Even his voice sounded small.

'Who should I call?'

'Your lawyer.'

'I don't have a lawyer.'

The cop sighed. 'Most college kids, they're hauled in here for public intoxication. Girls, they call their mamas. Boys, they call their daddies.' He scratched his chin and grunted. 'Rape and murder, better call your dad.'

'My *dad*?'

William shook his head then again hid his face in his hands.

'My dad's a fucking loser.'

16

TEN YEARS BEFORE

Chapter 1

'You're the best dad in the whole world.'

Could a twelve-year-old boy understand what those words meant to a man? No. He could not. Only another man could. Another father.

'And you're the best son in the whole world,' Frank Tucker said.

That's the way it is for a father. Your son is part of you, but you thank God that he got only the good part of you and not the bad part of you. Not the nose or the ears or the acne. Because you don't look at your son and think, I want him to be me. You look at him and think, I want him to be better than me. That's a father's dream for his son.

Frank tossed the football back to his son. William was in sixth grade, but he was big for his age. He was tall and strong with broad shoulders and big bones. If he grew into his hands and feet – which already seemed man-sized – he'd be six-three, maybe six-four. He could already throw a football from the other side of the playscape to this side of the big oak tree. Thirty-five yards. Frank had paced off the distance. Rusty, their golden retriever, barked at William; he wanted in the

19

game. William took an imaginary snap from center then bounced to his right to evade Rusty as if the dog were a blitzing linebacker, set his feet, and fired the ball back. A perfect spiral. With velocity. The leather stung Frank's hands.

'I'm going to be the Dallas Cowboys' quarterback,' William said. 'I'm going to be a star.'

That was a boy's dream for himself. Every twelve-year-old boy dreams those kinds of dreams. Frank had dreamt of being a pro golfer, another Jack Nicklaus, but he couldn't make a putt to save his life – or win a match. So he had gone to law school. Plan B, as they say. He wondered if William Tucker would need a Plan B.

He threw the ball back to his son.

William caught the ball, rolled to his left, quickly set his feet, and rifled the ball to his dad as if he were running an out route. He had the coolest dad in his school. The other dads, they were rich businessmen and doctors and even lawyers like his dad, but they weren't famous criminal defense lawyers like his dad. Of course, he didn't help bad guys who hurt nice people. He only helped good guys the police thought were bad, but they weren't really bad. He proved they were really innocent. He said his clients were mostly white-collar defendants, although William never understood what the color of their shirt collars had to do with whether they were guilty or innocent.

'I want to be famous like you,' William said.

Dad threw the ball back.

'I'm not famous.'

'You're always in the paper.'

'Because my clients are famous.'

William rolled right then threw a fade left.

'Like the senator?'

'Yes. Like her.'

20

His dad was in some big trial up in Austin. He had come home for the weekend.

'Why do famous people call you?'

'Because they're in trouble.'

'Why?'

'Because they made mistakes. Or because the prosecutor thinks they made mistakes.'

'But they're not bad people?'

'No. My clients are innocent.'

'What if they're guilty?'

'Then they're not my clients.'

'What if they're rich and can pay you a lot of money?'

'They're still not my clients.'

'Are we rich?'

'We're comfortable.'

He sometimes said things like that instead of yes or no. That's how lawyers answer questions.

'We live in a big house in River Oaks,' William said.

'It's not big for River Oaks.'

Dad wore white collars, too, but he wasn't a criminal. He was wearing a white shirt and a colorful tie and his suit pants and smooth leather shoes and trying not to step in Rusty's poop that William was supposed to have already picked up. Dad had rolled the sleeves of his shirt up. He had just driven in from Austin and pulled the Expedition into the garage and saw William out back, so he had just started tossing the ball, not even changing into play clothes first. He was like that. Suits and stuff didn't matter to him, even when he sweated like now. He was pretty old, forty-five, but he didn't look that old, like the other boys' dads did, pale guys with pudgy bodies and bald heads. He looked manly, like an athlete. He worked out at his law firm's gym. He said he stayed in shape to keep up with his son. They ran the streets of River Oaks on weekends and played golf together at the club. And Dad

21

still had his hair. Other moms looked at him when he came up to the school to have lunch with William or to attend William's games. William felt proud that Frank Tucker was his dad.

'Dinner's ready!'

Becky called from the back door. William jogged over to his dad and held up an open hand; Dad slapped his hand. A high-five. Dad said William had high-fived since he was a baby. Now it was their personal bonding thing, like Dad always kissed Becky on her forehead. William was way too old for his dad to kiss him. They walked around the pool and into the house. Rusty followed them in. They lived in a big two-story house in a nice part of Houston called River Oaks. Most people would probably call it a mansion, but most of his classmates had bigger homes. Mom wanted a bigger house. Dad made a lot of money; he said Mom spent a lot of money. Sometimes William saw in his face that he wanted to say more to Mom, but he didn't.

'Just keeping the peace, William,' he always said.

Frank walked through the back door and into the kitchen to his wife and daughter and the aroma of Lupe's enchiladas. He had been away for five days, but his wife did not rush to him from the other side of the kitchen. She did not embrace him. She did not kiss him. She seldom looked at him anymore. She had always preferred that people look at her. Elizabeth was still the blonde beauty queen at the University of Texas.

'I missed you, Daddy.'

His daughter gave him a big hug. He squeezed her then kissed her forehead. She smelled fresh and fourteen; unlike William, who had taken to showering every other day or so, Becky bathed daily. She wore her cheerleader uniform. The varsity football team played that night.

'How was your week, honey?'

'We lost both games.'

Becky was an eighth-grader at the same private school William attended. She played on the volleyball team and cheered for the other teams. She was blonde and blue-eyed like her mother but taller, almost as tall as Frank. She was a pretty girl, but not a beauty queen like her mother; she had gotten too much of Frank for that. But she was athletic. And smart. Mature for her age. She seemed to be raising herself; all he had to do was pay her tuition and feed her. He always said that she had been born thirty years old.

'Sorry I missed them.'

He seldom did.

'Don't be. We're terrible. Daddy, can we go to the beach tomorrow?'

They had a beach house in Galveston just forty-five miles south of Houston. It was just a bungalow that sat right on the beach on the West End where there was no seawall. The next hurricane would wipe the small structure off its stilts, but Frank had gotten it at a good price: a client had paid him in kind, with a deed instead of cash. He and the kids and Rusty loved the beach; not so much Liz. The sea air made for too many bad hair days. Frank Tucker belonged on a beach. One day he would live on a beach, maybe when the kids were grown.

'We can't this weekend. William's got a game tomorrow, and I've got closing arguments on Monday. I'll have to drive back to Austin Sunday afternoon.'

'Will you make my games next week?'

'The case will go to the jury Monday morning. We won't get a verdict until Thursday or Friday at the earliest. But you never know with juries, so I'll have to stay in Austin. Sorry.'

'You know, Father' – when she addressed him as 'Father' instead of 'Daddy' he knew she had been thinking seriously about something – 'if I went to public school, I could play on a good team, maybe get noticed by colleges. With Title Nine, I could get a scholarship.'

'To play volleyball?'

'Unh-huh. Colleges have to give girls the same number of scholarships as boys. Boys get eighty-five football scholarships, thirteen for basketball, and eleven-point-seven for baseball.'

'Eleven-point-seven?'

'Football and basketball are head count sports, but not baseball. So they can divvy up the total scholarships, give half scholarships to the players. Anyway, that's a hundred nine-point-seven scholarships they have to give to girls, and we don't have a big sport like football. So girls get scholarships for basketball, softball, soccer, swimming, diving, track, tennis, golf, gymnastics, rowing, field hockey, rugby, equestrian, indoor and sand volleyball, and bowling.'

'*Bowling?*'

She nodded. 'They've got to match scholarships, and they won't cut football.'

'Good,' William said. ''Cause I want one of those football scholarships.'

The U.S. Congress decided in 1972 that college sports required intervention by the federal government; members of Congress were apparently not busy enough bungling national defense and screwing up the economy. Feminist groups complained that girls didn't have enough athletic opportunities in college. So Congress enacted a federal law that divvied up athletic scholarships between boys and girls. In order to comply with Title Nine, colleges must provide an equal number of athletic scholarships for boys and girls, even if the boys' sports made money and the girls' sports lost money. Hence, bowling for girls.

'So what about it, Father?' his daughter said.

'You've already got a scholarship.'

'I do?'

He nodded. 'It's called Daddy. Full tuition and room and board at the college of your choice.'

24

'Wellesley. It'll cost sixty thousand a year by the time I go to college.'

Frank blinked hard. 'You really think you could get a volleyball scholarship?'

Lupe, their maid, cook, and nanny, walked over and handed Frank a cold Heineken. She knew him well after ten years.

'*Gracias*,' he said.

Frank took a long swallow of the beer. He was not a drinker; he had never acquired a taste for wine or hard liquor. Back at UT, he had consumed his share of Lone Star beer; now his alcohol consumption consisted of one cold Heineken with Lupe's Mexican food, a Friday night tradition in the Tucker household. After a long week in court and a three-hour drive, the beer went down easily.

'Frank,' his wife said, 'tell Rebecca she needs to go shopping.'

He turned to his daughter. 'Go shopping.'

'No.'

He turned back to his wife. 'She doesn't want to go shopping.'

'She needs a new party dress for the fall social,' his wife said.

Liz took her place at the head of the table. They were going to the football game after dinner, but Liz was dressed as if she would be competing in the evening gown competition. She sat with perfect posture waiting to be served by Lupe.

'No, I don't, Mother. Because I'm not going to the fall social.'

'Yes, young lady, you are going.'

'Mother, it's October. Football season. I'm a cheerleader. I play volleyball. I don't have time for socials.'

'Make time.'

Becky gave Frank a pleading look. He turned his palms up at her mother.

'Liz—'

'She's going, Frank. And all the girls will be wearing new dresses. Do you want your daughter to feel embarrassed?'

'Let me think about that.'

'Daddy, I can't stand the boys at our school,' Becky said. 'They're all rich snobs. Why do I have to socialize with them?'

'Good question.' Frank turned back to his wife. 'Why does she have to socialize with rich snobs she doesn't like?'

'The same reason I have to socialize with rich snobs I don't like.'

'So she'll be written up in the society section?'

Becky laughed, but Liz did not appreciate his humor. Frank walked over to the sink and washed up. Lupe stood at the stove and filled plates with enchiladas, tacos, refried beans, and guacamole. She wore a colorful Mexican peasant dress.

'How's your boy, Lupe?'

She was thirty-five, a single mother with a four-year-old boy. He had been born with a heart defect; fortunately for little Juan, Houston was home to many renowned heart surgeons and his mother's employer had put her and her dependents on his health insurance plan.

'He's fine, Mr. Tucker.'

William grabbed a plate and sat at the table; he attacked the food. He ate like a horse these days and smelled like one. Puberty will do that to a boy. Frank took two plates and served his daughter and wife then went back for his plate. He returned to the table and sat across from the kids. The house had a formal dining room off the kitchen, but they always ate in the kitchen. It was comfortable. Informal.

'Did you wash your hands, William?' he asked.

Through a mouthful of food: 'Why?'

'Hygiene.'

'I'm a football player.'

Frank folded his hands and said, 'Prayer.'

His son froze with a taco halfway in his mouth while Frank said the Tucker family dinner prayer. Then his son resumed his assault on the defenseless taco. Frank turned to his wife.

'Nancy's son deployed to Iraq,' he said.

Nancy was his longtime secretary.

'Oh, that's neat,' Liz said.

'I doubt it.'

'I looked at a house in the nice part of River Oaks today,' she said.

'The *nice* part?'

River Oaks was the richest part of Houston. Old money. New money. Oil money. Inherited money. But most of all, money.

'I'm not moving,' William said.

'Me neither,' Becky said.

With his head still bent over his plate and without breaking stride shoveling food into his mouth, William stuck a fist out to her. She bumped her fist against his. A fist-bump, a bonding ritual of athletes. Only two years apart, they seemed more like twins. The same hair, the same eyes, the same features. They watched out for each other. They had lived their entire lives in this old house. It was fifty years old with a big yard, the pool, and tall oak trees on a large lot, room for Rusty to roam and the kids to play. They each had their own bedroom and bathroom, which kept the peace upstairs. Hers were always tidy; his looked like a locker room. The house was just under four thousand square feet, small by River Oaks standards, and Frank could easily afford a bigger place, but it was four times as big as the house he had grown up in in a working-class suburb of Houston. And the kids were happy there. But Liz wanted a bigger house. She always wanted more.

'It's on Inwood just off the boulevard' – the River Oaks Boulevard – 'a block from the club,' she said. 'Eight thousand square feet, six bedrooms, seven baths. And only five million.'

She said it with a straight face.

'Liz, what would we do with seven toilets and eight thousand square feet?'

'Entertain.'

'We do.' He turned to the kids. 'You guys entertained?'

They laughed. Rusty barked. Lupe muffled a giggle. Liz gave him that stern look that used to mean, 'No sex tonight.' But sex had ended long before. He had not sought sex from other sources; perhaps he was too afraid or too lazy or too Catholic. He didn't think she was cheating on him; that would be too scandalous in Houston high society. Instead of climbing the social ladder she would become the subject of social gossip. So they now slept in separate bedrooms; he told the kids his back made him toss and turn and wake their mother up. William had bought it; but he was only twelve. Frank suspected that Becky had not; but she went along with it. At fourteen, she was his deputy, working hard to keep the peace in River Oaks.

Which was not easy with her mother.

They had married eighteen years ago. He was twenty-seven and already practicing with a Houston firm; she was twenty-two and just graduated from UT, a pretty girl who wanted to be a star. She had planned on parlaying her looks into local television stardom and then jumping to the networks; it didn't pan out. At forty, she wanted to be a Houston society dame. Her Plan B. They had grown apart, as they say. In fact, they had married too young to know themselves and too soon to know each other. By the time they knew who they were and who they were not, they already had the kids. Frank had contemplated divorce, often, but Liz would get custody of the kids. Unless she was an alcoholic or drug addict, the mother could be dating an NFL team and she'd still get custody. He would be the every-other-weekend dad. He couldn't bear the thought of that life. So he stayed for the kids. For himself. He needed to be close to them. To live with them. To see them every day. To be a part of their lives.

Frank Tucker was a family man.

Chapter 2

The varsity quarterback threw a wounded duck, a pass that wobbled in the air like a shot fowl. The defensive back intercepted at the thirty-yard line and returned the ball for a touchdown. The home crowd groaned.

'A pick-six,' William said.

The Houston skyline illuminated the night sky to the east and seemed to loom large over the small stadium. River Oaks occupied the south bank of Buffalo Bayou just west of downtown. River Oaks was a part of Houston, but it seemed completely apart. A different world. A two-square-mile island of wealth and white people surrounded by the two million residents who called the sprawling 627-square-mile city of Houston home. Originally excluding minorities and Jews, River Oaks' real-estate prices now excluded only those without money. Fourteen hundred families called River Oaks home. The Tucker family lived in River Oaks because it was the mother's dream and close to the father's office. Instead of commuting the congested freeways of Houston an hour each way, Frank had two more hours each day with the kids.

It was eight that night, and his daughter stood on the

sideline with the other cheerleaders. His son sat on one side of him and his wife on the other, on the front row of the small bleachers among other affluent white people whose children attended the Academy. Since racial integration of the Houston public schools back in the seventies, it was a given that River Oaks parents would send their offspring to private schools. Frank sent his children to private school because his parents could not; he wanted more for his children.

The River Oaks parents and children in the stands looked like models from a Neiman Marcus catalog (there were no Nike sweat suits in these stands) and the parking lot like a Mercedes-Benz showroom (with a few Ferraris and Bentleys thrown in for variety). The Academy was a small private school in River Oaks teaching pre-K through high school; tuition cost $40,000 per year, more than public colleges in Texas. But graduates of the Academy did not go to college at a public university in Texas; they went to the Ivy League. The Academy had become a feeder school for Harvard, Yale, Princeton, Smith, and Wellesley. A few went west to Stanford or stayed home at Rice. None went to the University of Texas or Texas A&M.

'Hi, William.'

Two preteen girls who looked as if they had stepped out of a fashion shoot strolled by in front of them. They did not distract William from the game.

'Hey.'

They giggled as girls did. Frank nudged his son's shoulder.

'Already got the girls' eyes, huh?'

'Girls are lame, Dad.'

His son was handsome with angular features, blue eyes, and curly blond hair that fell onto his face. But he had not yet reached the age when girls graduated from lame to alluring. Sports interested him much more than girls. Which was a good thing at twelve. For the boy and his father.

30

The first twelve years of William Tucker's life had been easy for Frank Tucker. It was more like having a younger brother, teaching William all the manly things Frank knew – how to throw a baseball and swing a bat, pass and punt a football, swing a golf club – or rather, pay the club pro to teach him; Frank would never impose his golf swing on his son – and how to spit watermelon seeds. Frank's father had taught him how to roof and paint a house, use and repair a lawnmower, snake and unclog a sewer line, and fix and change a tire; that is, useful life skills. A man did not pay another man to do work he could do. But Frank was a lawyer not a plant worker so he hired out that work so he would have time to teach his son the less useful life skills.

It had been a fun twelve years with William in his life.

But Frank knew the next twelve years would be more challenging for father and son. His son would go through puberty; his body would transform seemingly overnight from boy to man. But his mind would not. Physical maturity would come soon and fast; mental maturity would come later and slower. Studies suggest that the part of a boy's brain that controls judgment does not fully develop until his mid-twenties. And that gap between mind and body – a body that could suddenly do what a man could do and a mind that still thought like a boy – could put his son's future in jeopardy. Throughout the history of man, testosterone and stupidity had never joined together to produce a good result. Frank wondered if he could protect his son from himself. He put an arm around his son's shoulder.

'You going to get the senator off, Frank?'

The dad sitting behind them leaned in; his breath evidenced his taste for expensive wine.

'Gag order, Sid.'

'I can't believe you're representing a Republican.'

Sid was a rich Democrat – Houston was a Democratic hold-out in the state of Texas – but his children attended this elite private school so they wouldn't have to sit next to the brown children of poor Democrats in the public schools.

'I'm representing an innocent person.'

'She's guilty of being a Republican.'

The other team kicked off. The Academy player fumbled the ball. The opponents recovered and scored on the next play.

'Wow,' William said. 'They're terrible.'

The team was terrible. But the boys were nice. The coaches were nice. The parents were nice. No one was disappointed in their play because no one expected them to win.

'We may not have scored in two years,' Sid said from behind, 'but ten of our students aced the SAT this year.'

The apparent purpose of public high schools in Texas was to produce the best football players in the country. And they did. Division I-A college football coaches from across America journeyed each fall to Texas to fill their rosters. They did not stop at the Academy. Athletics at the Academy were employed to build character and camaraderie among the student body, not to produce D-I athletes. And they did not. No student in the fifty-year history of the school had ever won a D-I athletic scholarship. The Academy was a top-ranked academic school, not a top-ranked athletic school. Consequently, every season was a losing season. This season was no exception. But the parents still came to the games, and the cheerleaders still cheered.

'Two bits, four bits,
Six bits, a dollar.
All for the Armadillos,
Stand up and holler.'

No one stood. The students were engrossed in their electronic devices, and their parents in conversation about politics and the stock market. Of course, it was hard to get fired up for a football team called the Armadillos. But Frank stood, threw his arms over his head as if to start a wave, and yelled, 'Go

'Dillos!' Becky laughed from the sideline then hid her face behind her pompoms. His wife glanced up at him as if he were insane. But then, she wore perfume to a football game.

'It's over on Inwood,' she said to the equally perfect mother sitting next to her. 'It's only eight thousand square feet, but we don't want something too big. Just enough room for a charity event.'

Frank and William were watching the game; she was climbing the social ladder. She had never been off-stage since her first beauty pageant in high school. She always looked perfect, sat perfect, stood perfect. Perfect clothes, perfect posture, perfect makeup, perfect hair. As if she were still competing for a crown. Perhaps she was.

'We want cozy.'

William heard. He turned to Frank, made a face, and mouthed, 'Cozy?'

Frank shrugged then held an open hand out to him. They high-fived.

Elizabeth Tucker saw the envy in her friend's eyes. The same envy that had once resided in her own eyes. She had grown up on the wrong side of Houston with nothing. She hated being poor. She always looked at the society section of the newspaper, at the parties and social events and the beautiful people, and wondered what their lives must be like. To have something in life. When she began driving, she would often cruise the streets of River Oaks in the old family car. One day, she had always said. One day.

One day had come.

She had caught her husband's look when she said, 'cozy.' He didn't understand her. She had grown up in a family of nobodies. She needed to be somebody. He apparently did not. He was almost famous, like a B-movie star, but he seemed not to care. He had no desire to become an A-lister in Houston. She burned with such desire.

To be somebody.

But he made the money she needed to be somebody. To live in River Oaks, on the right side of Houston, in a house worthy of somebody. To make the society section. To be envied by others.

William focused on the football field. His buddies spent the games chasing each other around the stadium, but he preferred to watch the games with his dad. Fact is, he'd rather be with his dad than with his buddies. Watching the games, running around River Oaks, playing golf at the club, having their man talks – they could talk about anything, he and his dad. His dad understood him. He knew what was inside him, in a way his mom and Becky could not. Of course, they were girls. He and Dad were guys. Dad said girls didn't understand guys, and guys didn't understand girls; that's why God gave guys cable TV with a hundred sports channels.

William groaned. The varsity quarterback threw another interception.

'He missed the read.'

William didn't just watch the games; he studied the games. Analyzed the plays, the alignments, the defenses, what worked and what didn't work. What he would do when he played on the varsity in four years. This year's varsity fumbled and stumbled their way to a losing 0-40 halftime score.

'When's the last time we won a game, Frank?' the dad behind them asked. 'Back in ninety-seven?'

'Ninety-eight,' his dad answered.

'That'll change when William's our quarterback.'

Chapter 3

'They ought to put William on varsity now,' the dad sitting next to Frank said. 'He's already better than the senior quarterback.'

'He'll be playing for the Aggies in six years,' another dad said.

'Like hell,' the first dad said. 'He'll play for the Longhorns. Right, Frank?'

'Maybe Harvard,' Frank said.

They both regarded him as they might a Chevrolet cruising down River Oaks Boulevard.

'*Harvard?*' they said in unison.

It was the next afternoon, and Frank was again sitting in the same stands at the same football field. William's middle-school team was playing another private school. The Academy's classes were small, so the sixth, seventh, and eighth graders played together on one team against larger private school teams comprised mostly of eighth graders. William's team was equally as bad as the varsity, but he was good. Very good. Abnormally good. William Tucker was a prodigy, like Mozart or Bobby Fischer. Except his gifts were physical in nature. He was a natural athlete. He excelled at all the sports – basketball, baseball, soccer, tennis, golf – but what he could do with a football – what he could do on a football field – defied explanation. He was not a normal twelve-year-old boy. He was bigger, stronger, and faster than the fourteen-year-old boys. He had thrown three perfect passes for touchdowns, but his receivers had dropped the balls. He had run for four touchdowns. And he was now running for a fifth.

Frank stood to watch his son.

William had dropped back to pass. The defensive team had converged on him, and a sack was imminent. But at the last second, he spun around and broke wide, leaving the would-be tacklers grasping air. He hit the sideline and turned on the speed. His feet were fast, his gait smooth and rhythmic. No one touched him.

Touchdown.

The other dads whooped and hollered. There is something about football. Frank did not know what it was because he was not afflicted with the football virus, odd for a man in Texas. He had played in high school, as most boys do, but he had never dreamed of a football career. He hadn't been big enough, strong enough, or fast enough. His son was more than enough, but Frank did not live or die his son's football. Most men, even men who were successful at the law or medicine or business, want their sons to be like Frank's son. A man's desire for his son to be a star football player transcends race, religion, and socio-economic status. Whether a poor uneducated black man in the Fourth Ward or a rich educated white man in River Oaks, he wants his son to be the star quarterback. He wants to bask in his son's glory. To watch him do football feats he could never do. Success on a football field is different than success in the courtroom or boardroom or operating room.

Football is manly.

Consequently, men stand in awe of football ability. You can work hard and become a competent lawyer or doctor or businessman; such success is the stuff of hard work, not the stuff of God-given genius. Football success also requires hard work; but no matter how hard you work, if you're not big, strong, and fast you will fail as a football player.

Hard work won't make you six-five, two-thirty-five, and fast.

Frank Tucker's life was not wrapped up in a leather ball. Or in his son's football heroics. He did not need his son to resolve his father's football failures. Or to make his father's dreams come true. But, like other men, he watched great athletes and wondered what it felt like to hit a home run to win the World Series or score a touchdown to win the Super Bowl or hit a four-iron stiff to win the Open. Few humans will ever experience that feeling. And those who will cannot explain it to those who won't. Consequently, Frank stood among a dozen other fathers, and like them, he watched his twelve-year-old son running down the field and wondered what it felt like to be William Tucker.

William Tucker felt like that lion in the film they had watched in natural science class. The lion had stalked an antelope then chased it across the African savannah, pounced on it, bit into its neck, and then ripped it apart. It was gross, sure, but it was exciting to see that lion let the beast out. Did the lion think about what it was doing? No. It was just doing what came naturally. He had watched the film and thought, *That's me. That's what I do on a football field. What comes naturally*. On the field, he let the beast out. And it felt good. Really. Really. Really. Good.

★

'Frank, I've got another client for you.'

The game had ended, and Brian Anderson had walked up. He was an IPO lawyer in a large Houston corporate firm. Three years before, when the dot-com bubble had burst, the Feds had brought securities fraud cases against insiders who had cashed out their stock before the crash. When the market goes up and investors get rich on paper profits, everyone's happy and the economy hums along; when the market goes down and investors' profits become losses, they are unhappy and the economy stumbles. In order to distract the people, the government puts people in prison. Brian referred his clients to Frank. They had been indicted on technicalities in the securities laws, traps for the unwary or politically unconnected. They were twenty-something whiz kids who had dreamt up the next big thing; they became political sacrifices in a capitalist society like pagans sacrificing lambs to the sun god. After a three-week trial, the jury acquitted them.

'Who?'

'CEO. Dumped his shares right before a bad quarterly report.'

'That's called insider trading.'

'Not if he was a member of Congress.'

Congress routinely exempted itself from the laws it imposed on the citizens, much as the ruling parties in Russia and China do. Consequently, the five hundred thirty-five members of Congress could freely and legally trade stocks on inside information whereas the other three hundred million Americans could not. Frank disagreed with the law, but it was still the law.

'Is he guilty?'

Brian shrugged. 'He can pay.'

'Sorry, Brian.'

Brian turned his palms up and laughed. 'My God, how do you make any money, not representing guilty people?'

★

Criminal defense lawyers must make their peace with one harsh fact of life: most of their clients are guilty. They will devote their professional careers not to defending the innocent but instead the guilty: rapists, murderers, gangbangers, drug dealers, conmen, scammers, fraud artists, embezzlers, thieves, cheats, and liars.

Frank Tucker had never made his peace. He only defended the innocent. In Texas, there was no shortage of clients, of innocent defendants wrongfully accused by overzealous or misguided or politically ambitious prosecutors. Many such defendants now resided in the state penitentiary. Unless they were defended by Frank Tucker. He had never lost a case.

Of course, he had no quarrel with the constitutional principles that even guilty defendants were entitled to due process, a fair trial, and a competent lawyer. But they weren't entitled to him. And his children's rights trumped their constitutional rights: his children were entitled to a father they could be proud of, and he didn't think defending a brutal rapist would make his children proud. So he defended the innocent. For his children.

'Great game, William.'

'Thank you, sir.'

'Super run, William.'

'Thank you, sir.'

The dads had congregated on the field behind the bench to greet the boys. William's team had lost again. They were 0-6 this season. He shrugged it off. Few boys at the Academy were athletes. Like Ray. He stood four feet ten inches tall and weighed ninety pounds. His shoulder pads dwarfed him. His uniform pants hung so low that his kneepads protected his ankles. He couldn't run, block, or catch. Heck, he couldn't catch a football if it was made of felt and he was covered in

39

Velcro. But he was still William's best buddy. He walked over and sat next to Ray on the bench. He was bent over with his elbows on his knees and his chin in his hand. William tried to cheer him up.

'Good game, Ray.'

'My dad's gonna be mad.'

'Why?'

'He wants me to be a football player.'

William tried not to laugh. 'Seriously? What's he smoking?'

'On the grill?'

'Uh . . . no. Did he play?'

Ray shook his head. 'Does your dad want you to be a football player?'

'I think he wants me to be a lawyer.'

'But you're so good, William.'

He shrugged. 'I'm good at sports, but you're good at math. Man, you do math stuff that I can't even dream of doing. I wish I was as smart as you.'

Ray was captain of the math club. More Academy students tried out for a spot in the math club than on the football team. That's how bad it was at the Academy.

'You do?'

'Sure.'

'I am pretty good at math.'

'Everyone's good at something, Ray.'

'Being the star of the math club isn't the same as being the star of the football team. Dude, you're going to be a famous athlete one day.'

'Math people are famous.'

'Name one.'

He could not.

'But math people do all kinds of neat stuff,' William said. 'My dad said they invented the Internet.'

40

'Al Gore said he invented the Internet.'

'Who's Al Gore?'

'Algorithms, maybe.'

Ray laughed as if it were the funniest joke he'd ever heard. William didn't have a clue.

'Is that a math club joke?'

'Yeah.'

Ray sat up straight. He seemed happier now.

'You want to come over tomorrow, play video games?' William asked.

'Sure.'

'Right after the Cowboys game.' William stood. 'You okay?'

'Yeah. Thanks, William.'

William held his arms out to the smaller boy.

'Reel it in, buddy.'

Ray stood, and William gave him a buddy hug, like the pros do after a good play. Ray walked off just as William's dad walked up and stuck out an open hand. William slapped his hand against his dad's.

'Good game, William,' his dad said. 'Sorry y'all lost.'

'No big deal. It's fun to play with my buddies.'

They watched Ray drag his helmet over to his dad.

'What's that boy's name?'

'Ray.'

'Is he a nice boy?'

'Yeah. He's a little nugget, but I like him.'

Most of the boys at the Academy were little nuggets. Others, like Jerry, the school photography club, were Mc-nuggets. He hurried over with his big camera hanging around his neck.

'William, let me get a shot of you and your dad.'

Dad put his arm around William's shoulder pads, and they smiled for the camera.

Chapter 4

'He should've audibled into a hot route,' William said.

'Who?' his dad said.

'The Cowboys quarterback. Watch the Sam's feet.'

'Sam who?'

'The strong safety. In the NFL, they call him the Sam. Watch his feet, you can see he's going to blitz.'

'You can?'

Last Sunday they had thrown the football on the beach in Galveston, but this Sunday they were watching football in the den of the River Oaks house. William sat in front of the big-screen TV with the sports pages spread out on the floor. His dad sat in his leather chair next to the lamp. Becky lay sprawled out on the couch. William was watching the Cowboys play; his dad was working on his closing argument; his sister was reading about wizards. Dad had to drive back to Austin after the game. Closing arguments in the senator's trial were tomorrow morning. The game went to commercial, so William went back to the sports pages.

'Roger Clemens won his three hundredth game.'

Dad grunted.

'Sammy Sosa hit his six hundredth home run.'

Another grunt.

'Oh, shit – Kobe got arrested!'

That got Dad's attention. Kobe Bryant was a huge star in the NBA.

'Language, William. For what?'

William read the story.

'Rape.'

William knew generally what rape was – a man forcing himself on a woman – because he had asked his dad, but he wasn't entirely sure what 'forcing himself' meant. He had started to ask his dad – Dad's rule was, 'If you ask a question about stuff like that, I'll tell you the truth. Just make sure you want to know the truth' – but he wasn't sure he wanted to know that truth. Not yet.

'They say he raped a girl at a hotel in Colorado. Desk clerk.'

'Where?'

'His room.'

'Witnesses?'

'Nope.'

'He said, she said.'

'Huh?'

'Her word against his.'

'He'll win.'

'Why do you say that, William?'

'Because Kobe's special. He's a star athlete. No jury will convict him.'

'He might be special on a basketball court, son, but that doesn't make him any more special as a human being than that girl.'

His dad always said stuff like that – 'Innocent until proven guilty beyond a reasonable doubt' . . . 'No man is above the

43

law' ... 'Every person is equal under the law' – same as William's social studies teacher. But even kids his age knew adults didn't really believe all that stuff. They just said it because they were supposed to. Except maybe his dad. Sometimes William thought maybe his dad really did believe it.

'We're all God's children?' William said.

He remembered the priest's sermon from that morning.

'That's right.'

'Well, maybe so, Dad, but God must've liked His son Kobe a heck of a lot more than He liked His daughter the desk clerk.'

'Why?'

'Because He made Kobe six-six and gave him a killer jump shot. So he's a rich and famous basketball star. He didn't give that girl shit. So she's a desk clerk.'

Dad grunted. Which made William proud. Because when Dad grunted, that meant William had said something that made him think.

'Language, William.'

A thought struck him.

'Hey, Dad, maybe Kobe will hire you to be his lawyer. I bet he could pay you millions. You'd be really famous if you were his lawyer.'

'He doesn't represent clients accused of rape,' Becky said.

Frank Tucker represented wrongly accused defendants in white-collar criminal cases. Corporate executives and politicians. Corporate executives charged with various kinds of criminal fraud – Houston was home to thousands of multinational corporations; consequently, the white-collar criminal defense business was booming – and politicians charged with violations of state and federal ethics and campaign finance laws and official misconduct – this was Texas, so that business was always booming.

White-collar criminal defense attorneys seldom became famous like the defense lawyers who represented accused murderers. Everyone knew who Johnnie Cochran and F. Lee Bailey were after they had represented O.J. Simpson in his murder trial. But white-collar cases generally weren't as sexy as murder cases. Consequently, Frank Tucker had been well known only to other lawyers who referred their indicted clients to him. But he had made the leap to the front page the year before when he had represented an Enron defendant. Enron Corporation had been a high-flying energy trading company headquartered in Houston in the nineties. It had gross revenues of $100 billion. It had assets of $60 billion. It had a stock price of $90. It had engaged in pervasive criminal fraud. After the company collapsed in 2001, corporate executives, including Ken Lay, the chairman of the board, and Jeffrey Skilling, the CEO, had been indicted. Even Enron's accounting firm, the venerable Arthur Andersen, had been indicted for obstruction of justice.

Frank's client, a thirty-year-old vice president in title but in fact just a Harvard-educated paper-pusher, had been charged with criminal fraud. He was guilty only of criminal stupidity, and there weren't enough prison cells in America to incarcerate all the executives guilty of that offense. He was just a kid who had followed orders and believed in the company; he had put every dime he made into Enron stock. He had lost everything – his job, his savings, his retirement funds, his reputation – just like the employees. But he had been caught up in the wide net of justice thrown out by the Justice Department in response to political posturing by members of Congress. They netted the sharks but also the shrimp. After a four-week trial, the jury had acquitted his client, one of the few Enron defendants who weren't convicted. As he walked out of the courthouse after the verdict, angry former Enron employees spat on Frank. That was a first. Many Americans had cheered O.J.'s acquittal, but then, he had only been accused of brutally murdering two innocent people, including his ex-wife whose head had almost been cut off. Frank's client had been accused of financial malfeasance resulting in the loss of jobs and the value of Enron stock. But Frank had long ago learned that being a criminal defense lawyer meant having the courage to live with the fact that just verdicts often were not popular verdicts.

And that the hardest verdict to live with was his own verdict of himself.

Frank gave William a man hug and a high-five and Becky a bear hug and a forehead kiss.

'I'll see you guys Thursday or Friday. Becky, you're in charge until Mom gets home.'

His wife was house hunting.

He would rehearse his closing argument during the three-hour drive to Austin. He would face the jury at 10 A.M.

Chapter 5

'Ladies and gentlemen of the jury. Over the last two weeks, you have witnessed something that is not supposed to happen in America: a political persecution. A politically motivated criminal prosecution brought by a politically ambitious district attorney. Mr. Dorkin, the Travis County District Attorney, desperately coveted the seat in the United States Senate that the defendant, Martha Jo Ramsey, now holds. Mr. Dorkin, a life-long Democrat, sought support for a campaign run from the leading Democrats in Texas. But he received no support. So he plotted his revenge. Not against his fellow Democrats, but against the defendant. Against a Republican. He took trumped-up charges to two grand juries, both of which declined to indict. But as they say, the third time's the charm.

'He finally got his indictments.

'Four charges of official misconduct. Second-degree felonies. He claims that Senator Ramsey, while serving as Texas Secretary of State, used state employees to conduct her personal and political business and then ordered them to destroy records evidencing such acts.

'Wow. That sounds pretty serious, doesn't it? A corrupt politician in Texas. We've seen a few of those, haven't we? We've had politicians who bought prostitutes with state money. Who used inside connections to make profitable stock and land purchases. Who even stole state welfare funds. So what was the felony crime Senator Ramsey is alleged to have committed?

'She had her secretary write thank-you notes.'

Two jurors rolled their eyes. The senator was very well liked in the state of Texas. So Frank had tried not to alter that affection. Each morning on their way into the Travis County Justice Center, she had given interviews for the throng of reporters, smiled for the cameras camped out front, and signed autographs and taken photos with her constituents. She looked like a television mother, like the mom in that show Frank watched reruns of as a kid, *Leave it to Beaver*. Would June Cleaver intentionally break the law? Frank didn't think so. Neither would this jury.

'Thank-you notes, and now she stands before you, a sitting United States senator from Texas, indicted by a jealous prosecutor. Mr. Dorkin wants you to send her to prison for thank-you notes. To serve hard time with murderers, rapists, and drug lords. For thank-you notes.'

Frank Tucker pointed at the district attorney.

'He has wasted your time and your money to seek revenge against his rival. He is a failed politician taking his political frustrations out on an innocent defendant. He's like the school bully, using his power to abuse a classmate. Ladies and gentlemen of the jury, as American citizens, you are the senator's classmates. Are you going to stand by and let him bully your friend? Or are you going to stand up to the bully?'

*

48

Judge Harold Rooney charged the jury in the matter of *The State of Texas versus Martha Jo Ramsey* and sent the jurors to deliberate at 11:04 A.M. After the jury had left the district courtroom in downtown Austin, the judge motioned counsel to the bench.

'This could take a while, gentlemen. I'm thinking Thursday at the earliest.'

He turned to defense counsel.

'Frank, if you want to go home to Houston, I'll hold the verdict until you have time to drive back up. The senator should stay in Texas.'

'Thank you, Harold.'

Frank felt the district attorney's eyes boring holes in his skull. Dick Dorkin and he had been classmates at UT law school twenty years before. Frank had graduated number one in their class; Dick had graduated number two-thirty-three. Out of four hundred. Frank had hired on with a large Houston firm; Dick had hired on with the district attorney's office. Frank was a good lawyer; Dick was a good politician. Twenty years later, Frank was a name partner in the firm; Dick was the elected district attorney of Travis County. Having failed in his attempt at a Senate seat, word was he now had his eyes on the Governor's Mansion just a few blocks from this courtroom. A high-profile conviction could shorten that distance.

Dick Dorkin had been Frank's rival in law school; he had never really known why. Today, Frank Tucker had made him an enemy for life. But that is what a lawyer must do when an innocent defendant faces the loss of her freedom. A lawyer must fight for his client, even if that means making enemies. A lawyer must be able to live with himself. With his own verdict. Of himself.

'So, Frank,' the judge said, 'I hear your son's quite the football player down there in Houston.'

'He's twelve.'

'Only six years till he's playing for the Longhorns.'

The judge was also a UT law grad.

'Well, that's a long—'

'Excuse me, Judge Rooney.'

The bailiff had walked up to the bench.

'Yes?'

'The jury has a verdict.'

'A *verdict*?' He looked at the clock. It was 11:19. 'In fifteen minutes?'

The bailiff shrugged. 'Yes, sir.'

The judge looked at counsel. His eyebrows arched. He turned back to the bailiff.

'Well, bring them in.'

The jury acquitted the senator on all counts.

Chapter 6

The first college scout showed up when William was fourteen.

'He's the best I've ever seen, Frank.'

The last two years had been a blur. The case against Kobe in Colorado had been dismissed; the case against Enron in Houston had not. Kobe paid the desk clerk a reported $5 million to go away; the Enron chairman of the board and CEO were going away to prison. The U.S. Supreme Court unanimously overturned the obstruction of justice conviction of Arthur Andersen, Enron's accounting firm, but it was too late to save the company or its eighty-five thousand employees. Martha Stewart served prison time for insider trading; the speaker of the House of Representatives did not. George W. Bush won reelection, and then Hurricane Katrina inundated New Orleans and Bush's presidency. Tom Brady and the Patriots won their third Super Bowl. Major League Baseball instituted a steroid testing program after most of the record-breaking home run hitters of the nineties had been implicated in the performance-enhancing drug scandal. Lance Armstrong won his seventh straight Tour de France; at least there was one clean athlete in America. The wars in Iraq and Afghanistan waged on. Something called Facebook was launched, as if thousands of people were really going to put their entire personal lives on display for the world. Frank tried more white-collar criminal cases and won them all. William played more private school football games and lost them all. It was a Thursday afternoon in late October, and his eighth-grade team was losing again. His father stood along the chain link fence that surrounded the Academy field. Sam Jenkins stood next to Frank and smelled of Old Spice and tobacco. Sam was short and stocky and smoked a cigar. He was a college scout.

'He's fourteen,' Frank said.

'He's special.'

'He's a kid.'

'He's an athlete. With a big-time future. If you manage his career correctly.'

'His *career*?'

'That's right. His career. A career that could be worth a couple hundred million dollars, Frank. Top pro athletes make more than movie stars today . . . and a hell of a lot more than lawyers.'

'He's playing eighth-grade football.'

'He's four years from playing college ball, eight from pro ball, maybe six if he leaves college early.'

'He won't.'

'Play pro ball?'

'Leave college early.'

Sam nodded. 'That's what they all say. But when an NFL team offers millions, a college degree doesn't seem so important.'

'What are the odds of William playing pro ball?'

'What are the odds of winning the lottery? But someone always wins.'

Sam exhaled cigar smoke that lingered in the air.

'Frank, if William was a music prodigy – a pianist – would you nurture that gift?'

'Sure.'

'Well, he's a football prodigy.'

'How many pianists suffer concussions and long-term brain damage?'

'How many make ten million a year? Frank, your boy's got a gift. I've been scouting kids for thirty years now, I've never seen a fourteen-year-old boy like him.'

'You scout fourteen-year-old boys?'

'No. I scout twelve-year-old boys. Problem is, they're just hitting puberty, and half of the good ones come out of puberty no bigger than they went in. Normally I'd tell you to hold him back in school a year, maybe two, give him a chance to grow before varsity ball. But that's not an issue with William. He's already big – what is he, six foot?'

'Six-one.'

'What's his shoe size?'

'Thirteen.'

Sam whistled. 'Size thirteen at age fourteen. He'll go to size sixteen, maybe seventeen. I figure he'll top out at six-four, maybe six-five. How big are his hands?'

'Bigger than mine.'

'What does he weigh?'

'One-sixty.'

'In eighth grade. He'll go two-twenty, and he won't need steroids to do it. Which is always a concern. You look at sixteen-, seventeen-, eighteen-year-old bulked-up boys, and you always wonder if they're using.'

'High school boys are using steroids?'

Sam chuckled. 'You're spending too much time in the courtroom, Frank. Hell, yes, high school boys are juiced. They

53

get through puberty and realize they're not going to be big enough, decide to give their bodies a boost. Anything to live the dream. So I always check their hands and feet.'

'Why?'

'I see a pumped-up boy weighing two-twenty but wearing size ten cleats, I know that doesn't add up. Too big for his feet. Same with their hands. Boys grow into their hands and feet, not vice-versa.'

'You've got scouting down to a science.'

'Size and strength is science, but heart and guts isn't. A boy's got to have the guts to compete and the heart to win. You can't coach that.'

On the field, William ran left, juked two defenders, broke four tackles, and sprinted down the sideline for a touchdown. Sam regarded Frank's son with awe. He pointed the cigar at the field.

'You can't coach that either, Frank. A boy's either got it or he doesn't. Your boy's got it.'

Sam sucked on the cigar and again exhaled smoke.

'When I got started in the scouting business, my mentor was an old-timer who scouted Namath in high school. Said watching him play was like having an orgasm. I never understood what he meant. Until now.'

'An orgasm? You're scaring me, Sam.'

Sam smiled then spit a bit of cigar.

'Gives me chills, watching your boy play.' Sam ran his fingers over his forearm then held his arm out to Frank. 'Here, feel the goose bumps.'

'I'll pass.'

'Last time I got even half this excited watching an eighth-grader was Troy Aikman up in Oklahoma. That boy could play. I ranked him number one coming out of high school. He did okay in football: went number one in the NFL draft, won three Super Bowls with the Cowboys, made the Hall of Fame, earned millions. But he wasn't as good as William at fourteen. Frank, if you don't nurture his gift, give him a chance to live his dream, he'll hate you.'

'He'll hate me?'

Frank smiled. He assumed Sam was joking. He wasn't.

'He will.'

Frank couldn't imagine his son hating him.

'So what's your advice, Sam?'

'First, he's in a small private school. He's got no team around him to work with.' Sam gestured at the field. 'He can't develop with a bunch of losers.'

'Losers? They're nice boys.'

'They're lousy athletes. He's got no offensive line, no receivers who can catch. He only throws the ball ten times a game. He can't develop his quarterbacking skills playing an old-style offense that runs the ball. The forward pass is the game today, Frank. The pro game is all about passing, which means the college game is all about passing, which means the high school game is all about passing. That's why freshmen can start and excel in college, why they can go pro and start in the NFL. They've been running pro offenses since middle school. You need to put William in a big public school that runs a pro-style offense, throws fifty times a game, and has players around him, preferably black players with speed and skills. And an indoor practice field.'

'An indoor practice field?'

'It rains in Houston, Frank. Rain days are lost practice days. So all the big public schools in Texas build indoor practice fields.'

'I thought our public school system was broke?'

'There's always money for football. When they played the Super Bowl in Dallas, the teams practiced in indoor arenas at high schools.'

'But he loves his school.'

'Frank, families move across the country so their sons can play at the best public high schools running the best pro offenses.'

'You're kidding?'

'Do I look like I'm kidding?'

He did not.

'He's got to get on track now – if you want him to play in the NFL.'

'I don't care.'

'He cares.'

'He's fourteen. Every fourteen-year-old boy dreams of being a star pro football player.'

'Difference is, Frank, his dream can come true. He can be a star. He's got it. The size, the strength, the speed. Bigger stronger faster.'

He said the three words as if they were one.

'I read about you, Frank, that profile in the *New York Times* after you won the senator's case—'

Frank Tucker had become famous. The senator's acquittal had propelled him to the top of the heap of criminal defense lawyers in America. He could have specialized in defending members of Congress accused of ethics and criminal violations, but he didn't want to spend so much time in Washington away from his family. And there were plenty of white-collar defendants in Texas. Why travel?

'—how you've never lost a trial. Why do you win all your cases?'

'Because justice is on my side.'

Sam snorted. 'Yeah, right. You win because you're smarter. In a court of law, smarter beats dumber every time, right? That's the law of man. On a football field, bigger stronger faster beats smaller weaker slower every time. That's the law of nature.'

56

Frank gazed out at his son's smaller, weaker, and slower team losing to a bigger, stronger, and faster team.

'Second, he needs to spend his summers in quarterback school.'

'What's that?'

'Summer camps run by former pro quarterbacks and coaches. They work with the top prospects in the nation. Throwing motion, footwork, leadership skills, passing drills, reading defenses, recognizing coverage, calling audibles . . . They teach the boys how to play the position. He does that for a couple of summers, then goes to an Elite Eleven camp.'

'What's that?'

'Quarterback camp for the best of the best. They hold them all over the country, invite fifty or sixty boys to each camp. Maybe one boy from each camp moves on to the five-day Elite Eleven finals up at Nike's headquarters. They call it "The Opening."'

'How much does all that cost?'

'Thousands. Tens of thousands.'

'That's a lot of money.'

'They end up signing for millions.'

'What else?'

'You need to put him on a training program with a personal trainer. Chisel his body. Quarterbacks today, they're ripped. You ever see players at the combine meat market, standing up on stage in their skivvies so the owners and coaches can take a look?'

'Uh, no. I haven't. And I don't want to.'

Sam chuckled. 'It is a bit strange, white team owners and coaches eyeballing these big black studs same way white plantation owners used to eyeball black slaves being sold on the docks in Galveston – I saw a show on cable about that, struck me – but difference is, these black players are going to make millions, not pick cotton. Anyway, I can give you some names of trainers here in Houston. And a speed trainer, like Michael Johnson up in Dallas. Olympic gold medal guy, he trains NFL prospects and players to get that extra step for the combine. From four-five in the forty to four-four. One step faster can be the difference between playing in the NFL or working at Wal-mart.'

'How much will that cost?'

'Nothing a famous lawyer can't afford.'

'What else?'

'A nutritionist. Boys eat fast food, they build fat instead of muscle. He needs to be on a strict diet.'

'At fourteen?'

'He should've been on it at twelve.'

'Public school, quarterback school, personal trainer—'

'And seven-on-seven tournaments.'

'Which are?'

'Passing tournaments. A QB plus six receivers against seven D-backs. They run them all summer.'

'What about family vacations?'

'You vacation at the tournament locations.' Sam inhaled on the cigar and exhaled. 'Look, Frank, if you want William in the NFL, that journey starts now. His family's got to get on board, dedicate their lives to that one goal.'

'Why?'

'Because every other William Tucker out there, his family is. That's what it takes today.'

'Are there any other William Tuckers out there?'

'No. But their parents think they are.'

'Why do they do it?'

'Fame and fortune. There are thirty-two NFL teams. Thirty-two starting quarterbacks. Average salary is five million. By the time William is drafted number one, he'll get twenty million. A year. Guaranteed.'

'But he needs to get a good education, maybe at an Ivy League school, then—'

Sam laughed. '*Ivy League?* Shit, Frank, most high school teams in Texas can beat the hell out of Harvard's football team. Forget the Ivy League, Frank. William's got to go to a big D-One school.'

'—medical or law school.'

'And be a lawyer like his daddy?'

'Maybe.'

'When do you figure on retiring, Frank? Sixty-five?'

'Depends on how much my wife can spend between now and then.'

'NFL quarterbacks retire at thirty-five. You watch the Olympics?'

Frank nodded.

'You see those little gymnasts? They're sixteen, seventeen, eighteen, been living in dorms since they were ten, so they can be near their coaches, train every day for their one shot at glory. One shot at fame and fortune. One shot at a life. Sports today, it's younger than ever. You've got ten years max to make it. You're in the game at twenty-two, out at thirty-two. If you're lucky and don't get a career-ending injury. But if you play it right, you're sitting on a pile of money. You're set for life.'

'So it's about money?'

'It's about William doing what he was born to do. Play football.'

Frank watched his son play football. Was that what William Tucker was born to do?

'You ever been wrong, Sam? About a boy?'

'Sure. There was a boy named Montana. Skinny, slow, couldn't throw a football fifty yards. You wouldn't pick him for your high school team. But he had ice water running through

59

his veins. He won a national championship at Notre Dame and four Super Bowls.'

'I mean, on the downside. A boy you knew would make it, but didn't.'

Sam nodded. 'Many times. You can never be sure what's inside a boy. The heart and guts thing. Whether they'll thrive on pressure or fall apart. And there's always the injury factor. One injury and a promising career can be over.'

'What if you're wrong about William? You want him to give up a great education at the Academy and the Ivy League for football? What if he doesn't make it?'

'Plan B.'

'Which is?'

'His rich daddy. He can go back to college, maybe law school. No worries for William. It's the black kids, the ones without a Plan B, they're the ones I lose sleep over. Football's their only way out of the 'hood, it's all or nothing. A lot of them end up with nothing.' Sam stared at the field. 'But I'm not wrong about William.'

'So I'm supposed to make a major life decision for my son based upon your appraisal?'

Sam held his hands up as if in surrender.

'Hey, you're his dad. I'm just a scout.'

Sam chuckled then took a long drag on the cigar and blew out smoke.

'Frank, when you were a kid, did you dream of being a pro athlete? You sure as hell didn't dream of being a lawyer.'

Frank nodded. 'Golfer.'

'Did you love the game?'

'I did.'

'Were you any good?'

'Not good enough.'

'What if you had been? And not just good, but great. How

would that have felt? Would you have chased your dream? Would you have been mad if your dad had denied you that chance?'

Sam Jenkins answered his own question.

'You would've hated him. And William will hate you.'

Sam waved the cigar at the teams on the field.

'That's his dream, right out there. You gonna take that dream away from your son, Frank?'

A good father wouldn't take his son's dream away, would he?

William's team was losing. Again. He had scored five touch-downs, but the other team had scored nine. His team ran off the field. The linemen bowled over Ray and knocked him to the ground. All the water bottles he carried in his little carry rack went flying. Ray was now the team manager, aka, the water boy. William stopped and helped his friend up. He then picked up the plastic Gatorade bottles and replaced them in Ray's carry rack. It looked like an old-time milk-man's carry rack, except Ray carried bottles of Gatorade not milk.

'You okay, Ray?'

'Yeah. Thanks, William.' He nodded at the other players. 'They've got no respect for water boys.'

William stuck a fist out. 'Knucks.'

As in 'knuckles.' They fist-bumped.

Sam Jenkins had left, and Frank stood at the fence pondering the scout's advice when his cell phone rang. He checked the readout. It was an Austin number. He answered.

'Frank Tucker.'

'Frank. Scooter and Billy.'

Scooter McKnight was the athletic director at UT. Billy Hayes was the head basketball coach. They were on a

61

speakerphone. Frank had a feeling they weren't calling to offer game tickets.

'Can we talk?' Scooter said.

'Shoot.'

'Not on the phone. Can you come to Austin? Tomorrow?'

'Can't.'

'Saturday?'

'Scooter, I told my son we'd play golf—'

'It's important, Frank.'

Scooter was not given to drama. So Frank and William would play Sunday instead.

'All right. At your office in the stadium?'

'At the jail.'

'The *jail*?'

Scooter sighed into the phone. 'Watch the news.'

Frank disconnected and wondered what the meeting would be about. More specifically, whom it would be about. Frank had handled some high-profile matters for the athletic department, which is to say, he had represented athletes who had found themselves on the wrong side of the law. Most were just young and stupid and bulletproof, or so they had thought. They were living in those gap years, with bodies like men and brains like boys. Testosterone and stupidity had apparently joined up to produce another bad result. He knew Saturday's meeting would not be a happy affair. Happy people don't call criminal defense attorneys.

'We've got the society luncheon tomorrow.'

His wife's perfume announced her presence. He turned to her. She was forty-two now, but daily workouts and regular spa treatments had deferred her aging. She was still lean and fit; climbing the social ladder in Houston required stamina.

'What time?'

'Noon.'

'I can't.'

62

'You promised.'

'Nancy's son is coming home from Iraq.'

'So?'

'In a casket.'

Her son had died at twenty-two, only eight years older than William. Where would Frank's son be at twenty-two? Not dying from a roadside bomb in a foreign land to help people who hated Americans. Would he be playing pro football for Americans who loved the game more than life itself? Was his son's dream in Frank's hands? Was Sam the scout right? What would a good father do?

'Who was that you were talking to?' his wife said.

'On the phone?'

'No. That man.'

'College scout.'

'Why?'

'He came to see William play. Scouting a fourteen-year-old boy.'

'So what did he say?'

Frank recounted his conversation with Sam Jenkins to his wife.

'He really thinks William could be a star in the NFL?' she said.

'Apparently.'

'Then we've got to do it.'

'Hold on, Liz. We need to think this out, the consequences for William. Not just what he wants, but what he needs. What's best for him. He's as big as a man, but he's still just a kid without a clue.'

'What's a vagina look like?'

Frank spit out the beef from his beef taco. Becky covered her face.

63

'Oh – my – God! William, that is so disgusting. And at the dinner table.'

Liz had gone into the kitchen to check on Lupe. They were not sitting at the table in the kitchen in the old house. They were sitting at the formal dining table in the formal dining room in the new eight-thousand-square-foot house. They had sold the old house and moved into this house a year ago. It was new and austere and filled with marble, like a mausoleum. It did not feel like home to Frank. Or to the kids. Or to Rusty, one holdover from the old house. This new house had cost four and a half million dollars. Frank was carrying a two-million-dollar mortgage. All to keep the peace. To be with the kids. Becky, who was sixteen now and had only two more years at home, and William, whose size made him seem older when in fact he was just a fourteen-year-old boy working his way through puberty. Sometime in the last year, girls had become interesting.

'It's my one question,' William said.

About a year before, William had figured out that there was a secret world called sex, so he began peppering Frank with questions. A lot of anatomical and mechanical inquiries. Five, ten a day. Frank felt as if he were being deposed. So he reminded his son of the rule – if he asked a question, Frank would tell him the truth; but he had to be sure he wanted to know the truth – and then limited his sex questions to one per day. He couldn't deal with that much sex talk each day, particularly given that he was no longer a practitioner. But the preferred place for the daily question was not the dinner table.

'So how did this particular topic come up?'

'Some of the guys were talking about it at practice. Timmy McDougal said he had seen a picture online. Then his mother blocked porn sites on his computer. Petey Perkins said he had seen his sister's, but that made us all want to throw up.'

Lupe came in with a platter of Mexican food. She was the other holdover. The house was new and the furnishings were new, but their maid was two years older. She did not wear a colorful peasant dress but instead all black, like a waiter at a fine restaurant. Liz had decided that Lupe needed to upgrade to a uniform when they moved into the new house.

'So why do you want to know?' Frank asked.

'I'm the only fourteen-year-old kid who's never seen one, not even a picture. I should know that sort of thing.'

'Can we talk about something else?' Becky said.

'Why?'

'Because this is gross.'

'My question was directed to William.'

'All the other guys do. I feel stupid.'

Frank tried to recall when he had first seen a vagina. It was in a *Playboy* magazine another boy had smuggled into school like contraband. He was in ninth grade and never looked at girls the same way again. Answering his son's sex questions had fallen to Frank, father-son and all. Telling him there was no Santa Claus was easier. That talk had also fallen to Frank.

'All right. After dinner. We'll find a vagina on the Internet.'

Becky stared at Frank with her mouth gaped. Frank turned his hands up.

'What?'

'If I had asked to see a penis when I was fourteen, would you have shown me a picture on the Internet?'

'No.'

'Exactly.'

'And have you seen one?'

She pointed at her brother. 'His . . . but not recently.'

There was more for her to tell, but Frank could not summon up the courage to ask. She answered anyway.

65

'Don't worry, Daddy. I'm still a virgin. I'm not going to let a guy use me to make his high school memories. I'm smarter than that.'

Frank leaned over and kissed her forehead.

'Thank you.'

'For what?'

'For being a better daughter than I am a dad.'

'You're welcome.'

Everyone said the first child would be easy. Not so much the second.

'Can I ask a follow-up question?' William said.

'No.'

He did anyway.

'Jimmy said girls put IUDs up their vaginas so they don't get pregnant. But I told him that would be dangerous because your secretary's son died from an IUD in Iraq. Jimmy's dumb, isn't he?'

'He is,' Becky said.

'But not about that,' Frank said. 'Nancy's son died from an IED, an improvised explosive device. An IUD is an intrauterine device. A form of birth control women use.'

'Do they hurt?'

'Women? Yes.'

Frank smiled at Becky.

'Funny,' his daughter said.

'What's for dessert?' his son said.

William's cell phone buzzed. Incoming text. He checked it then jumped out of his chair and ran into the kitchen to the nearest TV. He clicked it on and found the local news. Mom stood next to him. She was mad because Dad wasn't going to some lunch with her the next day.

'Dad!'

Dad and Becky walked in a few seconds later. William pointed at the screen. The reporter was talking: 'Bradley Todd, the star UT basketball player, was arrested today in Austin and charged with the brutal rape and murder of a UT coed. He's being held without bail in the Travis County Jail. The D.A. is going to seek the death penalty.'

'So that's it,' Dad said.

'What?'

'The AD and coach called me today at your game. We're meeting Saturday morning. About this.'

'I thought we were playing golf Saturday?'

'Sunday.'

'Is he the son of the Todds of Highland Park?' Liz asked. 'The billionaire?'

'I don't know.'

She did.

'They're high in Dallas society.'

'His dad'll buy his way out,' William said. 'Just like Kobe bought his way out.'

'Kobe wasn't accused of murder.'

'You're not seriously going to be his lawyer?' Becky said.

'Depends.'

'Daddy, you can't represent a rapist and a murderer!'

'I'm not going to. I'm going to meet him, see if he's being wrongfully accused, if he's innocent.'

'And if he's not? Innocent?'

'He'll have to find another lawyer.'

Chapter 7

The Travis County Jail anchored the corner of Tenth and Nueces in downtown Austin. On any given day, several hundred men resided there; several thousand more resided in the long-term jail facility south of town. They all resided there involuntarily. They had been arrested and charged with violations of the Texas Penal Code. Assault. Robbery. Rape. Murder. Some could not make bail. Some were denied bail. All wanted out. Desperately.

Bradley Todd was one such man.

Sitting on the inmate side of the Plexiglas partition in the interview room, he did not look like a rapist or a murderer. He looked like a very tall Mormon missionary. But he was not a missionary. He was twenty years old and the star player on the UT basketball team. Coach Billy Hayes shook his head in despair.

'I finally find a white boy who can play D-One basketball, then he does this.'

'Did he?' Frank said. 'Do it?'

'Rape and kill her? No. I mean, get himself arrested.'

Scooter McKnight sighed. 'Book 'em Horns.'

'Hook 'em Horns' was the Longhorn slogan. After a number of UT athletes had been arrested in recent years for various violations of the law, the Austin media had taken to saying, 'Book 'em Horns.'

'He's a player,' Billy said. 'A real shooter. He could go pro, but he wants to be a doctor – you believe that? A false accusation like this could ruin his life. He's religious and Republican – Republicans don't rape and murder college coeds. Jesus, Frank, he goes to Sunday school. What basketball player does that these days? These girls, they throw themselves at star athletes. It's hard to say no when all you have to do is say yes. Then they claim rape.'

'How many claim murder?'

The coach gave Frank a look.

'You know what I mean. Look at him.'

They spoke in low voices. Frank, Billy, and Scooter were standing on the visitor side of the Plexiglas; Bradley's parents stood against the wall behind them. They were in fact the billionaire Todds of Highland Park. Their son stood six feet eight inches tall. His hair was short. He had no visible tattoos or piercings. He was engaged to a nice girl. He was white. Would Frank feel the same about him if he were black and accused of raping and murdering a white girl? If he had dreadlocks and tattoos and wore his pants below his butt? If his name was D'Marcellus or LaMichael? If his parents were poor?

'They can pay the full freight, Frank,' Scooter said. 'They live in Highland Park.'

Dallas' billionaires lived in Highland Park just as Houston's billionaires lived in River Oaks.

'You name your price, they'll pay. They want you.'

'Why?'

'The dad, he's buddies with Senator Ramsey. She told him to hire you.'

'You know my rule, Scooter.'

69

'He's innocent, Frank.'

'On the TV, the police chief said they had his DNA.'

Billy sighed and nodded. 'Semen. Like I said, these girls throw themselves at the players.'

Frank studied Bradley Todd. Was he a brutal rapist and murderer or a falsely accused innocent young man? Like the three Duke lacrosse players who made the mistake of going to a party where a stripper named Crystal Gail Mangum performed. After the party got out of hand, she accused the three players of raping her. The university, faculty, students, police, and district attorney (who was up for reelection) presumed their guilt. Feminists and faculty staged campus protests and demanded that the players be expelled. They were. The grand jury indicted the players for rape and kidnapping. Fortunately for the players, their parents had money; they spent three million dollars proving their sons' innocence. The North Carolina Attorney General declared that the three players had been falsely accused and revealed that District Attorney Mike Nifong had withheld exculpatory DNA evidence. Nifong was subsequently disbarred for prosecutorial misconduct and convicted of criminal contempt; he served one day in jail. The players sued Duke University, which settled with them, and enrolled in other colleges. Mangum wrote a memoir and was later convicted of murder after stabbing her boyfriend to death. Three innocent young men would be in prison still if a lawyer hadn't believed in them.

'I need to talk to him,' Frank said. 'Alone.'

'Why?' Billy asked.

'The attorney-client privilege doesn't apply if third parties are privy to our conversation. You could be called to testify.'

'But I'm his coach.'

'Sorry, Billy. There's no legal privilege for basketball coaches.'

'That doesn't seem fair.'

Frank repeated his request to Bradley's parents.

'I'm staying,' the father said. 'I want to hear what you have to say. I'm paying you.'

'If I take his case. And I can't decide if I'm taking his case until I talk to your son, Mr. Todd. Alone.'

The father stared at Frank, then surrendered.

'The judge denied bail. Said he's a danger to the community. If you take the case, can you get him out of here?'

'I can.'

'He's innocent, Frank.'

A father's undying belief in his son. Mr. Todd walked out of the interview room. His wife followed him. Scooter and Billy followed her. Frank sat in the chair facing Bradley Todd. His expression was that of a deer caught in headlights – and about to be run over. Being arrested will do that to an American citizen. When the police show up and slap the cuffs on you, read you the Miranda warning, and then haul you off to jail, fingerprint you, and take a DNA cheek swab, you are filled with the fear of God. The fear of losing your freedom. The fear of prison. Bradley Todd was full of all those fears. Frank picked up the phone on his side and gestured for Bradley to pick up the phone on his side.

'Bradley, my name is Frank Tucker. I'm a criminal defense lawyer. I usually represent white-collar defendants, not defendants accused of rape and murder. So if I'm going to represent you, you must tell me the truth, the whole truth, and nothing but the truth. Do you understand?'

'Yes, sir.'

'Did you rape and murder Rachel Truitt?'

Rachel Truitt had been an eighteen-year-old freshman at the University of Texas at Austin. She had been brutally raped and then strangled to death behind a bar on Sixth Street.

'No, sir, Mr. Tucker. I didn't rape her. I didn't kill her.'

'The police recovered your DNA from her body. Semen. You had sex with her?'

71

Bradley's eyes dropped.

'Yes, sir.'

'The same day she was murdered?'

'Yes, sir.'

'Where?'

'In the basketball arena, after the game.'

'In the arena? Where?'

'Girls' locker room. It was vacant.'

'I thought you're engaged to another girl?'

'I am. Sarah Barnes. She's a sophomore, too.'

'But you had sex with Rachel?'

'I try to resist, but they come on so strong. I'm only twenty, Mr. Tucker. I never had girls in high school. But in college, if you're a star athlete, it's like being a movie star.'

'You didn't wear a condom?'

'No one does.'

'You've never heard of AIDS? Sexually transmitted diseases?'

'We don't worry about that stuff.'

'You could give something to your fiancée.'

'I won't.'

'When did you first meet her?'

'My fiancée?'

'Rachel.'

'Ten minutes before we had sex. I didn't even know her name, till I read about her in the paper.'

'So, what, she came up to you after the game, and ten minutes later you had sex with her in the girls' locker room?'

'Yes, sir. I noticed her during the game. She smiled at me then waited for me after the game.'

'Is that a normal occurrence?'

'Oh, yes, sir. And not just for me.'

'What time was that?'

72

'Maybe five.'

'Her body was found that night at midnight. On Sixth Street. Where were you that night?'

'With my fiancée. At her apartment.'

'And she will so testify?'

'Yes, sir.'

'Will you take a polygraph?'

'Yes, sir, Mr. Tucker. Absolutely.'

'You took the case?'

District Attorney Dick Dorkin sat in the judge's chambers next to Frank. Judge Harold Rooney sat across his desk from them. It was that afternoon. Harold had come in on a Saturday because Frank had asked; the D.A. had come in because he had no family to spend his Saturdays with.

'He's guilty, Frank, and you don't represent guilty clients,' the D.A. said. 'Remember?'

'He's innocent.'

'How do you know?'

'I looked him in the eye and asked him if he raped and killed Rachel Truitt. He said he did not.'

'He's lying.'

'No twenty-year-old boy can lie that well.'

The D.A. turned to the judge. 'Harold, you can't let Todd out of jail. He's guilty, and he's a danger to the community. This is a death penalty case, for God's sake.'

'Frank,' the judge said, 'I could set his bail at five million, but his dad could pay that with a credit card.'

'So what's the point? That's why I'm asking for his release on PR.'

'Personal recognizance?' the D.A. said. 'For an accused rapist and murderer? Harold, you can't.'

The judge exhaled.

'Frank, we all know your reputation. Your rule. I'm relying on you. Don't make me look like a fool.'

'You won't, Harold.'

'PR,' the judge said.

Chapter 8

It was a 'he said, she said' case. She was dead. He was on the stand.

'Bradley, did you rape Rachel Truitt?' Frank asked his client.

'No, sir.'

'Did you have sex with her?'

'Yes, sir.'

Frank led his client through the details of the encounter with Rachel in the basketball arena locker room.

'After she left, did you ever see Rachel again?'

'No, sir.'

'Did you strangle Rachel that night until she was dead?'

'No, sir.'

The UT football team's winning the national championship at the Rose Bowl just two weeks before had faded from the front page of the Austin newspaper, replaced by *The State of Texas v. Bradley Todd*. Reporters and cameras camped out in the plaza fronting the Travis County Justice Center in downtown Austin. Spectators lined up early for available seats, as if the rape and murder trial were a reality show. Perhaps in

America of 2006, it was. Frank had thought the Enron case had been a circus, and it had been; but the trial of a star athlete was a three-ring circus.

It was early January, and Frank again found himself trying a criminal case before Judge Harold Rooney and against Travis County District Attorney Dick Dorkin. The D.A. had not gotten over the senator's acquittal two years before. Pretrial hearings had been contentious. The D.A. was determined to convict Bradley Todd. To beat Frank Tucker. To win the Governor's Mansion.

Frank had requested the earliest possible trial setting in accordance with the speedy trial law and refused all continuances requested by the D.A. When the prosecutor has no evidence, you push him to trial. Force him to either dismiss the charges or prove them in court. Bradley Todd's life had been put on hold – he had been suspended from the basketball team and the school after feminists and faculty had staged campus protests; he was innocent until proven guilty everywhere except at a liberal arts university – and would remain on hold until the jury had rendered a verdict. Which would happen in a matter of days now.

'Mr. Dorkin,' the judge said.

Travis County District Attorney Dick Dorkin stood and walked over to the witness.

'After you had sex with Rachel, where did you go?'

'To the men's locker room. I showered then went to Sarah's apartment.'

'Sarah Barnes? Your fiancée?'

'Yes, sir.'

'And where were you the rest of that night?'

'With Sarah, at her apartment.'

'You didn't leave her apartment?'

'No, sir.'

76

'Sarah is sitting outside this courtroom right now, waiting to testify after you, you know that?'

'Yes, sir.'

'Now, Mr. Todd, you know that if Sarah lies to protect you, she would be guilty of perjury?'

'Yes, sir. But she won't. Lie for me. She doesn't need to lie. We were together all night.'

'But if she did lie, and that was subsequently discovered, she could be charged and convicted. You know that?'

'Yes, sir.'

The police had Bradley's semen from the victim but no other physical evidence linking him to her death. They had found no evidence that put his alibi in doubt. And Bradley's fiancée would testify to his whereabouts at the time of the murder, that he was with her at her apartment. Frank had interviewed her as well. He had no doubt that she was telling the truth. But the D.A. remained convinced that Bradley Todd was guilty. That he had gone to Sixth Street that night. That he had met up with Rachel Truitt at a bar. That rough sex had turned into violent death. But he had no evidence. No witnesses. No surveillance camera images of Bradley. Nothing. The D.A. could have dismissed the charges and waited to find the evidence he was so sure existed and indict Bradley again in a year or five years or ten years; there was no statute of limitations on murder. But a dismissal would look bad in the press and would be brought up in the debates among the candidates for governor. So the D.A. pressed forward with the case. His only hope for conviction was to break Bradley's fiancée on the stand.

Sarah Barnes was cute and Christian. She wore a cross on a chain around her neck and swore to 'tell the truth, the whole truth, and nothing but the truth, so help me God' and meant it. She sat in the witness chair. Frank asked a few preliminary questions regarding her relationship with the defendant, and then he asked the only question that mattered.

'Sarah, was Bradley Todd with you at your apartment from six P.M. on the night of Saturday, October the eighth of last year through the following Sunday morning?'

'Yes, sir.'

'No further questions.'

The D.A. attacked.

'Ms. Barnes, did Bradley tell you that he had had sex with Rachel that same afternoon?'

'No, sir.'

'So he lied to you?'

'He didn't tell me. But, yes, that's the same as a lie.'

'He betrayed you.'

'Yes.'

'But you still love him?'

'Yes.'

'Even though he lied to you and betrayed your love?'

'Yes.'

'Why?'

'He's a good man. Or he'll be a good man when he becomes a man.'

'He's six feet eight inches tall. He's not a man?'

'No. He's just a big boy who happens to be able to play a silly game called basketball. Which, for some reason I don't get, makes him very attractive to college girls. Look at him – does he look like Brad Pitt? No, he does not. But girls, they'll drop their shorts for him – for any of the players – any time. I feel sorry for them.'

'The players?'

'The girls.'

'For girls who've had sex with Bradley?'

'Yes. I pray for them.'

'Why?'

'Because they need something. Something he can't give them.'

'What's that?'

'Love.'

'And you think he loves you?'

'I know he does. But he's just a twenty-year-old boy. I'm going to stick with him because when he grows up, he'll be a fine forty-year-old man. He'll be a fine father. And a fine doctor.'

She turned to the jurors; her eyes did not waver.

'Bradley was home with me that night. All night. I swear to God.'

The all-white jury acquitted Bradley Todd.

Truth of the matter, Bradley Todd was a wholesome, clean-cut white boy who said 'yes, ma'am' and 'no, sir.' His alibi witness was a pretty white Christian girl. If Bradley had been a tattooed black gangbanger with dreads who said 'yo' and ''ho' and whose body was covered with tattoos and whose pants sagged below his butt and whose alibi witness was a drug-addicted hooker, they'd have sent his ass to prison in a heartbeat. Frank knew that. But he also knew that Bradley Todd was innocent.

William sat in his room watching pro football on TV. The play-offs. Not the Dallas Cowboys. They had missed the playoffs again. He imagined himself wearing the silver-and-white uniforms with the number twelve on his back and a star on his helmet and leading the Cowboys to the Super Bowl. They had won two Super Bowls when Roger Staubach was their quarter-back back in the seventies and three Super Bowls in the early nineties when Troy Aikman was their quarterback, but they had never won a Super Bowl since William had been alive.

That was still his dream, to be the Dallas Cowboys quarterback. To be rich and famous. But he first had to play college football at a Division I-A school. Which meant he had to get a football scholarship. You don't walk on and start at quarterback on a D-I football team. Would D-I coaches come to the Academy to recruit William Tucker? Even if he was good? Really good? When his team was really bad?

His middle school team had gone 0-10. He hadn't really cared about losing, not at first, but by the end of the season, he was really tired. Of losing. Of being the best player on the field, every game, but losing every game. He hated losing. He figured he'd love winning, but he didn't know because he had never won a game. And the varsity team had lost every game, too, so it wasn't as if things would change next year. Or the year after that. Or ever. At the Academy, the athletic teams lost. It was just . . . expected.

But losing sucks.

Would he get a college scholarship playing for a losing team? A lousy team? If his varsity record was 0-40? He had thought about that a lot lately because he would be in ninth grade next year. High school. When boys become men. When they prove themselves on a football field. That they're good enough to play college ball. That they're winners. College coaches aren't paid to lose, so they don't recruit losers.

'Your room is a mess.'

William's mother walked into his room. The place was pretty messy, and at first he thought she was going to tell him to clean up his room. She walked around shaking her head as if disgusted; she stopped and picked up the framed photograph of William and Dad from two years ago, the one Jerry the photography club had taken after a game. After another loss. She replaced the photo and sat down on the bed next to him.

'You have a checkup tomorrow. Lupe will take you after school.'

'Does it involve shots?'

'William, you're too big to be afraid of needles.'

'If I wasn't afraid of needles, I'd have tattoos like the pros.'

'Then I guess it's a good thing you're afraid. But no shots tomorrow.'

'You're not lying again, are you?'

Last checkup, she had said no shots, but there were shots.

'Would your mother lie to you?'

'Yes.'

'Oh, your dad called. He won.'

'Really? Bradley Todd was innocent?'

'Apparently.'

'Wow. Dad's a great lawyer, isn't he?'

'Yes, he is. So do you want to be a lawyer like your dad when you grow up?'

William pointed at the TV.

'No. I want to be a pro quarterback.'

'Has anyone from the Academy ever made it to the NFL?'

He laughed. 'Are you kidding?'

'Well, then it's probably just a dream.'

'You don't think I'm good enough?'

'I think you could be. If you did what that scout said you should do.'

'What scout?'

'A college scout came to see one of your games this year. He talked to your father, gave him some advice.'

'Like what?'

'That we should get you a personal trainer and a nutritionist, send you to quarterback schools . . . and you should transfer to a big public school so you can play at a higher level. Develop your skills.'

'Public school? You said trailer trash goes to public schools.'

'If he gets to go to public school, so do I!'

Becky stood in the doorway.

'My volleyball team sucks as badly as his football team.'

'Are there professional volleyball teams?' his mother asked.

'No.'

'Then you're not going to high school with the trailer trash. You're staying at the Academy.'

'That's not fair! If he gets to go to school with the trailer trash, why can't I?'

'I have to leave my school?' William asked. 'My friends? Ray?'

His team lost every game, but he loved his school. And his friends.

'No, honey, of course you don't have to. You can stay at the Academy.'

'Good.'

'Unless you want to be a star athlete.'

Thing was, Mom wanted a star in the family. She had hoped to be a star, but she wasn't. Becky wasn't either; she wanted to be a writer. Dad was kind of a star, for a lawyer. But lawyers aren't stars like athletes. No one is.

'What does Dad think?'

'He thinks you should be a lawyer.'

Chapter 9

It's a conflicted day for a father when your son can finally hit a golf ball farther than you. On the one hand, you're proud that he can bomb the ball; on the other hand, you realize that he is no longer your little boy. He's now a little man. Or in William's case, a big little man. And you realize that you're past your prime physically.

'Dad, I want to be a pro quarterback.'

Summers in Houston were hot and humid, but winters were sunny and mild. You could play golf in January. Frank bent over and teed his ball. A Titleist Pro-V-One. A four-dollar golf ball. You didn't hit cheap X-outs at the River Oaks Country Club. Frank had joined the club when he had made partner at the firm.

'Okay.'

As if he had said he wanted to be an astronaut.

'Mom told me about the scout.'

'She did?'

'Yep.'

Frank had not.

'I want to go to public school with the trailer trash.'

He had talked to his mother.

'But you love your school. And your friends.'

'I love football more. Dad, I'm tired of losing. I want to be a winner. I want to play big-time high school ball then go D-One. Then the NFL. That's my dream.'

'I dreamed of being a pro golfer when I was your age.'

'Were you any good?'

'Not good enough.'

'But I am. Good enough.'

'You know that?'

'Yeah, Dad. I know that. I know I'm different from the other boys.'

'How?'

'I'm bigger, stronger, faster. Better.'

'At fourteen. You might not be at eighteen.'

'I will be. Once I grow into my hands and feet.'

He held an open hand out. Frank placed his hand against his son's, as if they were high-fiving. William's hand was bigger than Frank's.

'I'm as tall as you, and my feet are bigger than yours. I'll be big enough. I'm a freak of nature, like all athletes.'

'What do you mean?'

'I mean, normal people can't do what pro athletes do. LaDainian Tomlinson, LeBron, A-Rod – they're freaks of nature. To be that big, that fast, that strong, that good – it's not normal. I'm not normal.'

He wasn't.

'Dad, I love you and I'm proud of you, being a great lawyer, saving innocent people like Bradley Todd. But I don't want to be you. I want to be me. I want to let the beast out.'

'What beast?'

'The beast inside me.'

'And you do that on a football field?'

'I do. It's who I am, Dad. When I'm on that field, I know that's where I belong. Like I was born to play football.'

'How does that feel?'

'Perfect.'

Frank wondered if he had ever felt perfect. When the jury had rendered its verdict of not guilty in *The State of Texas v. Bradley Todd*, he had felt relieved, not perfect. There was nothing perfect about the American criminal justice system, even when an innocent person was acquitted. Because there was still an innocent victim. Rachel Truitt had been raped and murdered, and her murderer remained on the loose. Bradley had his justice, but Rachel had not had hers. Not yet.

'What if you get hurt? What if a knee injury takes your speed?'

'I can still throw with bad knees, like Joe Namath. But I won't get hurt.'

'How do you know?'

'I just know.'

Frank hit a good drive. At forty-seven, he still had some distance off the tee. It felt good. But not perfect. William teed a ball, stepped to the side, and cranked a drive that blew past Frank's on the fly. A perfect drive. Frank held out an open hand to his son; they high-fived. Sid and his son had stopped their cart to watch.

'Better make him give you strokes, Frank,' Sid said with a laugh then drove off.

'Dad, I don't want to be a lawyer.'

'You don't have to be a lawyer. But you need to be educated. The Academy is among the finest college prep schools in the country, a straight shot to the Ivy League.'

'You didn't go to the Ivy League.'

'My parents couldn't afford that for me. I can afford it for you. Harvard and Yale have football teams.'

'But I don't want to play for Harvard or Yale. I want to play for the best. UT. Notre Dame. Alabama. Dad, football is my destiny. That's where I belong. On a football field. I'm not smart like Becky. She loves school, but school is just a hobby for me. I'm a student of football, not math and science.'

Frank picked up his carry bag. They could ride in a cart, but a four-hour walk with your son, that's what golf is all about. It's not a sport; it's a way to be with your son without cell phones.

'What if I say no?'

William slung the strap of his bag over his broad shoulder and looked Frank in the eye. His voice was soft. Almost sad.

'I'd hate you. Not now. But later, when I'm older and looking back, wondering if I could've lived my dream. I'd hate you, Dad, for not letting me try.'

William Tucker attended public school the next year.

Chapter 10

It was the fifth day of August, and across the state of Texas tens of thousands of high school boys took to the football field for the first day of fall practice. Only it wasn't fall. It was summer. And it was hot. In Odessa, it was 112 degrees Fahrenheit. In Dallas, it was 105 degrees. In Houston, it was only 99 degrees, but with 95 percent humidity the air felt like a steam sauna.

William Tucker's body glistened in sweat, and practice hadn't even started yet. He wore only shorts and cleats; pads came next week. He was sixteen and stood six feet three inches tall and weighed one hundred ninety pounds with only 10 percent body fat. He worked out with his personal trainer five times a week. He ate a strict diet designed by a sports nutritionist. He honed his skills at quarterback school and his speed with an Olympic coach. He could bench press two hundred fifty pounds ten times. Squat three hundred pounds fifteen times. Run a 4.5-second forty. Throw a football seventy-five yards. He had a forty-six inch chest and a thirty-inch waist. His body was muscular, his skin bronze, and his hair blond and curly. The leather football he held seemed a part of his body.

He was a sophomore about to start his first year on varsity and sitting in the bleachers at his high school's new stadium. Seating capacity was twenty-five thousand. Parents camped out overnight at the admin building when season tickets became available; they became available only when a current season ticket holder forfeited his tickets – which never happened – or died – which didn't happen often enough to suit those waiting in line. Mounted atop the scoreboard in the north end zone was a huge high-definition video screen that showed instant replays during games. The turf was the same grass the pros played on. Behind the stadium stood the new indoor practice arena; it was air-conditioned, but the coaches made the team practice outside so their bodies could acclimate to the heat. That, or the coaches were just—

'Sadistic bastards,' Bobby said.

Bobby Davis played center. He stood six-four and weighed two-ninety. He had a dozen scholarship offers from D-I schools. He was a senior and used steroids. Consequently, he stunk. William always stayed upwind of Bobby.

'They're not happy unless someone passes out during practice,' he said. 'Puking used to be enough, but we lost in regionals last year. Two-a-days this summer are gonna be rough.'

'Really?'

Bobby laughed and shook his head.

'Private school kids. You guys come over here to play big-time ball, but you're like a bunch of altar boys going to a strip joint. So, William, you as good as they say?'

'Yep.'

'Hey, don't be modest or nothing.'

'You asked.'

'You get nervous before a game?'

'Is a shark nervous in water?'

Bobby laughed. 'If you play up to your ego, boy, you're gonna be all-American.'

'It's not ego if you can do it.'

Bobby grunted. 'You want some D-bol?'

Dianabol. Stanozolol. Nandrolone. Oxandrolone. Anabolic steroids. High school athletes knew the names like preteen girls knew Britney Spear's lyrics.

'I don't need it.'

'You should've seen some of the quarterbacks at the summer football camp I went to back in June. They're fucking animals. Hairy fucking animals.' Bobby laughed. 'So I go in there weighing two-seventy. I'm almost nineteen years old—'

'You're almost nineteen?'

'My dad held me back so I'd have time to get bigger before varsity.'

'It worked.'

'Anyway, this is a camp for elite players, guys like me holding D-One offers. I tell the offensive line coach I'm gonna start as a freshman. He laughs, says, "Not at two-seventy you ain't." Said I need to weigh in at three hundred to start in D-One-A. I said, "What do I do?" He said, "Bulk up, Bobby."'

'He told you to use steroids?'

'No. But I knew what he meant. Everyone knows. They told everyone the same thing, except those fucking fast-ass black receivers from the 'hood. Man, those guys could go pro straight out of high school.'

'So you put on twenty pounds with the juice?'

'Shit works. You should try it.'

'Like I said, I don't need it.'

They watched the cheerleaders practicing their routines down the sideline. Including Becky.

'Your sister's kind of cute,' Bobby said.

'Don't go there.'

He laughed. William didn't.

'Hey, sorry, man,' Bobby said. 'Didn't know you were so touchy about your sister.'

He was. After a moment, he calmed.

'You like this school?' William asked.

'I like playing football at this school. Not so much going to school.'

'What's your GPA?'

'One-point-seven.'

'That's low.'

'Not for a football player.'

'Do you study?'

'Football. Why waste my time on math and English when I'm going to college to play football?'

'Are your grades good enough to get into college?'

'There ain't any academic standards for athletes. If you can play, you get in.' He laughed. 'College coaches today, they don't worry about your academic transcript, just your criminal background check.'

Bobby leaned back and clasped his hands behind his head as if all that he saw was his.

'See, William, the rest of the world's got rules. We don't. If you can play football – I mean, really play – you're on a different level in life from everyone who can't play football. You live above the rules.'

A cute cheerleader bounced past; she gave them a finger wave and a smile.

'Hi, William.'

He didn't know her.

'She knows you.'

They watched her – she peeked back to make sure they did – all the way down the sideline to the other cheerleaders. Including his sister. When his dad allowed William to leave the

Academy and attend public school, Becky had demanded equal treatment. She played volleyball, and this public school's teams were great. She wanted a scholarship.

'Name's Chrissie. She's the team punch. You make the team, you make her.'

'Anyone on the team?'

'Starters. She ain't gonna screw a sub, William.'

As if he should know that.

'Girls line up for the starters.'

William knew he was ready to start on one of the top-ranked high school football teams in Texas, but was he ready for the cheerleaders? Bobby laughed and pointed.

'Look at rich-boy Ronnie.'

Another player had walked up to the cheerleaders and was obviously trying to flirt. He was an offensive lineman like Bobby, and he was big, but not in a ripped, muscular way; he was big in the 'he occupied a lot of space' way.

'Thinks he can buy his way onto a D-One team,' Bobby said. 'Ain't enough money in his daddy's bank for that.'

'What's he doing here?'

'Same thing as you. Another River Oaks rich boy slumming with the trailer trash, hoping to play big-time high school ball, develop his skills, get a D-One scholarship. It ain't never gonna happen for Ronnie.'

Down on the track, Ronnie's flirting had fallen flat with the cheerleaders. They had frowns on their faces and now ignored him. He was clearly not pleased. Becky turned away from him, but he grabbed her arm. The beast inside William roared to life. He jumped up, ran down the stands, and vaulted the railing. He landed on his feet and sprinted to his sister. She looked scared. The beast grabbed Ronnie by the throat, yanked him away from Becky, and then drove his fist into Ronnie's—

'Whoa!'

A massive arm wrapped around William's chest and pulled him back.

'Shit, William!' Bobby said. 'You're a fucking animal!'

William broke loose of Bobby's grasp and stepped toward Ronnie; he outweighed William by sixty pounds but he stepped back. William put a finger in Ronnie's face.

'Don't ever touch my sister again.'

Ronnie's eyes showed the fear of an antelope facing the lion. He turned and walked away. William turned to his sister.

'You okay?'

'Yeah. Thanks, William.'

Bobby Davis grinned. 'Man, it's gonna be a fun year with a beast like you playing quarterback for us.'

Bobby spread his arms out to the stadium where they would play their first game in three weeks.

'And you're gonna love it. We go undefeated for seven or eight games, you're not gonna believe this fucking place.'

Chapter 11

The stadium looked as if the Barnum & Bailey Circus had come to town.

The high-profile trial of a star athlete was a three-ring circus. But a football game featuring star athletes on two top-ranked high school teams on a Friday night in Texas was the biggest circus of them all. It was late October, and the heat and humidity of Houston had finally broken. The air was cool and filled with excitement and the sound of the bands competing from opposing bleachers across fifty-three and one-third yards of manicured green grass that rivaled the fairways at the country club. Twenty-five thousand parents and students and lovers of football filled the stands; thousands more without tickets stood outside the perimeter fence at the south end zone to watch the game on the video screen in the north end zone. Frank Tucker had a ticket. Two. Normally, he would have been put on a waiting list and waited at least five years to purchase season tickets. But parents of the players got moved to the front of the line. A perk of your son playing football on the number one ranked team in the state of Texas.

This public high school enrolled four thousand students in grades nine through twelve. Two thousand were boys. A football team played eleven boys on offense and eleven on defense. All the coaches needed were twenty-two athletes out of a pool of two thousand. They found them. Big white boys from working-class families, fast black boys from the 'hood, and a rich quarterback from River Oaks. The public school that served River Oaks also served the Fourth Ward. The inner city. Blacks and Latinos. Two-thirds of the students were minorities; one-third was white. One hundred percent were poor. The rich kids were in private schools. But not William Tucker. Because his father did not want his son to hate him. Football was his dream. For the other players, it was their way out of the Fourth Ward.

Cheerleaders in uniforms jumped and somersaulted and performed stunts on the sideline. Students roamed the open area around the home concession stand. Their parents sat in the stands.

It was not an Academy crowd.

The girls wore body-hugging clothes that seemed more befitting of street hookers than high school students. The white boys wore sweatshirts bearing college logos – UT and A&M, not Harvard and MIT – and the black boys wore hoodies and their pants below their butts revealing colorful undershorts. The parents did not wear the latest from Neiman Marcus but instead the latest from Nike and Adidas, as if they all had endorsement contracts. Sweat suits and sneakers and football jerseys. Caps on backwards and tattoos on their arms and ankles and lower backs. Pickups and SUVs made in America filled the parking lot. Video cameras made in Asia filled the stands; the parents captured their sons' glory days on tape for college coaches or posterity.

Frank stood along the sideline fence. Alone and without a video camera. He didn't know any of the other parents and Liz refused to come; this multicultural and working-class environment was too far below her social standing. She had encouraged William to transfer to this public school so he'd become a star, but she didn't want to personally witness his path to stardom, similar to wanting to be a politician but not be willing to dive into the filthy muck called fundraising. Frank had grown up in just such a working-class environment, but he did not feel at ease. The times and attire had changed. The people had changed. Many of the dads still worked in the petrochemical plants that lined the Houston Ship Channel and the moms at jobs that served the industry, but they did not seem like the moms and dads he had remembered as a boy. Those moms and dads seemed like TV parents, like Ward and June Cleaver. These moms and dads seemed like the Osbournes.

'Fuck you, asshole!' one of the dads yelled to the referees.

'Not exactly a River Oaks polo crowd, is it?'

Sam Jenkins, the college scout, stood next to Frank. He smoked a cigar and remained loyal to Old Spice. Polo was in fact played in River Oaks.

'Nope.'

Sam laughed. 'This is a football crowd, Frank. You don't get a lot of JDs and MBAs and PhDs at a high school football game, except at the Academy, and what those boys do doesn't qualify as football. This is your working class. NFL is built on the working class and Latinos. Shit, you been to a Texans game?'

The Texans were Houston's pro football team.

'No.'

William followed the Cowboys, so he had not pressured Frank to take him to the Texans' games.

'Like going to a bullfight in Juarez, everyone speaking Spanish. And in the high-dollar seats. They don't have health insurance, but they'll pay brokers a thousand bucks to watch a

95

pro football game. For the lower class, football's an escape from their fucked-up lives.'

'You're a psychologist now?'

Sam shrugged. 'Part of being a scout, figuring people out, what makes them tick. You see a boy, he's got all the physical tools, but you've got to figure his mind out, does he have ice in his veins, does he burn with the competitive desire, does he want to win more than live, does he have the confidence to be the man.'

William's new team was big, strong, and fast. Big, strong white boys and fast black boys. They ran a pro offense. William had thrown thirty-two passes in the first half and completed twenty-seven for two hundred seventy-five yards and four touchdowns. He had also run for another seventy-five yards and a touchdown. Eight games into his sophomore season, William Tucker was the top college prospect in the nation. He was sixteen years old.

'You did the right thing, Frank.'

'Did I?'

They had gone all in on William Tucker's career. A big public school with a pro-style offense and an indoor practice arena. A personal trainer and a nutritionist. An ex-Olympian speed coach. Quarterback school. Seven-on-seven passing tournaments. Tens of thousands of dollars. Frank Tucker had nurtured his son's gift, no expense spared. It had seemed so . . . American. To spend whatever it took – whether Ivy League tuition or speed training by a gold medal winner – to buy your children success. A better life. Their dreams. But, despite his misgivings, Frank had to confess that it had worked. William's improvement over the last two years was nothing less than remarkable. His skills soared. His size, his strength, and his speed increased dramatically. His footwork and throwing motion were now textbook. His vision of the field – twenty-one other players who seemed to be running around chaotically – was both omniscient and laser focused. His recognition of the pass coverage and thus which of his receivers would be open on the play was instant and unerring.

'He's a hell of a quarterback,' Sam said.

Perhaps his son was born to play football just as Mozart was born to write symphonies and Bobby Fischer to play chess. Perhaps we are who we were meant to be. Pushing a boy to be a football player when he wasn't born for it, that's wrong. But allowing a boy to be what he was born to be – how can that be wrong? Some people were born to be doctors and scientists and perhaps even lawyers? Why not athletes? Why not football players?

'I've kept tabs on William,' Sam said. 'Saw him at the quarterback schools.'

From his expression, Frank could tell that Sam was about to offer more career advice for his son. He gestured to the field where the teams were returning for the second half. The boys pounded their chests and held their arms out to the fans like victorious gladiators. Sam shook his head.

'People on TV talk about kids having no self-esteem. Complete bullshit. Kids today got self-esteems the size of fucking Wyoming. Self-esteem oozes from every pore on their bodies. They been told they're special since the day they popped out of mama and a hundred times a day since. They believe it. They haven't done a goddamn thing in their lives, but they know they're special. So when they fail at sports or school or life, it's not because they didn't work hard enough or they're just not smart enough or good enough. No, they're special, so it's got to be someone else's fault. They didn't fail. Someone made them fail. Now we've got an entire generation of fucked-up narcissists 'cause their mamas told them they're special.'

'What's your point, Sam?'

'My point is, it's not bullshit with William. He really is special.'

Sam smoked his cigar.

'Game program says William's six-three and one-ninety. That true?'

'It is.'

'Shoe size?'

'Sixteen.'

Sam grunted in obvious admiration of William's shoe size.

'And no tattoos.'

'He's afraid of needles.'

Sam chuckled. 'Everyone's got something that'll make them sweat. I hate snakes.'

Another puff on his cigar, which he then pointed at the field. At William.

'Time he's a senior, he'll be six-five, two-twenty. He's number one on my list. Hell, he's number one on every scout's list. He'll have his choice of schools.'

'We've already gotten dozens of recruiting letters.'

'You'll get more.'

Frank sighed. 'I wanted him to go to the Ivy League, but that's not what he wants. His dream is to play D-One. So, what, do we go to the schools to meet the coaches?'

'Nope. They'll come to William. Like wise men to baby Jesus.'

Sam breathed out cigar smoke.

'William's life is about to change, Frank. Big time.'

Becky Tucker stood down the sideline from her dad and a man smoking a cigar. She was eighteen and a senior cheerleader. The last few months, as the team had won more games and William had become the star quarterback, she had begun hearing rumors at school about her brother and the head cheerleader. Rhonda. She was a senior, too. She was not a virgin.

Not even close.

The thought of her little brother having sex with Rhonda made her want to throw up. He might be as big as a man, but he was still just a boy. And sophomore boys didn't need sex with senior girls. At the Academy, she had never heard of anyone having sex. Of course, some kids had to be doing it, but those who were didn't talk about it. At this school, that was all they talked about. Who was screwing whom. (Although no one said 'whom' at a public school.) And they took cell phone photos of their body parts and sexted each other.

Gross.

Becky had never bonded with the other girls. They were different. They were not girls. They were women. Sexually active women. Rhonda and the other cheerleaders were huddled together down the sideline, waving to the players on the sideline and then giggling. Gossiping. No doubt about who was screwing whom. Rhonda waved at the players. At a player.

'William!'

Becky saw her brother turn to Rhonda . . . and Rhonda blow him a kiss. That did it. Becky's anger rose inside her until she felt as if she might explode. She marched down the sideline and to the girls, put her hands on her hips, and glared at Rhonda, the bitch.

'Are you screwing my brother?'

Rhonda smiled.

'Yes.'

All the girls had answered as one.

99

Chapter 12

'Daddy, I'm worried about William.'

The next morning, Frank sat at his desk in the study on the backside of the house looking out at the pool. The kids were at home with him; Liz had gone to the funeral of Beverly Joiner, another socialite who had died of breast cancer. Frank didn't know her or her husband, Dale. All he knew about them was what Liz had told him: he was in oil and gas, and they lived in a fifteen-thousand-square-foot home abutting the country club. On the phone were a dozen messages from corporate lawyers in the biggest firms in Texas and two dozen more from sports agents for top college and professional athletes who had run afoul of the law and now sought Frank Tucker's representation. The Bradley Todd case had put Frank in the national press again. His fame had grown. As had his son's. On the desk sat a stack of letters addressed to William Tucker from the head football coaches at UT, A&M, Notre Dame, LSU, Florida, USC, UCLA, Ohio State, Alabama, and two dozen other Division I-A football schools in the country. Recruiting a sophomore in high school. Sitting on the other side of the desk as if she were a client was Becky.

'Why?'

'He's changing.'

'How?'

'He's becoming a star. It's changing him. His attitude. About himself. And girls. Daddy, he's having sex with the cheerleaders.'

'Which one?'

'All of them.'

'Pretty cool, huh, Dad?'

Becky had left, and William held a hand out for a high-five. Frank slapped his son's hand then they sat on opposite sides of Frank's desk. William was speaking of the recruiting letters, not sex with cheerleaders. He was drinking a protein shake.

'Sure, son, it's nice that all these coaches think you could play college ball.'

'They love me.'

'No. They don't love you, William. They need you. There's a difference. They're paid millions to win football games, so they need players like you to keep their jobs. They need you, but they don't love you. Your family loves you, win or lose. And we'll love you even if you throw five interceptions.'

'I've never thrown five interceptions in one game.'

'You will.'

Frank leaned back in his chair.

'Son, are you having sex?'

'Dad, did you see they indicted Barry Bonds for lying under oath to a grand jury about the steroids scandal?'

Barry Bonds was the all-time major league baseball home run hitter. His agent's message was on Frank's phone.

'Don't change the subject.'

'And Marion Jones confessed to doping during the Olympics in Sydney when she won five medals.'

She was facing prison time. Her agent's message was also on the phone.

'What about you? Are you confessing?'

'To doping?'

'To sexing?'

'Is that really a word?'

'It's a question.'

'Am I under oath like Barry?'

'You're under my roof.'

They regarded each other a long moment then William smiled and shrugged.

'What can I say? The girls love William Tucker.'

'You're speaking of yourself in the third person now?'

Another shrug. 'All the pros do.'

'You're not a pro. What's the girl's name?'

'What girl?'

'The girl you're having sex with.'

'Which one?'

'There's more than one?'

'Not at the same time.'

'You've had sex with more than one girl?'

'Dad, it's no big deal. It's like texting. Bobby said—'

'Bobby your center?'

'Yeah.'

'You're taking advice from an offensive lineman?'

'He's a senior.'

'That doesn't mean he's smart. Son, there are laws. If you have sex with younger girls—'

'They're older.'

'How old?'

'Juniors, seniors, college . . .'

'You're having sex with college girls?'

'They come home for the weekend.'

His son had stopped asking sex questions at the dinner table a few months before. Now Frank knew why: he was getting his questions answered by older girls. Frank decided that he had better ask a few questions of his own.

'William, you know if you impregnate a girl and she has the baby, you're responsible for child support for eighteen years?'

'All the girls are on the pill.'

'You can still contract a sexually transmitted disease, like AIDS.'

'They're good girls.'

'Are you using condoms?'

'Seriously?'

'Testosterone and stupidity strike again.'

'Huh?'

'Your body is acting like a man, but your brain is thinking like a boy.'

'What?'

'You're doing something stupid. You're playing Russian roulette with your life. I want you to stop.'

'Playing Russian roulette?'

'Having sex.'

William regarded Frank as if he had just said, 'Stop having protein shakes.'

'No way. Look, Dad, I know sex was a big deal back when you were my age, but it's not today. It's just a part of dating – go to the movie, get a burger, have sex. Everyone does it.' He smiled his movie star smile. 'Sex is good for William Tucker.'

Frank sighed. How could he protect his son from himself?

'Then at least wear a condom.'

Sex used to be good for Frank Tucker. His first thought was that he was jealous of his sixteen-year-old son. His second thought was that he should grill his son a thick steak – he couldn't keep that kind of sex life up on protein shakes alone.

But he quickly admonished himself for employing a double standard with his children. If Becky were having sex with several different boys every week, he'd be devastated, not proud. And he had to confess, he felt a twinge of pride in his son's sexual exploits. He shouldn't, but he did. His son was living every sixteen-year-old boy's dream, the same dreams Frank had entertained at sixteen. Should he criticize his son for succeeding where Frank had failed? He did not see that William Tucker had taken the first step to entitlement. But he did see his son take the second step.

'I need you to mow the lawn and wash the cars today,' Frank said.

William nodded, pulled out his new iPhone, and began texting.

'I'll get my people on it.'

Frank chuckled. 'You're a sophomore in high school. You don't have people.'

'Sure I do.'

He sent the text then sat back, as if waiting for a response. Thirty seconds later, he got one. He read the text then smiled.

'Two freshmen will be here in an hour to cut the grass and wash the cars.'

'You're kidding?'

'Nope. Freshmen volunteer to do stuff for the football players.'

'Why?'

'Because they can't play football. So doing stuff for us gives them a connection to the team. They want to help the team win.'

'By mowing your grass and washing your cars?'

'*Your* grass and *your* cars.'

'William, other people don't exist for your convenience. They're not just part of your entourage. Being a football player doesn't make you special.'

'Sure it does.'

'No, it doesn't.'

His son gestured at the recruiting letters.

'All those coaches think I'm special. Everyone does. The media, other players, parents, classmates, girls . . . Are they all lying?'

'No. But they mean you're a special football player – that's determined by what you do on the field – not a special human being – that's determined by what you do off the field.'

'How many human beings can do what I can do on a football field?'

'Not many.'

'So I'm a special human being.'

'No, William, you're a lucky human being.' Frank pointed a thumb in the direction of the medical center in downtown Houston. 'But you're no more special than a child over in MD Anderson's cancer ward. You're just luckier. There's a difference. Never underestimate the role luck plays in life.'

'I'd rather be big, strong, and fast than lucky.'

'William . . .'

'Dad, Ray is a math/science genius. He'll probably discover the cure for cancer, but I'll make a lot more money playing football than he's going to make doing that.'

'Do you still see him?'

William shook his head.

'Why not?'

'He still goes to the Academy.'

'He still lives right here in River Oaks.'

'And, you know, he's a nerd.'

'That didn't matter before.'

William shrugged. 'We grew apart. Like you and Mom.'

He was sixteen. He understood now why his father and mother slept in different bedrooms.

'People look at me differently,' his son said. 'Like I'm a star.'

'Who?'

'Everyone. I see the dads staring at me when I walk from the locker room to the field. They line up to look at me, like I'm an animal at the zoo. Do people line up to look at you when you walk into a courthouse?'

'No. Lawyers aren't heroes anymore. Athletes are our heroes now.'

'I'm a hero?'

'Some people might look at you that way, William, like you're a star or a hero, but you can never look at yourself that way. You have to know that it's not real. They don't love you.'

'Girls do.'

'No. Some girls are attracted to star athletes—'

He grinned. 'A lot of girls.'

Now he was bragging. Frank shook his head. It was tough when your sixteen-year-old son was getting more sex than you.

'Would they have sex with you if you were a math nerd like Ray?'

His son laughed. 'Nerds don't get laid.'

'William, what I'm saying is, you've got a lot of athletic ability, more than most boys. That ability makes you special on a football field, but nowhere else. You have to stay grounded. Fame and stardom can make a person lose their footing in life, slip and fall. Those people end up paying me to represent them. William, you're a great kid. Don't let the fact that some people worship athletes change who you are.'

'Like LeBron holding a national television special to announce his new NBA team?'

LeBron James was the best basketball player on the planet. When he decided to leave his original team, the Cleveland Cavaliers, and enter the free-agent market, he held a nationally televised event to announce where he would play basketball the next season, as if he were the president announcing that the country was going to war.

'Exactly like that. Other people might think you're special, but you can't believe that. There's a difference between being special and being lucky. You stay the William Tucker you are now, and you'll be a happy man no matter what happens for you in sports. Or to you.'

'LeBron seems happy.'

William's phone pinged. He read the message.

'My people are here early.'

'So what do these freshman boys get in return for being your people?'

'Protection. No one at school messes with them. And I give them autographed jerseys.'

'Boys at your school want to wear your autographed jerseys?'

'No. Their dads do.'

Frank sat back and sighed. He regarded his son. He was a good kid. But he was already falling into the celebrity athlete trap. How was his father to save him? How do you keep a boy grounded when the world kept putting him up on a pedestal? When the world told him daily that he's special? That he's a star? At sixteen, the fame snowball had already started rolling downhill for his son. And once it started rolling, it was hard to stop. It consumed everything in its path. And Frank worried that it might consume his son.

That William Tucker might be too good for his own good.

At forty-nine, life was good for Frank Tucker – apparently not as good as it was for his sixteen-year-old son, but good. He had two great kids. Becky would not win a volleyball scholarship, but she had won acceptance to Wellesley with a full scholarship from her father. Sixty thousand a year. She was worth every penny. And it was probably the only college tuition he would pay. William would win a scholarship to the school of his choice. His ticket in life. His sexual promiscuity at sixteen concerned Frank, but what could he do about it? Would he have stopped having sex with older girls when he was sixteen, even if his father had asked him? No. He would not have. Of course, he didn't have sex until his first semester at UT. And he hadn't stopped having sex until he was forty-three.

When he was twenty-seven, he was sure his wife loved him. The truth of the matter is, he had married up. In his prime, he was a good-looking man; but he was not great looking. At best, he was a five or maybe a six. Liz was a ten-plus. She was a beauty queen at the University of Texas, no small feat. He had met her when he was a third-year law student and she was still an under-grad; he had already accepted a job with a Houston firm. He asked her out on a whim and was stunned when she said yes. Because you learn at an early age where you fit on the human food chain. Where you fit in terms of looks and wealth. You date accordingly. A nerd doesn't ask the homecoming queen to the prom; the star athlete doesn't ask the class ugly duckling. A poor boy doesn't date a rich girl; a rich boy doesn't date a poor girl. Humans don't work that way. They order themselves according to looks and wealth. They date their own kind. You don't stray outside your place on the food chain. That's the rule.

Frank had always observed the rule. He dated cute girls. Sweet girls. Nice girls. But not beautiful girls. Not drop-dead gorgeous girls. Not girls like Liz. But he had asked her out, and she had fallen in love with him. He had broken the rule and had won the lottery.

Or so he had thought.

When you're young, you intentionally overlook such discrepancies. You convince yourself that she loves you for who you are, not how much you make. That you're her Prince Charming, not just her provider. Twenty years of marriage later, you realize she never really loved you. And you pray for that, for someone to love and someone to love you, hopefully the same person. You no longer want to have sex like a sixteen-year-old boy; you want to make love like a man.

He understood now that for Liz it was never about love, just about the cost of living. She wanted things. His profession was the law, but his job was to give her the life she wanted. The things she wanted. She had not given him love, but she had given him the children. And in the end, their love meant more to him than the love of a woman. Other men lived without money or success or children or good health. He had all that. So he lived without love and without complaint. He kept the peace.

Every man makes his own bed. And then sleeps in it. Frank slept alone.

It was an hour later, and Frank stood at the window watching two boys mow his grass. They were actually doing a good job. His son sat in a patio chair autographing jerseys.

Something was wrong with that picture.

Most dads would think it was a perfect picture. Their son the star quarterback. Having sex with cheerleaders and college girls. His entourage mowing his grass and washing his cars. That's the dream. For the son and the dad. But not for Frank. He knew what pressure could do to a human being, how it could push a good man – or woman – over the edge. Most of his clients were good people who had been pushed to the edge and then over by the pressure to succeed. Business was a high-pressure environment. Sports even more. Doping among professional athletes had become pervasive. Home run hitters hauled before Congressional committees then charged with perjury. Olympic track stars convicted and sentenced to prison.

109

Chapter 13

Frank drove to Austin Sunday afternoon. He checked into the Driskill Hotel in downtown, bought and read the local newspaper, and then went to the Travis County Jail. He asked to see Bradley Todd then waited in one of the cubicles in the interview room on the visitors' side of the Plexiglas partition. Bradley was now a senior star on the UT basketball team. He was charged with the rape and murder of Sarah Barnes, his ex-fiancée. She had been stabbed forty-seven times. The Bradley Todd who soon appeared before him was not the same Bradley Todd the jury had acquitted two years before. His eyes were different. He sat and picked up the phone.

'Hey, Frank.' Not Mr. Tucker. 'You want to earn another million bucks?'

Frank held the phone to his ear and the front page of the newspaper with Sarah's photo to the glass.

'Did you rape and kill Sarah?'

'Are you my lawyer?'

'Depends on your answer. But whatever you tell me is still confidential.'

111

He nodded.

'Why?'

'She broke it off a year ago, our engagement.'

'Why?'

'She said she got tired of all the other girls.'

'And?'

'And I kept trying to get her back. But she wouldn't come back.'

'What happened the night she died?'

'I went to her apartment and found her with another guy. I got pissed, her fucking around on me.'

'She broke off the engagement a year ago. She wasn't your fiancée.'

'Like hell. She was mine and she was always gonna be mine. That's what I told her.'

'So you raped and killed her?'

'I had sex with her.'

'Sex without consent is rape, Bradley.'

'We had sex while we were engaged.'

'It's not a lifetime pass. What happened then?'

'She tried to call the cops.'

'So you stabbed her? Forty-seven times?'

He shrugged. 'I got mad.'

As if that made it justifiable homicide. They stared at each other through the Plexiglas. Frank did not want to ask the next question, but he had no choice.

'Did you rape and murder Rachel Truitt two years ago?'

Bradley's eyes were void of remorse.

'Yeah.'

'You lied to me.'

Bradley shrugged again. 'You wouldn't have defended me if I had told you the truth.'

'And Sarah lied to protect you?'

112

'We were engaged.'

'Did she know you killed Rachel?'

'No. I told her I was partying on Sixth Street, which was true, but if she didn't say I was with her, the jury would convict me.'

'They would have. So she committed perjury for you. And now she's dead. I believed you, Bradley. I thought you were innocent. Now another girl is dead.'

'So are you going to be my lawyer?'

'No.'

Frank got drunk in the hotel bar.

Chapter 14

Six months later, Frank's cell phone rang. He answered.

'Mr. Tucker, this is the court clerk. Are you stuck in traffic? The judge and the jury are waiting for you.'

'Uh, yes, the traffic. I just pulled into the parking lot. I'll be right up.'

Frank unscrewed the top on the pint bottle of Jim Beam and took a long swallow. He screwed the top back on, grabbed his briefcase, and got out of the Expedition.

Almost two years before, the subprime mortgage market had collapsed. A year before, his client had been indicted by a federal grand jury for mortgage fraud. For doing exactly what the federal government wanted him to do: make home loans. Prop up the residential real estate market. The economy. Easy money kept the nation's economy humming along, the people employed, and the stock market high. Easy money was good for America.

But when the market crashes, someone has to be punished.

The politicians – the drug lords of easy money – are never punished; the mortgage brokers – the street dealers who implemented easy money – are. His client had approved mortgage loans guaranteed by the full faith and credit of the United States government to anyone who could fog up a mirror. Income to repay the mortgage was optional. Wall Street bankers bundled the mortgages into salable securities and sold them to mutual funds, pension funds, foreigners – to any sucker they could find. No one complained as long as real-estate prices marched upward; but, of course, what goes up must come down.

The housing market came down.

The politicians pointed fingers at the big banks before voters pointed fingers at them. But the government bailed out the Wall Street bankers then indicted the brokers. Including Frank's client. The trial had lasted two weeks. The jury had a verdict. Frank was late. He rushed into the courtroom in the federal building in downtown Houston. He hurried up the center aisle and sat at the defense table. The judge was not happy; he nodded to the bailiff. He disappeared through a door then returned with the jurors in tow.

The jury acquitted Frank's client of all charges.

After the jury had been dismissed and the courtroom had emptied, the judge motioned Frank to the bench. Frank walked over to the judge.

'Another acquittal, Frank. Congratulations.'

'Thanks, Melvin.'

The judge sniffed the air; more specifically, Frank's breath. In his rush, he had forgotten to use the breath spray after that last shot of Jim Beam.

'Frank, have you been drinking this morning?'

Like most drunks who didn't know they were drunks, he tried to laugh it off.

'Hell, Melvin, I've been drinking every morning.'

'You tried this case drunk?'

Frank shrugged. 'I still won.'

'You won, but not like you usually do. You never made mistakes before, Frank, but you made a lot of mistakes this time. You won because the prosecutor made more.'

The judge regarded Frank Tucker. He had gained weight. His complexion had reddened from the whiskey. He wasn't the man or the lawyer he once was.

'Frank, what the hell happened to you?'

'A girl died.'

Melvin sighed. 'I read about all that. Frank, it wasn't your fault. That's part of the job description. Your client might be guilty.'

The judge's expression turned judicial.

'Frank, showing up in federal court drunk . . . you crossed a line. You need help. And your clients need a sober lawyer, even if you are better drunk than most lawyers are sober. I've got no choice. I've got to report you to the bar association.'

'Melvin, please—'

'Frank, they'll suspend your law license.'

Chapter 15

Frank Tucker didn't start drinking because his client had raped and murdered Rachel Truitt, the first girl. That's a risk every lawyer takes when he takes a case, that the client might be lying. He was convinced that Bradley Todd was telling the truth. That he was innocent. That he was not a rapist and a murderer. He was wrong. But Bradley had already raped and murdered Rachel when Frank agreed to represent him. So he suffered no moral guilt over her death. Rachel Truitt's death had not occurred on his watch.

But the second girl's death had.

Sarah Barnes had died because he had won an acquittal for Bradley Todd in the first case. His client had been guilty of brutally raping and murdering an eighteen-year-old coed, but Frank Tucker had 'gotten him off,' as the newspapers referred to Bradley's acquittal after he was arrested for the second murder. So Bradley Todd wasn't on death row where he belonged, but on the streets, free to rape and murder another young coed. And he had. Sarah was twenty-one. She was sister to Ben and Carla. Daughter to Gary and Cindy. She was a cute Christian girl. A dead girl.

Her face haunted Frank Tucker.

He had found himself in the press again, but it wasn't favorable press. Travis County District Attorney Dick Dorkin finally had his revenge. He had been quoted in the Austin paper: 'Frank Tucker once called me a failed politician. Perhaps I am. But at least I don't have that girl's blood on my hands. At least my conscience is clear. At least I can look myself in the mirror each morning and know I'm not responsible for Sarah Barnes's death. I tried to put Bradley Todd on death row for raping and murdering Rachel Truitt. But his billionaire father could afford to hire Frank Tucker and pay him a million dollars to get his son off. And Frank Tucker did just that. He set Bradley Todd free to kill again. And kill he did. Frank Tucker got the verdict he wanted for Bradley Todd two years ago. I hope he can live with his own verdict of himself today.'

He could not.

He stared at Sarah's photo from the two-year-old story in the paper. He carried it with him always. He looked at her face daily. He downed another shot of whiskey straight up. Four shots would usually blur her image from his mind. He would pass out on the fifth shot.

William sat in a chair behind a table set up on the artificial turf inside the indoor practice arena. The head coach stood to one side, his mother to the other. His father was supposed to be there, but it was probably just as well that he wasn't. If he were drinking, he might make a scene on national television. Arrayed on the table in front of William were five caps bearing college emblems: UT, A&M, ND, USC, and F. The five finalists competing for William Tucker.

I am a star.

William was eighteen and a senior; he hadn't mowed the grass or washed his own car or gone a week without sex in two years. He had led his team to a third straight undefeated record – he loved winning – and a third straight Class 5A state football championship. He stood six feet five inches tall and weighed two hundred twenty pounds with 7 percent body fat. He had a forty-eight inch chest and a thirty-two inch waist. He benched three-fifty and squatted four-fifty. He ran a 4.4 forty. He wore a size seventeen shoe. He was a beast, a freak of nature, and the number one college prospect in the nation. And the nation was waiting for him to decide where he would play his college football. He would make that decision today and then graduate from high school next week, before the Christmas break. In January, he would enroll in college for the spring semester. For spring football practice.

'Two minutes,' the television producer said.

The world was mired in the Great Recession, but football-loving America – which is to say, most of America – took a timeout from their economic misery to watch ESPN that day. It was national signing day, the first day high school seniors could sign binding letters of intent to play Division I-A football on full scholarships at the colleges of their choice. The expensive and time-consuming process that had begun when the boys were twelve – the scouts watching their middle school games and charting their progress and size through high school; the recruiting letters to thousands of boys beginning in their freshman year; the on-campus visits by hundreds of boys; the head coaches' home visits to a select few – it all came down to this day. Today the process either succeeded or failed. Each school's recruiting class would be graded by college football analysts on cable television: A to F. Who won, who lost. Who had convinced the best football players in America to become student-athletes at their school for the next four years, although there was little student left in the student-athletes of today and few stayed long enough to graduate. The best players left school after their sophomore or junior years. Money awaited in the NFL.

'One minute.'

Aimed at him was the ESPN camera. He wasn't nervous. At eighteen, he had already given dozens of live TV interviews to local, state, and even national sports channels. Being the top high school football player in America, his signing would be carried live on national television. The sports cable channels ran twenty-four/seven; Americans were addicted to sports. But mostly to football. High school football, college football, pro football, fantasy football. Football had captured the nation's imagination. It was America's sport. Invented in America and played by Americans. On college campuses across the country, football in the fall brought alumni and money and perhaps the glory of a national championship to the school, much more than, say, a professor winning the Nobel Prize in physics; in the year after Johnny Manziel won the Heisman Trophy at Texas A&M, the school raised a record $740 million in donations. The signing of a star quarterback was far more important to a college's financial future than the signing of a star professor.

I am special.

Consequently, his choice held the nation's attention. Where would he go? Would he play quarterback for the Texas Longhorns, the Texas A&M Aggies, the Notre Dame Fighting Irish, the University of Southern California Trojans, or the Florida Gators? Each of the five schools had live feeds into its campus, similar to when the Olympic Committee announced the next host city. Coaches, students, players, and alumni gathered in front of their televisions. America awaited his decision. William Tucker's decision that day would determine which of those five schools would have a legitimate shot at the national collegiate football championship during the next four years. Which of those schools would reap a revenue bonanza from bowl games, TV contracts, ticket and skybox sales, and merchandising profits. Which of those schools would make or lose money on their athletic department. College football today was a big business worth billions.

'We're live.'

The anchor from New York: 'William Tucker, you're the star of this year's high school recruiting class. A special player indeed. You're going to be a hero to one of five colleges today.'

On the five monitors set up in front of him, William could see live shots of the crowds of students, coaches, and alumni at each of the schools, like Catholics waiting for the naming of the next Pope. Except these campus crowds featured sexy cheerleaders holding posters that read WE WANT YOU, WILLIAM TUCKER and COME PLAY WITH US, WILLIAM TUCKER and THESE STUDENT BODIES LOVE YOU, WILLIAM TUCKER.

'William, where are you going to play college ball?'

There was a drum roll. Seriously, the show did a drum roll.

'Will it be Texas, A&M, Notre Dame, USC, or Florida?'

The campus crowds on the monitors fell silent. Students put their folded hands to their faces as if praying. Coaches clenched their fists as if to will a decision for their school. Athletic directors dreamed of BCS bowl game revenues. Alumni envisioned bowl wins over their archrivals.

'I'm taking my football talents to . . .'

William reached out and hovered his hand over each of the caps for a few seconds, just to generate some suspense for the viewers, then grabbed the UT cap and put it on.

'. . . Austin, Texas. I will play for the Texas Longhorns.'

The crowd on the UT campus jumped for joy. Students screamed. Coaches threw their arms into the air and hugged each other. William Tucker was coming to Austin.

The losing crowds collapsed in stunned disbelief. Coaches cursed, and coeds cried. Athletic directors and alumni looked as if they had just been diagnosed with terminal cancer. William Tucker would not be playing for their team.

I am William Tucker.

Elizabeth Tucker stood next to her son. NCAA rules require that a parent sign the letter of intent if the player is under twenty-one years of age. She would sign as William Tucker's guardian. Her son would be the star she had never been.

She signed the letter of intent then smiled for the television camera. At forty-six and after a few minor nips and tucks, she was still photogenic. She wasn't the UT beauty queen that she had been twenty-four years before, but she was still a beautiful middle-aged woman.

But was she beautiful enough?

Beautiful enough to compete in Houston for a wealthy middle-aged divorced or widowed man? A man with money? They were hot commodities in Houston. So many women forty and older had had their husbands dump them or die on them that the competition for a man with money was fierce. At forty-six, her pool of men with money started with the fifty year olds. A man with money her age could marry a teenager in Houston. And beautiful though she still was, she could not compete with a teenager. And even a fifty-year-old man with money could reach down twenty years for a bride. Perhaps she would have to make do with a fifty-five-year-old. Or settle for a sixty-year-old man. But settle she would, for a man with money. Because her husband had bankrupted the Tucker family. Two years before, he had started drinking and never stopped.

Because of a dead girl.

They would lose the house. The cars. The club. Becky's college. Lupe. Everything. Hurricane Ike had already destroyed her husband's beloved beach house. Now her husband had destroyed his family. Once word had spread through the legal community that the great Frank Tucker was a drunk, the referrals had stopped. Rich clients don't hire drunks to defend them in a court of law. Not when their freedom is on the line. Not even if the drunken lawyer is Frank Tucker. The firm held out hope that he would return to form, but after a year they had fired Frank. Now Elizabeth Tucker's life – the life she had worked so hard to build the last twenty-four years – would be ripped from her being as brutally as a purse-snatcher ripping her Gucci handbag from her grasp. It would all be gone.

She had filed for divorce that very day.

William took a deep breath then blew it out and pushed the barbell up. Three hundred fifty pounds. Once. Twice. Ten times. He replaced the barbell in the rack and sat up on the bench. He was pumping iron in the school's weight room, which rivaled any of the college weight rooms he had toured on his recruiting visits.

'So I tell the coach that my jersey number is twelve, you know, 'cause it was Joe Namath's number. And he says, "Well, we have another player wearing twelve, but he's a senior, so you can have it next year." I said, "I've always worn twelve. It's my number." And he says, "William, I can't take his number away from him." And I say, "Sure you can, Coach. Just ask him if he'd rather wear number twelve or have me quarterbacking the team with a chance to win the national championship."'

His teammates laughed. But not Ronnie. He had not received any Division I-A offers. Or Division I-B offers. Or even Division II offers. His football career was over. After ten years of playing football from peewee through varsity, after thousands of hours of training and weight-lifting and drills, after taking steroids the last two years to get bigger – he still

123

only weighed two-sixty, tiny for an offensive lineman – Ronnie would be playing intramural flag football during his collegiate career. He would also attend UT just like William, but he would be watching the game from the stands.

He burned with jealousy of William Tucker.

'William,' Ronnie said, 'did you know my dad is president of the bank that holds the mortgage on your home?'

'So?'

'So he says your dad's in default. That the bank might have to foreclose. Maybe evict your family. You know what they do when they evict deadbeats who don't pay their mortgage? They send a bunch of goons to your house, break down the front door, and throw all your possessions into the front yard. It's a real sight to see. Wonder what that's gonna feel like? All because your dad's a fucking drunk.'

The weight room had fallen silent. The working-class white boys hated rich-boy Ronnie; he too had come to public school to develop his football skills, but that decision had turned out to be a bad bet. They would not come to Ronnie's defense. The black boys just wanted a fight. They played street ball and thrived on taunting opponents. They waited for William to make his move. He pushed himself up from the bench and walked over to Ronnie. Without saying a word, William punched the bigger boy in the face so hard that his knees buckled and his two-hundred-sixty-pound body collapsed to the floor.

'Wonder what that feels like, Ronnie?'

Becky Tucker sat on her bed in her dorm room at Wellesley College outside Boston. She had just watched her brother on national TV. It seemed unreal. He was only eighteen and still in high school. She was twenty and a junior in college. She had made straight As her first two years and the first semester of her

124

third year. It was almost Christmas break. Admin had sent her an email that morning. Tuition for her spring semester had not yet been paid. She called her dad. After a dozen rings, he picked up. He sounded groggy. She knew why.

'Daddy, are you awake?'

It was noon Texas time.

'Uh, yeah, honey, I'm awake. Sort of.'

She explained the tuition situation.

'Oh, uh . . . well . . .'

'Daddy, I don't need to go to Wellesley. I can pack up my stuff and ship it home. I can finish college at UT or A&M, a public college, someplace closer to home, to save money.'

'I don't know . . . maybe . . .'

His voice drifted off. She heard his snoring.

'Daddy!'

She started crying.

'It wasn't your fault, Daddy.'

William walked in through the back door and found his father sleeping on the couch in the den. He still wore his bathrobe. He hadn't showered or shaved. The phone, an empty whiskey bottle, and Rusty lay on the floor next to the couch.

His dad was a fucking drunk.

Becky had escaped to Boston; he would escape to Austin. William would graduate early from high school so he could enroll at UT for the spring semester. UT, like all the big football powerhouses, enrolled its top recruits for the spring semester so they could get acclimated to college life – of course, it wasn't as if they were seventeen-year-old newbies; most had been held back one or two years, so they were nineteen or older – and participate in spring training. Learn the system. Work out in Austin over the summer. Be ready to start in the fall. William Tucker's journey to the NFL began in three weeks.

His life at home ended in three weeks.

Which was good. Mom and Dad fought constantly now; or rather, Mom constantly yelled at Dad now. He didn't go to the office anymore. He had no office; his firm had fired him. Mom was panicked that she'd lose the house. Be foreclosed on. Get evicted. William would go to UT, but where would she go? Becky had already gotten out. William wanted out. UT was his way out. Football. The only thing he could depend on his entire life. Football was always there for him. His dad stirred awake. He wiped his nose on the sleeve of his bathrobe and struggled to sit up. He saw William standing there.

'Hey, William.'

His dad held up a hand as if to high-five. William did not take a step in his father's direction.

'You missed the signing.'

'Oh, shit. Was that today?'

'Yeah. It was today.'

'Sorry.'

The doorbell rang. William walked to the front of the house and answered the door. A man stood on the porch; he held a folded-up document. He looked up at William.

'Frank Tucker?'

'That's my dad.'

'Is he home?'

'Yeah.'

'May I see him?'

William shrugged. 'Why not?'

William led the man into the den. He pointed at his dad.

'That's him.'

The man stepped closer.

'Frank Tucker?'

126

'Yeah.'

The man tossed the document to William's dad. It hit his leg and fell to the floor.

'You've been served.'

The man turned and walked out. William heard the front door shut. He stepped over and picked up the document. He unfolded it and read the heading: 'Petition for Divorce.'

'What is it?' his dad asked.

'Mom's leaving you.'

William dropped the document in his father's lap. He started to walk out but turned back.

'You didn't kill that girl, Dad. Bradley Todd did. He was guilty, and the jury put him on death row. You were innocent, but you put yourself on death row.'

William wiped away the tears that now came.

'We were innocent, too, Dad.'

Chapter 16

William rifled the ball to D-Quan on a Train route. Fifty yards downfield, the ball dropped into his favorite receiver's hands; D-Quan never broke stride. Coach Bruce tossed William another football; he dropped back three steps, set his feet, and rifled a pass to Cuz on an out pattern. Perfect. Another ball. Another perfect pass to Outlaw on a crossing route. And another perfect pass to Cowboy on a curl.

William Tucker was as close to perfect as a quarterback could be.

It was 10:30 on a November Saturday morning in Austin, Texas. The sun was shining on the stadium and on William Tucker. The team was warming up – jogging, stretching, throwing, catching, kicking, punting. The band was tuning up. The cheerleaders were jumping up. The fans were arriving in burnt orange shirts and caps and jerseys. It was college football game day in America. It was glorious. The Longhorns would play a home game against Texas Tech at noon on national television. Cameras occupied various strategic points around the stadium to capture every bit of action on the field and off. They always cut to the stands between plays to catch gorgeous young coeds bouncing up and down; middle-aged men watching from home loved bouncing breasts, and bouncing breasts brought higher ratings. The coeds knew that the best chance of getting on national TV was to wear revealing clothes.

And bounce.

The Texas Tech cheerleaders bounced past William. They glanced his way. He wore the tight uniform pants but only a snug sweat-wicking sleeveless T-shirt that clung to his muscular body. His long blond hair blew in the breeze. He was a star. And the girls loved the stars. They just couldn't help themselves. They grew up wanting to be Cinderella at the ball, plucked out of obscurity by Prince Charming and given the perfect life. And today, a big, tall, handsome, and rich star athlete was as good as it gets when it came to Prince Charmings. Consequently, William Tucker did not have to seek out girls. They sought him out. He called out to the cheerleaders.

'The Dizzy Rooster on Sixth Street. Tonight. Be there.'

They giggled. He watched them across the field to the visiting side. He had had sex with most of the UT cheerleaders, so he was now working his way through the opponents' cheer squads. He was twenty years old, a sophomore, and on top of his world.

'Focus, William,' Coach Bruce said.

He was the quarterback coach, which is to say, William's personal mentor, confidant, sports psychologist, best friend, and coach. They spent every practice together, working on the game plan and plays, techniques, audibles, and passes. He called and texted William several times each day outside of practice. He would always ask a football question, but he was just checking up on his star quarterback. Trying to keep him out of trouble. Which usually began with girls and ended in a bar on Sixth Street.

William just smiled and threw the ball downfield. The ball seemed to travel through the air with even greater velocity. He was pumped. The adrenaline, the testosterone, the girls, the game. God, it was great to be young. Talented. Handsome. Bigger. Stronger. Faster. When he had first stepped on this field last year, he was already the best college quarterback in the nation. He had been a finalist for the Heisman Trophy last year; he was the frontrunner this year. The team was undefeated after seven games – after seven perfect games from William Tucker. But he couldn't have a single bad game. One bad game, and he could kiss the Heisman goodbye; one loss, and the team would drop out of contention for the national championship. But he didn't have bad games. He had great games and even greater games.

It was good to be William Tucker.

'William.'

'Yeah?'

Coach Bruce nodded past him toward the home sideline. William turned and looked that way. At his father. Who was stumbling drunk. He tripped over some equipment and fell to the turf.

'Shit.'

William flipped the football to Coach Bruce then ran over to his father. His father held up a hand as if to high-five, but instead William lifted him up as if he were a bag of feathers. He was only fifty-three, but he looked like an old man.

'Hey, William.'

His words came out slurred. He embraced William; he smelled the whiskey on his father's breath, like other dads reek of aftershave.

'Dad, please, I'm getting ready for the game.'

'Just wanted to say good luck.'

More slurred words. He had gone deeper into the bottle after the divorce. After Mom left him. After he lost everything.

All because of a dead girl. All because he blamed himself. The jury had sentenced Bradley Todd to death. But Frank Tucker had sentenced himself to a worse fate: life without forgiveness. One of the equipment guys walked by. William grabbed his arm.

'Bennie, take my dad up to a skybox, get him some coffee, something to eat.'

Bennie nodded.

'Dad, go with Bennie. He'll take care of you.'

'Okay. See you after the game, son.'

Bennie took his dad's arm and led him away, like a nurse helping an old person. William watched his father stagger away then turned back to the field. All action had stopped. Every player and coach stared at William Tucker a long awkward moment then abruptly turned away. As if from a train wreck.

His dad was a drunk.

Joe Namath was arguably the greatest quarterback to ever play the game. He was certainly the most celebrated. He was the first superstar celebrity athlete, back in the sixties, when he played for the New York Jets. 'Broadway Joe,' as the press had dubbed him, was young, talented, and handsome. He threw passes on the field, and women threw themselves at him off the field. He was a man's man and a ladies' man. He had it all. Including numerous knee injuries. He played in pain most of his career. He turned to alcohol to ease the pain. By the time he retired, he was an alcoholic. Joe hit rock bottom in 2003 when he showed up drunk at a Jets game honoring him and during a sideline interview with a female reporter, he begged her for a kiss. On national TV. All of America cringed for Joe.

Just as all of William's teammates now cringed for him.

He jogged back over to Coach Bruce and the receivers. Coach Bruce tossed a ball to William. He yelled, 'Hut!' D-Quan ran downfield and broke to the sideline on a fourteen-yard-out. William took three steps back, set his feet, and fired the ball.

It sailed ten feet over D-Quan's head.

William threw five interceptions that game. He fumbled twice. The Longhorns were losing 28-21 with 2:03 left in the game. William dropped back to pass, but the middle of the field opened up, so he ran. Fast. Ten yards. Twenty. Thirty. A touchdown would tie the game. They could still win in overtime. They could remain undefeated. They could remain in the hunt for the national championship. He could remain the frontrunner for the Heisman. He could see the end zone.

He did not see the strong safety.

The strong safety was running full speed – twenty-two miles per hour – when he launched his two-hundred-twenty-pound body helmet first at William's head. His helmet impacted William's helmet from the side with the force of a freight train. William's brain slammed against the left side of his skull then ricocheted back and hit the right side of his skull, causing William to suffer traumatic brain trauma. Bruising of his brain. A concussion. William didn't remember anything after that. His head was spinning, and his ears were ringing. He was lying flat on his back on the turf. Through the fog he could make out blurry figures standing over him.

'William. William. You okay?'

'Dad?'

'Oh, shit. Let's get him up and to the bench.'

They pulled him up. Someone held William's right arm over his shoulders; someone else held William's left arm over his shoulders. They led him to the sideline. The crowd groaned. They put him on the bench. Someone got in his face.

'William, it's Coach Bruce.'

132

'I can play.'

'You sure?'

'Yeah.'

'Where are we?'

'Dallas.'

'What team do you play for?'

'Cowboys.'

'What team are we playing?'

'Giants.'

'What's your name?'

'Troy.'

William bent over and threw up. He heard a different voice above him.

'Can he go?'

'No,' Coach Bruce said. 'Probably has a concussion. He thinks he's playing for the Cowboys against the Giants.'

'Does he think he's Roger Staubach?'

'No. He thinks he's Troy Aikman.'

'Good. If he thought he was Romo, I'd take him out. Send him back in.'

William went back into the game and fumbled on the next play.

Frank Tucker had sobered up by the time he walked into the emergency room at the hospital in downtown Austin. He stood just outside the open door to his son's room. William lay propped up in the bed; a white bandage was wrapped around his left elbow. A coach and a nurse stood next to the bed. No one noticed Frank. Their eyes were locked on a television perched on the wall; it was tuned to a sports channel. Two analysts sat behind a desk in the 'college football game day control room' in New York City; they were conducting a post-mortem on the UT-Tech game in Austin, Texas.

'It was a humiliating defeat for Texas today,' one analyst said. 'An embarrassing game for William Tucker. The Longhorns lost any chance at a national championship, and William Tucker lost any chance at a Heisman Trophy. The Longhorns' season ended today with the worst game William Tucker has played in his entire life. Three fumbles and five interceptions. There's not a lot of love for William Tucker in Austin today. God, he had a terrible game.'

'Hard to focus on football when his dad shows up stinking drunk for his game.'

A video clip ran showing Frank before the game, stumbling over equipment and falling down . . . William running over and helping him up . . . the equipment guy escorting Frank from the field.

'How embarrassing is that? With a dad like that, you don't need opponents.'

William's eyes fell from the television and found Frank. The coach and the nurse looked his way, glanced at each other, and walked out past him without making eye contact or uttering a word. Frank stepped into the room. His son seemed utterly defeated. What does a father say in such a moment?

'Next game will be better, son.'

Not that. His son glared at him.

'You destroyed yourself, Mom, Becky . . . and now you're trying to destroy me. You're not going to take me down with you, Dad. Go away. And stay away. I don't ever want to see you again.'

His son wiped tears from his face.

'I'm a winner, Dad. You're a fucking loser.'

THE PRESENT

Chapter 17

Two types of men find their way to Rockport, Texas: fishermen and losers. Frank Tucker did not fish. He drank. Whiskey. Vodka. Beer. Pretty much anything with alcohol content. Every day. All day. And night. Until he fell asleep.

Only then did he find peace from the past.

Frank opened his eyes then averted them from the morning sun shining through the open windows. The present beckoned; he was not yet conscious enough for the past to torment him . . . for her face to haunt him . . . to hear her pleading . . . as Bradley Todd raped her . . . and her screams . . . as he stabbed her . . . forty-seven times . . . her cries as she lay dying . . . her last gasps of life. No, he still had precious time not to think of Sarah Barnes. He wiped drool from his mouth and shivered against the sea breeze. He had slept in his clothes again, shorts and a T-shirt. Rusty had taken the blanket. Again.

The dog barked.

Frank's head pounded like the surf against the seawall. Only there was no seawall on this isolated stretch of sand fronting the Gulf of Mexico. Rockport was a small fishing town on the

137

Texas coast, about halfway between Galveston and Brownsville but a long way from River Oaks. A long fall. He had started falling and hadn't stopped until he landed in that sand. Face first. Drunk. He had passed out on the beach almost two years ago and had never left.

Or stopped drinking.

You do that when your life falls apart. When everything you worked for the last thirty years is suddenly gone from your life. When your wife leaves you for another man, a richer, sober man. When your children no longer answer their phones when they see your name on the caller ID. When the state bar association suspends your license to practice law because you showed up for trial drunk. Three times. When a man invests everything he has – everything he is and everything he ever will be – into his family, and then his family is abruptly ripped from his life like his wallet being snatched by a thief on the street, he is left adrift in a harsh world. He becomes a castaway.

And he drinks.

The local motto was *Rockport: A drinking town with a fishing problem.*

Frank sucked in the salt air. He was running the beach with Rusty. He still wore the same clothes. They were both bare-footed. He had once run five miles every day, either on a treadmill at his downtown club or around River Oaks on weekends; but now one mile proved too much for his body. Being fifty-five years old and a drunk will do that to a man.

He stopped short and threw up.

He spit the last of the bile then stood and stretched to the sun. His morning detox. He stepped into the surf, unzipped his shorts, and peed. In front of God and everyone, except there was no one else in sight. Only a few seagulls witnessed his act of public indecency, and they wouldn't talk. He and

Rusty walked the last four miles to the rock jetty that jutted out into the sea and then the two hundred paces to the point. The waves hit the rocks and splashed man and dog. He stared out at the endless sea.

If this wasn't the end of the world, he was close to it.

Where the hell's the shampoo? Frank felt the bottom with his toes – rock, wood, stone, another rock—

'Shit!'

Not a rock. He lifted his leg until his foot cleared the waist-deep water. A crab had clasped its claw onto his big toe and wasn't letting go. Frank yanked the crustacean loose and flung it into the surf. He searched with his foot again until he found the plastic bottle then ducked underwater; he emerged with the shampoo. He squirted the gel into his palm and applied it to his shaggy hair. He needed a haircut. He bathed in the Gulf of Mexico each morning because the sea was warmer than the shower; the water heater had broken, and he couldn't afford a new one. He scrubbed his hair then shampooed his body. He had put on weight. A liquid diet would do that to a middle-aged man.

Frank regarded his beachfront estate sitting just beyond the high tide line. The sea wind had caused the wood structure to cant landward, making it appear as if it might fall over at any moment; a strong gust could finish the job. The eight-hundred-square-foot bungalow – which sounded more romantic than 'shack' – had been paid to him in lieu of legal fees in his final case. He had tried the case drunk but had still won an acquittal. His client was happy, but the judge was not amused; he reported Frank to the state bar. The third judge to do so. Three strikes and Frank Tucker was out. His license was promptly suspended pending substance abuse counseling and rehabilitation.

Which was still pending two years later.

One day a developer would come along and put up condos along this stretch of beach, and the town would declare his bungalow uninhabitable to make room for yuppies from Houston or refugees from Matamoros. Until that day came, this was home to Frank Tucker. And Rusty. The dog bathed only once a week, so he chased gulls on the beach while Frank bathed. He went underwater to rinse his hair and body. Another crab scurried along the bottom – or was it the same crab? They all look alike. Frank grabbed the shampoo and stood; he wiped the water from his eyes and combed his hair back with his fingers then walked out of the surf and onto the sand. A white-haired couple wearing wraparound sunglasses had wandered onto his part of the beach wielding long metal detectors – more tourists searching for lost Spanish treasure. Good luck with that. Frank walked past them; they recoiled as if they had seen a ghost.

'Morning,' Frank said.

They stood speechless. Not the friendly sorts, he assumed. Must be from Dallas. That or they had never seen a grown man naked.

'We've got a big day, buddy. Need to protein up.'

Frank filled Rusty's bowl with a high-protein feed then prepared his breakfast. He first brewed a pot of coffee. Then he set up the blender. Into the glass pitcher he dumped a scoop of Ion Exchanged Microfiltered Hydrolyzed vanilla flavored whey protein ... a cup of frozen organic blueberries ... a cup of frozen organic strawberries ... one large organic banana ... a cup of unsweetened organic almond milk ... two cups of organic plain nonfat Greek yogurt ... and a shot of vodka. The breakfast of champions. He blended the concoction then drank directly from the pitcher. He stepped the few paces to the small television and turned it on. Reception was fuzzy, so he adjusted the rabbit ears. He found the *Today* show and sat down in his favorite albeit ratty chair. *Good Morning America* on ABC was too perky for early morning and the CBS morning show too boring, so he watched *Today*. He liked Al. He downed the smoothie in long gulps while watching a segment on Buzz Bissinger, the famous author of *Friday Night Lights* and father of three, who had confessed in *GQ* to being addicted to Gucci clothes – $5,000 leather pants and $22,000 leather jackets – wearing women's underwear, makeup, and six-inch stilettos, and having dabbled in S&M on the side. Shit, he could have kept that to himself. The guy wrote a hell of a book about Texas football, which became a hell of a movie about Texas football and then a hell of a television series about Texas football, but he felt compelled to embarrass his children in the national media. Of course, it did make Frank feel somewhat better about himself: he had only embarrassed his son by showing up stumbling drunk at his nationally televised football game. He placed the empty pitcher on the plank floor next to the chair. The fruit and protein gave renewed vigor to his body, but the vodka made him . . .

He fell asleep in his chair.

Rusty barked him awake. The sun shone through the east-facing windows so it was still morning. Which meant either the dog had to pee or—

'Do we have an appointment?'

Rusty doubled as his secretary. Frank cleared his vision and pushed himself out of his chair. He rinsed a mug and poured coffee then stepped outside. A young man in a suit sat in one of the plastic lawn chairs on the porch. He stood and stuck a hand out. They shook.

'Frank.'

'How're you doing, Ted?'

'Not so good.'

'Well, let's talk about it in my office.'

Ted kicked off his shoes and pulled off his socks and rolled up his trouser legs. He kept his coat and tie on; a lawyer could get only so casual. They walked to the sand and turned toward Galveston. Rusty bolted ahead to clear the beach of seagulls. The first lawyer had shown up about six months after Frank had landed in Rockport. Word quickly spread up and down the coast that the great Frank Tucker now resided in Rockport. He could no longer practice law, but he could still consult with lawyers who could.

'Prosecutor's being an asshole,' Ted said.

'That's redundant.'

'What?'

'You said a lawyer's being an asshole. That's the same as saying a lawyer's being a lawyer or an asshole's being an asshole.'

'Huh?'

'Never mind. What's he doing?'

'Withholding exculpatory evidence . . . I think.'

'Wouldn't be the first time.'

Ted was a criminal defense lawyer in Corpus Christi thirty miles down the coast. He was defending a seventeen-year-old Mexican national against federal drug conspiracy and murder charges; an undercover DEA agent had been killed in a buy-bust gone bad. With the border drug war invading north across the river, it was an emotionally charged high-profile case. Ted was thirty-two, and this was the biggest case of his young career. He practiced alone; he had no senior partner to advise him. So he came to Frank. Often.

'But the judge has denied every motion I've filed to force discovery.'

'Why?'

'His son was killed five years ago. Went into Mexico on spring break, didn't come back. Mexican police said he tried to buy drugs down there, cartel murdered him.'

142

'And you think his son's murder is causing the judge to be biased against your Mexican client, an alleged cartel member and murderer?'

'Seems that way.'

They walked in silence through the wet sand where the high tide had left seashells and shrimp and fish out of water. Rusty returned with a stick; Frank threw it sidearm, and the dog raced after it.

'My client isn't getting a fair trial, Frank.'

'It's your job to see that he does.'

'What should I do?'

'Is he innocent?'

'Yeah. He is.'

'You sure?'

Ted nodded. 'He's just a kid who was in the wrong place at the wrong time. All he wants is to get the hell back to Mexico.'

'File a motion for recusal.'

Ted regarded Frank as if he had just advised him to swim to Cancun.

'You want me to ask a federal judge to withdraw from the case? Shit, Frank, he's the only federal judge in Corpus. He could destroy my career.'

'He could send an innocent boy to prison.'

Ted stopped and picked up a shell. He flung it into the sea.

'Is that what you would do, Frank?'

'It is.'

'For a Mexican?'

'For anyone.'

'Why?'

'Because that's what lawyers do. Defend the innocent.'

Ted dug his toes into the sand for a time then looked up at Frank.

'Frank, I don't mean any disrespect, but defending the innocent is what put you on this beach.'

'No, Ted, defending the guilty is what put me on this beach.'

They walked a bit more then returned to the bungalow where another man in a suit sat on the porch, his shoes and socks off and his trouser legs rolled up. Ted paid Frank with a $50 dollar bill. In Houston, he had charged $1,000 an hour.

'Thanks, Frank.'

Ted headed up to his car on the road but turned back.

'Hey, Frank – I hope your son wins the big game up in Dallas today. I hate Oklahoma.'

Frank Tucker was a family man. But he had no family. His wife had divorced him and remarried a man with money. She was now Mrs. Dale Joiner; he was the oilman whose wife had died of breast cancer. Liz was fifty; Dale was seventy. But he was also a billionaire, which lessened the age difference considerably.

His daughter had come home from Wellesley and finished school at a public college. Becky now taught English in a Houston public school. She had never needed her father, but she drove three hours once a month to spend an afternoon on the beach with her old man. He saw the disappointment in her eyes.

He hadn't seen his son in two years.

Or talked to him. Or communicated with him by mail, email, or text. Before his cell phone plan expired, Frank had called his son several times a week and left messages. He had even called collect – he had been past due on the bill – on the old landline in the bungalow. But his son had never called back.

William Tucker had no need for his father.

Who could blame him? His father had shown up drunk for his big game; which became his worst game. His son had banned his father from his life. But Frank Tucker had kept up with his son's personal life through his daughter and his son's football career through the sports pages. What father wouldn't? William had won the Heisman Trophy his junior year and was a sure bet to win it again his senior year. He had led his team to an undefeated record. They had four games left in the season, but for all intents and purposes the game that afternoon against Oklahoma would decide the national champion. Frank turned the television on, switched channels until he found the game, and then adjusted the rabbit ears until the reception was almost clear. The camera caught number twelve running onto the field. Rusty barked.

'Yep, there's our boy.'

It seemed like yesterday when William was his boy. Twelve years old and throwing the football in the backyard. Dreaming of being a pro quarterback. Thinking his dad was the best dad in the whole world. Those are the times a father remembers and then regrets that they didn't last longer. That they had ended. That the twelve-year-old boy had grown up and become a man. That he wouldn't always be your boy.

That he wouldn't always think that you're the best dad in the whole world.

But he does grow up. And the boy who hugged you tightly when you came home from an out-of-town trial, who sat in the stands with you and watched the varsity play, who wanted to be with you, who was proud of you, who looked up to you – no longer does. When he's twelve, you want him to be better than you; when he's twenty-two and realizes that he is better than you, he has no reason to look up to you. He sees his dad not as a hero but as a human. With faults and frailties and failings and fears. And he moves on with his life. Away from your life. And your life is less.

145

Without a son.

William's star had risen as far and as fast as Frank's star had fallen. He was twenty-two and movie star handsome. He possessed extraordinary athletic ability. He was big, strong, and fast. He was the best college quarterback in the country and would be the number one pick in the NFL draft in April. He would soon be a very rich young man.

Frank would soon be drunk.

He and Rusty watched the game. Texas versus Oklahoma was one of the biggest rivalries in college sports. Longhorns versus Sooners. Burnt orange versus bright red. Each side of the Cotton Bowl Stadium in Dallas was filled with the respective school colors. Ninety thousand fans. Millions watching on television. Watching William Tucker play football. Perfectly. Amazingly. He ran for two touchdowns and threw for three more. But Oklahoma recruited most of its players from the state of Texas too, and they had come to play, so the game came down to the final play for William and the Longhorns. Fourth down. Eight seconds left. Losing by four points. Fifty-four yards to the end zone. They didn't draw up plays for that situation. The camera caught William in the huddle, calling the play and firing up his teammates for one more big play.

Frank's heart pounded. He did not want his son to fail.

The team broke the huddle and hurried to the line of scrimmage. William stood back in a shotgun and barked out the signals. One receiver went in motion across the formation. The center snapped the ball back to William . . . his receivers raced downfield . . . a linebacker blitzed, but the halfback cut his legs out . . . William rolled right . . . to the sideline . . . he set his feet . . . raised the ball . . . stepped forward . . . and threw the ball deep down the far sideline . . . to the end zone . . . to D'Quandrick Simmons . . . touchdown. Frank jumped out of the chair.

'Yes!'

He low-fived Rusty's paw and fell back into his chair. That's what perfect looked like. His son was a thing of beauty on a football field. That first college scout eight years before – What was his name? Sam Jenkins? – had been right after all: William Tucker was born to play football. He was special. But the scout had been wrong about one thing: Frank had followed his advice to the letter – public school, personal trainer and nutritionist, quarterback school, speed coach – but his son still hated him.

The fans swarmed onto the field and surrounded William. He threw his arms in the air. His face showed the pure joy of perfection. The television crew stuck a camera in his face and a female reporter yelled a question over the crowd noise. His son took no credit. Instead, he gave all the credit to his coaches and teammates and—

'The Good Lord.'

Frank felt proud even from a distance of four hundred miles. His son had grown into a fine young man. Modest. Respectful. Not your typical star athlete. The kind of young man any father would be proud to call his own. But William Tucker had done it without the need for a father.

Frank Tucker had never felt more useless in his life.

Frank again woke to Rusty barking. The sun shone through the west-facing windows and cast long shadows.

'Another appointment?'

Rusty dropped a golf ball in Frank's lap.

'Oh, is it our tee time?'

Frank Tucker teed up a Pro-V-One ball, the choice of your top touring pros. A four-dollar golf ball. He pushed his left hand into a Footjoy cabretta leather golf glove, his last one. He pulled his driver from the small carry bag and removed the head cover. It was a Titleist D210 with a Diamana Whiteboard 73 stiff shaft, which kept the ball down in the wind, a must on the difficult beach course. The sea lay to his right, and the wind was off the sea, so he played for a draw. He turned his cap backwards and adjusted his sunglasses he wore on a red cord around his neck. He stepped to the side of the ball, placed the driver behind the ball, adjusted his foot position, waggled once, and swung the club. The ball rocketed off the tee and into the blue sky and out over the water, where it hung for a long suspenseful moment . . . until the wind carried it back into the middle of the fairway.

Rusty barked his approval then raced ahead to the ball.

A lot of your exclusive country clubs don't allow members to play barefooted or dogs to serve as caddies. But being that Frank was the founding member of this particular club, he could play without shoes and with a canine caddie. He picked up his can of beer and the carry bag that contained seven clubs – he had found that the regulation fourteen clubs were not necessary on the beach course; he did carry a sand wedge – and slung the strap over his shoulder. Even at fifty-five, he enjoyed walking a golf course. The sand was wet and cool under his bare feet. The beach course was not the River Oaks Country Club, but there were no monthly dues. And he could just walk on.

He paced off two hundred and forty-seven yards. All carry. You didn't get a lot of roll on these fairways. Rusty stood guard next to the ball so a hungry seagull did not mistake it for food. Frank couldn't afford to lose another Pro-V-One. He was down to his final dozen. The last remnant of his River Oaks life.

'What's the yardage?'

Rusty barked.

'One sixty?'

Frank dropped the bag then grabbed a handful of sand. He tossed the sand into the air and gauged the sea breeze.

'Pin's on the right side of the green. I'm going to have to hold the ball in the wind with a cut. What do you think, seven-iron?'

Rusty barked.

'Six-iron? You really think so?'

Another bark.

'Okay, you're the caddie.'

Frank took a swallow of the beer then pulled the six-iron and set up for a cut. He swung the club. The ball bored through the wind and held its line to the green. It hit the sand and stuck. Stiff.

'Greens are holding today.'

Rusty barked.

'Yeah, you made a good call on the six.'

A caddie who demanded credit. They walked to the green. The sand was wet and smooth; the ball would run true. But you had to putt around shells and dead fish. They were not considered loose impediments but instead part of the course. Local rule. Rusty dug a little hole fifteen feet away.

'I believe I was closer than that.'

Rusty held his ground.

'Fine. A stickler for the rules of golf.'

Frank yanked the putter from the bag. He lined up the putt and put a smooth stroke on the ball. He skirted a deceased jellyfish, but the ball broke left just before the hole. Rusty barked.

'Hey, how many times did Nicklaus have to putt around a jellyfish at the Masters?'

They walked to the tee box on the second hole, a par three. Frank tried to play nine holes every day. Never know, there was still the senior tour. Plan C. Thoughts of which he entertained until he duck-hooked a drive on the ninth hole into the Gulf of Mexico – against the wind. Rusty ran into the surf and dove for the ball, but to no avail. Damn, a Pro-V-One. The sea was a lateral hazard, so Frank suffered only a one-stroke penalty. But he got his four-iron approach shot up in the wind; it sailed into a dune right of the green. Sand shot. He pulled the sand wedge and pitched on; he two-putted. Double-damn-bogey. His caddie knew to keep his snout shut.

'Let's go up to the clubhouse. Time for a drink.'

The sun sat low in the sky and transformed the wispy clouds hanging at the horizon into an orange-and-yellow masterpiece of nature. The sunsets always gave Frank hope; he had survived another day. They collected sand dollars on the walk back.

'We're in the chips now.'

Frank tossed two sand dollars into the pile in the center of the card table.

'Whoa, we got us a big spender tonight,' Dwayne said.

Frank was holding only a pair of fours, but Dwayne was always a sucker for a bluff.

'Practiced a little law today,' Frank said. 'Hence, the Jim Beam.'

He had ridden the bike – he had no car, just a big-wheeled Schwinn with a basket up front, and there was no law in Texas against biking while drunk – to the store in town and bought four T-bone steaks and a fifth of whiskey for their Saturday night card game. Chuck had grilled the steaks on the Weber, and now they played cards and drank bourbon on the back porch of the bungalow. They each wore reading glasses; the curse of middle age. Dwayne smoked a cigar, Chuck a cigarette, and Chico a joint. Being a drunk himself, Frank tried not to judge, so long as Chico stayed downwind. A single sixty-watt light bulb dangled from above and illuminated the table sufficiently to make out the cards. Willie Nelson's 'Phases and Stages' drifted out the open windows.

'I liked him better when he was young,' Chuck said.

'He's eighty,' Dwayne said. 'You weren't alive when Willie was young.'

Dwayne Gentry was fifty-six and an ex-homicide cop from Houston. Born and raised in the Fifth Ward, he was big and black and educated by the U.S. Army. Twenty-two years on the job, he had taken early retirement; in fact, he had been kicked off the force for being drunk on duty. Frank had known him from the old days; he was a good cop. He got the bad guys. He did the job the right way. But he had fallen hard for the wrong woman. A married white woman. And he had fallen alone; when he hit the ground, he didn't get up. Instead, he started drinking. He was already a bona fide drunk by the time Frank picked up the bottle, but Frank was a fast learner. Dwayne had stumbled into Rockport a year ago.

'Your son, that was a hell of a pass,' Dwayne said. 'Last second win over Oklahoma, that's got to feel good.'

'Man, I'd love to get a tape, break the game down,' Chuck said.

Chuck Miller studied game film as if he were still coaching. He was white, forty-nine, and stocky. He had grown up in Uvalde and won a football scholarship to SMU, back before the NCAA had given the school the death penalty in the eighties when it came to light that boosters (including the governor of Texas) had paid players. Chuck had played strong safety and was known for leading with his head; consequently, he had inflicted and suffered numerous concussions. He had been a good player, but not good enough to be paid by the boosters or the pros. After graduating with a degree in football, he hired on at a Houston high school to coach football. He promptly fell head over heels for the nineteen-year-old senior drum majorette. Her mother discovered their affair and reported him to the principal. He was promptly arrested for having an 'improper relationship between an educator and a student.' It was consensual sex with a female above the age of legal consent; she was an adult under the law and dated men older than Chuck. But those facts were not defenses to the offense. She was a student; he was an educator (although his lawyer had argued that a football coach could not be considered an educator under any known definition of the word). Which made their affair a second-degree felony under Texas law. For him, not her. He was a twenty-three-year-old coach just out of college and working his first job. It would be his last. The judge gave Chuck probation; the school district gave him a termination notice. Twenty-six years later, he still harbored dreams of getting back in the game. But it was hard enough to get hired in Texas after coaching a losing season, much less after screwing the drum majorette. He would never get back in the game. Chuck had found his way to Rockport five years before Frank fell face down in the sand.

'I'd've given my left nut to be as good as your boy,' Chuck said.

'Hell, you could've given the right one too, much as you're using them,' Dwayne said.

Chuck grasped the football he always carried as if to throw a pass. He carried the ball like old women carried poodles; he thought it kept him in the game.

'You know how rich your boy's gonna be in a few months? And playing quarterback for the Cowboys, man, he's gonna have to beat those Dallas girls off with a stick. Wonder if the team still bans the players from dating the cheerleaders? Always seemed like a harsh rule to me.'

'That kind of wondering about cheerleaders is what put you on this beach.'

'She was a majorette.'

'She was a student.'

Chuck shrugged. 'Girls are my weakness.'

'When's the last time you were with a girl?'

'In what sense?'

'The Biblical sense.'

'Does phone sex count?'

'Those call-ins you pay for?'

'Yeah.'

'No. In-person sex.'

'Oh. Well, that really limits the sample size. Let's see, that would've been eleven years ago. No . . . twelve. I think.'

'Girls ain't your weakness, Chuck. Delusional thinking, that's your weakness.'

'Least my delusions aren't married.'

'My wife's married,' Chico said. 'But not to me.'

Chico Duran was fifty-two and an ex-con. He started his career in crime knocking over ATMs and then quickly graduated to bank robbery. The electronic variety. He never stuck a gun to a bank teller's head; just a few mouse clicks, and he transferred $50,000 to the Cayman Islands. Thirteen times. Chico maintained that he was simply striking a blow for working class Americans. 'The government loans the big banks trillions at zero percent interest rate, then they turn around and charge 30 percent on our credit card debt. What is that but highway robbery? But I go to jail?' He did. Five years in a federal penitentiary. He remained indignant over his conviction to that day. He had called Rockport home the longest.

'Frank,' Chico said, 'how much money you make lawyering other lawyers?'

'Fifty bucks per session.'

'On a monthly basis.'

'Good month, five hundred.'

'Five hundred? Man, I can get you a thousand, and you don't have to meet with lawyers.'

Like a doctor saying you didn't need a digital rectal exam this visit.

'Tax-free money, Frank. Everyone's riding that government gravy train. You ought to jump on before all the gravy's gone.'

Chico had found a less detectable crime than bank robbery: Medicaid fraud. Specifically, obtaining disability payments through false pretenses. He had forged the necessary documents, and eight weeks later received his first disability check. That was four years ago.

'Two months, I'll have you on the payroll. Lifetime benefit.'

Frank had always declined Chico's offer. He still held out hope of getting sober and his law license reinstated. A federal Medicaid fraud charge wouldn't further the cause.

'And the beauty of it is,' Chico said, 'so many folks are doing it, you get lost in the pile. Almost no chance of getting caught.'

'Almost.'

'Ain't no guarantees in life, Frank.'

An ex-cop, an ex-coach, an ex-con, and an ex-lawyer. All the exes of life. Castaways adrift in a harsh, unforgiving world. Each a loser in his own right. Everyone gets the opportunity to screw up his life, some more than others. Each of them had taken full advantage of his opportunities. Each dreamed of recapturing his old life, but then, dreamers and losers were next of kin.

'Panama,' Dwayne said.

Chuck and Chico groaned. Dwayne was always researching foreign locations to live where his police pension would go farther than in the U.S. Chuck and Chico said nothing; they knew not to encourage him. But Frank enjoyed Dwayne's calculations. Sometimes he sounded almost rational.

'Panama?' Frank said.

'Yep. They use the U.S. dollar as their currency, but it's worth a lot more. You can live like a king down there. Everything's cheap. Housing, food, whiskey' – he held up his stogie – 'cigars, cost you nothing down there. It's like going back to the fifties.'

'You want to live in Panama?'

'I want to live someplace I can afford to live. Hell, I came down here figuring it would be cheaper than Houston, but all the Houston people are moving here, driving up the price of whiskey.'

'If you want cheap,' Chuck said, 'why don't you move to Cambodia, eat fish and rice?'

'No cable TV.'

Chuck grunted. 'No ESPN, that would be a deal-breaker.'

'But if you put your money in a bank in Panama,' Frank said, 'it might not be there tomorrow. There's no deposit insurance, and those governments down there, they're like Greece – one day you wake up and the government decides to take 10 percent of everyone's bank account.'

Dwayne shook his head. 'You don't take your money down there, Frank. You leave it here. I'm not gonna offshore my money – I'm gonna offshore myself.'

'Offshore yourself?'

'Yeah. See, rich guys like Romney, they stay here but send their money offshore. Poor folks like us, we leave our money here and send ourselves offshore.'

It almost sounded rational. Dwayne tossed his cards on the table.

'I'm busted.'

155

He stood and pulled out his small Mag flashlight as if pulling his weapon on a suspect. Beyond the light from the bungalow, the beach lay dark.

'I'm gonna have to dig up some more chips.'

He took a step toward the sea just as a phone rang. Frank and Chuck did not react because neither had a cell phone. Dwayne and Chico checked theirs.

'Not mine.'

'Or mine.'

Another ring.

'It's from inside,' Dwayne said. 'I didn't know your landline worked, Frank.'

'News to me. I thought they had pulled the plug for nonpayment.'

Another ring. Frank was content to let it ring, but Dwayne was already up. He stepped inside and found the phone; he answered.

'Tucker estate.'

He said nothing for a moment.

'*Jail?* Your one call?'

He returned to the porch with an odd expression on his face.

'Frank . . . it's your son.'

Chapter 18

The desk sergeant sniffed the air like a bird dog on a hunt then eyed the four men as if they were suspects.

'Smells like a brewery. You boys been drinking?'

It was the next afternoon. They had piled into Chico's 4x4 SUV that morning and driven the two hundred miles to Austin. Four drunks in one car for three and a half hours. Who would still be sober?

'We're drunks, Sergeant,' Frank said. 'So, yeah, we've been drinking.' He gestured at Chico. 'Well, he's been smoking dope.'

The sergeant regarded Chico over his reading glasses. Chico gave him a stoned grin.

'Little old for that sort of thing, don't you think, *amigo*? Just 'cause you got that ponytail, don't make you Willie.'

The sergeant had amused himself. They had parked on Tenth Street in front of the old courthouse in downtown and walked through the plaza and a gauntlet of cameras with logos not of news networks but of cable sports channels; consequently, a carnival atmosphere prevailed on the plaza. They did not appear important in their beach attire, so their presence warranted no media attention. They now stood at the public reception desk inside the Travis County Jail; the sergeant stood on the other side. His nametag read 'Sgt. Murphy.' His red Irish face said he was no stranger to alcoholic beverages.

'Just the lawyer.'

Frank turned to Dwayne (clamping an unlit cigar in his teeth), Chuck (holding a football), and Chico (eating Cheetos) and then back to the sergeant. He tried to keep a straight face when he said, 'They're part of the defense team.'

The sergeant could not keep a straight face.

'Defense team? They look like the Beach Boys on their fifti-eth reunion tour.'

He had amused himself again.

'Boys, they were good. *Dead Man's Curve,* I loved that song.'

'That was Jan and Dean,' Frank said, 'not the Boys.'

'Really?' The sergeant grunted. 'Aw, hell, it's Sunday, no one's here. All right.'

He waved them all back but gestured at Chuck's football and shook his head.

'He won't sign it. Asked him to sign a ball for my boy, promised I wouldn't put it on eBay – he told me to drop dead.' Back to Frank: 'Your son, he's a bit of a jerk, but he is a hell of a football player.'

'White boy gonna play football for the Huntsville Inmates 'stead of the Dallas Cowboys. Gonna score license plates instead of touchdowns. Gonna get paid two dollars an hour instead of two hundred million. Gonna—'

'Kick your ass if you don't shut the fuck up.'

The other guests of the Travis County Jail fell silent. The black dude with the big mouth looked as if someone had told him his father was white.

'What . . . what you say?'

'You're stupid. Are you deaf too?'

William stood in one corner of the large holding cell. The black dude sat in the opposite corner with his homeboys. He pushed himself up off the concrete floor and sauntered over with his pimp roll. He was lean and muscular, a street thug. William was bigger, stronger, and younger.

'What you say?'

'I said, I'm gonna kick your ass if you don't shut the fuck up.'

'You a tough white boy, is that it?'

'Tough enough to kick your black ass, homey.'

'*Homey?*'

The dude grinned. But not because he thought William's comment was funny. William had lived with black guys from the 'hood the last four years – like all major college football powerhouses, UT recruited black players from the inner cities of Houston and Dallas because they were the ticket to bowl game revenues – so he knew every move in the 'hood book. There were no rules on the street; there were only predators and prey. The dude's first move would be to fake the grin and then laugh—

He laughed.

—and then he would turn back to his bros and turn his palms up, as if saying, What am I supposed to do with this silly-ass white boy?—

He turned back to the other black inmates and turned his palms up.

—which move he hoped would lure William into a false sense of security, which security would be brutally violated when he suddenly whipped around and sucker punched the silly-ass white boy. Sure enough, the dude's right fist clenched behind him and his shoulders started rotating toward William and his fist came up and around and his head spun around and—

159

William drove his huge fist into the dude's chin so hard he heard the jaw cartilage crack just as he had heard so many knee cartilages crack on the football field. The dude was out before his body hit the floor. William stared at the dude's bros.

'Anyone else want to fuck with me?'

'William Tucker!' the jail guard shouted. 'Your lawyer's here.'

Sitting in the chair on the visitor's side of the Plexiglas partition in the interview room, Frank felt a distinct sense of deja vu. As if he had been there before. His brain fought through the fog of whiskey and found the memory. He had been there before. In this same cubicle. Facing Bradley Todd.

But it wasn't the same. Bradley Todd was not his son.

Frank hadn't spoken to or seen his son in two years, except on the old television. When the guard escorted an inmate wearing a green-and-white striped uniform into the interview room, Frank almost didn't recognize his son. At twenty, he had been a boy, albeit a big boy, lean and sinewy; at twenty-two he was an action-figure, with a massive chest, broad shoulders, and thick arms with veins that looked like blue cords. His bulky body stretched the uniform to the breaking point and filled the space in the cubicle on his side of the glass. He remained standing. Frank wanted desperately to embrace his son, but more than the one inch of glass separated father and son. William spoke, but Frank couldn't hear him. He picked up the phone on his side and pointed to the phone on his son's side. William put the phone to his face and spoke again.

'This is bullshit! I didn't kill anyone! I didn't rape anyone! These fucking idiots got the wrong guy! I'm innocent!'

Frank had come to the jail as a father even though he hadn't been much of a father to his son since he had started drinking six years before; and he likely wouldn't be his son's lawyer because his license was suspended. The father in him knew that his son

160

could never have committed such violent acts against a girl; but the lawyer in him wanted to ask that question – 'Did you do it?' – so he felt a sense of relief to hear his son say those two words: *I'm innocent*. Those words led in one direction – dismissal of the charges before trial or acquittal at trial – while *I'm guilty* would have led in another direction – a plea and prison.

'They act like they don't know who the hell I am! I can't believe they made me stay here overnight – they didn't even give me a private room!'

As if he were on a road trip with the team instead of in the county jail.

'Get me the fuck out of here!'

Not 'Hi, Dad. Good to see you after two years.' But perhaps that was expecting too much. His son was in jail charged with rape and murder. He was breathing hard. Blood spotted the knuckles on his right hand.

'What happened?'

'Fight. Back in the cellblock.'

'You okay?'

'This time. Next time I'll have to fight five brothers.'

William dropped the phone and paced the cubicle; he was hyped up on adrenaline and anger. Frank gave him time to calm. After a few minutes, William's respiration noticeably eased; he sat down hard in the chair on his side and blew out a big breath. The adrenaline resided, and his big body calmed. Frank leaned forward in his chair, but his son leaned back, as if trying to escape. But there was nowhere to go. He regarded Frank a long moment then picked up the phone.

'You look old.'

'Being a drunk will do that.'

'Do what?' Chuck said.

The guys stood behind Frank; they could only hear Frank's side of his conversation with William.

'Make you look old.'

Chuck turned to Chico. 'Do I look old?'

Chico shook his head. 'Just ugly.'

Frank's son now regarded Dwayne, Chuck, and Chico.

'Who are they?'

'Your defense team.'

'Are they drunks, too?'

'They are.'

'Get me out of here.'

The Austin newspaper said his son was being held on a $5 million bail. His father was a broke drunk, but his mother's new husband was a sober billionaire.

'I'll try.'

'They said I killed a girl. A Tech cheerleader. Two years ago.'

The newspaper story said a Texas Tech cheerleader had been murdered after UT's game against Tech in Austin, the same game two years before when Frank had shown up drunk and embarrassed his son. His son had played the worst game of his career; then he had banished his father from his life.

'I'm innocent.'

'I know,' Frank the father said.

Over two hundred thousand males were behind bars in the state of Texas. Did their fathers know they were innocent, too? Bradley Todd's father had known his son was innocent. But he wasn't. Frank held the front page of the newspaper with the image of the dead girl up to the Plexiglas. Her name was Dee Dee Dunston.

'Did you know her?' Frank the lawyer asked.

His son leaned in and studied the image. He slowly shook his head.

'You don't recognize her?'

'No. I've never seen her before in my life. I swear.'

'Did he know her?' Dwayne said.

'No. Says he's never seen her before.' Back to the phone and William: 'The newspaper said the police recovered your DNA from her body.'

'*How?* I don't know her, I never met her, I didn't have sex with her. How could they get my DNA?'

From his saliva, sweat, semen, secretions, skin . . .

'Why was your DNA in the database?'

'A month ago, a bunch of us were partying over on Sixth Street, a cop got mouthy with us, we got mouthy with him. He said he was going to arrest us for public intoxication, I told him to fuck off. So he arrested me for resisting arrest. Hauled me down here. Soon as they found out who I was, I signed a few autographs, took a few photos, they let me go. But they did a cheek swab.'

Anyone arrested in Texas for a serious crime – and resisting arrest qualified – will have his or her DNA collected and input into the national database.

'Why'd they have his DNA?' Dwayne said.

'Arrested. Public intoxication and resisting arrest.'

Dwayne grunted. 'That'll do it.'

Back to William: 'So they input your DNA, and the database matched it to an unsolved murder.'

'That's what the cops said.'

'William, tell me everything you did that day.'

His son shook his head. 'I can't.'

'Son, everything you tell me is confidential. I'm not just your father, I'm your lawyer. Sort of. And they're working for me, so the privilege applies to them as well.'

'Are we getting paid?' Chuck asked.

'No,' William said. 'I mean, I can't remember what happened.'

'Why not?'

'I don't remember anything from that day. Concussion. The whole day is gone.'

'You don't remember anything?'

'No.' He shrugged. 'Every time I've had a concussion, that day, most of the next week, it's just a black hole.'

'He had amnesia?' Chico asked.

'Concussion,' Frank said.

'I had amnesia after my concussions,' Chuck said. 'Still got it.'

'He's going with an amnesia defense?' Dwayne said. 'That ain't gonna fly.'

Back to his son: 'How many concussions have you had?'

'Four or five. Six. Maybe seven.'

'Seven concussions? And they still let you play?'

'I don't tell the coaches.'

'Why not?'

'They won't let me play.'

'Maybe you should stop playing.'

'Maybe I should stop breathing. I'm a football player. That's who I am. What would I be if I stopped playing?'

'My son.'

'That won't get me a hundred-million-dollar guaranteed contract.'

It would not. Being Frank Tucker's son was not worth much in this world. Only slightly more than being Frank Tucker.

'What was your normal schedule for a game day?'

'That was a day game, wasn't it?'

'Yeah.'

Frank had been drunk, but he had not suffered a concussion. He remembered that game day.

'I usually get up around eight, eat breakfast in the athletes' dining hall, walk over to the stadium.'

Frank had woken at ten that morning, hung over at the hotel. Not the five-star Driskill Hotel in downtown Austin, but a cheap hotel fronting the interstate not far from the UT

164

stadium. He had passed out the night before and slept like a baby; the whiskey drowned out the traffic noise. He had his usual breakfast of vodka and orange juice – not too much orange juice – then a liquid brunch and an early liquid lunch. He was too drunk to drive, so he walked over to the stadium. His son had given him a sideline pass – the star quarterback could do that for his father – so Frank Tucker received VIP treatment just like Matthew McConaughey and other UT alumni who had achieved celebrity status. By the time he entered the stadium, Frank Tucker was stumbling drunk. But he still thought his son would be happy to see his dad on the sideline. When you're a drunk, you think things like that.

'Then what?'

'Pre-game stuff. The trainer tapes my ankles, I suit up but no pads, go out onto the field and warm up. Stretching, jogging, passing drills. That was the game you came to, wasn't it?'

It was.

Frank Tucker stumbled down the sideline past the TV cameras and reporters and celebrities and cheerleaders and into the team's equipment. He fell to the turf as if he had been tackled. The next thing he knew, his son was helping him up and placing him in the care of a guy named Bennie. He took Frank upstairs to a suite and got him a hamburger and coffee. A lot of coffee. Frank had sobered up by the fourth quarter when William suffered a brutal helmet-to-helmet hit. And a concussion.

'Worst game of my career. Five interceptions.'

'You remember?'

'Read about it. Couldn't bear to watch the film. Cost me the Heisman.'

'After the game, they took you to the hospital. You remember that?'

William shook his head. 'Coach said they gave me a brain MRI, stitched up my elbow.'

'What happened after I left?'

After his son had told him to leave and stay the hell out of his life. After he had said his father was a fucking loser. The truth hurts.

'Coach Bruce said he got me some dinner, took me back to the dorm, put me to bed.'

'Did you stay there all night?'

'Must not have. Guess the guys decided I needed some fresh air.'

'What guys?'

'Back then, would've been Cowboy and Red.'

'They're your best friends?'

'They're the guys.'

'Who's your best friend?'

He pondered a moment.

'Coach Bruce, I guess.'

'You don't have a steady girlfriend?'

'You mean, like, someone I'd take home to meet my . . . sister?'

'Like that.'

'No. Those girls don't groupie for athletes. And I don't have time for commitments in my life, except football. No distractions, focus on football. That's the ticket to the NFL.'

'What about life?'

'Football is my life.'

And perhaps it should be at twenty-two.

'Where did Cowboy and Red take you?'

'Sixth Street, I'm sure.'

'Did you drink?'

'I'm sure.'

'At the Dizzy Rooster?'

166

The victim's body had been discovered in the alley behind that bar.

His son shrugged. 'We go there a lot. But I don't remember if we went there that night.'

'Was he there?' Dwayne said.

'Doesn't remember.'

'That ain't gonna fly.'

Back to William. 'You don't remember anything?'

'When you get a concussion, you're in a fog for days, like a dream you can't remember when you wake up.'

'How can you go to a bar in that condition?'

'Hell, I've played entire games in that condition. Your body just goes on autopilot.'

'Did you meet this girl?'

'I told you, I've never seen that girl before in my life.'

'Did you meet other girls?'

He shrugged again. 'I'm sure. I'm William Tucker. I always meet girls. Or they meet me.'

Just as a matter of fact.

'Did you have sex with a girl that night?'

'I don't remember.'

'Because of the concussion?'

'Because there's been too many girls on too many nights. Even without the concussion, I couldn't remember a girl from two years ago.'

'You just go into a bar and pick up a girl and have sex?'

'Wow,' Chuck said from behind.

'They pick me up.'

'Do you always wear a condom?'

William shook his head. 'I never wear a condom. No one does.'

'He doesn't wear rubbers?' Chico said. 'Man, that's *loco*.'

'I don't wear condoms,' Chuck said.

'Yeah, but you can't catch nothing from your hand.'

'True.'

'AIDS, STDs, pregnancy,' Frank said to his son, 'any of that mean anything?'

'Not really. But I went to bed early that night. The guys took me back to the dorm.'

'You were back in your dorm? What time?'

The newspaper said the girl had been killed between midnight and two A.M.

'Around midnight.'

'You remember that?'

'The guys told me.'

'What time?' Dwayne asked.

'Midnight.'

'Convenient. He don't remember nothing except he was in his dorm when the crime was committed.'

'Get me out of here,' his son said. 'I've got a game Saturday.'

Frank didn't have the heart to tell his son that his season was over.

'Your bond is five million. I'll try to get it reduced, but—'

'Call Mom. She's in Europe with Dale. He's a billionaire. Tell her I need money for bail and to hire a lawyer.'

Frank Tucker used to be the lawyer every accused wanted to hire.

'You have her number?'

'It's on my cell phone. In my dorm room. Jester West, room five-twenty-one.'

'The cops probably took your phone when they searched your room.'

'They searched my room?'

'Standard police procedure. Is there anything you wouldn't want them to find?'

His son shrugged. 'No.'

168

Father and son regarded each other across six feet of Plexiglas-partitioned space. A father always sees the twelve-year-old boy who thought he was the best dad in the whole world; he never sees the twenty-two-year-old man who thinks his dad is a loser. A man can't handle that truth. Frank reached out and placed the palm of his right hand flat against the glass then waited for his son to match hands, a jailhouse high-five. And waited. His son stared at his father's hand then at his father. He stood.

'Frank, get me the fuck out of here.'

'*Frank?*'

'What do you want me to call you – *Dad*?'

His son hung up the phone and turned his back on his dad. He walked out of the inmates' side of the interview room. The four men on the visitor's side remained quiet for a long awkward moment until the silence was broken by Dwayne's voice.

'Not the kind of kid you like right off, is he?'

169

Chapter 19

'So, Frank, you get over that drinking thing?'

'No.'

He had drunk his daily protein-and-vodka breakfast shake just to get the day going, beer on the drive up from the beach, and then a quick shot of whiskey before facing the Travis County District Attorney. The last time the two men had been in the same room, it was a courtroom upstairs in this same building when the not-guilty verdict had been read in Bradley Todd's first trial. Frank had won, but the district attorney had been right. He didn't figure his bitter, lifelong legal rival would fail to remind him of that fact. Hence, a shot before meeting the D.A.

Dick Dorkin sat behind a massive wood desk in his office on the first floor of the Blackwell-Thurman Criminal Justice Center at Eleventh and San Antonio Street; the office befit the most powerful politician in Travis County, Texas. He wore a suit and tie, but not because he had just come from church that Sunday. Frank occupied a visitor's chair across from him. The guys occupied the sofa along the wall behind Frank. After he had left his son at the jail, Frank had asked the desk sergeant for the homicide detective in charge of the case. But the sergeant informed him that the case had already been referred to the district attorney's office. The D.A. had already taken the case to the grand jury. And William Tucker had already been indicted for rape and capital murder.

'Well, at least you got a nice tan, lying on the beach.'

Frank was not dressed in a suit and tie, but in jeans and a T-shirt. His hair was ragged and too long for a lawyer. His sunglasses hung on a cord around his neck. He wore no wedding ring. He did have a nice tan.

'I've dealt with these prima donna athletes before, Frank, too many times, as you well know. They think playing football or basketball means they don't have to play by any other rulebook. But there's no exemption for star athletes in the penal code. Your son's had some run-ins with the law before – public intoxication and resisting arrest, DUI, solicitation—'

'Solicitation?'

The D.A. shrugged. 'Coeds moonlighting on Sixth Street.'

'Coeds? Like at the Chicken Ranch?'

Back in the seventies, rumor had it that the infamous Chicken Ranch whorehouse in La Grange sixty miles southeast of Austin employed UT coeds; it made for a good Broadway musical, but no one actually believed the rumors. Apparently those rumors had come home to Sixth Street.

'—but he played the star card every time. Signed a few autographs, took some photos, and the cops released him. A Heisman Trophy will do that for being drunk and stupid, even resisting arrest. But not for rape and murder.'

'I just came from the jail. William swears that he's never seen the victim, never met her, never had sex with her.'

'Defendants lie, Frank. As you are well aware.'

Frank knew Dick Dorkin would wield the Bradley Todd case like a sledgehammer.

171

'And that he was back in his dorm by midnight, before the time of death.'

'Careful what you think you know, Frank.'

As if he knew something.

'How'd you get his DNA if he didn't have sex with the victim?'

'We didn't get his semen. We got his blood.'

'*Blood?* On her clothes?'

'On her skin. She fought him, hard enough to bring blood. Traces were found on her arms and thighs. DNA doesn't lie. People do. He's guilty, Frank.'

'His blood doesn't prove guilt beyond a reasonable doubt.'

'Tell that to the jury. And then explain how his blood got onto her body. Only one way: direct physical contact. As in forcible rape. And then murder by strangulation.'

The D.A. had come in on a Sunday for a news conference that afternoon; hence, the media throng in the plaza. The circus outside played out on a flat-screen TV mounted to the wall. William Tucker's arrest for rape and murder constituted news. National news. Cases like this didn't come along often, so a politician couldn't afford to squander his moment in the spotlight. You never wanted to get between an ambitious politician and a news camera.

'No semen but he raped her?'

'Maybe he wore a condom.'

'How many rapists wear condoms?'

'Ask your son.'

'He said he doesn't use condoms.'

'Oh. Okay. Then I'll dismiss the case.'

'Wow, that was easy.'

Chuck's voice from the sofa.

'He don't mean it,' Dwayne said. 'It's called sarcasm.'

'Ohh.'

172

The D.A. chuckled. 'Where'd you find these guys, Frank? Alcoholics Anonymous?'

'We don't believe in that,' Chico said.

'Being an alcoholic?'

'Being anonymous.'

Which elicited another chuckle from the district attorney.

'Comedians.' He frowned and pointed a finger at Chuck. 'Why does he have a football?'

Frank could only offer a lame shrug before he asked, 'No witnesses?'

'The only witness is dead.'

'Did they recover his skin tissue under her fingernails?'

'Nope.'

'Saliva?'

The D.A. shook his head.

'All you have is his blood?'

'*All?* That blood is more than enough to convict your son.'

The D.A. stared at Frank as he processed that information. William's blood on the victim, but not his semen inside her.

'I'll consider a plea offer,' the D.A. said. 'Life in prison.'

'He's innocent. We'll take it to a jury.'

The D.A. picked up a remote and pointed it at the TV and the circus outside. The volume came on. A middle-aged woman in a crowd of middle-aged women was being interviewed.

'I watched every episode of the Casey Anthony trial.'

'*Episode?*' the reporter said.

'But this show isn't going to be on TV, so we came down to the studio.'

'*Show? Studio?* You do understand that this is a murder case?'

'Oh, yes. Those are the best shows.'

The D.A. muted the volume and turned to Frank.

'There's your jury pool, Frank. You want to put your son's life in her hands?'

No. He did not.

'Can we get into his dorm room?'

'We?' The D.A gestured at the sofa behind Frank. 'You and the Three Stooges going to investigate the case?'

'The defense team.'

'That's funny,' the D.A. said.

'What about the dorm, Dick?'

'Sure, why not? Knock yourself out. The detectives searched his room, and it's not a crime scene. And you're his father.' He paused. 'Are you his lawyer?'

'He's going to hire a lawyer.'

The D.A. nodded almost as if he were embarrassed for Frank. But Frank knew he was not.

'Must be tough, even your own son doesn't want you to represent him.'

'Will you agree to a reduction of his bail?'

'He's accused of a brutal rape and murder, and his DNA was on the victim. I couldn't reduce bail for my own son, if I had a son. And I'm up for reelection. My Republican opponent would crucify me. And what if he raped and killed another girl, like Bradley Todd?'

'Five million is unreasonable bail.'

'Capital murder, he's lucky to get bail.'

'I'll take it to the judge.'

'*You?* You mean, William's lawyer? Well, good luck with that. Judge Rooney's got the case, and he's up for reelection, too. He can't let an accused rapist and murderer back on the street – he's got to show he's tough on crime, even in Austin.'

Austin was the blue hole in the red Texas donut. But even liberals feared violent crime.

'And Harold won't forget that he let Bradley Todd out on bail because you were his lawyer and as we all knew, you only represented innocent people. You made him look like a fool, Frank.'

'Then you'd better segregate my son from the other inmates or you won't have a defendant to try – he's already been in one fight – and your opponent will enjoy asking you why a suspect was killed in jail.'

The D.A. pondered the political ramifications then nodded.

'All right. I'll call over to the jail, get him transferred to the solitary cellblock.'

'I want the homicide file.'

'I don't have to give you the file.'

'The lawyer for the accused is entitled to every piece of exculpatory evidence the state possesses.'

'True, but you're not his lawyer, Frank. You're not even a licensed lawyer at the moment.'

'I'm his father.'

At forty-five, Dick Dorkin had been a short, pudgy little prick. At fifty-five, he was a short, even pudgier little prick. But he held the fate of Frank's son's life in his hands. So Frank tried to mend fences.

'Look, Dick, I know we've had our differences, but—'

'Our *differences*?' The D.A. laughed. 'I hate your fucking guts, Frank.'

'Because I called you a failed politician? Because of Bradley Todd? Because of the senator?'

'Because of Liz.'

'*Liz?* What the hell does she have to do with anything?'

'She picked you over me.'

'You knew her back then? When we were in law school?'

He nodded.

'You asked her out?'

Another nod.

'She turned you down?'

Another nod. As if he were still shocked by Liz's rejection. Frank almost laughed out loud. Talk about violating the natural order of men and women. Even as a young law student, Dick Dorkin had been a two at best in the male rankings, one being the guy in *Sling Blade*; he didn't have a snowball's chance in hell of snagging a date with a ten like Elizabeth Barton, UT campus beauty queen. But there was no accounting for the male ego.

'That's how this lifelong grudge started, back in law school? Because my ex-wife rejected you?'

'Ex?'

'She divorced me and married a billionaire oilman.' Frank snorted. 'Hell, Dick, I did you a favor. You should be thanking me. You would've gone broke supporting her.'

'How do you know?'

'Because I did.'

The D.A. regarded Frank across the wide expanse of wood. After a moment, he sighed.

'All right, Frank. But find him a lawyer fast, or the judge is going to appoint a PD. The arraignment's Tuesday morning at nine.'

'I'll be there.'

Frank stood and walked to the door.

'And Frank—'

He turned back.

'—try to show up sober.'

Chapter 20

Camera crews accosted every student-athlete entering the Beauford H. Jester Center-West dormitory on the University of Texas campus north of downtown Austin.

'Do you know William Tucker?'

'You think he killed the girl?'

'How did he treat girls on campus?'

Frank, Dwayne, Chuck, and Chico didn't look like students or athletes, so they were allowed to pass without being stopped and questioned. They went inside and took an elevator to the fifth floor; they found William's room. A Hispanic worker wearing a uniform screwed new door hinges into the door-jamb.

'Looks like the arrest warrant was executed with a boot,' Dwayne said.

William's door was not sealed off with yellow crime-scene tape but someone apparently thought he was a criminal: *RAPIST* and *KILLER* had been scrawled across the door like graffiti.

'So much for being a campus hero,' Chico said.

'Damn, we didn't have coed dorms when I was at SMU,' Chuck said.

Fit girls wearing skin-tight Spandex short-shorts and leggings bounced past the four middle-aged men and down the corridor. Chuck, Chico, and Dwayne stared at their departing backsides, but firm female bottoms could not distract Frank's mind from his son. The worker allowed them entry after Frank identified himself and Chico had translated his English into the worker's Spanish. They stepped inside the room; the worker shut the door behind them. Frank had been in his son's bedroom at home hundreds of times a year for eighteen years; now he felt as if he were entering a stranger's home. He found the wall switch and flipped on the lights; they were greeted by a huge color blowup of William Tucker on the opposite wall. It was an action shot of number twelve throwing a pass during a game. He was literally bigger than life. More action photos of his son adorned the other walls.

'Boy likes to look at himself, don't he?' Dwayne said.

'What are we looking for?' Chico said.

'Cell phone,' Frank said. 'And evidence.'

'Of what?'

'Innocence.'

They spread out to search the room. Chico took the desk, Chuck the dresser, and Dwayne the closet. The police had already conducted a cursory search; contents of drawers and boxes had been tossed and left in disarray. But the crime had been committed two years before and not in this room, so they had left it as they found it. And they already had all the evidence necessary to convict William Tucker: his blood from the victim's body. Frank had learned that cops stopped searching when they had their man. Or thought they did.

'Wow,' Chuck said.

He held up a tiny black thong in one hand and a tiny red one in the other.

'He's got a bunch of these. Wonder why?'

'They're like notches on a gunslinger's six-shooter,' Chico said. 'Laptop.'

'They put notches on laptops?'

'Man, you had one too many concussions. I *found* his laptop.'

'Ohh.'

'The cops didn't take his laptop?' Frank asked.

'Apparently not.'

Chuck held up a football. 'Frank, can I have this?'

'You want his football?'

'He signed it.'

'You want a football signed by my son?'

'We could sell it on eBay,' Chico said. 'Make some serious money.'

'Really?'

'You bet. A football signed by a famous athlete and now he's accused of murder . . . sorry.' He hesitated. 'I've sold lots of stuff on eBay, and I didn't even own most of it. That ball, it's worth its weight in gold.'

Frank heard voices speaking in Spanish outside – the worker and a female – and the door opened on a middle-aged Hispanic woman dressed like a maid, as if the dorm were a high-end hotel. She froze at the sight of the four men rummaging through the drawers and closet.

'It's okay,' Frank said. 'I'm William Tucker's father.'

Her expression remained unchanged. Chico stepped over and spoke to her in Spanish. She answered.

'What'd she say?'

'Said she cleans his room. They got cleaning and laundry service. The athletes.'

'Ask her if she knows anything about William.'

Chico again spoke to her in Spanish. He frowned.

'What?'

'Uh, she said she don't like him.'

'Something of a consensus is building,' Dwayne said.

'Why not?' Frank asked.

Chico spoke to her in Spanish, and she spoke back. Then she left and the worker shut the door.

'Says he's an animal, he's a slob, and he treats her like his personal maid. Says she's gonna come back later.'

'Anyone want a beer?' Dwayne said. 'Or a Red Bull?'

He had squatted down and opened the small refrigerator lodged under the desk. It was filled with cans of Coors and Red Bull. He popped the top on a Coors.

'Don't mind if I do,' Chuck said. 'Beer.'

'Ditto,' Chico said.

'Might help my headache,' Frank said.

Dwayne tossed cans of Coors to the defense team. They resumed the search. Except Chuck, who plopped down into William's recliner that fronted a flat screen on the wall and pointed a remote at the screen as if this were any other Sunday afternoon to be spent watching pro football. The television flashed to life.

'Man, he's got the premium subscription, every sports channel in the country.'

Chuck clicked through the NFL games, pausing to watch a bit of each game.

'Cowboys versus the Giants . . . Romo's thrown two interceptions in the first half . . . Cowboys got a billion-dollar stadium and a hundred-dollar quarterback. But when William's playing quarterback for them, they're gonna—'

Dwayne threw a beer can at Chuck.

'*What?*' He realized his error. 'Oh. Sorry.'

'Cell phone,' Chico said.

'The cops left his phone, too?' Dwayne said. 'Man, when I

executed a search warrant, I took everything that wasn't nailed down, just in case.'

'Check out the phone,' Frank said.

Chico did not need an invitation. He was already tapping on buttons and running his fingers down the screen.

'His photos look like a *Playboy* magazine. Lots of naked girls. Sexting.'

'Always wanted to try that,' Chuck said.

'Please don't,' Dwayne said.

'Chico, look through his contact list,' Frank said.

'Who am I looking for?'

'My ex-wife.'

'Got a speed dial for "Mom."'

'That would be her.'

Chico handed the phone to Frank. He pushed the call button and waited for it to ring through. But it went to voicemail. He didn't leave a message. Instead he checked the contact list again and found a number for 'Home.' After three rings, a familiar voice came across.

'Joiner residence.'

'Lupe?'

'*Mr. Tucker?* Oh, my God, I thought you were dead.'

'Just drunk. Lupe, can you get Liz?'

'Mrs. Tucker . . . I mean, Mrs. Joiner, she's in Poland.'

'Poland? Why?'

'With Mr. Joiner. A business trip.'

'Do you have a number? I need to talk to her.'

'About William? I saw it on TV.'

'Yes. About William.'

'Let me find their hotel number.'

The line went silent, so Frank turned his attention back to the search of his son's room. Dwayne was experienced in such matters; he was conducting a thorough search.

181

'You find any drugs?' Frank asked.

'Nope.'

'Alcohol? Other than the beer?'

'Nope.'

'Performance enhancers?'

'Nope. You thinking 'roid rage?'

'Always a possibility with an athlete. If Lance was dirty, anyone might be.'

'His shelf looks like a health food store, but just vitamins and protein bars and protein mix, stuff like that. No PEDs and no condoms.'

Lupe came back on the line and gave him the number for the Mamaison Hotel Le Regina in Warsaw where Frank's ex-wife and her replacement husband were staying. Frank thanked Lupe then disconnected her and dialed the overseas number. He figured his son would soon be rich enough to pay the charge . . . or he would be in prison and the carrier would have to eat the charge. While waiting for the call to go through, he admonished himself for allowing that thought entry into his mind. The hotel clerk answered in Polish.

'Do you speak English?' Frank asked.

'Yes, sir, I do.'

'Elizabeth Tucker's . . . Elizabeth Joiner's room, please.'

'One moment. Yes, here it is. I will connect you.'

His wife answered after a few rings.

'Hello.'

'It's me, Liz.'

'*Frank?* What . . . why?'

'You haven't seen the news?'

'What news?'

She had not heard about William. The Polish people apparently did not care about American football players who had been accused of rape and murder. Frank gave her the bad news.

'My God. His blood was on her? Frank, you don't think . . .?'

'No.'

'What are you going to do?'

'First thing is to get him out of jail. He needs money for bail.'

He did not need to add, 'And I'm broke.'

'How much?' she asked.

'Five million. And a million more for a lawyer.'

'You're a lawyer.'

'A lawyer whose license isn't suspended.'

Six years before, Frank Tucker could have secured the bail money and saved his son himself. Now he was asking his ex-wife to ask her new husband for six million dollars to save his son. Their son. Frank had never been Liz's Prince Charming; he had been her provider. He was to give her all the things she wanted in life. When he could no longer provide her material needs, she found someone else who could. He had been angry at first – twenty-four years of providing faithfully then she had dumped him after only two years of being a drunk – but now he actually felt good about her decision. Her billionaire husband could afford their son's bail and legal fees.

'Lawyers charge a million dollars?'

'Justice doesn't come cheap. It's going to be a high-profile trial. A media circus. Only a few lawyers in the country are up to that sort of trial. And proving his innocence will take a lot of money.'

'I thought the prosecutor had to prove his guilt?'

'Most people think that. Until they're in the system. Then they learn the truth. Can you get Dale to wire the money A-S-A-P? It's Sunday here. What time is it there?'

'Seven-thirty.'

'Is Dale there?'

'He's sleeping.'

'Exciting life.'

'It was, for six months.'

'Banks are closed. Can he wire the money tomorrow?'

She did not speak.

'Liz? You still there?'

'I'm here. Frank . . . we don't have that much money.'

'Dale's a billionaire.'

'Not anymore.'

'What happened?'

'Gas prices plunged. From eleven dollars per whatever to less than two.'

Dale Joiner was in the business of drilling for natural gas, specifically shale gas through fracking, as hydraulic fracturing had become known. Texas was the biggest fracking state in America, and Dale one of the biggest frackers in Texas.

'He lost a billion dollars?'

'Two. He still owns the gas, but it's not worth as much now. It's like a stock market crash. He's trying to hang on until prices rebound.'

'You could put up your house. It's got to be worth more than six million.'

'Fifteen. But Dale already took out a home equity loan and used the money to keep his company afloat, pay his employees and bills.'

'What are you doing in Poland?'

'Dale's trying to get a contract with the government to frack here. It'll save him.'

'Not in time to save William.'

'Can't you represent him?'

'Not with a suspended license.'

After a few more minutes of meaningless talk – 'Yes, I'm still drinking' . . . 'No, I'm not remarried' – Frank disconnected. There was no five million dollars for bail. Unless the judge reduced his bail at the arraignment, William would remain in jail until the verdict. And there was no million dollars for a top-notch criminal defense lawyer. Who would represent his son? His son's father had once been the best criminal defense attorney in the state, maybe in the nation, but he had decided to become a drunk instead. His son had not needed his father in too many years; now, when he finally needed his father, his father could not give him what he needed most: a defense to a murder charge.

'Look.'

Chuck gestured at the television screen – at the image of Travis County District Attorney Dick Dorkin standing before a clump of microphones in the plaza outside the Justice Center. The press conference. Chuck increased the volume.

'Almost two years ago to the day,' the D.A. said, 'Dee Dee Dunston, an eighteen-year-old freshman cheerleader at Texas Tech University, came to Austin to cheer at the UT-Tech football game. She never returned to Lubbock. Dee Dee was brutally raped and strangled to death that night. Her body was discovered behind the Dizzy Rooster on Sixth Street where she had been seen that night. Blood traces were recovered from her body. Investigators ran DNA tests on the blood and then a search in the national DNA database, but no matches came up . . . until a month ago. The match was a well-known college athlete. As is my policy in cold cases, I ordered a retest. The results confirmed the match. I took the case to the grand jury. An indictment for rape and capital murder against one William Tucker was handed up Saturday morning. A warrant for his arrest was issued that afternoon. Mr. Tucker was arrested last night in his dorm room without incident. He is being held in the Travis County Jail on a five-million-dollar bail. Arraignment will be at nine A.M. Tuesday before Judge Harold Rooney. Questions?'

The reporters shouted questions.

'Did William confess?'

'Not yet.'

'Is he claiming innocence?'

'At this time.'

'Are you certain William Tucker raped and killed this girl?'

'We are certain that the DNA results are accurate and that William Tucker's blood was on the victim's body. Given that no one else's DNA was recovered from her body, we are confident that William Tucker is the killer.'

'Are you going to seek the death penalty?'

'Yes.'

The four men sat in silence in the accused's dorm room on the University of Texas campus as the two words sunk in: death penalty.

'Son of a bitch didn't tell me that,' Frank said.

'I could hack into his bank account, clean him out,' Chico said.

'Can we get a drink?' Dwayne asked. 'A real drink?'

Chapter 21

'Daddy, the death penalty? It's all over the news down here.'

'Becky, he's innocent. He's not going to be convicted or sentenced to death.'

'You were sure Bradley Todd was innocent.'

'William's your brother.'

'He's not the same brother. He changed. When he became a star.'

Frank ended the call to his daughter. He stood at the upper falls at McKinney Falls State Park in southeast Austin along Onion Creek. The creek is an outflow of the Colorado River; the Colorado runs east out of Austin, the Onion southeast. The water flows over limestone formations that create an upper and lower falls, below which sit small pools. The park is a popular summer destination when the temperature hits a hundred degrees, but not so much in October. Campsites run $20 per night; their beer and whiskey ran twice that. The last time he had tried a case in Austin, Frank had stayed at the five-star Driskill Hotel in downtown in a $750-a-night suite with a king-sized bed. This time he had a sleeping bag on the ground.

He tossed a stick into the pool; Rusty raced to the water and dove in. The dog needed to run after a day in the car.

'Burgers are ready,' Chuck said.

Ever since he had won the Weber grill in a hotdog eating contest on the beach a few years back, Chuck had become something of a grill master. He watched cooking shows about grilling; he read books about barbecuing. He knew more about basting and barbecue sauce than any man alive, or so he maintained. He flipped the burgers with the spatula in his right hand and the William Tucker-autographed football in his left hand. They had stopped at the Whole Foods in downtown and stocked up on supplies and beer before heading out to the park. They had packed their own camping gear and Jim Beam up from the beach. Chico and Dwayne sat at the picnic table. Frank joined them and handed William's cell phone to Chico. On the table was a box holding the spoils of their search of William's room. Chico fiddled with William's cell phone; Dwayne thumbed through the homicide file the D.A. had surrendered and jotted notes on his cop pad with a Sharpie. He smoked a cigar and wore reading glasses. Frank drank his Coors. They had taken the beer and protein bars from William's room. Chuck slapped hamburgers on paper plates in front of them. Burgers, potato chips, beer, and bourbon for dessert.

'Five million bail,' Frank said. 'If the judge won't lower it, he's going to sit in jail until trial. Couple of months in there, he won't come out the same boy.'

'Might not be a bad thing,' Dwayne said. 'He ain't exactly Miss Congeniality.'

'He could come out worse.'

'We could break him out,' Chico said. 'Hightail it down to Panama, live like kings.'

He seemed serious.

'Are you serious?' Chuck asked.

'Sure. Course, we gotta make our move while he's still in

county lockup, before they convict him and ship him down to the state pen in Huntsville. County jails, they're like Swiss cheese.'

'We should've got some Swiss cheese to put on our burgers,' Chuck said.

'No county jail could hold me,' Chico said.

He had escaped six county jails in the course of his career. Consequently, Chico Duran fancied himself another Cool Hand Luke, although he didn't look like Paul Newman. More like Cheech Marin with a ponytail.

'I think we should work within the criminal justice system for now,' Frank said.

'System is broke, Frank, and you know it. You say your boy is innocent – how many innocent people are sitting in prison today? You gonna let him spend the rest of his life in prison or take the needle for a crime he didn't commit? Because the judge and the D.A. want to get reelected?'

Frank did not know what he would do if William were convicted. What does a father do if the system wrongfully convicts his son? Does he say, sorry, son, the system didn't work in your case, so you'll just have to die in prison. It hadn't worked for scores of other defendants in Texas; fifty black men had been released in the last decade when DNA tests proved their innocence, some after serving twenty or more years. But what if DNA proved his son guilty?

'I think we can win inside the system.'

Chico shrugged. 'You're Anglo. You gotta believe.'

'So what did we find in William's room?' Frank asked.

'Laptop and phone,' Chico said. 'I'm seeing if his text messages go back two years.'

'Still don't figure that,' Dwayne said. 'Cops not taking the good stuff.'

'Not all the good stuff,' Chuck said.

He reached into the box and held up a tiny black undergarment.

'You took a thong?'

'Three.'

'Why?'

'That's kind of personal, Frank. Oh, I found this, too.'

Chuck again reached into the box then held out a small, framed photograph. Frank took it and looked at the image of himself and his son. It was after a middle-school game at the Academy when William was only twelve. When he was still just a boy dreaming of being a man. The Cowboys quarterback. A star. He had not dreamed of being an accused rapist and murderer.

'He's innocent,' Frank said. 'You guys don't know him. I do. It's not in him to hurt someone.'

'Frank,' Dwayne said, 'just playing the devil's advocate here, but you believed that Todd boy was innocent, too. You were wrong.'

'I'm not wrong about William.'

'His blood on the victim, that ain't good, Frank. Ain't good at all.'

'Look, if you guys want to go back to the beach, it's okay.'

'Do we look like we're going back to the beach?' Dwayne said. 'But if we're gonna defend your son, we got to be honest with each other. Say what we think. So we don't miss nothing.' He tapped the homicide file with his finger. ''Cause the prosecution won't.'

'Well, I don't know if your boy raped and killed that girl,' Chico said, 'but I sure wouldn't want him coming around my girls.'

Chico guarded his teenage daughters' virginity like the Secret Service guarded the president. Which was not easy since they lived with their mother in Corpus Christi.

'What'd you find?'

'Texts back and forth with his buddies, talking about coeds that put out, rating them on a one-to-ten scale, and not in terms you'd want your daughter mentioned.' Chico shook his head. 'Good thing we got his phone, Frank, might not be good for that asshole D.A. to have these messages. Jury wouldn't like him much.'

'The D.A.?'

'Your son.'

'Like I said, boy ain't gonna win Miss Congeniality, that's for sure,' Dwayne said. He exhaled cigar smoke then turned to Frank. 'So what's our next move, counselor?'

Frank pointed at the file in front of Dwayne.

'William gave me his timeline for that day. Now we take that file and reconstruct the victim's last day of life. See if they intersect.'

'How much you want to bet?'

His son sat in jail, charged with raping and murdering an eighteen-year-old girl named Dee Dee Dunston. Frank ate half his burger and drank his beer and then went straight to dessert. He had vowed to stay off the hard stuff, but his head was pounding with a headache. So he downed a shot of bourbon; it wasn't that different from taking Advil to relieve the pain. But just one. Shot. Or maybe two, so he'd sleep that night. He needed to sleep to work the next day. To think. But no more than three shots, that was his absolute limit.

Just as the light of day was fading into the dark of night, the worst day of Frank Tucker's life would soon fade into the fog of Jim Beam.

William had been moved to a solitary cell. The upside was, he wouldn't have to fight a brother each day; the downside was, there was barely enough floor space for him to exercise. But he had tried: five hundred pushups, five hundred sit-ups, one hundred jump squats, and one hundred lunges. Twice. But he felt unsatisfied. He needed iron plates. Hundred-pound weights. Barbells and dumbbells. He needed to feel the pump of the blood through his body. He needed to push his muscles to the max. He needed a real workout. He needed to prepare for Saturday's big game.

'Hey, man, you wanna talk?'

191

The cramped space contained a cot and a toilet. It was late; he lay on the cot with his eyes closed. He strained to recall the girl, but her face drew a blank. As did that entire day. And night. Normally he could remember every play of every game, but not that game. Not that night. Not that girl. There had been so many girls and so many nights lost forever to alcohol and concussions. Sometimes it seemed as if he had no memories of college.

'Worst thing about solitary, no one to talk to. I like to talk.'

William was a naturally confident player. But he had to admit: this unexpected turn of events in his game situation – rape . . . murder . . . DNA . . . prison – had jolted his confidence in a way that throwing five interceptions could not. It was as if he could feel the momentum of his life shifting. For almost twenty-three years, the momentum had carried him forward, faster and faster. Now he suddenly felt adrift.

'You the white boy?'

The solitary cellblock sat silent, except for the whispered voice from the cell next door. William sighed and whispered back.

'Yeah. I'm the white boy.'

'Football player?'

'You don't know who I am?'

'We don't get no Twitter in here.'

'Yeah, I'm the football player.'

'Heard you cold-cocked Coco Pop.'

'Who the hell's Coco Pop?'

'The homey you cold-cocked.'

'Is that his given name?'

'That the name we give him, 'cause he always eating them Coco Pops cereal. Too much sugar for me. I like that Shredded Wheat and cold milk, 2 percent. Skim taste like water. Course, you don't come here for the food.'

'I'm not supposed to be here.'

'Me neither. But that asshole homey ratted me out.'

'Coco Pop?'

'No, man. Eugene. He took a plea, say I killed that cop.'

'But you didn't?'

'No, I did. But Eugene ain't supposed to rat me out, so I ain't supposed to be here.'

'I didn't kill her.'

'Who?'

'That girl.'

'What girl?'

'Cheerleader.'

'Aw, man, a cheerleader. What she do, fuck around on you? Them cheerleaders, they like that.'

'No, she wasn't . . . I mean, I don't know. I didn't know her. They've got the wrong guy. I'm innocent.'

'That sound good. Keep saying it, just like that. Sound sincere.'

'I didn't kill her.'

'Shit, I'm starting to believe you my ownself. You good, homeboy, real good. I was good too, crying and telling everyone I was innocent, that I didn't kill that cop. Got me a new trial. Course, I got convicted again. Fuckin' jury.'

'But you killed him?'

'Damn straight. Fuckin' punk-ass undercover cop gonna bust my ass? I don't think so. I shot that motherfucker right between his eyes with my Glock nine. *Boom!* He dead. But that jury, they wouldn't believe me no how, gangbanger from the 'hood all tatted up and looking bad. But you a white boy, they might buy your bullshit. You might beat it, walk out that courtroom a free man. It could happen.'

'You really think so?'

'Nah.'

The gangbanger next door laughed.

193

Chapter 22

Dee Dee Dunston woke at 6:30 A.M. on the morning of Saturday, November 12, 2011. She was eighteen years old and a freshman cheerleader at Texas Tech University in Lubbock in West Texas. But that morning she woke in Room 310 at the Omni Hotel in Austin, Texas. The Tech football team, cheerleaders, band, and fans had traveled the three hundred seventy-five miles from Lubbock to Austin for a game against the Texas Longhorns that day at noon. Dee Dee Dunston teemed with excitement. She had never been to Austin. She did not know that she would never leave Austin.

She would be dead in eighteen hours.

Dee Dee jumped out of bed and into the shower before her roommate woke. Cissy was a sophomore and liked to sleep late; she was a city girl from Fort Worth. Dee Dee was a country girl from Sweetwater. She had grown up on a ranch where animals and humans woke at dawn. She wore boots and jeans and cowboy hats. She rode horses and branded cows and castrated calves. She was a cowboy; anyone who called her a 'cowgirl' got a punch in the nose, and she could punch. She didn't wear makeup until college. She never knew she was a pretty girl; neither did the other cowboys.

But they knew now.

She blew her short blonde hair dry then dressed in her cheerleader outfit: a red top that came just below her breasts and a short red skirt that rode just below her navel, revealing her lean torso, and black Spandex shorts underneath. White bow in her hair. She was a member of the coed squad, thirty boys and girls. The coed squad performed at football games, but they also competed in collegiate cheer tournaments. The days of cheerleaders offering bouncing breasts and fluffy pompoms were long gone; cheerleading today was physical and demanding, more gymnastics than cheerleading. Back in high school, she had played softball and volleyball and trained in gymnastics, which led her into competitive cheering. She had won a spot on the Tech squad at the tryouts the previous May. Tumbling, stunts, basket toss, game day spirit and motion techniques, and the interview. It was like winning the Miss America pageant, only harder. Her abs were ripped, her legs muscular, her arms lean. Cheerleading today was not for soft-bodied girls. It was for athletes.

Dee Dee Dunston was an athlete.

'What time is it?'

She had come out of the bathroom to find Cissy stirring.

'Seven-thirty. I'm going down for breakfast.'

Sweetwater's population was ten thousand; Lubbock's was two hundred forty thousand; Austin's was a million. Dee Dee had never been to the big city. She felt as if she had spent the entire time in town gazing about in awe with her mouth gaped open. The tall buildings, the homeless people panhandling for hand-outs, the colorful tattooed people with piercings all over their bodies, and the cross-dressers parading about. It was like going to the circus, except this show wasn't under a big tent. It was everywhere in Austin.

And now she felt her mouth drop open again as they walked across the football field at the UT stadium. The Mustang Bowl, the Sweetwater High School stadium, seated six thousand; the Texas Tech stadium sixty thousand; the UT stadium one hundred thousand. The stands rose high into the blue sky, and there was a huge video screen in the south end zone where they would show instant replays.

'Big,' Cissy said.

'Amazing,' Dee Dee said.

'He is.'

'I'm talking about the stadium.'

'I'm talking about him.'

'Who?'

Cissy nodded in the direction of the Longhorn team warming up on the field. Dee Dee looked that way.

'William Tucker.'

He wore his white uniform pants but only a tight sleeveless orange shirt. His body was muscular, his long hair blonde, his smile big and bright when he looked over at them. His voice was strong and manly when he called out.

'The Dizzy Rooster on Sixth Street. Tonight. Be there.'

Cissy and the other girls giggled. Dee Dee did not. She stood as if her sneakers were embedded in the grass field. Cissy tugged at her arm. Dee Dee finally moved, but not before she had made a decision.

She would be there. That night. At the Dizzy Rooster.

The Dizzy Rooster offered live music seven days a week. It was loud, it was crowded, it was filled with neon beer signs, and it was fun. The female bartenders wore red and pink tutus and corsets and stockings with garter belts, which explained all the

196

guys at the long wooden bar, that and the two girls dancing on the bar. Dee Dee stood at the bar with Cissy and four other Tech cheerleaders. They were drinking beers. The legal drinking age in Texas was twenty-one, but like most underage college students, Dee Dee possessed two driver's licenses: the real one she gave to cops when they stopped her for speeding the highway between Sweetwater and Lubbock, and the fake one she gave to bouncers at bars. The fake one showed her age as twenty-one.

She finished her beer and ordered another; she felt a hand on her arm. She whirled around ready to tell another Tech player to drop dead and came face to face with him. She stared up at his face. The face all of America had seen so many times on television. The face that had been all around campus the past week as the excitement over the big game with Texas grew each day. The face of—

William Tucker.

'She fought him,' Dwayne said.

It was Monday afternoon. They had retraced Dee Dee Dunston's every step that day based upon the homicide report from two years before: Omni Hotel . . . UT stadium for the game . . . back to the hotel for dinner . . . partying on Sixth Street . . . the Dizzy Rooster bar. Frank and the others now stood at the crime scene behind the bar where Dee Dee's short life had ended.

'Detectives back then, they were pros,' Dwayne said. 'Tracked her minute by minute that day. To this bar. She was last seen inside the bar at approximately midnight. She came out here through the back door. Of her own volition.'

'What's that mean?' Chuck asked.

'Means he didn't drag her. She came out here of her own free will. Only one reason she'd come out here with the killer. Sex. Consensual sex turned rough and then violent. It happens.'

The alley behind the bar was bleak and bare; it was not a place where a young girl's life should end. Where any life should end.

'Time of death was between midnight and two A.M.,' Dwayne said. 'Cause of death was strangulation. Cleaning crew found her the next morning, about six. Cops collected all the evidence there was to collect, couldn't match the DNA. Put out her photos around Austin and on the Tech campus, asked for leads. None came. Became a cold case.'

Dwayne squatted; he puffed on his cigar and pondered the crime scene like a Sioux hunter tracking his prey. He was a homicide cop again, a pro from the mean streets of Houston. He held out the color crime scene photos one by one, matching each up with the reality of the crime scene. Frank looked over Dwayne's shoulder at the final photo – Dee Dee Dunston in an awkward sitting position in a corner where this building met the adjoining one, as if she had slid down the brick wall, her face bloody and her blonde hair messy, her red cheerleader outfit out of kilter, her legs splayed, the bright white sneakers with the little red pompoms entwined in the laces incongruous with the rest of her body, her blue eyes wide open. Staring at her lifeless image, Frank Tucker was certain of one thing.

My son did not do this to her.

'Whoever did this to her,' Dwayne said, 'he was big and strong. 'Cause she didn't go down easy. She fought him, hard. She punched, she kicked . . . she didn't want to die.'

An image flashed through Frank's mind of Dee Dee fighting for her life in this small space, trapped in this corner, slapping her fists against her attacker's thick arms while his big hands grasped her neck and strangled her. Fighting but losing. They all stared at Dee Dee's death photo. Chico made the sign of the cross.

'Can we get a drink?' Chuck said. 'Seriously, I need a drink.'

★

'I need a protein shake,' William said to the guard. 'So I need someone to go to my dorm and get my supplements and whey protein. And I've got to get in a real workout today. I've got a game Saturday.'

The fat-ass guard pushed the food tray through the slot in the bars. From the looks of him, he hadn't even driven past a gym in two decades.

'Oh, okay. Let me call down to the fitness center, make you an appointment.'

'Thanks.'

The guard laughed.

'What?' William said.

'Boy, you some kind of bullshit prima donna, ain't you? This ain't no fucking spa, stud. You in that cell twenty-three hours each day. You get one hour outside on the concrete inside the fences with the electric wires up top. Ain't no working out in here. There's just working off the time.'

'You know who I am? I'm William Tucker.'

'And you think that makes you special?'

'Yeah. I do.'

'Your mama tell you that? You a special boy? Well, let me tell you something, William Tucker – ain't no special in here.'

The guard chuckled and walked off. William heard him mumbling.

'"I want to workout," he says. Hell, I want a fuckin' raise.'

The gangbanger next door giggled.

'White people are funny.'

Chapter 23

There was a time when black cops could not be homicide detectives in the South. But times had changed. In Houston and in Austin. Herman Jones was black. He was the detective in charge of the Dee Dee Dunston murder case, two years ago and today. He refused to give Dwayne Gentry the time of day until Dwayne flashed his Houston police department badge.

'You on the job?'

'Early retirement.'

'Drinking?'

'That obvious?'

Detective Jones nodded. 'You got that look. And the breath.'

They had soldiered up on the drive over.

'I'll have both too in ten years,' the detective said. 'Part of the job description.'

'Amen.'

Detective Herman Jones appeared to be mid-forties, maybe ex-military like Dwayne. He looked Dwayne over then sighed.

'Come on back.'

Herman led Dwayne into a large room filled with desks where the homicide detectives worked. Herman sat behind his desk; Dwayne sat in the chair to the side. The guys had dropped Dwayne at the Austin Police Department in downtown before they drove to the UT stadium to meet William's coach. Dwayne hoped Herman would treat him like a colleague instead of an adversary. Like a brother in arms.

'Dee Dee was a party girl,' Herman said. 'Partied with the wrong guy that night. Bad deal.'

'We retraced her steps this morning. You did a good job.'

'Thanks.'

'Did William Tucker's name ever come up back then?'

'Nope. Still can't believe it. But I handled the Bradley Todd case, still can't believe that.'

'Neither can his dad.'

'Heard he was in to see his boy. He was a great lawyer. I sat through the Todd trial. The first girl. He made the D.A. look like a fool.'

'The D.A. hasn't forgotten.'

'Nope. He's got a hard-on for the dad. Heard he started drinking after Bradley killed the second girl.'

'Yep.'

'Hard thing to live with. Even for a lawyer. But, hell, Bradley's girlfriend had me convinced he was innocent. He shouldn't blame himself.'

'It's what good men do.'

'I guess. What do you want to know?'

'The homicide file tells me you're a pro, Herman. So why didn't you take William's phone and laptop when you executed the search warrant on his dorm room?'

'No comment.'

'Come on, man, don't "no comment" me. I would never have left the prime suspect's phone and laptop.'

Detective Herman Jones sighed.

'Sorry, Dwayne. Gag order.'

'From the judge?'

'The D.A. Like I said, he ain't exactly buddies with the boy's dad. He taking his boy to trial?'

'Yep.'

'Gonna be another O.J.'

'You can't help me, Herman?'

Herman regarded Dwayne, obviously wondering if he were seeing his own future.

'Tell the dad, the D.A.'s playing to win. And he's got the ethics of a pit bull.'

'No dogs in the locker room,' Coach Bruce said.

He meant Rusty.

'He's a trained police dog,' Frank said.

'He'd better be potty-trained. He craps on this carpet, I'm in a heap of shit. So to speak.'

Frank diverted the coach's attention from Rusty.

'William said you're his closest friend,' Frank said.

Coach Bruce nodded. 'It's that way, quarterback coach and quarterback. We spend a lot of time together, especially during the season. He's a dedicated athlete, Mr. Tucker. Never stops training, always working to get better. That's why he's the best there is. Best there ever was. Would've won the Heisman his sophomore year, except for that game . . . and now this.' He seemed solemn. 'We've had players in trouble with the law, all the big football schools do, but the death penalty? Shit, that wouldn't be good for the program.'

'Or him.'

Coach Bruce Palmer looked to be about forty; he was lean and fit, as if he had once played and still could. He wore a burnt orange Longhorn sweat suit and sneakers and a UT cap.

202

'What's your opinion of my son?'

'He's a great quarterback.'

'As a man.'

'He's a star.'

'What's that mean?'

'Means it's different for him. For every star.'

'In what way?'

'In every way. They don't have the typical college experience. First day they walk onto this campus, they're celebrities. Other students treat them like gods. And if they happen to be the best college football player in America, like William, it's a crazy life. Hard for him to have close friends, he never knew if his friends had an agenda. You know, does this girl like him or the attention she gets being his girlfriend? And there's a lot of attention living in William's world. Believe me, I know that for a fact. We've all been living in William's world the last four years.'

'So a girl would date him to move up in the world?'

He shrugged. 'It happens. Remember last year, the BCS Championship Game, they showed the Alabama quarterback's girlfriend in the stands on national TV. Good-looking gal. Next thing you know, she's got a gig reporting at the Super Bowl. That's what can happen to the star's girlfriend, kind of like winning *American Idol* except she doesn't have to sing.'

Coach Bruce was giving Frank and the guys a tour of the athletic facilities at the stadium – the one-hundred-thousand-seat stadium, the twenty-thousand-square-foot weight room, and now the lavish locker room that offered gaming stations.

'We didn't have anything like this when I played,' Chuck said.

'Or when I played,' Coach Bruce said. 'But we make more money than any other football program in America, and we spend more. Best of the best. Winning the national championship back in oh-five changed everything. The money just poured in after that. Hundred fifty million we made last year, from TV revenue, merchandising, ticket sales, luxury suites, and premium seating . . . we've even got our own cable TV channel, the "Longhorn Network." And we don't have to pay taxes.'

'It's not considered business income unrelated to education?' Frank asked.

'Nope.'

'Why not?'

'Politics. Every state has a UT – a big public university that wants to be number one in football. That takes money. A lot of money. If we had to pay taxes on our business income like everyone else, we couldn't offer all this to top recruits. So Congress exempted athletic income from taxes.'

'I exempted myself,' Chico said. 'Haven't paid a dime in taxes in years.'

Coach Bruce's expression said he wasn't sure if Chico was joking. He wasn't. He lived his life off the books.

'This was William's locker . . . is his locker,' Coach Bruce said.

Since Dwayne wasn't there, Chico, having the most personal experience in the criminal justice system, played cop and frisked the locker. He came up empty-handed. The space was filled only with football cleats, uniforms, protein powder, protein bars, protein drinks, vitamins, supplements, and footballs. Coach Bruce picked up a football and gripped it as if to pass. His emotions got the best of him.

'He was the best I've ever coached.'

'He didn't die,' Frank said. 'He was arrested for a crime he didn't commit. He'll play again.'

That perked Coach Bruce up.

'This season?'

'Maybe not.'

His face fell. 'Damn. We don't have a prayer without William.'

They turned away from William's locker, but Coach Bruce quickly turned back.

'Put that ball back.'

Chuck had taken one of the footballs from William's locker. 'Dang.'

He put the ball back. Coach Bruce gave Frank a look. He shrugged.

'We're not related.'

'Can you ask him to stop?'

Coach Bruce gestured at Chico, who was now playing at one of the game stations. It was like taking the kids on a road trip. Fortunately, the inside tour ended, and they returned outside to the stands. The stadium was a monument to football. Rusty bounded down the stands and leapt onto the grass. He crapped.

'Great,' Coach Bruce said.

'Fertilizer,' Frank said.

The coach's eyes drifted off Rusty and around the stadium.

'What William could do on that field . . . unbelievable.'

'You've been here all four years with William?'

Coach Bruce nodded.

'So you were at that game two years ago?'

Another nod. 'I saw you on the sideline. Bad day for you. And William. Really upset him, threw him off his game.'

'I know.' Frank sighed. 'So after the game, you took him to the hospital?'

'The docs gave him an MRI.'

'They diagnosed a concussion?'

'Yep.'

'Did he remember anything from the game?'

205

'Nothing. Thought he was Troy Aikman.'

'Roger Staubach's my favorite Cowboy quarterback,' Chuck said.

'Are you serious?' Chico said. 'Don Meredith, he was the man.'

'Well, he was the best on *Monday Night Football*, sure, but Staubach won two Super Bowls.'

'True, but . . .'

Coach Bruce looked from them to Frank with a confused expression. Frank could only shrug.

'And then you took him back to his dorm?'

Coach Bruce nodded. 'I got him dinner first. Told him to stay in and sleep. Never knew he didn't until he got arrested Saturday night, read the story in the Sunday paper. That was a shock.'

'He said his buddies came by, took him out. Cowboy and Red.'

'Red graduated last year.'

'Where would we find Cowboy?'

Coach Bruce checked his watch.

'Dining hall.'

Ty Walker, aka 'Cowboy,' was a cowboy from Amarillo. A big cowboy. He wore a T-shirt, Wrangler jeans, and cowboy boots. He looked as if he had just ridden in from the range. He was handsome in a rugged way. They found him eating a steak in the athletic dining hall. He sat alone at a round table. Spread on the table in front of him was the Austin paper with images of William Tucker and Dee Dee Dunston. They sat down without an invitation.

'What kind of sauce they put on that steak?' Chuck said.

Cowboy glanced up from the paper and gave Chuck a look.

'Steak sauce.'

'Ahh.'

'Who the hell are you guys?' Cowboy asked. 'You don't look like cops or reporters.'

'I was a cop,' Dwayne said.

They had picked him up after their stadium tour.

'I'm Frank Tucker, William's dad. These are my friends.'

'Did he do it?'

'You have to ask?'

'These days, you never know.'

'You don't seem surprised that he got arrested.'

Cowboy shrugged. 'Part of the game. Players get cut, get hurt, get arrested . . . you just suit up the next game and play. That's just the way it is now. Problem is, the backup quarterback sucks.'

'Are you and William close friends?'

Cowboy cut a piece of steak and stabbed it with his fork. He stuffed it in his mouth then answered Frank's question.

'Close? We drank and chased girls together – well, I chased. He didn't have to. But I don't know that he has any close friends.'

'Why not?'

'Because we're just players – he's a star. Like when Garth was still singing – there was Garth and there was everyone else.'

Cowboy assaulted the steak with a serrated knife.

'So how would you describe your relationship with William?'

'I'm just part of his entourage.'

'Anyone else on the team he hung out with?'

'Nah.'

Cowboy waved his fork at the dining hall. Other tables were occupied by big boys but seemed segregated by race. All white or all black.

'Most of the players are black now. We don't hang out together much.'

'Racism?' Dwayne said.

'Music. We don't like rap, they don't like country.'

'What about Latino music?' Chico asked.

'Mexicans don't play our kind of football.'

'So you eat alone?'

'This was our table, me and William. Left the other chairs reserved for the girl athletes.'

'Did you chase girls with William after that game?'

'We chase girls after every game.'

'At the Dizzy Rooster?'

'Good place for girls.'

'Did you take William there that night?'

'Maybe. Too many games and too many bars to remember.'

'Do you remember taking him home that night?'

Cowboy shook his head. 'Too many nights. He doesn't remember?'

'He got a concussion that game.'

'Oh, yeah. He got his bell rung good.' Cowboy shrugged. 'It happens. Football's a collision sport.'

Frank pointed at Dee Dee Dunston's photo in the newspaper.

'You ever see William with that girl?'

Cowboy stared at the photo then shrugged. 'Shit, I don't know. All their faces blur together after a while. And that was too long ago.'

'Only two years.'

'That's a lifetime of girls.'

Chapter 24

'The State of Texas versus William Tucker. Arraignment.'

The media now knew who Frank Tucker was. So the defense team had to fight their way through the gauntlet of cameras and reporters on the plaza outside the Justice Center. The murder trial of William Tucker, Heisman Trophy winner, promised to be the biggest judicial media circus since the murder trial of O.J. Simpson, Heisman Trophy winner, back in 1995. O.J.'s trial had been racially charged – he was black; the victims and the cops were white – with the N-word tossed about by one of the detectives. His defense counsel played the race card; the prosecutors played inept. O.J. was acquitted. William Tucker could depend on neither the race card nor inept prosecutors: he was white, the victim was white, and the prosecutors were skilled and savvy. They would not make mistakes. And their boss needed a win to assure his reelection.

'All rise,' the bailiff said.

Judge Harold Rooney entered the courtroom through a door behind the bench. Frank stood at the defense table; the guys sat in the spectator section like bored retirees. The D.A. and three assistant district attorneys who looked like ex-Navy Seals stood at the prosecution table. No one in the spectator pews rose. Courtroom decorum had gone the way of business attire. The judge arranged himself at the bench, shuffled through papers, and without looking up said, 'Make your appearances, gentlemen.'

'Travis County District Attorney Dick Dorkin, for the state.'

'Frank Tucker, for the defendant.'

Now the judge looked up – at Frank. He stared a long uncomfortable moment – Frank had suffered such stares prior to his relocation to the beach, when old colleagues in Houston encountered him in public – and then motioned the lawyers up to the bench. The prosecution team wore dark suits and dark ties and short hair; Frank wore jeans, a Hawaiian print shirt, and scraggly hair. The judge regarded Frank over his reading glasses then turned the microphone away and leaned forward. This conversation would be off the record.

'You look like hell, Frank.'

With images of Dee Dee Dunston, deceased, fresh in their minds, they had drunk whiskey late into the night at the campsite.

'Nice to see you too, Harold.'

'Frank, I'm real sorry about your son. I hope he's innocent.'

'He is.'

'Is your law license still suspended?'

'It is.'

'So you are appearing today in what capacity?'

'Father.'

Harold sighed and regarded Frank as one does an old friend who's fighting cancer. You remember him as he once was – young and strong and unbroken – not as he is now – old and weak and broken in mind, body, and spirit.

'Even hung over, you're probably the best criminal defense lawyer alive, but as far as this court is concerned, you're not a lawyer. I can't let you represent your son.'

210

'Harold, I'm broke. I don't have the money to hire a lawyer for William. And my ex-wife's husband is broke, too. He's in Poland trying to save himself. He can't save my son. I can.' He pointed a finger in the D.A.'s face. 'And this son of a bitch didn't tell me he was seeking the death penalty.'

The D.A. smirked. 'Surprise.'

'Fuck you, Dick. He's my son.'

'Gentlemen, this *is* a courtroom.' Back to Frank: 'Can he borrow the money?'

'A million bucks? He's a college kid.'

'Who'll go number one in the NFL draft in a few months.'

'Hard to play quarterback on death row,' the D.A. said.

Frank again pointed a finger at the D.A. 'Harold, I'm gonna punch him.'

'Please don't.'

Harold exhaled and looked to the back of the courtroom; he gestured someone forward. Frank and the D.A. turned to see a young woman, mid-thirties perhaps, wearing a suit and low heels, walk up the center aisle. She had shoulder-length curly black hair that bounced and muscular legs. She sported the gait of a runner, as if she might break into a sprint at any moment. When she walked past the row on which the guys were sitting, Chuck leaned out from his aisle seat, obviously checking out her backside, but he leaned too far and fell onto the floor. The D.A. chuckled.

'The Three Stooges.'

The woman continued through the gate and up to the bench. For a lawyer, she was a gorgeous woman. The D.A.'s eyes searched her body like a cop patting down a suspect for contraband.

'Frank,' Harold said, 'this is Billie Jean Crawford. She's a public defender. I'm appointing her to represent your son.'

She regarded Frank as one does a movie star past his prime – way past – and offered more pity than admiration. She stuck a hand out to Frank.

'Mr. Tucker, it's an honor to meet you. We studied your cases in our trial advocacy course.'

'He's a living, drinking legend,' the D.A. said.

'I'm gonna punch him, Harold,' Frank said.

Harold turned to the D.A. 'Dick, don't be a—'

His eyes cut to Ms. Crawford and he thought better of it. She still held her hand out to Frank.

'Harold, you're appointing a PD to defend my son when the state is seeking the death penalty? He's entitled to an experienced death penalty counsel.'

'That would be you, Frank. I believe the Bradley Todd case was a death penalty case, and as I recall, you won.' He paused and shook his head at the memory. 'Wish you hadn't. For both our sakes. And for the second girl.' He leaned even closer to Frank, almost as if to give him a buddy hug over the bench. 'It wasn't your fault, Frank. You did your job.'

Frank fought his emotions.

'Let me do my job now, Harold. Please.'

'I'm trying to, Frank. But I'm a judge, so I feel that I should follow the law whenever possible. I'm appointing Ms. Crawford to officially represent your son.'

'Harold—'

'But – I'll allow you to participate in the trial as her assistant.'

'Her *assistant*?'

'Best I can do, Frank. Take it or leave it.'

That was the judge's deal: Frank could defend his son at trial, but only if the judge could cover his ass with the appeals court by appointing a public defender with a current law license. Frank looked Billie Jean Crawford over; her eyes were amber and her hand remained extended to Frank. He grasped her hand.

'I'll take it.'

'Let's do this.'

Harold returned to his role as Judge Rooney and counsel to their respective tables. Frank whispered to Ms. Crawford.

'First murder trial?'

'First trial.'

Before Frank could respond, a side door opened and his son appeared. William wore the green-and-white striped jumpsuit and shackles on his hands and feet. He waddled over, flanked by two armed deputies, and stood next to Frank.

'Mr. Dorkin,' the judge said.

The D.A. read the indictment. It was painful to hear that a grand jury of twelve citizens had voted to indict your son for the rape and murder of a young woman. William leaned down to Frank and whispered.

'Did they get this shit straightened out?'

As if he hadn't just heard the charges of rape and murder against one William Tucker.

'Am I getting out of here today? I've been in here three nights. They don't even have a gym. I've got to work out, get prepped for the game.'

'Not now,' Frank whispered.

'Did Mom send money?'

'No.'

'Why not?'

'Dale's broke.'

'*Broke? How?*'

'We'll talk after the arraignment.'

William nodded past Frank to Ms. Crawford. 'Who's she?'

'Your lawyer.'

'William Tucker, how do you plead to the charges against you?' the judge said.

'Not guilty,' Frank whispered to his son.

'Not guilty,' his son said.

Frank turned to Ms. Crawford. 'Ask for a trial setting within the speedy trial statute.'

'Why?'

'Just do it.'

She spoke up. 'Your Honor, defense requests a setting within the speedy trial statute.'

The judge regarded her over his reading glasses then cut his eyes to Frank. He knew Frank Tucker's standard trial strategy: push the prosecution to trial. Fast.

'You sure about that?'

'Are we?' Ms. Crawford whispered to Frank.

'Yes.'

'Yes, Your Honor. We're sure.'

'All right. Trial is set for Monday, December ninth. Six weeks. Is that too soon?'

'Is it?' Ms. Crawford whispered.

'No,' Frank whispered back.

'No,' she said to the court.

'Now ask for a reduction in bail,' Frank whispered.

She did.

'Denied.'

Frank decided to test out his new role.

'Your Honor, as Ms. Crawford's assistant, I would ask that my . . . that the defendant be treated like any other defendant without regard to his celebrity status and the media attention. This is a circumstantial evidence case. The defendant has never been accused of a violent crime. The defendant is neither a danger to the community nor a flight risk. We are more than agreeable to appropriate bail conditions such as GPS monitoring. Thus, I would argue that five million dollars is unreasonable bail under the Supreme Court's ruling in *Stack v. Boyle*.'

The D.A. jumped in. 'Your Honor, the defendant's DNA – his blood – was recovered from the victim's body. The perpetrator brutally raped her and strangled her with his bare hands. He looked into her eyes as he killed her. I think that makes the defendant a danger to the community.'

'I have to agree,' the judge said. 'Taking into account the nature of the offense, to-wit, a violent forcible rape and manual strangulation of the victim, and the circumstances of the offense, to-wit, behind a crowded bar in downtown Austin on a Saturday night, which evidences a perpetrator unrestrained by any fear of capture, the defendant does in fact present a danger to the community. Therefore, bail is revoked.'

'*Revoked?*' Frank said. 'Your Honor, the crime occurred two years ago. If the defendant were a risk to the community, he certainly hasn't demonstrated any violent tendencies during the last two years.'

'He was arrested a month ago for resisting arrest,' the D.A. said.

'It was a public intoxication charge,' Ms. Crawford said. 'How many college kids are arrested for public intoxication on Sixth Street every Saturday night?'

'The police report says the defendant became belligerent, that the officer was in fear of the defendant,' the D.A. said.

'The defendant's blood on the victim establishes that he had close personal contact with her that night,' the judge said. 'Explain that, Mr. Tucker.'

'I can't,' Frank said.

'When you can, I'll reconsider bail. Until then, the defendant shall remain in the Travis County Jail pending trial.'

William had stood silent throughout the arguments, almost oblivious to the fact that they were arguing over his personal freedom. But now he understood. He exploded.

'But I've got a big game Saturday! Kansas State!'

The judge regarded William Tucker almost as if saddened by the sight.

'You've played your last college game, son.'

215

'*What?* I've got to play! If I don't play, I won't win another Heisman Trophy! Or the national championship!'

'Mr. Tucker, you should not concern yourself with winning trophies and championships. You should concern yourself with staying off death row.'

'*Death row?* What the hell are you talking about?'

The judge glanced at Frank – he had not yet told William – then back at Frank's son.

'Mr. Tucker, the state is seeking the death penalty.'

'*The death penalty?*'

The judge banged his gavel. Court was adjourned. The deputies grabbed William's arms and pulled him away. He looked back at Frank with an expression of shock.

'Take him to the interview room.'

The deputies gave Frank a 'we don't work for you' look; but they would take him across the plaza to the jail and deposit him in the interview room. Frank told Ms. Crawford to meet him in the interview room then followed the judge into his chambers. The judge knew what was on Frank's mind. He shut the door behind them and removed his black robe.

'Why, Harold? Is this because of Bradley Todd? Because I made you look like a fool?'

'No, Frank. That happens. That's the chance we take – a lawyer when you take a case, a judge when I make a decision – that we're wrong about the human being standing in front of us. We try our best to see into his soul, but we can't. We're like surgeons – you're going to lose some patients on the table. We're going to be wrong about some clients and defendants. We were both wrong about Bradley Todd. But I don't blame you.'

'Then what's this about?'

'Your son.'

Harold sat in his chair and regarded Frank not as a judge but as a friend.

216

'You know what I see when I look at your son? A twenty-two-year-old boy who thinks he's entitled, that he's above the rules, that he's more special than the rest of the world, that he can do whatever the hell he pleases just because he's the best damn football player in the country. This isn't the first time he's run afoul of the law, Frank. All minor incidents, sure, and I know the resisting arrest charge was bullshit. But this isn't. This is serious, Frank. He might be innocent . . . but he might be guilty. Right now, I don't know. So he stays in jail until I do know. And even if he is innocent, a little jail therapy could be just what he needs. Six weeks till trial. He spends those six weeks in jail, maybe he'll have time to think about his life. Maybe he'll realize he isn't special, just lucky. Maybe he'll come out a man. A better man.'

The judge exhaled.

'I'm doing your son a favor, Frank.'

The judge saw William Tucker as the man he was today – a twenty-two-year-old prima donna athlete who thought the world revolved around him; but Frank saw him as the twelve-year-old boy who thought his father was the best dad in the whole world. A son never changes in his father's eyes. And the son was as scared as a twelve-year-old boy right now.

'*The death penalty?*'

'The D.A.'s trying to pressure you to take a plea deal.'

'I'm innocent! I've never seen her before in my life! I didn't rape her! I didn't kill her! Why don't they believe me?'

He was as convincing as Bradley Todd had been. He put his face in his hands on the other side of the Plexiglas. When he looked up again, the first signs of defeat appeared on his face. Jail could do that to a man. Especially a young man.

'You got to get me out of here, Frank. If I don't play Saturday, I can kiss the Heisman goodbye. And the national championship. How can the judge keep me in here when I've still got three games left in the season? Why can't we deal with this during the off-season? Does he know how many Longhorn alumni he's gonna piss off? It's been eight years since UT won a national championship.'

'Son, your season's over.'

'So I'm not getting out?'

'Not unless we can explain why your blood was on the victim.'

'I don't know how my blood got on her. But I'm not a murderer.'

'The voters think you are.'

'Why?'

'Because the police arrested you, the D.A. charged you, and the grand jury indicted you.'

'What happened to innocent until proven guilty?'

'It was never the reality. It just sounds good. The D.A. and the judge are both up for reelection. You don't get reelected by letting accused rapists and murderers back on the street.'

They sat on opposite sides of the Plexiglas partition with phones to their ears. Ms. Crawford sat next to Frank; she could not hear William's voice. The guys sat outside; only the lawyers were allowed in that day.

'Did they move you to solitary?'

His son nodded. 'Dale's broke?'

Frank recounted what Liz had told him.

'Your wife left you for a fracker?' Ms. Crawford said.

Frank frowned at her and put a finger to his lips. 'Shh.'

'How am I going to hire a lawyer?'

Frank gestured to himself and Ms. Crawford. 'We work for free.'

The prospect of two free lawyers did not seem to perk up his son's spirits.

'A drunk ex-lawyer and a public defender who's never tried a case? That's all that stands between me and the death penalty?'

'I've tried a hundred cases. I used to be a good lawyer. I can be again.'

William stood but still held the phone to his ear.

'But can you stay sober?'

'I can. For you, son, I can. I will. I promise.'

Frank stood and again placed his palm against the glass. His son stared at Frank's hand then hung up the phone and walked out of the interview room.

Travis County District Attorney Dick Dorkin stood at his first-floor window fronting the plaza and the jail on the far side. He watched the great Frank Tucker exit the jail and walk across the plaza with the public defender.

Not so great now, are you, Frank?

Frank Tucker had always had the perfect life. The perfect wife. The perfect family. The perfect career. And Dick Dorkin's life had always been less than perfect. No wife, no family, a public service career. He had been Frank's backup for thirty-three years, since their first day of law school. Frank was the star of the class, a fact that became evident early on. Their classmates gravitated to him, not to Dick. Frank had graduated number one and then had gone on to a storied career as a defense attorney – defending the innocent.

Until Bradley Todd.

He had defended the guilty, and the guilt had destroyed Frank Tucker's perfect life. His wife had left him, his career had vanished, and his son had abandoned him. He was a broken-down beach bum. A drunk. A lawyer without a license to practice law. A loser. Now it was Dick Dorkin's life that seemed perfect. He was the righteous prosecutor fighting for justice. He got the good press now. And he wanted this conviction bad.

A death warrant for William Tucker was his ticket to the Governor's Mansion.

Chapter 25

'Teach me, Mr. Tucker.'

'Frank.'

'Teach me, Frank.'

'You've never tried a case?'

'I've never *had* a case. I just got my law license.'

'I've tried a hundred cases, but I lost my law license.'

'I've got what you need, Frank, and you've got what I need.'

'I need a drink.'

He stood and got a drink. A Shiner Bock beer. Like an appetizer before the main course. But he had promised his son. William needed a sober lawyer. So there would be no whiskey for Frank. He would go cold turkey on Wild Turkey. And Jack Daniels. And Jim Beam. And all his other buddies. He would wean himself off whiskey with beer; he wasn't sure what he'd use to wean himself off beer. Something equally addictive – ice cream, maybe. They all sat at the picnic table. Chico fiddled with William's cell phone. Dwayne flipped the pages of the homicide file and Chuck the signed football into the air. Ms. Crawford typed notes on her iPad with the candy apple red cover, same as the paint job on her convertible Mustang.

'We read the transcript of your closing arguments in the senator's trial,' Ms. Crawford said. 'Brilliant. You got the jury to blame the prosecutor instead of the defendant, made the D.A. look like a fool. He's not the type to hold a grudge, is he?'

'I'm afraid he is.'

'Well, that explains his courtroom demeanor.'

'No, that's just because he's an asshole. The grudge stuff will come later.'

Ms. Crawford had come out to their campsite to plan their defense strategy. Frank drank his beer and regarded his co-counsel. She was an extremely attractive woman; the others had already noticed. They eyed her as if she were a fifth of bourbon on a liquor store shelf. The good stuff. She had a pretty face and a throaty voice, like that actress, the one who used to be married to the *Die Hard* guy. She had removed her jacket and wore a sleeveless white blouse. Her arms were muscular for a woman.

'You work out?' Chuck asked her.

'Every day. At the Y by the lake, then I run five miles around the lake.'

'What do you wear?'

She frowned at his question.

'Forgive Chuck, Ms. Crawford—'

'Billie Jean.'

'—emotionally, he's still in high school. So, Billie Jean, how did you find your way to the public defenders' office?'

'Law firms don't hire forty-year-old associates.'

She didn't look forty years old.

'This is my second career,' she said.

'What was your first?'

'Stripper.'

'I like her already,' Chuck said.

221

'Some girls call themselves exotic dancers, but there's nothing exotic about taking your clothes off and putting your privates in strange men's faces.'

'Always seems exotic to me,' Chuck said. 'You ever do the olive oil thing?'

'I've never *heard* of the olive oil thing.'

Chuck grunted as if surprised. 'All the strippers in Mexico know about it.'

She stared at Chuck for a beat then shook her head as if her brain were an Etch A Sketch and she was trying to shake the image clean from her mind. It took a moment for her to regain her train of thought.

'Anyway, I'm a single mom. I have a daughter, she's in college now. I married a bum when I was young and stupid. He was my Prince Charming, tall and handsome, a minor league baseball player on his way to the majors.'

'Did he make it?'

She shook her head. 'He was a minor-league player all his life. Turned out, he was a minor-league man, too. Played a doubleheader while I gave birth. First thing he said to me when he got to the hospital was, "Shit. I went oh-for-eight." He left us right after she was born.'

'Where is he now?'

'California, last I heard.'

'Doing what?'

'Screwing up someone else's life, I'm sure. Some other stupid woman looking for her Prince Charming. Why do we do that?'

'Ask my ex-wife.'

'Anyway, I went back to school, got a degree in criminal justice, working nights. Then law school.'

'You put yourself through college and law school on tips from stripping?'

222

'I was a very good stripper.'

'Now I'm in love,' Chuck said.

'My stage name was Candy because I always wore a candy apple red G-string.'

'You're killing me,' Chuck said.

'Hence, the candy apple red convertible,' Frank said.

'Reminds me of where I've been . . . and where I don't want to be again.'

She must have seen something in Frank's eyes, but it wasn't what she thought.

'I wasn't a prostitute, so don't judge me.'

'Billie Jean, we're all drunks who've screwed up our lives royally. Do we look like the types to judge?'

'Frank, I want you to teach me.'

'How to be a prostitute?'

She smiled. She had a nice smile.

'How to be a lawyer. I'm a fast learner. I want to be a good lawyer. You're the best. Or you were.'

Frank finished off the beer then stood and walked over to the cooler and popped the top on another can. He wanted a shot of whiskey. He addressed the defense team.

'The clock's ticking on my son's life. We're all that's standing between him and death row six weeks from now. Good news is, he's innocent. Bad news is, we've got no money to defend him and it's his word against his own DNA. That story ends on death row. We've got to find the truth.'

'Give him a polygraph,' Dwayne said.

Frank had never made Bradley Todd take a polygraph. He had wished so many times since that he had. Should he make his son take a polygraph? A father did not need proof that his son was innocent.

'Where? In his cell? And even if the D.A. allowed it, he'd know we gave him one. If he passes, they know we'll tell them, but they won't dismiss the charges because they've got his blood. If he fails and we don't tell them, they'll know they've got the right guy.'

'At least we'd know.'

'We already know. He's innocent.'

'Frank, you ain't buying his amnesia defense, are you?'

'I got no short-term memory 'cause of my concussions,' Chuck said.

'They got his blood off the girl,' Dwayne said. 'That's kind of hard to explain away. You've got to at least consider the possibility that he did it.'

'I can't.'

'Why not?'

'He's my son.'

'Frank, I understand but—'

'No. You don't understand. You can't understand. None of you can.'

'Why not?'

'None of you have a son.'

Frank took a deep breath and a long swallow of the beer. Dwayne inhaled on his cigar and then exhaled smoke circles.

'You're right,' Dwayne said. 'You're his father, and we're your friends. We're here to help you help him.'

'Thanks. Okay, Chuck, you're the football guy, so I need you to go to Lubbock and talk to the other players and coaches. You can relate to them.'

'You want me to go to Lubbock by myself?'

His expression seemed pained.

'You're forty-nine, Chuck. You can do it.'

'But, Frank, I'm a little worried . . . you know, the memory thing. And I don't think so good these days.'

Chuck's numerous concussions in college caused him to worry that he had suffered brain damage, as many ex-football players were discovering they had suffered. Repetitive concussions have been linked to memory loss, impaired thought processes, early-onset dementia, and irreparable brain damage.

'Six NFL players committed suicide the last two years,' Chuck said. 'And now McMahon—'

Jim McMahon, the Super Bowl-winning star quarterback of the Chicago Bears back in the eighties.

'—and Bradshaw—'

Terry Bradshaw, who won four Super Bowls as the Pittsburgh Steelers quarterback in the seventies and eighties.

'—they're both suffering memory lapses. Man, I don't want to get lost in Lubbock.'

'Chuck, you smoke those cancer sticks like a chimney,' Chico said. 'You should be worried about getting cancer, not getting lost.'

'At least with cancer I'd just die. Better than wandering the beach not knowing how to get home.'

'Sorry, Chuck,' Frank said. He knew better than to ask Chuck to go out of town alone. 'Dwayne, you go with him. Track down all the witnesses named in the file – cheerleaders, players, coaches. Recheck their stories, see if the detectives missed anything. Better that way, you can look after each other.'

'Two drunks watching each other? There's a recipe for disaster.'

'Or fun,' Chuck said.

They fist-bumped.

'Problem is, my truck's in Rockport,' Dwayne said.

'Take mine,' Chico said.

'How will you guys get back home?' Chuck asked.

'I'll drive them,' Billie Jean said. 'I'm on the team, too.'

'Uh, Frank,' Dwayne said, 'traveling to Lubbock, staying in a hotel, that costs. I'm tapped out till my next pension check.

We need money to fund this investigation – hell, to pay for gas to Lubbock.'

Frank glanced at the members of the defense team: Dwayne Gentry, an ex-cop who supplemented his police pension working as a part-time security guard at a mini-storage facility . . . Chuck Miller, an ex-coach who refereed peewee football games, but only the ones run by organizations that didn't require criminal background checks . . . Chico Duran, an ex-con who fraudulently received federal disability benefits and delivered pizzas on weekends . . . Billie Jean Crawford, an ex-stripper turned public defender. His eyes rested on her. Her eyes narrowed, then she shook her head.

'Don't even think about it. I'm not stripping again.'

Their moneymaking opportunities were limited. But defending a client against a capital murder charge carrying the death penalty required money. Frank saw no options . . . until Chuck flipped the signed football into the air again.

'Sell the ball,' Frank said.

Chuck caught the ball and frowned at Frank.

'Do we have to? I've gotten attached to it.'

'Get unattached. Chico, put that ball on eBay. Pronto.'

Dwayne smiled. 'An expense-account trip, even if it is to Lubbock.'

'No bars.'

Now he frowned. 'Well, that takes a lot of the fun out of a free trip.'

'No, I mean there are no bars in Lubbock. It's dry.'

'My God.'

As if Frank had just said the world would end the next day, Chico made the sign of the cross.

'Billie Jean,' Frank said, 'draft a subpoena. Copies of all DNA tests, all physical evidence reports, autopsy results, the game film, anything else they've got.'

'You want a copy of the game film?'

'I want Chuck to review the tape, see if it caught the girl on the sideline. Maybe someone talked to her during the game.'

'I'll break it down,' Chuck said.

'I don't care about the offensive and defensive schemes, just the cheerleaders.'

'That's what I meant.'

'I've never written a subpoena,' Billie Jean said.

'Look in the form books. You draft it, I'll review it.'

'Okay, I'll email it to you.'

'No email.'

'For security, so the D.A. can't intercept our communications?'

'Uh, no. I don't have email.'

'Why not?'

'I don't have Internet connection.'

'Why not?'

'I live in a shack on the beach.'

'Oh. Okay, I'll fax it.'

'No fax.'

'Mail?'

'Not that I know of.'

'I'll drive it down.'

'Chico, you go through his laptop and phone.'

His eyes remained locked on William's phone like a kid playing a video game.

'On it.'

'And no drinking, guys.'

That brought Chico's eyes up; they all eyed Frank a long moment then broke into laughter.

'That's a good one, Frank,' Dwayne said.

'Anyone know the area code for Lubbock?' Chico said.

Billie Jean typed on her iPad.

'You've got three-G?' Chico said.

'Four.'

'Damn.'

'Eight-oh-six,' she said.

'I was afraid of that.'

'Why?' Frank said.

Chico pressed buttons on the phone then put it to his ear and listened.

'Shit.'

'What?'

He pressed buttons again and engaged the speakerphone. He held the phone out. They could hear the call ring through and then a perky voice answering.

'Hi, this is Dee Dee. I'm out having fun so leave a message and I'll call you back. Bye.'

The message beeped. Chico disconnected. Frank could barely speak the words.

'Her number is on William's phone?'

'He lied, Frank,' Chico said. 'He knew her.'

'Play it again.'

He did. William knew the victim. He had lied to his father. Just as Bradley Todd had lied to his lawyer. Frank needed a drink. A real drink.

'It's been two years,' Billie Jean said. 'Why is her phone still working?'

'Because parents, they never let go,' Dwayne said. 'Seen it all the time. Her room at home, bet it looks exactly like the day she left for college.' He puffed on the cigar. 'Her folks probably kept her phone on their family plan. It don't cost much.'

'Why would they do that?'

'To hear her voice.'

*

'Hey . . . William Tucker.'

The whispered voice of the gangbanger next door came through the cell bars.

'Fuckin' death penalty, huh? Shit, that sucks.'

'This can't be happening to me.'

William felt as if he had taken a blow to the head. His thinking was foggy, his thoughts lost in the fog of fear. The death penalty.

'Sure it can. Happen to me.'

'You were on death row?'

'Five years, till I got me a new trial. Now I'm going back. Back home.'

'What's it like?'

'Boring. Goddamn, the boredom just eats at you, almost make you wanna kill yourself, save them the trouble. But you don't, man, 'cause you wanna live. You never know how much you wanna live till someone say you gotta die. That's why they strap you down, 'cause folks wanna live. Brothers on both side of me, they took that walk to the death chamber. Talked big shit, saying, "Hell, I'm gonna spit in the man's eye." But when the day come, they crying for they mama, scared to stop living. Least it ain't like the old days, sitting in that electric chair. You imagine that? They wire your ass up and hit the voltage, say your eyes pop outta your skull, that's why they put a hood over your head. *Shit*. That scary. Now you just go to sleep. Fuckin' forever. But don't you worry none, William, all the mandatory appeals they do, take ten years minimum. You gonna live a long time on death row. Being bored. Eating bad food. Waiting.'

William heard the gangbanger sigh.

'Man, if I just hadn't of gotten all these tatts, I might've got off. Them jury people, they see a black dude with tatts all over his arms and neck, they scared. That a good thing on the streets, see, but it ain't so good in a courtroom. You got any tatts?'

'No.'

'You play football but don't got no tatts?'

'I'm afraid of needles.'

The gangbanger next door laughed. 'That funny.'

'Why is that funny?'

'D.A. want to sentence you to death, but you afraid of needles. That ain't no defense.'

He laughed again, but William was confused. His foggy mind could not comprehend the joke.

'What?'

'You get the death penalty, they don't electrocute you no more, William Tucker. They stick a needle in you and shoot the poison into your veins. That's how they kill you now, with a fuckin' needle. And, hell, we all afraid of that needle.'

Chapter 26

'Hi, this is Dee Dee. I'm out having fun, so leave a message and I'll call you back. Bye.'

Frank played Dee Dee's voice message for William on the interview room phone. Billie Jean had driven Frank downtown to the jail the next morning in her candy apple red Mustang with the top down. It had wide tires and a 420-horsepower V-8 engine. She liked to go fast, which did not help his hangover. She now sat next to Frank, but she could only hear Frank's side of the conversation.

'That's on my phone?' William said.

'It is. You said you didn't know her.'

'I don't.'

'Then why's her number on your phone?'

'You think I'm guilty, don't you?'

'No.'

'What'd he say?' Billie Jean said.

Frank held up a finger to her.

'Her phone number doesn't mean I raped and killed her!'

'It means you knew her. When did you meet her?'

'I don't know.'

'It had to be that same night. She went to school in Lubbock.'

'I guess.'

'How can you not remember her?'

William gestured at his cell phone. 'A, I had a concussion. I don't remember that night. And B, I bet I've got five hundred girls' numbers on that phone, maybe a thousand. But I don't know them.'

'How can you not know them if you put their numbers in your phone?'

'I didn't.'

'What?' Billie Jean said.

Frank turned to her. 'He said he didn't put her number into his phone.'

'Then who did?'

Back to William: 'Then who did?'

'She did.'

'She did?'

'Look, Frank, here's how it works when you're a star athlete in America.'

As if there were a book setting out the rules.

'Anytime I leave my dorm and go out in public – to a bar, a restaurant . . . hell, to the post office – girls, they throw themselves at me. They're groupies. I'm like a celebrity on campus, anywhere in Austin. Even out of town. When we travel, girls hang out in our hotel lobby, hoping to get picked up. Coaches always remind the team to be careful with these girls. When we played in the Alamo Bowl last year, this girl went up to a room with two players, they had sex, then she claimed rape. Girls are just part of the job description.'

Billie Jean tugged on Frank's T-shirt sleeve.

'He says groupies swarm him in public.'

232

She gave a knowing nod. 'Same with my ex, and he was only in the minor leagues. The allure of celebrity.'

Back to William: 'Okay, I understand that. But her number was in your phone. Explain that.'

'So these girls, they grab my phone and input their numbers and they say, "Text me sometime. Anytime."' His son shrugged. 'They're my subs.'

'Your *subs*?'

'You know, if I need a girl, because it's not working out with the girl I'm with or I'm just bored watching sports on TV, I can text one of those numbers, and a girl will show up at my dorm room in ten minutes. I can call in a sub.'

'For sex?'

'Why else would I text a girl?'

'What'd he say?' Billie Jean said.

'They're subs.'

'The girls? Subs for what?'

'Sex.'

Frank studied his twenty-two-year-old son. His view of girls had taken root when he was sixteen. When the notion that he was special had taken root in his mind. When he began looking upon other people not as fellow human beings but as members of his entourage. Boys existed to mow his lawn and wash his cars; girls existed to provide sex. Frank had tried back then to explain to his son that his view was wrong, but why would his son believe his father when the world was telling him that his view was right? When boys were happy to serve him and girls were happy to have sex with him?

'But you never texted or called her?'

'No. I swear.'

'But that means you met her if she put her number into your phone, even if you can't remember meeting her.'

'I've met hundreds, thousands of girls. I don't remember them either.'

'You must have met her that night.'

'I can't remember that night.'

If the doctors had kept him in the hospital overnight for observation, William Tucker would not be in jail today.

'You've got to believe me. I didn't rape her, and I didn't kill her.'

'I believe you.'

'Because you think I'm innocent?'

'Because you're my son.'

William's massive body seemed to grow smaller.

'This isn't good, is it? My blood on her, her number in my phone. I'm not going to win this game, am I? They'll convict me, won't they? They'll give me the death penalty.'

'I won't let that happen.'

What else could he say? Truth was, in Texas it was possible. Probable. Likely even. Three hundred inmates sat on death row in Texas. Some were guilty.

'You won't let that happen? You're a fucking drunk, but you'll save me from the death penalty. Really?' His son regarded him with disdain. 'You look like shit, Frank.'

Frank felt like shit. Dee Dee's number on his son's phone had thrown him off the wagon before he was even officially on the wagon. He had drunk whiskey until he had passed out the night before.

'Couldn't stay sober for twenty-four hours, could you?'

He could not. Frank stood and started to put his palm against the glass again, but his son had already walked out of the room.

'I've got to be honest, Frank,' Billie Jean said. 'I'm having a hard time liking your son. I mean, *subs*? Really?'

234

Chapter 27

Rusty's bark felt as if someone were committing a home invasion on Frank's head. But not because he was hung over. Because he hadn't had hard liquor in thirty hours, his longest stretch in six years.

'Shut up.'

Rusty shut up. For a few minutes. Then he barked again. Frank threw the pillow at the beast. Sobriety put him in a foul mood.

Billie Jean had driven him back to the beach the day before. He couldn't stay at the campsite indefinitely, even at $20 per night. He had to get back home to counsel other lawyers. He had to earn his income, such as it was. He had to get sober. Frank ran half a mile down the beach then puked. He spit bile and gazed at the Gulf. Could he really stay sober for his son? After six years of never being sober? It didn't seem possible. Nor did running the five miles down the beach to the rock jetty. But he would do it. Somehow. For his son.

'Let's go.'

He ran down the beach with Rusty.

Frank bathed in the sea then dressed in the bungalow. He fixed his protein drink – whey protein, yogurt, blueberries, strawberries, banana, almond milk – and grabbed the vodka bottle out of habit. He stared at the clear liquid – the alcohol that would clear his head, improve his mood, make him feel alive – then replaced it on the kitchen shelf. He blended the concoction and drank from the pitcher. He almost spit it out.

'People drink this shit?'

He took a nap before the first lawyer arrived. They walked the beach. Frank listened and counseled and earned $50. Times three lawyers. He deposited the cash in the defense fund, aka, a cigar box.

Then he took another nap.

Rusty barked him awake for their tee time. But he did not play a round of golf that day. Golf did not encourage sobriety; it was the kind of game that demanded alcohol afterward. To stay sane, if not sober.

So Frank ate one of the protein bars they had taken from William's dorm room and worked out instead. Pushups on the porch. Eleven. Then he rolled over onto his back and did thirteen sit-ups. Which made him nauseous. He struggled to his feet and did twenty-five jumping jacks. Which made him dizzy. He grabbed hold of the crossbeam on the porch and did seven pull-ups. Which made him throw up.

Should've waited on the protein bar.

He sat in his chair on the porch and turned on the radio. The oldies channel. Buddy Holly was singing 'That'll Be the Day.'

*

Buddy Holly was born in Lubbock, Texas, in 1936. Not much has happened there since. With a population of two hundred forty thousand, Lubbock is the big city for West Texas. Ranchers and farmers travel to Lubbock for doctors and lawyers and the stock show and rodeo; their sons and daughters travel to Lubbock for higher education. They study in the College of Architecture, the College of Media and Communication, the College of Agricultural Sciences and Natural Resources, and, until 1993 when the name was changed, the College of Home Economics.

Thirty thousand students attend Texas Tech University in Lubbock.

They all show up for the football games. A, there's nothing else to do in Lubbock on a Saturday afternoon; and B, the Red Raiders football team is damn fun to watch. The team invented the NASCAR offense: a full-speed, nonstop, no-huddle, run-and-gun, pass-happy, all-out offensive attack. On any given day, the Red Raiders could beat any team in America. They usually didn't, but opposing coaches always worried they might when journeying to Lubbock. Dwayne Gentry and Chuck Miller were worried too as they entered town. But not because of the football team.

Because the whole damn place was dry.

'You can't buy alcohol anywhere in the city?' Chuck said. 'That's un-American.'

'We're in the Bible Belt, buddy.'

'But we're sinners.'

'True enough.'

'And I really want to sin today.'

'I know you do.'

Dee Dee Dunston was a sinner, too. They couldn't find alcohol in Lubbock, but they found Cissy Dupre. She had just finished her cheer practice when they approached her on the Tech campus. The investigating officers had interviewed her two years before.

'Cissy Dupre?'

She stopped and gave them a once-over.

'Yes.'

'We'd like to talk to you about Dee Dee Dunston.'

'No.'

She started to walk away, but Dwayne flashed his badge. He carried the badge in case he got pulled over when drinking; once the cop saw he had been on the job, he usually cut Dwayne some slack.

'Official police business, Cissy.'

It wasn't, but the badge had the intended effect: she stopped.

'I've never seen a policeman smoking a cigar on the job.'

'You've never been to Houston.'

'I already talked to the police.'

'Two years ago?'

'Two weeks ago.'

'Detective Jones?'

'I think so.'

'Black cop?'

'Yeah.'

'Well, we just have a few follow-up questions.'

She sighed. 'What do you want to know?'

'I want to know if it's true you can't buy a drink in Lubbock?' Chuck said.

'You can now. They voted the county wet a few years back.'

'Oh, praise the Lord.'

Cissy frowned. 'That's what you wanted to know?'

'No,' Dwayne said. 'We want to know what happened to Dee Dee.'

She shook her head and looked as if she might cry.

'I guess William Tucker killed her.'

'No. Before that night.'

'Oh.'

Now a few tears came.

'You ever see that show "Girls Gone Wild"?' she said.

'Oh, I love that show,' Chuck said. 'I've got all the seasons on DVDs.'

Like a kid who had all the *Barney* episodes.

'Well, that was Dee Dee – girl gone wild. She was this country girl from Sweetwater, but she got here and just went ape.'

'How so?' Dwayne said.

'Sex. I mean, everybody gets a little wild, first semester at college, away from your parents, all the boys, the parties, the alcohol. But not like her. She was as sweet as sugar, but she loved sex. I mean, loved it. She was like a sex athlete.'

'She was what you would call promiscuous?'

'She was what I'd call a nympho.'

'With anyone in particular?'

'Athletes. Star athletes.'

'Did you tell the investigators this back then?'

She shook her head. 'I didn't want to hurt her family. I met them. They were really nice people. They went to church. But I told that black detective two weeks ago.'

'You and Dee Dee roomed together that weekend in Austin?'

She nodded.

'After the game, you went out?'

'A bunch of us cheerleaders did.'

'To the Dizzy Rooster?'

Another nod.

'Did you see William Tucker there?'

'He came in after we had been there a while. When he walked into the bar, there was a lot of commotion, people taking cell phone photos of him, that sort of thing – it was like Channing Tatum had walked in.'

'Who?'

'Movie star.'

'Oh.'

'But he saw us – we were still wearing our cheerleader outfits—'

'Why?'

'So the UT players would see us. He walked right up to us. Dee Dee latched onto him, so I flirted with some other UT players.'

'So you personally witnessed William Tucker meet Dee Dee that night at the Dizzy Rooster?'

'I personally witnessed them groping each other like horny high schoolers.'

'Right there in the bar?'

'Right there at the bar.'

'Did they stay at the bar all night?'

'No. When I looked for her again, they were heading to the back.'

'Back where?'

'Back of the bar. I figured they were going somewhere to hook up.'

'Hook up? Meaning, to have sex.'

'Yes.'

'Did you see them again?'

'Him. Later I hear this noise, I turn around and he's puking at the bar.'

'William threw up in the bar?'

'Yeah.'

'But Dee Dee wasn't there?'

'No.'

'What time was this?'

'I didn't check my watch. You lose track of time when you're drunk.'

'Were you drunk?'

'We all were.'

'Dee Dee too?'

'Sure.'

'Did you tell the police she had met William?'

'No.'

'Why not?'

'Why?'

'You didn't think the fact that she had hooked up with William Tucker might've been important to their investigation into her death?'

'No. When they came to my room the next morning, said Dee Dee was dead and had been raped, it never occurred to me that William Tucker might have raped and killed her.'

'Why not?'

She offered a shrug. 'He's a huge star athlete. He didn't have to rape her.'

'Ain't no sex in prison. Not the kind you want, anyway.'

The gangbanger next door. William lay on his cot in the dark. The cellblock was quiet. Two words pounded in his brain: death penalty. And two lawyers stood between him and death row: a drunk and an ex-stripper. She was an unproven rookie. He was a past-his-prime star who had lost the skills he once had, who had let himself go, who could no longer compete. Who threw his career away for the bottle, just as so many star athletes had thrown their careers away for drugs. Did he want Frank Tucker quarterbacking his team? With his life on the line? No. He did not. But he didn't have the money to go into the free-agent market and buy a better lawyer. Which meant he didn't have a prayer. Just as his team didn't have a prayer against Kansas State the next day. They would lose. He would lose. The team would go home. He would go to prison. To death row.

'Was she pretty?'

'Who?'

'That girl you killed?'

'I didn't kill her.'

'Okay. Was that girl you didn't kill pretty?'

'I don't remember her.'

'That don't work, William.'

'What?'

'Saying you don't remember nothing. Jury say, he gotta remember something.'

'I had a concussion.'

'For real?'

'I played a game that day. Strong safety clocked me, helmet to helmet. My coach said I thought I was Troy Aikman playing for the Cowboys against the Giants.'

'I always like Troy. Romo, he drive me fuckin' nuts, but Troy, he a player. I remember that game, he got a concussion, linebacker hammered his helmet into Troy's jaw, almost bit his tongue off, bleeding all out his mouth, still threw the winning touchdown. You do that?'

'No. I threw . . . I threw up.'

'Ain't you supposed to go to the hospital?'

'I did. They released me.'

'And you went straight for the pussy?' The gangbanger laughed. 'Man, you must got that high testosterone, too. Shit, you'd be a good brother, fit right in. We the same way. We like the pussy. But that all over now, William Tucker. For both of us.'

The gangbanger sighed.

'Ain't no pussy in prison.'

242

Chapter 28

Frank woke the next morning in wet clothes and a wet bed. He had sweated through the night. Consequently, he had not slept well. And one thought occupied his mind: whiskey. He craved a drink. Just one.

But he fought the urge.

He went to the bathroom, changed into dry clothes, drank some water, put his sunglasses on, and walked outside. He ran. Almost a mile before throwing up. He was still bent over with his hands on his knees when Rusty barked. He had noticed something down the beach. Frank stood straight and focused on the object in the distance.

'What the . . .?'

A horse ridden by a woman galloped toward them. Frank tried to shake the image from his head. Hallucinations were one of many possible alcohol withdrawal symptoms. Hell, he had suffered the shakes and the sweats, why not hallucinations? The horse and the woman came closer. She appeared to be naked. Well, at least he had interesting hallucinations. He and Rusty stood frozen as the horse and woman galloped past them. She was in fact naked.

'Morning,' she said.

Frank grunted. At least he wasn't hallucinating.

He bathed, drank his protein shake, napped, counseled a lawyer, napped again, and worked out. Fifteen pushups, ten pull-ups, twenty sit-ups, and thirty jumping jacks. He ate another protein bar. And he thought about his son's blood. And Dee Dee Dunston.

'How's the detox coming?'

Billie Jean called that afternoon.

'I'm fighting it.'

'Any ideas on the blood?'

'No. But I can't think clearly right now.'

'It'll get better once you've cleansed your brain of the alcohol.'

'I hope so.'

She fell silent. But she had something to say.

'What?'

'Frank, if William can't remember meeting Dee Dee that night – and he did, her number's on his phone – what else about that night can't he remember?'

'He can't remember because of the concussion, but the concussion didn't make him violent.'

'I was just thinking out loud. You don't have to be grumpy.'

She hung up. Frank turned the TV on to watch the UT game. He did feel kind of grumpy. But hell, he was a drunk trying to sober up. That'd make anyone grumpy.

'Adams takes the snap . . . looking for a receiver . . . throws across the middle . . . intercepted!'

'Shit!' William said.

In exchange for his autograph on a jersey, the fat-ass guard had loaned William his small radio so he could listen to the

Texas–Kansas State game. Third quarter and the Longhorns were losing thirty-five to nothing. There goes the national championship . . . unless he could get out this week and play Saturday. They could still go 11-1. That might be good enough for a shot at the title, if Alabama lost to Auburn. There was still a chance for the championship. And the Heisman.

On the radio: 'He breaks open . . . touchdown!'

Forty-two to nothing. UT's backup quarterback had thrown more completions to the K-State D-backs than to the Longhorn receivers. He was only a freshman, and this was his first game action. With William at quarterback, the team couldn't recruit top quarterback prospects – they knew they'd sit on the bench until he graduated. No one expected him to be sitting in jail.

'Man, they jumping his throws 'cause he's staring at his receivers. He need to look 'em off.'

The gangbanger next door. As if he played.

'You ever play?'

'Hell, yeah, I play.'

'What position?'

'Q-B.'

'Really? Where?'

'Houston Yates.'

'They're good.'

'Damn straight we was. I was. Run a four-four forty, throwed six touchdown passes in one game. I had skills.'

'You get any offers?'

'From colleges?'

'Yeah.'

'Nah.'

'Bad transcript?'

'Bad rap sheet.'

'In high school?'

Chapter 29

'You haven't had a drink in twelve days?'

'Not even a beer.'

By his twelfth day of sobriety, Frank ran two miles before he threw up. He pushed up (twenty-five times), pulled up (fifteen), sat up (twenty-five), and jumped jacks (fifty). His strength and stamina were coming back; his mind was working better; he felt alive again. But he still fought the cravings. Every minute. Of every day.

'I'm proud of you, Daddy.'

Frank fought his emotions. Men who aren't fathers think dads want their children to make them proud. Not true. A dad is always proud of his children. What he really wants is his children to be proud of him. But how could Frank's children be proud of him when he wasn't proud of himself? He had killed a girl. He was as much to blame as Bradley Todd.

'You look good. Have you lost weight?'

'Ten pounds.'

His daughter threw the tennis ball far down the beach. Rusty raced to fetch it. It was the first Sunday in November, only five weeks until the trial, and the defense team had gathered at the beach bungalow to prepare his son's case for trial. And to play poker. On the porch around the table sat Dwayne, Chuck, and Chico trying to take Billie Jean's sand dollars; but she had learned more than stripping in her prior life. She was also a card shark.

'I'm writing a novel,' Becky said.

She had returned home from Wellesley and completed her degree in English and creative writing at Texas State University in San Marcos thirty miles south of Austin. She studied under Denis Johnson and Tim O'Brien, two National Book Award-winning authors teaching at a public college in Texas.

'What's it called?'

'*The Autobiography of Rebecca.*'

'What's it about?'

'A dysfunctional family. The father is a famous criminal defense lawyer in Houston, but he becomes a drunken beach bum after he wins an acquittal for a star college athlete charged with rape and murder only to learn that he was in fact guilty and then he kills again. The mother is a former beauty queen turned social climber who divorces him and marries a billionaire oilman only to see him lose everything when the gas market collapses. The son is a star football player who's always gotten all the family's attention and now finds himself accused of rape and murder. And the father finds himself faced with the same case again – but this time it's his own son who claims innocence.'

'So it's fiction?'

'Of course.'

'And who is Rebecca?'

'The daughter who never got any attention. Who was the perfect child who helped keep the peace between the mother and father. Who's still trying to figure out where she fits in the family.'

Frank reached over to her and put his arm around her shoulders. He pulled her close.

'Right here.'

She wiped tears from her face.

'You were the perfect first child. You raised yourself. It seemed that you didn't need much attention.'

'I did.'

'I'm sorry. I tried to be a good dad, to both of you. There was just so much I didn't know. But I love you, Becky. I've always loved you.'

'As much as William?'

'Yes. He just seemed to require so much attention, like he sucked all the air from the room.'

'He's bigger than life.'

'Not anymore. Life reached up and pulled him down into the muck where the rest of us live.'

'I wish it hadn't.'

'I know, honey.'

They walked on the sand and inhaled the sea. They thought of William, her brother and his son, and now alleged rapist and murderer.

'*The Autobiography of Rebecca* . . . I like that. So does the story have a happy ending?'

'I don't know yet.'

They returned to the bungalow to find a fifth player at the poker table on the porch: Ted, with his shoes and socks off and his trouser legs rolled up. They stood on the sand as Ted tossed sand dollars into the pile in the center. They all put their cards down; the four men threw their hands up. Billie Jean scooped the pile of sand dollars to her side. Dwayne stood and trudged down to the sand.

'She cleaned me out. I gotta dig up some more money.'

'She's a good poker player,' Frank said.

'Is she a good lawyer?' Becky asked.

'She will be.'

'You were.'

'Past tense.'

'You can be again.'

'I know I disappointed you. I'm sorry.'

'You didn't disappoint me. You could never do that. I hurt for you because you disappointed yourself.'

'You were always the smartest member of the family.'

'I know.' Her expression turned serious. 'She's in Hungary now. Mom.'

'Covering the Eastern Bloc.'

'Father—'

'I like "Daddy" better.'

'Sounds dumb for a grown woman to call her father "Daddy".'

'Not to her daddy.'

She smiled.

'Daddy—'

Now he smiled.

'—I understood about you and Mom back then. You two just didn't fit together. I always felt sorry for you.'

'Why?'

'Because she was getting what she wanted from you, but you weren't getting what you needed from her.'

'What's that?'

'Love.'

'Did I mention that you were always the smartest member of the family?'

'Yes. Do you think she can give you what you need?'

'Your mother?'

'Billie Jean.'

'She's too young for me.'

'You're not too old for her. She's interested in you.'

'How do you know?'

'I'm a woman.'

'You are, aren't you?'

They watched Billie Jean deal cards as if she were manning a table in Vegas.

'I'd better head back to Houston,' Becky said.

Frank hugged her and told her he loved her. Dwayne walked up with a handful of sand dollars; they watched Becky up to her car and waved when she drove off.

'Got a text from Herman Jones, the Austin detective on the case,' Dwayne said. 'Said I should come see him. Soon. He must have something.'

'What?'

'Whatever it is, it ain't good for William.'

Dwayne returned to the poker game. The alcohol on Dwayne's breath gave Frank pause; he inhaled the lingering scent. He really wanted a drink. But he waved Ted down to his office. They shook hands.

'Ted.'

'Frank, sorry to hear about your son. UT's lost two in a row without him.'

'So how's your case going?'

'Better.'

'What happened?'

'I filed the motion for recusal.'

'And?'

'The judge went apeshit. Called counsel into chambers, screamed at me like I was in grade school.'

Frank grunted.

'Then he broke down and started crying. Talked about his son. He apologized. Ordered the prosecutor to hand over all evidence. They were hiding a surveillance tape.'

'And it proved your client was innocent?'

'No. He was guilty, Frank. Surveillance camera caught the crime. He did it. He killed the agent. They weren't hiding exculpatory evidence – they were hiding incriminating evidence to surprise us at trial. After my client took the stand and cried and claimed innocence, they would show the tape on the big screen and the jury would see him shooting the DEA agent pointblank in the face. They'd give him the death penalty for sure. When I confronted my client with the evidence, he laughed.'

'He laughed?'

'Yeah. Because I believed him. He's a seventeen-year-old stone-cold killer, and I bought his bullshit.'

They walked in silence through the sand.

'I wanted to believe him, Frank.'

Ted paid Frank's $50 fee and left. Frank sat on the porch step and stared at the sea. Two thoughts fought for prominence in his mind: one, could his son possibly be feeding his father a line of bullshit as Ted's client had fed him? And two, was the D.A. playing the same game with Frank as the Feds had played with Ted? Was the D.A. hiding incriminating evidence in plain sight? He finally answered his questions: no and yes.

His son was innocent. The D.A. was guilty. The investigators had downloaded all the content from William's laptop and phone. They had found Dee Dee's phone number on the phone. The D.A. knew it would be a damning rebuttal to William's testimony in court:

'I swear I never met her.'

'Then why is her phone number on your phone?'

A jury of middle-aged men and women would not understand the ways of young men and women. That hooking up was considered normal. That girls were happy to be subs, to be texted for sex. That sex was no more an emotional commitment than a peck on the cheek after a date back in their time. The jury would sentence William Tucker to death.

The law requires that the district attorney disclose all exculpatory evidence to the defense; it does not require that the district attorney disclose all incriminating evidence. That's why the D.A. had left William's laptop and phone in his room. The phone contained incriminating evidence: the victim's phone number. The D.A. was required to allow Frank access to the phone, which he did, but not to lead Frank through the hundreds of phone numbers and point out the girl's number. That was Frank's job. The D.A.'s plan was to surprise the defense with her phone number at trial. Most bad prosecutors hide exculpatory evidence; this prosecutor was hiding incriminating evidence that would inflame the jury and assure the death penalty. Hiding evidence in plain sight, right there on the phone. All Frank had to do was find it.

He realized then that there was more to find.

'Chico, what'd you find on the laptop?'

'Nothing much. Video clips from his games, videos of girls stripping—'

'At strip clubs?'

'Dorm rooms, his and theirs. And homemade porn.'

'William?'

'Yep.'

Salacious but not incriminating or admissible. There was more to be found.

'Check the phone again. We're missing something.'

'There's nothing more, Frank.'

'There's something more.'

'What?'

Frank's mind processed the evidence they had and the evidence the D.A. must have had in order to be so assured of

253

his son's guilt. It finally came to him – it should have come to him when they found the phone, but his mind was too clouded by whiskey.

'How many photos are on his phone?'

'Hundreds, maybe a thousand.'

'Her photo is on his phone. That's why the cops left the phone. The D.A. is hiding incriminating evidence in plain sight.'

Billie Jean had driven down to Rockport a few days after the arraignment with her draft subpoena. She had done a good job. Frank had approved it, and she had filed it. That day she had driven down early with the results of the subpoena: DNA test results, autopsy report, trace evidence report, and a CD of the football game. The DNA test results showed conclusively that William's blood was on Dee Dee's body. The autopsy report showed that Dee Dee had been forcibly raped, that cause of death was strangulation, and that time of death was between midnight and 2:00 A.M. The trace evidence report showed no other evidence recovered from Dee Dee's body – no semen, no skin tissue, no saliva, no one else's blood.

Frank had looked over the discovery then he and Billie Jean had walked the beach while waiting for the rest of the defense team to arrive. She was easy to talk to. It had been a long time since he had talked with a woman. His only conversations with Liz had been about what he could afford for her to buy and the kids' schedules the next week. Money and parenting, not life and love.

They were now back at the bungalow. Chuck studied the game tape on William's laptop. Chico browsed the hundreds of photos on William's phone. Dwayne reported on their investigation in Lubbock. He held his cop pad in his left hand and a Sharpie in his right.

'Dwayne,' Chico said, 'why do you always carry that Sharpie?'

'Oh, this was my trademark back in the day, when I was the top homicide cop on the Houston PD.'

'Trademark?'

'Yeah, like that TV homicide cop always sucked on a Toot-sie Roll Pop.'

'Magnum?'

'No. He was a PI. The bald guy.'

'Bruce Willis?'

'No, the one—'

They could go on forever, so Frank steered the discussion back to the Lubbock trip.

'So you met this Cissy girl?'

'Oh, yeah. Most of the players and cheerleaders back then, they've already graduated and moved on. We could spend months and more money than we got tracking them down. No need to, they can't take William's blood off the girl's body. But we found Cissy Dupre.'

He recounted their conversation with Dee Dee's roommate, all the way through Dee Dee meeting William Tucker at the Dizzy Rooster.

'He said he had never met her,' Frank said. 'But he did since her number was in his phone.'

'And now the D.A.'s got a witness to say they met that night at that bar. And that they groped each other like . . . what did she say, Chuck?'

'Horny high schoolers. She saw them heading to the back of the bar, they disappeared, then she saw William later, puking. Couldn't put a time on it.'

'Where?'

'Right there in the bar.'

'He didn't say he was sick.'

255

'You know, Frank, when I was in the Army, the lifers, they always said they puked after their first kill.'

'Where was Dee Dee when he was throwing up?'

'Cissy said she never saw her again.'

Frank considered the news. So far, all the news had been bad. His son's blood on the victim and the victim's number in his son's phone. But the worst news was that his son might have—

'He lied, Frank,' Dwayne said.

'I can't believe that.'

'Believe it,' Chico said.

He turned William's cell phone so they could see the screen, on which was a color image of Dee Dee Dunston with a 'Dizzy Rooster' sign in the background.

Chapter 30

'I didn't lie. I just don't remember her. I don't remember anything from that day. I got the concussion.'

While probably medically true, it would be a tough sell to a jury. William felt well enough to go partying that night, but he didn't remember anything? The D.A. would exploit that at trial, ask him a hundred questions that would require an 'I don't remember' answer. If, that is, William testified. He could decline to testify, but it's a risky strategy. Juries want to hear the defendant tell his side of the story. And juries don't trust a defendant who can't recall his side of the story.

'I just can't remember.'

The next morning, Frank and Billie Jean sat in front of William in the interview room. Frank put the phone with Dee Dee's image on the screen to the Plexiglas.

'You don't remember taking this photo?'

'I didn't take it.'

'What'd he say?' Billie Jean said.

She sat next to Frank, but could not hear William.

'Said he didn't take the photo.'

257

'Ask him who did.'

Back to William: 'Who did?'

'She did.'

Frank turned the screen back and studied the girl's image.

'He said she took it herself.'

Billie Jean looked closely at the image.

'Could be a selfie.'

'A selfie?'

'Self-photo. Kids take their own photos, post them on Facebook and Twitter.'

'Why?'

'I don't know.'

Back to William: 'Why would she do that?'

'So I'd remember her. So I'd text her.'

Frank felt a sense of sadness. College thirty-five years ago was simpler; boys dreaming of sex but not getting much sex. College years filled with random sex with complete strangers did not seem all that wonderful. William shook his head.

'Her phone number, her photo, my blood . . .'

Frank hadn't had alcohol in thirteen days. His hands trembled. His son's hands trembled too, but not from alcohol withdrawal. From fear.

'Do the police know about her photo?'

'I think they do.'

William looked noticeably thinner. Almost gaunt, if a man his size could look gaunt. His blue eyes floated in dark circles.

'Are you sleeping?'

'Not much.'

'Eating?'

'Not much.'

'Exercising?'

'Why? My season's over – did you see the game yesterday? Two losses in a row. No Heisman, no championship. My career's over. My life's over.'

Frank regarded his son. Trial was four weeks away. Would he make it four more weeks in jail?

'Dwayne went to Lubbock, talked to the girl's roommate named Cissy. She was at the bar that night, too. She said you and Dee Dee disappeared, she figured you two had hooked up.'

'We did?'

'You don't remember that either?'

'No.'

Frank again put his palm to the glass, but his son put his face in his hands.

'I'm gonna die in prison.'

A few blocks away at the Austin Police Department headquarters, Dwayne Gentry sat next to Detective Herman Jones's desk. Herman seemed pained.

'You need to know about your boy,' he said.

'What?'

'He killed the girl.'

'He said he never met her.'

'But he did. Her phone number's on his phone.'

'And her photo.'

Herman smiled. 'You found it? I told the D.A. you would. But he figures he's the smartest guy in the room. Likes to play games.'

'But that's explainable. That's how kids roll these days, texting and sexting. Wish to hell I was a kid today.'

'Amen, brother.'

The two men smiled at the thought. As they say, youth is wasted on the young.

'And he got back to his dorm before the time of death,' Dwayne said.

Herman's smile turned into a frown.

'That's why I said you should come see me,' he said. 'The boy lied.'

Herman inserted a CD into his laptop and tapped the keyboard. He turned the screen so Dwayne could see. A video clip played. It showed William Tucker and Ty Walker, aka Cowboy, entering the Jester dormitory's front door.

'Check the time stamp,' Herman said.

'One-thirty-eight A.M. Eleven-thirteen-eleven. November thirteenth, two thousand eleven.' Dwayne blew out a breath. 'Well, shit.'

'The law says I have to disclose exculpatory evidence. It doesn't say that I have to disclose incriminating evidence or that I have to lead you through the evidence and point out the good stuff. You've got to do some of the work yourself, Frank.'

'You want the death penalty that badly, hiding the victim's photo and phone number in plain sight. You're an asshole, Dick.'

Dick Dorkin shrugged. 'I can live with that. But can your son live with a death sentence?' He exhaled. 'You know, Frank, I liked you better drunk. You're so intense sober.'

He grinned. Frank did not.

'Well,' Dick said, 'so now you know and you know it's bad.'

'Did you subpoena his phone records from back then?'

'Yep.'

'Any texts or calls from him to her?'

'Nope.'

'What's that tell you?'

'Nothing. She died that same night. He wouldn't call a dead girl.'

'Doesn't mean he killed her.'

260

'Means he met her that same night in that same bar. Frank, the evidence proves they were together inside the bar the same night she died outside the bar. According to the eyewitness, Cissy Dupre, they kissed and groped. She saw them heading to the back of the bar where there's a door leading to the alley outside, the same alley where she was found – with his blood on her body. The witness saw William again that night, but not Dee Dee. All that adds up to murder, conviction, and a death sentence.'

'Circumstantial evidence.'

'Most evidence is, you know that. One question you've got to answer, Frank: how did his blood get on her body? Explain that. You can't. Because there's only one explanation: his blood got on her when he raped and strangled her.'

'He wasn't even there when she was killed. Autopsy report says time of death was midnight to two A.M. He said he was back in his dorm before the time of death.'

'He lied.'

'How do you know?'

'Right now, Detective Herman Jones is giving your man a CD of the dorm surveillance tape from that night which shows your son entering the dorm at 1:38 A.M. He was out when she was killed. Frank, your son's another Bradley Todd.'

Frank Tucker looked as if Dick had just kicked him in the balls. It was fun holding all the aces in the deck. It rarely happens in a criminal case; the defense usually holds an ace, sometimes two. Or three. That's when prosecutors often venture into that murky realm known as 'prosecutorial misconduct.' When they inadvertently misplace a piece of exculpatory evidence or forget to file a contradictory witness account or, if necessary for a conviction, simply destroy a document that might make the jury question the defendant's guilt. Many prosecutors figure it's best not to confuse the jurors with the facts. Frank was still squirming in his chair, so Dick turned to the PD named Billie Jean. She was a sexy broad. Word of her past had spread through the Travis County criminal justice system faster than two cops through a box of donuts.

'You're the stripper?'

'I *was* the stripper.'

Dick grunted. 'One of my assistant D.A.s, he's getting married, the boys are holding a bachelor's party for him, if you want to make some extra cash.'

The stripper smiled and held up a middle finger.

'That's a no?'

Dick chuckled and turned back to Frank.

'Hey, did you catch the ESPN segment on the case?' He picked up a remote and pointed it at the screen on the wall. 'I TiVo'ed it.'

The segment began with the UT-Texas Tech game from two years before. Dee Dee Dunston cheering . . . William Tucker playing . . . and Frank Tucker stumbling over equipment on the sideline. Dick chuckled at Frank Tucker's expense.

'There's a memory.'

He froze the image on the screen and turned to Frank.

'So the great Frank Tucker's famous trial strategy backfired this time, didn't it? Thought you'd push me to trial, gain the upper hand. I'm ready for trial, Frank – I take it you're not?'

'I'm gonna punch you before this is over, Dick.'

'You'll have to get in line,' Billie Jean said.

Dick grinned. He was having the best time imaginable.

'Get him to plead, Frank, I'll agree to life without parole. At least your son will still have his life.'

'Life in prison isn't much of a life.'

★

'They said all my clients would claim innocence but be guilty,' Billie Jean said. 'They said we're just a Sixth Amendment right to counsel formality.'

Frank and Billie Jean sat outside on a bench in the plaza between the Justice Center and the jail. All the evidence said his son was guilty, but Frank knew he was innocent. He knew it. He just had to prove it. The burden was no longer on the state to prove the defendant guilty; it was on the defendant to prove himself innocent. The American criminal justice system had long been predicated on a simple belief: 'It's better to let a hundred guilty people go free than to convict one innocent person.' But not anymore. Now the prevailing philosophy was, 'It's better to convict a hundred innocent people than to let one guilty person go free.' Crime had changed America. Americans. They feared criminals, and they wanted to be safe. So they elected district attorneys and judges who put people in prison, and they criticized juries that didn't. But they didn't know that one day all that might stand between them and a prison cell is a district attorney or judge who put justice ahead of reelection or twelve citizens doing their legal duty and requiring the prosecutor to prove their guilt beyond a reasonable doubt. But they never think it will happen to them. Or to their sons or daughters.

Until it does.

'What if they're wrong? What if one of your clients is in fact innocent? What if you let an innocent person go to prison? That would haunt you forever.'

'Like getting a guilty person off only to see him kill again?'

'Like that.'

Chapter 31

Dwayne inhaled on his cigar, Chuck his cigarette, and Chico his joint. They exhaled in unison. Their emissions blended together and created an odd manly-sweet-toxic aroma. Fortunately, the sea breeze blew it away. It was two days later, a Sunday, and they had gathered on the back porch of Frank's bungalow because they had nothing better to do – it wasn't as if they were going to take up yoga that day – and they knew Frank had alcoholic beverages stashed away even if he were not partaking at the moment. Chico drank a beer, Dwayne a Jim Beam with a shot of Coca-Cola, and Chuck his Gatorade-and-vodka sports drink. Frank was running the beach with the dog.

'I'm thinking about frying a turkey for Thanksgiving,' Chuck said.

Dwayne frowned. 'A *fried* turkey?'

'Yeah, I've been reading about it. You drop the whole bird into a pot of peanut oil, fry it up.'

'Why you figure on frying a bird?'

'I can't grill a turkey. Won't fit on the Weber.'

Dwayne grunted. 'Well, I like just about anything that's fried, long as beer goes with it.'

'Well, of course beer goes with fried turkey. Beer goes with all your food groups.'

Chico sucked on his joint, held it for a five count, and then exhaled.

'So what do you think, Dwayne?' he said. 'You're the ex-cop.'

'About fried turkey?'

'About the Federal Reserve's decision to keep interest rates low. The hell you think – William Tucker.'

'I ain't buying his amnesia-by-concussion defense. He remembers. He just don't want to remember. 'Cause he did it. He killed that girl.'

'Ditto.'

'Yeah, me, too,' Chuck said. He exhaled cigarette smoke. 'All these star football players, they think the rules don't apply to them, find out the hard way they do. That Giants receiver, Plaxico Burress, he wins the MVP of the Super Bowl then carries a loaded handgun into a New York bar. Has it in the waistband of his sweatpants, like the elastic is gonna hold up a big ol' Glock nine millimeter. The gun falls down, hits the floor, and discharges – he shoots himself in the foot.'

'Literally,' Dwayne said.

'Lucky he didn't shoot his dick off,' Chico said.

'Spent two years in prison for criminal possession of a firearm,' Chuck said.

'He should've spent two more for criminal stupidity,' Dwayne said.

'Who's he playing for now?' Chico said. 'Philadelphia?'

'Pittsburgh,' Chuck said.

He kept up with those things.

'And O.J.,' Chuck said.

Orenthal James Simpson, aka, O.J., Heisman Trophy winner and NFL Hall of Fame halfback, was tried and acquitted in 1995 of murdering his ex-wife and another man but was tried and convicted in 2008 for armed robbery and kidnapping and sent to prison for nine-to-thirty-three years.

'He's just bad,' Dwayne said. 'A criminal who could play football.'

'He was good.'

'Real good.'

'And Nate Newton, he played on the Cowboys Super Bowl teams, retired, and took up drug dealing.'

'Dumb.'

'And Michael Vick, that dogfighting deal.'

Vick was a star NFL quarterback for the Atlanta Falcons who ran an illegal dogfighting ring on the side. He pleaded guilty and spent two years in prison. Upon his release, he returned to the NFL to play for the Philadelphia Eagles. Star athletes always get second chances. And third chances.

'Dumber.'

'And that Patriots player, Hernandez, they indicted him for murder. I saw an interview just the other day, he said he was a role model for Hispanics.'

'Only if they live in Nuevo Laredo.'

'More dumber.'

'And now William Tucker.'

'Most dumber.'

'Might cause a man to drink,' Chico said. 'Or start drinking again.'

'That's gonna be hard on Frank,' Chuck said.

'Harder on his boy, when they punch that needle into his arm,' Dwayne said. 'Too many lies, too much DNA. Says he never met her, but her roommate witnessed them meeting at that bar that night. Her phone number in his phone, but he

266

says he didn't input her number, says she did it. On his phone. You ever put your number in someone else's phone?'

'Nope.'

'Me neither. Her photo on his phone, but he says she took it herself. You ever take your own photo?'

'Nope.'

'Me neither. Says he got back to his dorm around midnight, but the surveillance tape shows him entering the dorm at 1:38, right in line with the time of death. Boy's lied every step of the way. But DNA don't lie. He had direct physical contact with the girl, that's the only way his blood got on her. No other explanation.'

'Makes you wonder why we're trying to save the boy,' Chico said.

'We're not saving William Tucker,' Dwayne said. 'We're saving Frank Tucker.'

'Frank seems convinced his boy is innocent,' Chuck said.

'Three things in life are certain: death, taxes, and a father's love for his son. What dad can accept that his son's a cold-blooded killer? Seen it many times in Houston, we got the killer dead to rights, but his daddy's saying, "My boy wouldn't hurt no one. He's a good boy." And I'd say, "Well, sir, your good boy stuck a gun to a convenience store clerk and pulled the trigger 'cause he wanted a pack of cigarettes." Fathers, they just can't believe they raised a killer.'

Was he a murderer? And a rapist? Was he innocent? Or was he guilty? That night had forever been wiped from his mind. The helmet-to-helmet hit had banged his brain against the inside of his skull, causing a traumatic brain bruising and putting him in a cloudy dreamlike state for days. He didn't tell the coaches or the doctors because he didn't want to be benched the next game; you don't win the Heisman Trophy sitting on the bench.

You've got to play. And in football, you play hurt. Bad knee, bad shoulder, bad brain – you still play.

But you don't remember.

Hell, he had thrown touchdown passes he couldn't remember and won games he couldn't remember. He had played entire games on autopilot. On instinct. His bell had been rung, but his instincts had played on. He couldn't remember those games, and he couldn't remember that night. Not the Dizzy Rooster, not the girl, not anything. If he couldn't remember being there or meeting her – which he obviously was and did – what else could he not remember?

'William Tucker, you awake?'

The whispered voice of the gangbanger next door. William was awake. He was always awake. He couldn't sleep. Or eat. Or think. He couldn't put a complete sentence together in his head. Or even a phrase. Only two words registered in his mind: death penalty.

'What did I do to deserve this?'

'Ain't no deservin', William. There's just destiny.'

'This isn't my destiny.'

'Yeah, it is. You just ain't accepted it yet. Took me a while, too, had to spend a lot of time thinking 'bout it. One thing about prison, you got lots of time to think. You ever think about dying?'

'I do now.'

'Me, too. How old are you?'

'I'll be twenty-three in two weeks. How old are you?'

'Twenty-five. I ain't gonna see twenty-six. Second time around, ain't no appeals, no stays of execution. Man, they got that needle ready for me. Course, my name been on that needle since the day I was born. That always been my destiny.'

Chapter 32

Twenty-six days without alcohol in his system. Frank Tucker had undergone a complete physical detoxification. But not a mental one. He still wanted to drink. Desperately. He stopped and puked after three and a half miles.

'You okay?'

He nodded and waved Billie Jean on. They were running the beach. Well, she was running; he was jogging. Rusty barked at Billie Jean racing down the sand.

'Yep, that girl can run. Go ahead, I'll catch up.'

The dog ran after the girl.

'Have you lost weight?'

'Yeah. Can't sleep. Can't eat. Can't think. Except about the death penalty.'

'Dad will save you.'

'How? He can't save himself.'

'He stopped drinking. For you.'

'He'll start again. For himself.'

Becky Tucker sat on the visitor's side of the glass partition and held the phone to her ear; her little brother sat on the other side with a phone to his ear. He was an inmate in the county jail accused of rape and murder. They had once been so close, brother and sister. Now he seemed so distant. So different.

'What motivates you, William?'

He groaned. 'Don't start that creative writing bullshit with me, Becky. I'm not a character in your book.'

'Of course you are. You're the protagonist.'

'Really? Am I the action-hero?'

'You're the tragic hero.'

'That doesn't sound good.'

'The protagonist is blessed with all the athletic talent required to become a star football player in America and to live a life few people can even dream of—'

'Are you writing my life story?'

'No. I'm writing mine. Anyway, he loses it all because of his fatal flaw.'

'Which is?'

'He doesn't understand the difference between being special and being lucky.'

'Bullshit, Becky. I understand the difference.'

'Which is?'

'I'm special. All the fans who get to watch me play are lucky.' He seemed serious.

'Oh, and he's got an ego bigger than Montana.'

'Try winning a football game with low self-esteem. The game's all about the quarterback, Becky. It's all on me. I have to make the decisions on the field that mean winning or losing. I have to make the correct reads and the perfect passes. I have to scramble when the protection breaks down. I have to make it happen out there. I have to lead the team to victory. It's all about me.'

'And he likes himself a lot, as evidenced by his repetitive use of "I" and "me" and "my" and "mine."'

270

'Can I sue you if you say something bad about me?'

'A good character has to be bigger than life but brought down to life because of his flaws. That's why you're such a great character, William.'

'Because I'm so much bigger than life?'

'Because you have so many flaws.'

'Funny.'

'The truth. But you're still my little . . . very big brother, and I still love you.'

'No one else does. Nobody comes to see me.'

'Not your coaches?'

'No.'

'Teammates?'

'No.'

'Girls?'

'Hell, no.'

'So who else comes to see you?'

'Frank.'

'*Frank?* You don't call him "Dad"?'

'Dads don't show up drunk at your game.'

'But they show up when you're in jail. What does that tell you?'

Her little-big brother pondered that a moment then said, 'I didn't pay a lot of attention in my English Lit class, but doesn't the tragic hero always die at the end?'

He could kill these little punks.

Dwayne Gentry stomped on the accelerator and steered after the perps. He had the vehicle running all out, lights flashing, racing over the pavement; but these boys were runners, even packing the backpacks stuffed with the stolen contraband. They were making for the line where his jurisdiction ended; once across they were home free. So he decided to cut them off at the pass. He veered hard to his left and took a side alley; the

271

vehicle scraped the exterior walls of the structures, but Dwayne had trashed his share of official vehicles in his career. He cleared the alley and cut the wheel hard to the right, too hard, and—

'Oh, shit!'

—the vehicle's right two tires left the ground. He leaned his big body to the right, and the vehicle came back to earth and bounced hard – which cost him valuable seconds. He punched the gas and headed directly to their escape route. One more corner – he veered left – and he'd be right on them—

'Damn!'

He slammed on the brakes and skidded to stop. The perps flung the backpacks over the perimeter fence then scurried up and over like squirrels up a tree. They dropped to the other side. Outside his jurisdiction. They grabbed the backpacks and ran a safe distance then turned back. Dwayne could no longer point a gun, so he pointed his cigar.

'I know who you are! You punks better stay the hell out of my mini-storage park!'

The teenage boys held up middle fingers.

'Hey, fuck you, Dwayne!'

Boys got no home training. Dwayne Gentry plopped down onto the vinyl seat of the golf cart with the little yellow flashing light and watched the perps running off with the contraband. Now he would have to explain to the boss how they managed to break into another storage unit in broad daylight. He checked his watch. Straight-up noon. Oh, lunchtime. Maybe pizza.

Chico Duran held his cell phone with his left hand, texted with his right hand, and drove with his knees. Sure, it was a bit dangerous for his fellow drivers and pedestrians, but he was not worried: he had no insurance. Or assets. His net worth consisted entirely of his next tip and his next disability payment. Which didn't technically belong to Chico Duran.

He screeched the 4x4 with the portable neon sign atop that read 'Pizza Man' to a stop in front of a big house in the nice part of Rockport. Where rich folks in Houston had bought week-end homes on the canals cut into the shore to allow boat access to the bay. Big-ass homes. He got out and grabbed the heat pack with the pizza boxes inside. Two extra large pepperonis. The twenty-two-inch monsters, extra cheese, extra pepperoni, came to $28.50 plus a $5 delivery charge. Plus a tip.

He walked up the sidewalk and rang the doorbell. A teenage girl wearing a T-shirt, a short blue jean skirt, and an iPhone answered.

'Pizza's here,' she said into the phone.

'Thirty-three fifty,' he said.

'You're a bad boy.'

'I am?'

She frowned at Chico and gestured at her phone.

'You want me to do what? Ooh, you really are a bad boy.'

Like she liked him being a bad boy.

'Right now? I gotta pay the pizza man. Well, okay.' To Chico, she said, 'Just a sec.'

She held the phone out as if she was giving it to him, but she wasn't. She put a real sexy look on her face then clicked a button on the phone. She took her own photo. The look disappeared, and she checked the phone. She frowned and turned the screen to Chico.

'You think this is a sexy pic?'

It was.

'Yeah. That's sexy.'

'It's for my boyfriend.'

The bad boy.

'Pizza's getting cold.'

She turned back to the house and screamed, 'Jacy, bring money for the pizza!'

Girl's got some lungs.

Then she bent over a little and stuck the phone up her short skirt. Chico heard the same click and saw a flash of light under her skirt. The girl took a picture of her privates. Damn. She was sexting. She stood straight and looked at the phone's screen. She frowned again.

'Uh, you want me to check out that pic, too?' Chico said.

Without looking up, she said, 'As if.'

Must mean no.

'Pizza's getting cold.'

'Jacy!'

'*What?*'

Another teenage girl appeared in the doorway. She gave Chico two twenties and grabbed the pizza. The sexter slammed the door in his face. Six-fifty tip, not bad.

Chuck Miller blew his whistle and halted the game.

'We got a facemask on White. Ten yards. Touchdown is called back.'

'You're full of shit!' a parent from the sideline yelled.

Peewee football. Kindergartners in pads and cleats trying to make their daddies proud. Hell, the pads were bigger than the boys, and the boys could barely keep from peeing in their pants, but their parents went apeshit over every call he made. He stepped off ten yards against the White team. Chuck wore a black-and-white striped referee's shirt and a black cap. And sunglasses to hide his bloodshot eyes. A player tugged on his shirtsleeve.

'Georgie's bleeding.'

'What?'

'He's bleeding. Georgie.'

Chuck followed the player to the White huddle. Another player was holding his arm and staring at his elbow. Blood seeped out of a cut. Chuck blew his whistle again.

'Bodily fluid timeout,' he called out to the coaches. One time he had to call a bodily fluid timeout when a kid crapped his uniform. It happens. Chuck grabbed the sports bottle he carried in a waist pack and sucked on the pop-top. He loved orange-flavored Gatorade, especially when he mixed in a little vodka. Okay, a lot of vodka. He swiped his sleeve across his mouth and said to the bleeder, 'You gotta go to the sideline and get that cut bandaged.'

The boy waddled over to the sideline where his mommy greeted him in full-blown hysterics, as if he had suffered a punctured artery and blood was spurting out. Hell, it was just a little cut. As he watched the mother tending to the boy, a thought tried to take shape in Chuck's mind but try though he did, he could not connect the dots in order to fashion a complete sentence. He felt the familiar beginning of a panic attack coming on – *oh, shit, it's the brain damage* – but a sudden realization calmed him just before he dropped to the turf and curled up in the fetal position: it wasn't the brain damage preventing a complete thought; it was the vodka. A sense of relief washed over him. *I'm just drunk!* He took another long swig of his sports drink.

'Any ideas on the blood?' Billie Jean asked. 'Only three weeks till trial.'

Frank had found her waiting for him at the point of the jetty. With man's best friend. Running the five miles from the bungalow to the jetty was his goal. When he could do that, he would be back. He would again be the man he used to be. But would he ever be the lawyer he used to be? That was the question. They were walking the beach back to the bungalow.

'No.'

'His blood, her phone number and photo, the surveillance tape, the fact that they met that night, Cissy Dupre testifying that they groped . . . it doesn't look good, Frank.'

'There's an answer out there somewhere, we've just got to find it.'

'How can I help? I don't feel I'm doing enough.'

'You will. Before this trial is over, you'll play a big role. Everyone on the team will.'

The tide was out, and the beach filled with an assortment of sea matter and dead fish. He tossed a stick for Rusty, and the dog raced ahead. It was nice to have someone to walk with who could talk.

'So why'd you come down?'

'I like the beach. I like being on the beach with you. And I like you, Frank.'

Frank felt awkward. A beautiful woman saying, 'I like you,' had not been on his day planner for that Sunday.

'I'm not sure what to say.'

'Well, you could say, "I like you, too, Billie Jean." If you do.'

'I like you, too, Billie Jean. But it won't work. Us.'

'Why not?'

'You're a ten.'

'I'm a four.'

'Not your dress size. Your ranking.'

'My ranking? You mean, like one to ten in beauty?'

'Yeah. You're a ten, and I'm a five. At best.'

'I'm less than a ten, and you're more than a five. Maybe a six. Six and a half.'

She smiled. By the time Frank had explained his human food chain theory, how men and women date according to their respective positions on the wealth and beauty ranking, she was not smiling.

'You're not serious?'

'I am.'

'So you've developed this goofy little theory about love and life – were you drinking when you came up with this? – because your ex-wife was too stuck up and stupid to see what a good man she had, and now you're going to push me away because of this bullshit theory, to use the West Texas vernacular.'

'Does George Clooney date girls who are fives?'

'No.'

'Does Amy Adams date guys who are fives?'

'No.'

'*Ergo*.'

'*Ergo* what?' She shook her head. 'I can't believe you're telling me I'm too good looking for you. What if I make myself look like a three?'

'Not possible.'

'You've never seen me in the morning.'

'True.'

'Your theory's stupid, Frank. Now shut up and hold my hand.'

He held her hand. It felt good. They strolled hand in hand down the sand and watched the seagulls searching the sea for their breakfast.

'I always wanted to live on a beach.'

'Why?'

'I grew up in Dalhart.'

'That would do it.'

'Did you always want to live on the beach?'

'Yes. But by choice, not by whiskey.'

'Sometimes the best choices are the ones made for us.'

'Try being a drunk.'

The beach seemed brighter sober.

'How's he holding up? William.'

'He's not. Facing a death sentence, sitting in that cell . . . he's panicking.'

'That's understandable.'

'We're coming up Sunday, for his birthday.'

'Can I come?'

'Well, I guess so. We're holding hands.'

'You're a good father, Frank.'

'I was, until I started drinking. But I never had to strip to pay the bills. Does your daughter appreciate what you did for her?'

'I think so.'

'Is she like you?'

'She's better.'

'I'd like to meet her.'

'You will.'

They walked in silence and breathed in the sea air.

'Frank, I hope William appreciates you.'

He shook his head. 'Doesn't work that way. I didn't appreciate my father until I became a father. But it was too late to tell him – he had already died. That's how things work with fathers and sons. You don't appreciate your old man until you are an old man.'

'William Tucker, you ever meet you daddy?'

The gangbanger next door.

'Uh . . . yeah.'

'I never did. Seen him one time, think it was him anyway. Last I heard, he in prison up north somewhere. Chicago, maybe. Crack dealing. Your daddy in prison?'

'No. He's in the bottle.'

'Alcoholic?'

'Yeah.'

'My mama, she a wino. Love that grape juice. My daddy a crack head. Ain't exactly what you call "Leave It to Beaver."'

The gangbanger next door laughed, but not as if it were funny.

278

Chapter 33

Frank Tucker woke with a clear head and without a headache or aches and pains. Not too many, anyway. He felt good for a fifty-five-year-old man. He looked down at his dog sleeping on the floor.

'Let's do it, Rusty.'

He strapped on his running shoes – he could only run so far barefooted – and his sunglasses. He stepped onto the porch and stretched. Thirty-two days without a drink. Thirty-two days of running and working out. Thirty-two days of puking. Thirty-two days of stopping before the jetty.

But not that day.

He jumped down to the sand and ran. A nice easy pace at first; he wasn't trying to win a race, just finish it. A five-mile marathon. The morning air felt good in his lungs, and the morning beach felt different to his eyes. As if he had never really seen the beach all this time. As if he had lived his life in a haze of whiskey and vodka and beer. But he saw it now, this beach he lived on and this life he still had. He had felt dead for so many years. Now he felt alive again.

His son needed him. A woman liked him.

The first mile passed easily. The second mile almost as easily. The third mile not so easily. His body was weakening, but his mind was not. His mind remained strong. Sobriety had brought strength. To his body, but even more to his mind. He could think again. He would need to be strong, mentally and physically to save his son. A murder trial is a grueling endeavor. Some trials last six weeks, some six months. If your body fails, your mind will follow. And an innocent person might go to prison.

The pain came in the fourth mile. His legs hurt. He sucked oxygen hard. His body begged to quit, but his mind refused. He would not quit on himself. Or on his son.

Rusty barked. He saw the jetty first. Now Frank could see it, like a mirage in the distance. Less than a mile to go. Weeks of running and working out . . . pushups, pull-ups, sit-ups, jumping jacks . . . one hundred of each . . . twice a day.

Half a mile and he spit bile.

A quarter of a mile and he couldn't breathe.

Two hundred yards and he sucked hard for air.

One hundred and he felt faint.

Fifty and he couldn't feel his feet.

Frank's feet left the sand and hit the surface of the concrete that had been poured between the rocks of the jetty. He did not slow his pace. He pushed himself harder. He ran down the center of the narrow jetty all the way to the point. He stopped. Rusty barked. The waves hit the rocks and splashed over them. Frank felt like Rocky Balboa. He threw his arms into the air. He was the man he used to be. Now he wanted to be the lawyer he used to be. He needed to be that lawyer again.

To save his son's life.

Chapter 34

William Tucker turned twenty-three that Sunday. So instead of running the five miles to the jetty that morning, Frank had driven to Austin. He was worried about his son. William had called him regularly since his incarceration; but the calls had stopped that week. Frank had called the jail but had not been put through. He left messages, but William had not returned them. With each call, William's emotional state seemed to be spiraling downward. Faster. His last call he had said it was his destiny to die in prison.

'I can break him out of here,' Chico said.

Dwayne, Chuck, and Chico had come along. Billie Jean and Becky had been waiting for them in the plaza. The open space was free of media; apparently, testosterone and stupidity had joined together to produce a bad result for a pro basketball player, so the sports cable channels had decamped Austin for Chicago. Becky brought a birthday cake she had made herself. Frank promised to save a big piece for the desk sergeant, so he allowed them to take the cake into the interview room. Frank put the cake on the table in front of the glass partition and lit the candles. His son would celebrate his birthday in jail.

'Now don't look shocked at his appearance,' Becky said. 'He doesn't eat or sleep, so he's lost weight. He looks like hell.'

'He's in hell,' Chico said.

They stood before the cake like a choir. The door on the inmate side opened, and a guard stepped in. Frank started singing loudly enough that William might hear on his side of the glass; the others joined in.

'Happy birthday to you,
'Happy birthday to you . . .'

Frank felt as if he were singing to his twelve-year-old son again. The birthday boy bounded into the interview room with a bounce in his shackled step and a big smile on his face. Their voices fell from their surprise. And confusion.

'Happy birthday dear William,
'Happy birthday to you.'

William waved at everyone like a kid at his surprise birthday party then grabbed the phone on his side. Frank picked up on his side.

'Hey, you remembered my birthday. Becky bake that cake?'

'She did.'

'Tell her thanks.'

Frank did. Back into the phone: 'Happy birthday, son. Uh, what's going on, William?'

'I feel great. Worked out today – pushups, sit-ups, jump squats. Gotta get in shape. I'm going to play pro football next year.'

'How?'

His smile got bigger.

'You're not going to believe it.'

'What?'

'I got a movie deal.'

'A movie deal?'

'He got a movie deal?' Becky said.

Frank nodded at her.

'For my life story,' William said into the phone.

'From jail? How?'

'Okay, so my college career is over, right, like the judge said? The season will be over before the trial. And, hell, they've lost every game without me. Shit, they lost to Baylor. Anyway, I'm not worried about losing my amateur status. So I hired an agent.'

'An agent? Who?'

'He got an agent?' Dwayne said.

Frank nodded at him.

'Warren Ziff,' William said. 'He's a real asshole, reps half the starting quarterbacks in the NFL.'

'How'd he find you in jail?'

'Everyone in America knows I'm in jail. ESPN runs daily updates.'

'You get cable in there?'

'No. Warren told me. Agents have been calling me since my freshman year, trying to sign me up. A lot this year, until I got arrested. Warren came to the jail last week.'

'And then?'

'He sold my life story to Hollywood for a million bucks.'

'A million dollars?'

'He got a million dollars?' Chuck said.

Frank nodded again.

'Do we get paid now?'

Back to William: 'And he's shopping a book deal. I'm gonna hire Becky to write it. Frank, I'm saved. Warren hooked me up with a big-time lawyer. He says he can get me out of here.

It's too late for the Heisman, but not for the NFL draft. I've got time to get in top shape again, blow the pro coaches away at the combine. I can still go number one.'

'You hired another lawyer?'

'He hired another lawyer?' Billie Jean said.

Frank nodded at her. Into the phone: 'Who?'

William pointed past Frank.

'Him.'

Frank turned to see Scotty Raines standing there. Raines was mid-forties and high profile in Austin, the second-best criminal defense lawyer in Texas, until Frank became a drunk. Now Scotty was the best. He wore a crisp button-down shirt, sharply creased slacks, and shiny shoes, apparently his Sunday casual attire. Frank wore a T-shirt, jeans, and deck shoes. No socks. Scotty looked him up and down with a bemused smile.

'Frank.'

'You're representing my son?'

'I am.' Scotty checked his watch. A Rolex. 'And I need to confer with him before I see the D.A. Privately.'

Frank glanced back at his son; he offered the same big smile. Frank turned back to the others.

'Becky, guys, why don't y'all step outside while—'

'Uh, Frank,' Scotty said. 'Sorry. Attorney-client privilege. If you sit in, the privilege is waived, you know that.'

'I'm a lawyer, too, Scotty.'

'Not anymore. At least not a licensed lawyer.' Scotty gestured at Billie Jean. 'And I don't need an ex-stripper on the defense team.'

'I need a drink,' Frank said.

'You need a son worth giving a shit about,' Dwayne said.

'I changed my mind,' Chico said. 'I don't want to break him out.'

The six of them and the birthday cake sat on a bench in the plaza.

'He fired you?' Becky said. 'His own father?'

'He fired me, too,' Billie Jean said. 'And I work for free.'

'So you guys are off the case?' Becky said.

'We are.'

'I told you he changed, Daddy. He became a star. He doesn't give a shit about anyone except himself now. We're all just his fucking entourage!'

She never cursed. She wiped her eyes.

'No, he's doing the smart thing. Scotty Raines is a top defense attorney with a big firm. They're connected.'

'To whom?' Billie Jean said.

'The D.A. And all the judges.'

'How?'

'Money. Campaign contributions. That's how the system works in Texas. Lawyers give judges campaign contributions, and judges repay the favor.'

'And they send us to jail,' Chico said.

'So?' Billie Jean said.

'So Scotty can get his bail reduced, maybe to PR. He can get him out of jail.'

'But can he get him acquitted?'

Frank Tucker had fallen so low that even his own son didn't want his counsel. He desperately wanted a drink.

'What are we going to do now?' Billie Jean asked.

'Go home.'

And dive into a whiskey bottle.

Scotty Raines exited the Justice Center and waved as he walked across the plaza. Billie Jean gave him the finger.

'Who wants cake?' Frank said.

Chuck raised a hand, but Becky grabbed the cake, walked over to a trash bin, and threw it in.

'Damn,' Chuck said. 'I like cake.'

'I'll be back,' Dwayne said.

Dwayne picked up the defense team's briefcase and walked back inside the Justice Center.

Dwayne told the desk sergeant he needed to see William Tucker. He went into the interview room and waited. When the guards brought William back in, Dwayne put the phone to his ear. William did the same.

'What do you want?' William said.

Dwayne opened the briefcase and tossed newspapers and magazines bearing the image of William Tucker onto the table in front of the glass partition. He read the bylines.

'"Another OJ" ... "All-American Psycho" ... "Number One in the Death Row Draft" ... They all think you're guilty. Hell, I think you're guilty. Only one person in this world believes in you, stud, and that's your old man. He thinks you're innocent. I hope for his sake you are. If you weren't Frank's son, I'd be happy to see you rot in prison. Or take the needle. One less spoiled egotistical jock who thinks the world revolves around him. Where's the world now, stud? Where are all your fans now? Your coaches and teammates? Those college coeds? Who's standing with you now? Your father. He's the best man and lawyer I've ever known, drunk or sober. He's a good man got run over by that dump truck called life. Now you dump on him? If that's the way sons treat their dads, I'm fucking glad I didn't have a son. You might be innocent of murder, but you're guilty of being one sorry-ass prick of a son. You understand that everyone comes in contact with you can't stand you? Hell, I don't even know you and I can't stand you. You don't have a fucking clue.'

'But it's my life. Scotty Raines can save my life.'

'He might get you off, stud, but your life ain't worth saving.'

★

Only thirty-two men in the world are special enough to be starting quarterbacks in the National Football League. More people are qualified to be president of the United States of America – to lead the Free World than to lead a pro football team. Fact is, being president is a hell of a lot easier job. Try giving a State of the Union speech while a three-hundred-pound son of a bitch is trying to face plant you into the floor of the U.S. Congress. That's the workplace of an NFL quarterback. A small five-square-foot pocket formed by his large offensive linemen fighting off the equally large defensive linemen, with a blitzing linebacker or D-back thrown in for good measure. In that small space on a football field, during a three-second window, the quarterback must read the defense, choose the open receiver, and make a strong, accurate throw, while ignoring the massive arms and legs and bodies flailing all around him and trying to face plant him in the turf. An NFL quarterback must possess the physical skills to throw the football thirty yards downfield into an opening the size of a can of soup with precise timing so that ball and receiver arrive simultaneously at the same spot on the field and the mental temperament to take the blame when the receiver screws up. He must have the confidence to throw five interceptions in the first half and then a touchdown pass in the last seconds to win the game. He must be physically tough enough to take the beating and mentally tough enough to take the beating. He must be a very special sort of athlete. Which meant Dwayne was wrong.

William Tucker was special.

William Tucker's life was worth saving. Because he was a special athlete, which is to say, a special human being. He had proved it in high school, he had proved it in college, and he would prove it in the NFL. Next season, he would be one of those thirty-two starting quarterbacks.

'*A movie deal? For a million dollars?* Who the fuck are you?'

The gangbanger next door.

'I'm William Tucker.'

'Who the fuck's William Tucker?'

'The best football player in America.'

'No shit? What the fuck you doing in here?'

'I'm getting out, that's what I'm doing. I won't be here tomorrow night.'

I am William Tucker. And I am special.

Chapter 35

'All rise!'

Judge Harold Rooney entered his courtroom, sat behind his bench, and put on his reading glasses. The first entry on that day's docket sheet read *The State of Texas v. William Tucker*, Motion for Reinstatement and Reduction of Bail. He glanced over at the district attorney at the prosecution table and then at the defendant at the defense table with his lawyer.

Scotty Raines.

'I see a new face. Mr. Raines.'

Scotty stood. 'Your Honor, I've been retained by William Tucker to represent him in this case.'

'I see. And what about his prior counsel? Ms. Campbell and Mr. Tucker?'

'He no longer needs their services.'

Harold turned to the defendant. 'Is that correct, Mr. Tucker? You no longer need Ms. Crawford? Or your father?'

The boy smiled. 'No, sir. I don't need them.'

Harold grunted. The boy didn't need his father.

'All right, Mr. Raines, you're now counsel of record. You are aware that this is a death penalty case?'

'Yes, Your Honor.'

'You have submitted a motion to reinstate and reduce bail to ten thousand dollars.'

'That's correct, Your Honor.'

'Mr. Dorkin, your response.'

'State has no objection, Your Honor.'

Harold sighed and thumbed through the document before him. The motion cited all the cases and made all the arguments for the defendant's release – a canned motion. Harold had seen the same one a thousand times. But the most compelling argument favoring the defendant was not written in the motion: Scotty Raines' law firm had contributed hundreds of thousands of dollars to the district attorney's political campaigns – and to Harold's. You don't write those things down. And now Scotty expected to be repaid. To collect a favor. Dick Dorkin owed him and had paid his debt off. Harold owed him, and Scotty now expected the debt to be paid in full.

Scotty Raines's law firm had bought the district attorney, just as the firm had bought Judge Harold Rooney. In Texas, district attorneys and judges were politicians elected in partisan elections. Democrat or Republican. Conservative or liberal. It wasn't about justice or injustice, it was about getting reelected. Democracy and justice were often distant relatives. Because elections cost money. But citizens did not contribute to judges' campaigns because 99.9 percent would never see the inside of a courtroom. Lawyers would. They did. Courtrooms were their playing fields and judges the referees. It was good to have the law and the facts on your side, but it was better to have the judge. Lawyers have a vested interest in which judges they face each day, and they want the judges they face to be indebted to them. Some years back, the Texas supreme court proposed a judicial rule that would have allowed either party to disqualify a judge if the other party or lawyer had contributed $5,000 or more to his last campaign. Lawyers in Texas voted down the proposal overwhelmingly. Therein lies the truth: as Scotty Raines himself often quipped (to much laughter) at bar meetings, 'Texas has the best judges money can buy.'

So Scotty stood there with a smug look on his face, knowing that he had bought this judge and this judge would give him what he wanted: freedom for his client.

Or would he?

Harold Rooney had sat on the bench in Travis County for sixteen years now. He had won four elections. He had collected hundreds of thousands of dollars in campaign contributions from lawyers. He had paid them all back.

But he had never saved a life.

The typical criminal defendants who came before him – gangbangers, drug dealers, sex offenders, child abusers – their lives were beyond saving. The only lives he could save were their future victims. And they were not represented by the Scotty Raineses of the bar. They were represented by public defenders who could not afford to contribute to his campaigns. So he locked their clients up for as long as the law allowed and then some. He was a judge but he couldn't save their lives.

Just as he couldn't save his own son's life. He had called in his own favors, back when he was practicing with a large firm that made generous campaign contributions to judges, and gotten his own son released on PR on a drug charge. His son had promptly overdosed on heroin. Died. Twenty years old. If he had only left his son in jail, practiced a little tough love instead of hard lawyering, his son might be alive today. Harold had never forgiven himself. A father can't forgive that kind of mistake.

Now he saw the same mistake being played out again, in his own courtroom this time. A connected lawyer calling in favors.

William Tucker's life might be saved. Could be saved. If he were innocent; and in his gut, Harold thought he was. Of course, he had thought the same about Bradley Todd. And he had been wrong. Dead wrong.

But if he were innocent. If he came out of this trial a changed man. If this experience taught him the value of life – his life and other people's lives. If he learned that he was not special, just lucky. Lucky to have been born in America where pro athletes make $20 million a year. Lucky to have been blessed with unusual size, strength, and speed, and remarkable athletic ability. Lucky to have been given the chance to succeed as an athlete.

Lucky to have Frank Tucker as his father.

Five weeks behind bars, William Tucker had learned nothing. So Judge Harold Rooney would try again to save the boy's life.

'Motion denied.'

Chapter 36

Frank woke with a fierce hangover. He had drunk whiskey until he had passed out the night before. A lot of whiskey. It was so easy to fall off the wagon. One shot, and the warmth of the whiskey inside his body just eased the fall. It was like coming home for Christmas, except it was only Thanksgiving.

Frank did not run that morning. He did not work out. He did not bathe in the Gulf. He went straight to his protein shake, with two shots of vodka. He was off the case and off the wagon. He was back to his old life. Back to drinking hard liquor. Back to being a worthless beach bum of a lawyer.

His son no longer needed him.

Becky stepped out onto the back porch of the bungalow.

'Anyone want coffee?' she asked.

'*Coffee?*' Chuck said, as if she had said broccoli. 'Caffeine's bad for your health.'

'And whiskey and cigarettes aren't?'

'You have to make choices in life, Becky.'

She had driven down from Houston to spend Thanksgiving on the beach with her father. And his friends. Dwayne, Chico, and Chuck – she liked them. They were great characters in her book – so many flaws. Tragic flaws. Like her father. But she didn't want Frank Tucker to be a tragic hero. Just her hero.

'Ecuador,' Dwayne said.

The others groaned.

'Ecuador?' Becky said.

'Everything's cheap, and they got beautiful beaches.'

'And girls?' Chuck said.

'Oh, yeah.'

'I'm in.'

Becky sat down with her cup of coffee, opened her laptop, pulled up her manuscript, and typed fast. Her book was racing to the end now. But how would it end?

Billie Jean pulled up in her candy apple red Mustang at noon. The top was down, and the sun was out. She got out and scanned the beach. She spotted Becky and Frank walking far down the sand and tossing sticks for Rusty. About fifty feet from the bungalow sat a deep fryer, apparently placed there so as not to endanger the bungalow and its inhabitants. Chuck was up to something for Thanksgiving dinner. Strung from the fryer to the bungalow was a long orange extension cord. Billie Jean was pretty sure that didn't meet code. Just as she was pretty sure that she would find Dwayne and Chico sitting on the back porch and smoking tobacco and marijuana, respectively. Billie Jean Campbell was forty years old, and she now found herself in a place she thought she would never be in her life. Actually, two places: Rockport, Texas, and in love.

She was in love with an older man. A broken-down lawyer. Life had kicked her to the ground before; she knew how it felt.

She had bared her body to survive. But survive she had. She had pushed herself up off the ground, and then she had kicked life in the balls. That's the kind of girl she was. Which is to say, not the kind of girl most men would find appealing. But Frank did. Find her appealing. She thought. She hoped.

But if his son went to prison, Frank would do the time with him. He would never be free of guilt. Never free to love and live. With himself or with her. She wanted to help him. And his son. Because she was the son's court-appointed lawyer. And because she was in love with his father.

'You got that turkey fried yet?' Dwayne said. 'I'm hungry.'

They were all lounging on the back porch. Chuck checked his watch.

'Should be done.'

Chuck stood, stepped down to the sand, and headed to the fryer. He had assured Frank that he knew what he was doing; he had seen a turkey fried on cable. Frank had his doubts, but he figured Chuck couldn't hurt himself too badly.

BOOM!

The force of the explosion knocked Chuck back and down to the sand.

'Shit!' Dwayne shouted.

Frank jumped up and off the porch in time to see the fried turkey fly through the air and land in the surf.

'And they say turkeys can't fly,' Chico said.

'You okay, Chuck?' Frank asked.

Chuck rubbed his face free of sand. 'Yeah. Might've got the peanut oil too hot. Should've stuck to Crisco.'

Becky laughed loudly. Then she typed fast.

'You can't make this stuff up,' she said.

Frank shook his head. 'You're in the book, Chuck.'

★

The defense fund had a balance of $325 so they decided to celebrate Thanksgiving with fried shrimp and cold beer in town. Billie Jean volunteered to be the designated driver. Dwayne, being the biggest of the bunch, sat in the passenger bucket seat up front. The four others squeezed into the back seat. Becky was almost in Frank's lap, as if she were still his little girl.

'Mom and Dale are in Romania now,' she said.

'Chico, blow that smoke the other way,' Dwayne said. 'I'm starting to feel young.'

'That's why they call it medicinal, my friend. And it's cheaper than an antidepressant prescription.'

'You depressed?' Chuck asked.

'Spending Thanksgiving with you guys instead of my girls, playing poker with sand dollars, my wife married to another man—'

His wife had left him for another man while he was incarcerated, but he still loved her.

'—hell, yes, I'm depressed.'

He sucked hard on the joint. It was night, and they were playing poker on the back porch. Becky had left for Houston and Billie Jean for Austin. But Frank could summon up no interest in playing poker with sand dollars. He was hard into the bottle these days, so his emotions had sunk to the bottom of the Gulf of Mexico. He pushed his sand dollars to the pile and tossed his cards on the table.

'You're not going to try to bluff me?' Dwayne said.

Frank stood and walked through the sand to the surf. He stared out to sea. He had climbed out of the gutter to save his son. He had put the bottle down. He had a purpose in life. He felt needed again. A man needs to be needed. At least by his family.

But his son didn't need him.

He sat on the beach where the tide kissed the dry sand. And he cried. He cried for himself, and he cried for his son.

'Man, this turkey good. I like dark meat.'

The gangbanger next door laughed. William did not. He did not laugh, and he did not eat. Motion denied.

'Thought you say you leaving me, William Tucker?'

'My lawyer said he could get me out of here. He didn't.'

'They lie. Take your money, don't do shit. And they call us criminals.'

Chapter 37

The next morning, William Tucker shuffled in shackles into a private interview room to find his lawyer and agent awaiting him. He sat down across the table from them.

'Why do you get a private room?' William asked.

'I've got pull around here,' Scotty said.

'Not enough to get me out of here.'

His lawyer shrugged like a receiver who had dropped a touchdown pass.

'Some judges just won't stay bought. What can I say?'

'I'm gonna die in here.'

'No, you're not, William. I can guarantee that.'

William felt his spirits perk up. 'How?'

'I made a deal.'

'A deal? What kind of deal?'

'A plea deal.'

'*Plea?*'

'You plead guilty to negligent manslaughter, you get two to five years. With good time, you're out in two years max.'

'You want me to plead guilty?'

'You'll only be twenty-five, plenty of years to play ball.'

'I'll be an ex-con.'

Warren the agent shrugged. 'So is Michael Vick. And he's making thirteen million. There's life after prison, William, if you're a star athlete.'

'Vick abused dogs. I'll be a convicted killer.'

'Not premeditated or intentional. See, what we'll do is, put you out there doing community service with kids in schools, telling them not to drink, that if this could happen to you, it can happen to them. The public loves redemption. I can market that.'

'Market a killer?' William turned to Scotty. 'I thought you were going to defend me?'

'That's what I'm doing.'

'By telling the world I killed her?'

'Not intentionally. You were both drunk, you had sex with her, it turned rough, got out of hand.'

'But I wasn't drunk, I didn't have sex with her, and I didn't kill her.'

'Look, William, your blood was on her body. Her photo and phone number were in your cell phone. The surveillance video from your dorm shows you got back in at 1:38, which is after the time of death. You were seen together that night at the Dizzy Rooster acting like two horny teenagers. Her roommate saw you and her heading to the back of the bar. Her body was discovered in the alley out back. You go to trial with that evidence against you, you're on death row. I guarantee it.'

'You told the D.A. I'd take a plea – now he thinks I did it.'

'He thought that before I said anything, William. Like when your DNA matched the blood found on the girl.'

'If he's got a slam dunk, why would the D.A. agree to this plea deal?'

Scotty smiled. 'We dug up dirt on the girl. She was basically screwing her way through the Texas Tech athletic department. Her folks are begging the D.A. to take the deal so their daughter isn't smeared at trial.'

'By who?'

'Me.'

'You would do that?'

'That's what lawyers do, William. You put the victim on trial, show her death wasn't such a loss to society – unless you're a college kid who likes to fuck cheerleaders.'

'My dad never did that.'

'Fuck cheerleaders?'

'Smear victims.'

'Well, he's a drunk, remember?'

'What about the judge? Why's he agreeing to this deal?'

'He hasn't yet. But he will. Because he owes me. Campaign contributions. Judges get reelected on contributions from lawyers, same as politicians get reelected on contributions from special interests. The judge wants to stay on the bench, and the D.A. wants to be governor. I'm connected, William, that's why I got this great deal for you.'

'*Great?* Confessing to a crime I didn't commit? I'm innocent.'

His lawyer and agent exchanged a glance.

'You don't believe me, do you?'

'Doesn't matter what I believe, William.'

'It matters to me. Tell me.'

'Honestly? No. I don't believe you.'

'You think I'm guilty, but you're still representing me?'

His lawyer laughed as if William had told a joke.

'If I didn't represent guilty clients, I'd have no clients.'

'My dad only represented innocent clients.'

'Not all of his clients were innocent, were they?'

300

'He believes me.'

'The jury won't. They won't buy your amnesia-by-concussion defense. They will sentence you to death, William. I can also guarantee you that.'

William Tucker wanted to be twelve years old again and throwing the ball in the backyard with his dad. He wanted his dad to protect him. To defend him. To save him. But his dad couldn't save himself. How could he save William?

'My own lawyer doesn't believe me.'

'They like that. They lie, so they figure everyone lies.'

'Did you lie to your lawyer?'

'Hell, yeah. But I'm black. They never believe us anyways. My mama only person in the whole world believe I'm innocent.'

'But you're not.'

'Still, I want my mama think I am. So you copping a plea?'

'I don't know. Scotty Raines said I won't get the death penalty if I plead.'

'Uh-huh, I see how it is. White boy got hisself a big-name lawyer, think he gonna plead out and escape that needle, is that it? Don't bet on it, boy.'

William Tucker lay crying on his cot in his cell in the solitary cellblock. His only friend in the world was the gangbanger next door.

'What do you mean?'

'What I mean is, the judge, he don't have to take the deal. See, William, your lawyer, he made a deal with the D.A., not with the judge. The D.A. can't change his mind, but the judge, he can do whatever he wanna do. 'Cause you can't make no deal with a judge. The judge, he decide what the deal gonna be. He might okay the deal, he might make his own deal. 'Cause once you plead guilty, he own you. He might say, "You

301

done confessed to killing that home girl. Now the Bible say an eye for an eye, so you gotta die. You gotta take the needle. You gotta face the Lord's wrath." Them crazy-ass judges in Texas, they say shit like that. They Bible-beaters. We takin' bets on you, homeboy. Five to two, you goin' to death row. It's your destiny, boy. Your name's on that needle, too, William Tucker.'

Chapter 38

It was the next day, and Frank and Rusty were watching the UT football game on the old television. Frank was drinking his protein-and-vodka shake, and the Longhorns were losing to TCU. They had lost every game since William's arrest. The first half ended, and they went to the studio in New York. The byline below the announcer read: *Breaking News*.

'We have breaking news from Austin,' the announcer said. 'Confidential sources at the Travis County Justice Center tell us that William Tucker will plead guilty to manslaughter – which is just a legal term for killing – in the death of the Texas Tech cheerleader two years ago. He will plead in open court on the ninth of December, nine days from today.'

The other announcer shook his head.

'They all claim innocence, but they're all guilty.'

Becky called Frank within the hour. She had heard on the radio that her brother would plead guilty. She was crying.

'Daddy, he can't be guilty.'

'He's not.'

'Then why is he going to plead guilty?'

'Because he's scared.'

'But he didn't do it?'

'No, honey. Your brother is not a killer. Or a rapist.'

'If he pleads guilty, everyone will think he is.'

'I know.'

'Daddy, you can't let him plead. I don't want his story to end like that.'

Chapter 39

Billie Jean arrived at the beach bungalow early Sunday morning. She had called the day before to let him know she was coming, but she had come early. So Frank was still bathing in the sea when she parked on the road above. Which left him in a bit of a dilemma: he could make a run for the house or he could hope she had a sense of humor. The water was cold in late November.

But she chose door number three. Once she had appraised the situation, she had wisely decided to take a walk down the beach with Rusty. When she returned, Frank was dressed and ready to leave. They were driving back to Austin to see his son. To beg William Tucker not to plead out.

'You drive,' Billie Jean said. 'I just drove three hours down.'

Frank got behind the wheel of the red Mustang. The seats were black leather buckets with a six-speed stick shift. He felt as if he were back in high school watching Steve McQueen in *Bullitt* at the drive-in movie theater with Mary Katherine Parker, his sweetheart. It didn't seem like thirty-seven years. Last he had heard, Mary Katherine had seven children.

305

Frank had the Mustang cruising the highway, the top down and a beautiful woman sitting next to him. He liked Billie Jean Crawford next to him. But he was fifty-five and a drunk; she was forty and not a drunk. She was a ten; he was a five. He glanced at her; her hair blew back in the breeze, and the sun on her face made her glow. She looked so much younger than he felt. He glanced at himself in the rearview mirror – the beach cap, the sunglasses, the wrinkle lines; the sun on his face high-lighted his weathered skin. An old man with a younger woman.

'I feel like I'm in a Viagra commercial,' he said.

The younger woman laughed. 'You're not that old.'

She reached to the back seat and retrieved a CD case.

'I've got Imagine Dragons, One Direction, Lorde . . .'

'You got any Marshall Tucker?'

'Who?'

'Bachman–Turner Overdrive?'

'Who?'

'Golden Earrings?'

She stared at him.

'How old are you?'

'Fifty-five.'

'Shit, you are old.' She laughed again. 'But not too old.'

'I feel too old.'

She frowned. 'Do you need Viagra?'

'I honestly don't know.'

'It's been that long?'

'And then some.'

'When I was stripping, old guys would sit alone at the stage. They weren't creeps – the young guys, they were the creeps. The old guys, they were just lonely. Like my dad after my mom died, only he didn't go to strip joints. At least I don't think so. Anyway, the old guys, they never tried to touch me. They tipped me just so I'd smile at them – is that sad or what, tipping a stripper for a smile? They weren't hoping for intercourse, just interaction. I always wondered how they got there, to that point in life, sitting alone and watching a woman strip. I don't want you to end up there, Frank.'

'I won't. I can't afford to tip strippers.'

'You shouldn't be alone, Frank.'

'Not many women banging on my door these days.'

'Do you still think about having a woman in your life?'

'Not anymore. When a man marries the wrong woman – a woman who doesn't love him – he can never recover.'

'Why not?'

'Because when you have kids, their lives become more important than yours.'

'I married the wrong man, but I recovered.'

'But you got your girl. Men don't get the kids. So a man who loves his kids, he sacrifices his love life to love them. To be with them.'

'You stayed with your wife to be with your children?'

Frank nodded.

'I didn't know men did that.'

'I did.'

'Your children are grown now, Frank. You don't have to sacrifice anymore.'

'I'm too old for love.'

'You're fifty-five, Frank. You're not dead yet.'

'I feel dead.'

'Maybe you just need a jumpstart. You know, Frank, I haven't had sex in so long I can't remember what it's like. But I still think about it. I still want it. Do you still want sex, Frank?'

'No.'

'You want to go the rest of your life without sex?'

'No.'

'I don't understand.'

307

'I don't want sex. I do want to make love. Once before I die, I want to have sex with a woman I love and who loves me. That's what I want.'

He felt her staring at him from the passenger's seat.

'Maybe I can help with that,' she said.

'I'm too old for you, Billie Jean.'

'If I was thirty and wanted children, maybe. But we've both had our children. They're grown. The rest of our lives belong to us, Frank. We decide how to live our lives. And with whom. I don't want a young man. I want a man who's old enough for life to have kicked all the bullshit out of him. Who's wise enough to appreciate life and old enough to appreciate love. And me. I'm a good woman, Frank, and I need a good man.'

'Most women your age are still waiting for Prince Charming to come along and sweep them off their feet and make their lives perfect.'

'I'm not that teenager anymore, in love with a fictional character. I'm not looking for Prince Charming, and I especially don't want a man who thinks he *is* Prince Charming. I want a real man. A really good man. That would be you.'

'You're a beautiful woman, Billie Jean. Is a good man good enough for you?'

'He is. You are. I've got what you need, Frank, and you've got what I need.'

'What's that?'

'Love.'

'Billie Jean—'

'I'm banging on your door, Frank.'

'You're my only son. I love you. I would trade places with you if I could. I would stand trial for you, I would go to prison for you, I'd take that needle for you. I would do that for you. But

308

I can't. Son, once you stand up in open court and tell the world that you killed Dee Dee Dunston—'

'I have to do that?'

'Yes. You do. Pleading guilty means just that – standing up in court and confessing guilt. You have to say, "Yes, I killed Dee Dee Dunston." And once you say those words, William, your life will never be the same. You will always be a confessed killer. You can never recover from that. No one will believe that you pleaded guilty to avoid the death penalty.'

'You said so yourself, prisons are full of innocent people. I don't want to be one of them.'

'You're innocent, William. I know that. I believe you. Fight. Don't quit.'

'But Scotty says I'll be out in two years at the most. I'll be free.'

'Son, if you confess to killing Dee Dee, you'll never be free. You will always be in that prison.'

'But Scotty believes—'

'Does he believe you're innocent?'

'No.'

'I do.'

'Why?'

'Because you're my son. Because you're part of me. Because I raised you from the day you were born. Because I know you don't have it in you to hurt someone.'

'But my agent says I can still play ball when I get out.'

'William, this isn't about playing football.'

'That's my life.'

'No. Proving your innocence is your life.'

'How? How do I prove I'm innocent? All the evidence says I'm guilty. Hell, I can't even remember that day. Maybe I am guilty.'

'No, you're not. You could never hurt someone. You're big and you're strong, but your heart is soft and gentle. That hasn't changed, William.'

309

'I don't know.'

'William, please believe in justice. Believe in yourself. Believe in me.'

'Have you been drinking again?'

'Yes.'

'Why?'

'Because you fired me.'

'I'm sorry.'

'I can stop again. Just don't plead.'

His son slumped in his chair. His jaws clenched. He was fighting his emotions. He lost. And then Frank lost. He wanted to embrace his son. Hold him. Make things right. He wanted to wrap his arms around his boy again. William put his massive palm against the glass on his side. Frank matched his hand to his son's.

'Save me, Dad.'

Billie Jean wiped her eyes. Maybe there was hope for William Tucker after all.

'We're back on the case,' his father said.

'Not until he fires Scotty Raines.'

'He will. We've just got to find the killer before next Monday.'

'Not much time.'

They exited the jail and drove to her townhouse in north Austin. They ate dinner and drank iced tea. After dinner they sat on her back balcony with the lights of the downtown skyline sparkling in the distance and the three-hundred-foot tall UT clock tower bathed in orange light. They talked about their children and their mistaken marriages, the choices they had made in life and the choices they wished they had made. Billie Jean got up for a tea refill but stopped. She bent down and kissed Frank.

'Open the door, Frank.'

Come to find out, he didn't need Viagra.

Chapter 40

'We're missing something,' Frank said.

He had gone to bed the night before craving a drink and had woken that morning craving a drink. He drank coffee instead. A lot of coffee.

'What?'

'I don't know. But it's like the photo on the phone – it's right there in front of us, in plain sight. We're just not seeing it.'

Billie Jean had driven Frank back to Rockport and stayed over. They spent the day going over their trial strategy.

'We can explain her phone number and photo to the jury—'

'If the jurors aren't old-timers,' Billie Jean said.

'So in jury selection, we go for the youngest in the pool.'

'I've never picked a jury.'

'I have. You look in their eyes. If they look back, you take them. If they look away, you don't.'

'Why?'

'Because they've already made up their minds. They think he's guilty.'

'What about the surveillance tape? He got in late enough to have killed her.'

'Hundreds of men were on Sixth Street that night. Any of them could have seen Dee Dee in her cheerleader outfit.'

'But none of their blood was on her body.'

'How the hell did you let this happen, Dwayne?'

Dwayne Gentry, former top homicide cop on the Houston Police Department and renowned interrogator of bad guys, stood in the small wooden shack that served as the operations headquarters for the mini-storage facility and suffered interrogation at the hands of Bob, the proprietor. They were studying the surveillance camera tape the day the three punks broke into a unit. On the screen, the camera caught the punks climbing over the perimeter fence, crowbarring storage unit number 124, and stuffing their backpacks with stolen contraband.

'Those little pricks were brazen, to try that in the middle of the day.'

'*Try?* They did it.' Bob shook his head. 'You left for lunch, didn't you? They had you under surveillance, saw you leave, and then made their move. Isn't that what happened, Dwayne?'

'No, it ain't what happened. I was here the whole morning.'

Bob pointed at the screen. 'They breached the perimeter fence at 12:35 P.M., made entry into the subject unit at 12:45 P.M., and escaped back over the fence at 1 P.M. The video don't lie, Dwayne.'

'Yeah, it does. When they took off with the contraband, it was straight-up noon. I checked my watch.'

Bob frowned. 'But the tape says one.'

'The tape's wrong. It was an hour earlier.'

'An hour earlier?' Bob snorted like a feral hog. 'Aw, shit, I know what happened. Robbie didn't turn the clock back on

312

the camera when we came off daylight savings time. Spring forward, fall back. The little dope.'

Robbie was Bob's son. He was a little dope.

'Okay, they breached at 11:35. You were still on site. Not your fault, Dwayne. What I need to do, see, is electrify the fence, maybe two-twenty volts. Those little fuckers try to breach my fence again, they'll be in for a little shock.'

Bob thought that was funny.

Chico Duran laughed. 'I shit you not, man, she took a picture of her privates and texted it to her boyfriend. He probably put it on his Facebook page, now half the world's seen her pussy.'

Keith, the nineteen-year-old delivery boy with tattoos and piercings all over his body, shrugged. 'I do that all the time.'

'Post photos of girls' privates on your Facebook page?'

'Get photos of girls' privates.'

'They sext you?'

'Yep.'

'Who?'

'Every girl I know.'

'Why?'

'It's social media, man. You take self-photos and share yourself with the world.'

'Why?'

'Why not?'

Chico shook his head. 'By the time I was your age, I was already conning people out of their credit card numbers. Kids today, you're spoiled, got no ambition, bunch of narcissistic little bastards spending your time taking photos of yourself, as if anyone gives a shit.'

Chuck Miller blew his whistle.

'Offsides on black. Five yards.'

313

'Shithead!' a parent screamed.

Chuck picked up the ball and stepped off five yards. He was about to blow the whistle to restart the game when one of the players said, 'He's bleeding again.'

'Who?'

'Georgie.'

'Shit, he might be one of them bleeders.'

'You're not supposed to say "shit" at peewee games. We're little kids.'

'Your fucking parents do.'

'Just our fucking dads.'

Chuck called a bodily fluids timeout and sent Georgie to the sideline. He took a good long swallow of his Gatorade-and-vodka sports drink. That same thought – *blood* – tried to take form in his brain again, but he still could not put the thought into a complete sentence, or even a recognizable phrase.

There was something about the blood.

'Harold went ethical on you, Scotty. It happens.'

'Not very often.'

'Nope. But Harold's always had an ethical streak in him.'

Dick Dorkin downed his drink. He and Scotty Raines were having drinks at the Capitol Club, the favorite watering hole for state politicos and judges and the lawyers who financed their careers.

'So is the boy taking the plea bargain or not?'

'He'll take it. Frank came in yesterday and got him all fired up to fight the charges, but I brought him back down to earth with my "come to Jesus" speech. He'll plead.'

'Come to Jesus?'

'If he doesn't plead, he's gonna come to Jesus.'

Dick laughed. 'Still, I'm not sure I wouldn't be happier if he didn't plead. I wanted that death sentence so bad I could smell his flesh burning.'

'A few drinks and you wax nostalgic, Dick. What do you want more – revenge on Frank Tucker or the Governor's Mansion?'

'It's a closer call than you might think.'

'Jesus, Dick, this isn't personal. This is business.'

'Maybe to you. But me, I'd like to stare at Frank Tucker while they empty that syringe into his boy's arm.'

William Tucker's six-foot-five-inch, two-hundred-thirty-five-pound body lay curled up on the cold concrete floor of his cell. He wanted to die. He wanted to close his eyes and die. The tears poured out of his eyes and the snot out of his nose. His massive body shook uncontrollably. He was big, strong, and fast, but he never felt so small, so weak, and so slow in his life. He always knew where life was taking him; now he felt lost.

'Help me, God.'

'Ain't no God in here,' the gangbanger next door said in his soft whisper. 'You in hell now, William Tucker.'

If he went to trial and lost, he'd get the death penalty. If he pleaded out, he would always be a convicted killer.

'Please, God. Save me.'

The gangbanger sighed. 'Man, you got it bad, William. Think God gonna come down here and pluck your white ass outta this jail, 'cause you His special child, like your mama told you since the day you popped out between her legs. Think He gonna come down here and save you. Shit, man, God ain't got no time for that.'

William cried harder.

'Mm, mm, mm. Big boy crying now. Wishing this ain't his destiny. Wishing God had gave him a better life, hadn't put him on this path from birth. I said them same prayers, I wished the same thing. All my life, I wish I had a better life. Some folks, they born into heaven. Us, we was born into hell.'

William swiped snot from his face and said, 'I estranged myself from my father.'

'Uh-huh, my daddy a stranger to me, too. I always wonder, what if my mama had of married my daddy, made us a regular family like that Bill Cosby show on TV. Wonder if I would be in this cell today, if that happened? Maybe me and my daddy, we'd of throwed a football in the backyard and talked about being a man 'stead of a criminal. Maybe we'd of had a real home, sit around a table and eat food with my family, and everyone ain't saying "fuck this" and "fuck that" instead we be sayin' grace before eating instead of "pass the fuckin' steak sauce," you know what I mean? You know I ain't never done that in my whole life, eat food with my family, say grace at the dinner table. My homies in the gang, they was my family. We want something to eat, we go to fuckin' McD's, get a Big Mac and fries, the double order, drink malt liquor when I was eight years old. You ever wonder what that kind of childhood be like, to have Bill Cosby be your daddy?'

'I know what it's like.'

'You know someone live like that?'

'Yeah.'

'Who?'

'Me.'

'Say what?'

'That was my childhood.'

'Wait. You saying you lived like that, like that Bill Cosby show?'

'Yeah.'

'You had a daddy at home? You eat food with your family? You say grace at the dinner table? You throwed the ball in the backyard?'

'Yeah.'

'Then how the fuck you end up in that cell?'

His voice rose, almost as if he were mad at William.

'I thought you was like me, with a fucked-up life. That why you in here. But you sayin' you had all that, a mama and a daddy and dinner at a goddamn table every fuckin' night of your life and you fuckin' end up in here? I dream of that life, but all I got was a fucked life, drugs and guns and gangbangers. You born in heaven but you put yourself in hell? What the fuck wrong with you, boy? I didn't choose to be here. It ain't my fault I'm here. I didn't kill that cop – my destiny did!'

He was almost screaming now.

'You the luckiest motherfucker ever live! You got a fuckin' mama and a daddy! You got a fuckin' family! You got a fuckin' dinner table with real fuckin' food! You stupid fuckin' white boy! I hope you fuckin' die!'

His voice cracked, as if he might be crying, too.

'I don't want to talk to you no more, William Tucker.'

The young men's soft sobs were the only sounds of the solitary cellblock that night.

Chapter 41

At five the next morning, William Tucker's court-appointed public defender woke to her cell phone ringing. She slapped her hand around in the dark until she found her purse. She dug inside and grasped the phone. She answered.

'Hello.'

'Billie Jean?'

'William?'

Frank switched the lamp on and rolled over to her. She put a finger to her lips.

'William, why aren't you sleeping?'

'I never sleep.'

'What's wrong?'

'What's wrong? I'm gonna die on death row, that's what's wrong.'

'No, you're not. Your dad's going to save you, William. He'll find a way.'

'Tell him I'm sorry.'

She motioned Frank closer; he put his head against hers and listened to his son.

'For what?'

'For kicking him out of my life. For abandoning him. For forgetting what a good father he is. For not understanding what he went through with Bradley Todd. For not sticking with him like he always stuck with me. For being a piece-of-shit son. For calling him a loser.'

She heard him sobbing.

'For taking the plea deal.'

Frank grabbed the phone and yelled, 'William – no!'

But his son was already gone.

Chapter 42

'Six days from today, my son is going to stand up in court and plead guilty to a crime he didn't commit . . . because he's afraid he'll get the death penalty. Once he does that, there's no going back. His life is over. We're not going to let that happen.'

William Tucker would take the plea deal. Innocent people do that. More often than people would imagine because fighting a prosecutor possessed of unlimited resources dedicated to putting you in prison is daunting and expensive. Few people can afford to wage that fight. In 2002, Brian Banks, a seventeen-year-old star high school football player with a scholarship to the University of Southern California and dreams of an NFL career, was falsely accused of rape by a classmate; she claimed he had assaulted her on their high school campus. He was innocent, but his lawyer advised him to plead guilty. 'You're a big black male,' she said. 'The jury will convict you.' He faced a forty-year sentence. So he pleaded guilty and got five years. His accuser sued the high school and won a $1.5-million settlement. Four years after his release from prison, his accuser contacted him on Facebook and asked to meet. Brian videotaped their meeting; she admitted that she had lied in order to sue the school.

It happens.

Frank could not let it happen to his son.

It was ten that morning, and the defense team had gathered on the back porch. They drank strong coffee and brainstormed with those few brain cells they hadn't previously killed with alcohol.

'Now, look, I know you guys think William is guilty, but—'

'He's innocent,' Dwayne said.

Frank studied the ex-cop smoking a big cigar.

'You changed your mind?'

'Yep.'

'Why?'

'The surveillance tape at his dorm is wrong. It's time-stamped 1:38 A.M., but it was really 12:38 A.M. They didn't turn the clock back when daylight savings time ended the week before.'

'How do you know?'

'I checked with the company that runs security for the dorms.'

'They told you? Just like that?'

'They told Detective Gentry, Houston homicide. Frank, William got in at 12:38 that night. Means he would've been hard pressed to kill her downtown at midnight, go back inside the bar and puke, then get back to his dorm – all in thirty-eight minutes. He's innocent.'

'Ditto,' Chico said.

Frank turned to Chico Duran. He was smoking a joint.

'You too? Why the change of heart?'

'Social media. Kids take self-photos of themselves, their body parts, to show the world. Don't ask me why, but they do it. If I ever catch my girls sexting, I'm gonna . . .'

321

He caught himself.

'Well, anyway, Dee Dee Dunston did it that night, with William's phone. He didn't take her photo. She did.'

He showed Frank the image of Dee Dee on William's phone.

'See, her arm's extended. She took her own photo. He didn't lie. He's innocent, Frank.'

'Dwayne, Chico . . . thanks, guys. But there's still the blood.'

'I think I can help with that,' Chuck said.

'How?'

Chuck sighed. 'I should've put two and two together a long time ago – course, I usually come up with five – you know, Frank, I don't think so good these days 'cause of all my concussions and the whiskey sure as hell don't help to clear my mind and—'

'Chuck . . . focus. The blood.'

'Oh, yeah. Well, anyway, this kid in my peewee games, name's Georgie—'

'Georgie?'

'They're five-year-old kids. They're all named Petey or Bobby or Jimmy or Georgie. Anyway, he's a bleeder. Every game, he bleeds. I mean, he falls to the turf, the little fucker bleeds. I gotta call a bodily fluid timeout, send him to the side-line, get him bandaged up so his blood don't get on another kid, and course his mama's hysterical . . . peewee football's a fuckin' zoo.'

'What's this Georgie kid got to do with William?'

'Check out this play.'

Chuck had been studying the game tape for the hundredth time. He turned the laptop so the others could watch the video.

'I've watched this video more times than I can count. And every time, I've been focusing on the sideline and not on the field.'

'No shit, Sherlock,' Dwayne said. 'Dee Dee's on the sideline. She was a cheerleader, not a player. She ain't on the field.'

'But William's blood is.'

'What?' Frank said.

'Watch the game. It's ugly, William played awful.'

'His dad showed up drunk, made a fool of himself before that game.'

'Oh. Well that explains it.'

Chuck clicked the mouse, and the video resumed playing. On the screen, William dropped back to pass then broke out of the pocket and ran; the three Tech linebackers converged on him. Chuck froze the frame and zoomed in.

'Okay. Look closely. All four players' arms are bare. Their jersey sleeves are cut up high, that's the fashion these days, to expose their biceps. And there's no visible blood on any of them.'

He resumed the video. The Tech players gang-tackled William high and low and hard and drove him into the turf. William jumped up as if he didn't feel the brutal tackle. Chuck froze the frame.

'Look.'

He clicked the mouse several times and zoomed in on William's left arm.

'His left elbow,' Chuck said. 'He's bleeding.'

Blood ran down his arm.

'When I saw him in the hospital after the game,' Frank said, 'his left elbow was bandaged up. He said he got stitches.'

'Nasty cut,' Chuck said. 'Probably took a facemask right on the bone, busted some of those capillaries, they'll bleed pretty good. One time I got cut on my forehead, face looked like I been shot.'

'The video.'

'Oh.'

Chuck resumed the video. William hurried back to his team's side of the ball and called the next play from the line of scrimmage without huddling up. The game clock was ticking down, the pace of play was frantic, offensive and defensive players ran on and off the field, and the referees raced around to keep up.

'Why didn't the refs call a timeout so he could get bandaged?' Chico asked.

'They're supposed to, in case he's got AIDS.' Chuck shrugged. 'I guess they didn't notice in all the confusion. This is late in the game, William's running a two-minute offense, trying to take the team down for a score to win. Things are moving fast. Few plays later, he gets his concussion.'

On the screen, William again dropped back to pass then again ran. The same three Tech linebackers converged on him; just before they tackled William, Chuck froze the frame and zoomed in on the Tech players.

'Their arms are clean,' he said.

He resumed the video. They tackled William then got to their feet. Chuck froze the frame again and zoomed in on one of the Tech players, number fifty-two.

'Now he's got blood on his arms.'

Chuck ran the tape again. Number fifty-two ran and jumped into the air where he was met by number fifty-five; they did a body bump, shoulder to shoulder and arm to arm. He repeated the gesture with number fifty-one. Chuck paused the video and zoomed in on each player.

'Now all three have blood on their arms.'

'William's blood?'

'No one else was bleeding before that tackle.'

'Transference of trace evidence,' Dwayne said. 'It happens. And it doesn't take much blood for the crime scene guys to capture his DNA. That's why they call it trace evidence.'

'That's good thinking, Chuck.'

Frank stuck a fist out to Chuck; they fist-bumped.

'Thanks, Frank.'

'I don't mean to ruin the party,' Billie Jean said, 'but wouldn't they have noticed the blood on their arms?'

'Shit,' Chuck said, 'when I played we got blood, spit, puke, piss, tobacco juice – hell, one time I got shit on me – not mine. That's football. It's a dirty game.'

'Okay,' Billie Jean said, 'so your theory is, William's blood got transferred from William to number fifty-two, from fifty-two to fifty-five, and from fifty-five to fifty-one? And then from one of those players to Dee Dee Dunston?'

Chuck shrugged. 'You got a better theory?'

'No. And actually it's not a bad theory. I remember one time, I was stripping, and this guy – young guy, one of the creeps – he reaches up with a twenty-dollar bill . . . they wouldn't just toss it on the stage, they had to slip in inside my G-string, that's when they'd always try to cop a feel. So I squat down a bit so he can reach it – my G-string—'

She demonstrated, sticking her right leg out and squatting.

'—and he slips the bill inside then his forearm slid down my leg, left his sweat – the creeps always sweated – all the way down my thigh. I could feel it and see it shiny and wet in the spotlight. I thought, yuk.'

'That was your candy apple red G-string?' Chuck said.

'Are you sweating?'

'Uh, we're on the coast.'

'It's December.'

'Oh.'

She shook her head clear.

'So this creep got his DNA on me just like that?'

'He did,' Dwayne said. 'And blood's easier to transfer than sweat 'cause it's sticky. And it dries on skin.'

'But I showered after my shows – God, I scrubbed my skin raw to get the cooties off,' Billie Jean said. 'Wouldn't those players have showered after the game, washed the blood off?'

Chuck shrugged. 'Maybe. Maybe not. They're linebackers. Barely domesticated wild animals.'

They stared at the frozen images of the three Tech players on the screen.

'That's it,' Frank said. 'That's how William's blood got on the dead girl.'

'That means—'

'One of those Tech players killed Dee Dee Dunston.'

'You guys are going to chase down those three players from two years ago?' Billie Jean said.

They stood at her car on the road. She would drive back to Austin; they would travel to Lubbock.

'It's our only hope. William's only hope.'

'Be careful, Frank. If one of them killed Dee Dee, he'll kill again to stay out of prison.'

'Truth is, my life doesn't matter all that much. My son's life matters a hell of a lot more.'

'Your life matters to me, Frank.'

'John Smith, Darrell Jackson, and Bo Cantrell,' Chico said. 'I searched for the rosters back then. Those are the players. Smith was a sophomore, Jackson and Cantrell were seniors.'

'We've got to track those guys down,' Frank said. 'Fast. Where do we start?'

'Lubbock.'

'That's a nine-hour drive,' Dwayne said.

'No time to drive. We need to fly.'

'Four plane tickets? We've run through all the money we got from selling the signed football.'

'We need to sell something else on eBay.'

'What?'

'Another ball.'

'I've got a ball,' Chuck said.

He tossed up his football.

'It's worthless without William's signature.'

'Give me the ball,' Chico says.

He tapped on William's laptop and retrieved the close-up photo of William's signature on the ball they had previously put on eBay. Then he held out an open hand to Dwayne like a surgeon to an OR nurse.

'Sharpie.'

Dwayne slapped his Sharpie into Chico's hand. Chico studied the photo then signed the ball: 'William Tucker.' He held the ball out for their inspection. They compared the fake signature to the real one.

'That's good,' Chuck said. 'Real good.'

'You forged my son's signature?'

'Frank, I forged dead people's signatures on Medicaid documents. This is a fucking football.'

'And now we're going to sell a football with a fake signature on eBay? That's fraud.'

Chico gave him a look. 'I'm an ex-con, Frank. I can live with that.'

Two hours later, they had sold the ball for $7,500. Apparently news that William Tucker would plead guilty to raping and killing a college coed made the ball more valuable. Only in America.

Chapter 43

They drove to Corpus Christi then flew to Lubbock early the next morning. They had five days to track down three football players from two years before, figure out which one was the killer, and then convince him to confess.

There was no time to waste.

They rented a car at the Lubbock airport and drove to the Texas Tech campus. They went directly to the football stadium. They parked and walked to the main entrance. The gate was locked.

'Wednesday, they'll practice today,' Chuck said. 'But not in the stadium.'

A maintenance man pointed them in the direction of the practice fields. They crossed Mac Davis Lane—

'Man, I loved his songs,' Chuck said.

He tried to sing a Mac Davis song but fumbled the lyrics.

'Damn concussions.'

'Mac was born right here in Lubbock,' Chico said, 'just like Buddy Holly.'

'Played the quarterback that was supposed to be Don Meredith in *North Dallas Forty*,' Chuck said. 'Best movie ever made.'

Dwayne gave him a look of disbelief.

'You're saying it's better than the *Die Hard* movies? You are brain-damaged.'

'Well, maybe not the first one. That's a classic.'

'Damn straight it is.'

'That's what I said.'

The athletic complex building sat across the street. Behind the building were the practice fields. They stood at the fence and watched the team.

'There he is,' Dwayne said. 'Number fifty-one. John Smith.'

They stayed until the practice ended an hour later then waited out front of the athletic complex building for John Smith. When he exited the building, they approached him. He was stocky and muscular with short blond hair. Wet hair. He wore a sweat suit and sneakers.

'John Smith?' Frank said.

The player stopped. 'Yes, sir?'

'Hair's wet – you just shower?'

He recoiled. 'Hey, if you're one of those creeps like that Penn State guy, likes to hang out in gym showers—'

'I'm Frank Tucker. William Tucker's father.'

John Smith held a hand out and started to walk off. 'I don't want to talk about that.'

Dwayne flashed the badge. 'Police business, son.'

John Smith stopped and surrendered. But his face did not register guilt. Instead, he offered a sad shake of his head.

'Sorry, Mr. Tucker. That was a strange question.'

'Here's another one: Texas versus Tech game two years ago in Austin, did you shower after that game?'

'Not sure why you're asking, but I did. I shower every day. Did William really kill Dee Dee? I guess he did. He confessed.'

'He didn't. Confess or kill her.'

John frowned. 'But they said on TV that—'

'They're wrong. Did you know Dee Dee?'

'Yes, sir. Everyone did. She was a sweet girl.'

'Was she promiscuous?'

John pondered a moment then nodded. 'That's what I heard.'

'You didn't have sex with her?'

'Mr. Tucker, I'm a Mormon. And a virgin. Like Tebow.'

'I've got two daughters I want you to meet,' Chico said.

'You see Tebow signed with the Patriots?' Chuck said. 'No way he's beating out Brady.'

Everyone stared at Chuck. He turned his palms up.

'Just saying.'

Frank returned to John Smith. 'Did you know Darrell Jackson and Bo Cantrell?'

'Yes, sir. The three of us, we were the starting linebackers back then. They were seniors.'

'Did they have sex with Dee Dee?'

John sighed. 'Darrell had sex with every girl on campus, from what I heard. He was this handsome cowboy. He modeled for book covers, romance novels, had copies in his room.'

'What about Bo?'

'Bo, he was . . .' John shook his head. 'A swamp rat from the bayou.'

'Did they shower after the games?'

'I didn't keep tabs on that, Mr. Tucker. You'll have to ask them.'

'We will. Where are they now?'

'Last I heard, Darrell is back cowboying on his family ranch in Wink, and Bo is up in Omaha.'

'Doing what?'

'Playing pro ball, for the Wranglers.'

'Thanks, John.'

'Yes, sir. I hope William is innocent.'

330

They watched John walk off.

'He ain't the killer,' Dwayne said.

'How do you know?' Chico said.

'I've interviewed a hundred killers in my time, and none of them were Mormon.' He paused. 'Course, sometimes they fool you.'

'I know,' Frank said.

Chapter 44

'Looks like a bigger version of Roy Rogers,' Dwayne said.

'Who's Roy Rogers?' Chuck said.

Frank and Chico had flown to Omaha to find Bo Cantrell. Dwayne and Chuck had driven the one hundred seventy miles from Lubbock to Wink to find Darrell Jackson. They had. On the Lazy River Ranch outside town. Darrell rode up on a big white horse just as they pulled up to the ranch house and got out of the rental. He did look like a male model.

'Help you?' Darrell said.

'Nice looking horse,' Dwayne said.

'You a rancher?'

'Cop. Ex-cop.'

'What brings you out here?'

'Dee Dee Dunston.'

Dwayne almost hoped that Darrell would yank on the reins and gallop off. Because then William Tucker's life would be saved. Which would save Frank Tucker's life. If the boy went to prison, Frank would never be free. He was a good man and a good friend, and Dwayne Gentry was down to three friends in the whole world. He couldn't afford to lose one.

'We understand you knew her,' Dwayne said, 'in the Biblical sense.'

Darrell dismounted. He jingled.

'Wow, cowboys really do wear spurs,' Chuck said with a kid's grin.

Darrell frowned at Chuck then turned to Dwayne.

'I knew her. But I didn't kill her, if that's why you're here.'

'It is.'

'I thought William Tucker confessed?'

'Nope. He didn't kill the girl.'

'Paper said his blood was on her.'

'It was on you, too,' Chuck said.

'You an ex-cop, too?'

'Coach.'

'An ex-cop and an ex-coach.'

'You wore number fifty-two back then, didn't you?' Dwayne said.

'Yep.'

'William was bleeding at the end of that game. When you tackled him, his blood got on John Smith, Bo Cantrell, and you.'

'How do you know?'

'Game film,' Chuck said. 'Got a real neat zoom feature.'

'Did you shower after the game?' Dwayne said.

Darrell recoiled and seemed a bit amused.

'Odd question.'

'Mind answering it?'

'Yeah, I showered after the game. Always did. I may be a cowboy, but I'm not a cow. I got a degree in engineering, and I know how a shower works.'

Dwayne and Chuck exchanged a glance. Darrell pushed his hat back on his head.

333

'So you two fellas came all the way out here to ask if I showered after the game? Hell, you could've called.'

'What about Bo Cantrell? He shower after the game?'

Darrell laughed. 'Bo Cantrell was a half-crazy, juiced-up coon-ass from Louisiana who suffered one too many concussions. And he stunk worse than cow shit. His idea of bathing was swimming in the swamp.'

'Tell us about him.'

'We came up together, started all four years. He was middle linebacker, I was outside. He was dead set on going pro, but he was only two-thirty. Pro linebackers are two-sixty. So he got on steroids junior year. Made him meaner than a rattlesnake. And the concussions didn't help his disposition.'

'You didn't partake?'

'Nope. I never figured on going pro. I'm a cowboy. I had this ranch to come back to. Bo, he didn't have anything waiting back in Louisiana for him. If he didn't go pro, he was back hunting gators in the swamp. I always figured I'd read about him in the paper.'

'Sports pages?'

'Obituaries. Figured he'd commit suicide, like those other brain-damaged pro players.' He shook his head. 'Well, I'd better go look for some cows.'

Darrell Jackson stuck a cowboy boot into a stirrup and mounted the big horse. He jerked the reins as if to gallop off, but didn't. He turned back to Dwayne and Chuck.

'By the end of our senior season, Bo's head just wasn't right. The juice, it made him paranoid. You go looking for Bo, you watch yourself. He started carrying a gun.'

Bo Cantrell had been taken by Omaha in the third round of the NFL draft two years before. He was now a starting linebacker for the Wranglers. He sported a shaved head and tattoo sleeves on both arms. When he walked out of the Wrangler's training facility after their Tuesday practice, Frank called out to him from across the parking lot.

'Bo!'

He glanced their way but kept walking and yelled over his shoulder, 'No autographs.'

Frank and Chico caught up with him.

'We don't want your autograph.'

Still walking. 'Good.'

'We want to ask you about Dee Dee Dunston.'

Bo stopped. He turned and looked them over. And Frank looked him over. His head seemed oversized, his neck was thick, and his shoulders were wide and lumpy with muscles. He had acne. He was not a handsome human being. He wore a Wrangler T-shirt, sweat pants, and sneakers. Grass was in his hair; his thick arms were matted with dirt and sweat. His body odor was stifling.

'You cops?'

'I'm Frank Tucker. William Tucker's father.'

Bo maintained his stern expression, but Frank saw something in his eyes. Guilt.

'Way I hear it, your boy's done confessed to killing Dee Dee.'

'You heard wrong, Bo. He didn't kill her.'

'Then who did?'

They locked eyes. Dwayne had reported in on their meeting with Darrell Jackson. Only one suspect remained.

'You did.'

Bo's massive neck muscles clenched. His breathing came faster, and his face flushed. He was the killer.

'You didn't shower after practice, Bo.'

'So?'

'Habit. You didn't shower after the UT game two years ago either.'

'So?'

'So William's left elbow got cut at the end of the game, when you and Darrell Jackson and John Smith tackled him. He

335

bled down his arm. His blood got on their arms and your arms. But they showered after the game, washed the blood off. You didn't. His blood was still on your arms when you raped and murdered Dee Dee that night out back of the Dizzy Rooster.'

'Prove it.'

'We can. We can prove that you killed Dee Dee. It's over, Bo.'

Bo Cantrell stepped toward Frank as if to hit him.

'Fuck you.'

He turned and walked fast to a jacked-up four-wheel drive pickup, got in, and sped off. Chico took a photo of the license plate with William's cell phone. Then Frank called Dwayne. When he answered, Frank said, 'You and Chuck drive to Midland, fly to Omaha. It's Bo Cantrell.'

'How are we going to get Bo to confess?' Chuck asked.

Frank and Chico had picked up Dwayne and Chuck at the Omaha airport that night and driven back to the hotel.

'We're gonna haunt his ass,' Dwayne said. 'When you know who the bad guy is, and the bad guy knows you know, you gotta get in his head, let him know you're watching him, make him look over his shoulder, get him scared.'

'Of us?' Chico said. 'An ex-lawyer, ex-cop, ex-coach, and ex-con?'

'Good point,' Frank said.

'I've dealt with his kind before,' Dwayne said. 'He ain't the brightest bulb in the box, see, but he figures he got away with murder. And rape. Now it's two years later, and he likes his life. Wants to keep it. He'll do anything to keep it. Even kill again. 'Cause he's got nothing to lose.'

'Kill again?' Chico said. 'That would be us?'

'It would,' Dwayne said.

'That calls for a drink.'

Chapter 45

At eight the next morning, Friday, they were parked directly across the street from Bo's home in an upscale Omaha neighborhood. It looked like the Tuckers' old house in River Oaks, which is to say, completely unbefitting Bo Cantrell.

'He's gonna see us,' Chuck said.

'We want him to,' Dwayne said. 'This ain't a surveillance. This is a haunting.'

'What's the difference?'

'Surveillance, you try to be stealthy, not let the suspect know you're watching him. A haunting, you want him to know he's being haunted.'

'Ohh. But that sounds more dangerous.'

'There is that.'

Bo Cantrell pulled out of his driveway at nine. He saw them and sped off in his truck. They followed him to the Wrangler's training facility. They watched him walk inside. He glanced back at them at the door.

'Who wants coffee?' Chico said.

'Starbucks?' Dwayne asked.

'Of course.'

'Venti decaf Mocha Cookie Crumble Frappuccino with extra whipped cream,' Chuck said. 'One shot.'

'Espresso?'

'Whiskey.'

'Grande pumpkin latte, one shot, and a doughnut,' Dwayne said. 'I always ate donuts on stakeouts.'

'What kind?'

'Whiskey?'

'Donuts?'

'The kind with sugar.'

'I'll have a donut, too,' Chuck said.

'A scone,' Frank said. 'Regular tall coffee, no whiskey.'

'Call me if Bo comes out,' Chico said. 'I'll be back in ten.'

Bo came out at three that afternoon. Frank waved to him. He did not wave back. He drove to a liquor store—

'Now he's teasing us,' Chico said.

—and then to a strip joint.

'Now he's taunting us,' Chuck said.

They did not enter the establishment. Bo might have friends in low places. They waited. And waited. A few hours later, he exited the joint with a stripper.

'There's a cash transaction,' Chico said.

They followed him back to his house. He entered with the girl, but they saw him peeking out the window at them.

'That's good haunting, boys,' Dwayne said.

Chapter 46

The next morning, they were again parked outside Bo's house.

'You sure this will work?' Frank asked.

'Pretty sure,' Dwayne said.

Saturday went much the same as Friday except Bo stopped to eat before going to the strip joint. A Cajun food place. He sat by the window. Frank waved to him. He gave Frank the finger.

'Jesus, he eats like a pig,' Chico said.

'Cajun,' Dwayne said.

'The food?'

'Bo.'

'I wonder, could I grill crawdads?' Chuck said.

Chapter 47

On Sunday, Omaha played the Patriots in the Wrangler Stadium. They acquired four tickets behind the Omaha bench from a scalper outside the stadium. Inside, Chuck bought a Wranglers football—

'I wonder if I can get some of the players to sign it after the game?'

'You're a groupie, aren't you?' Dwayne said.

—Dwayne an orange team color plastic cowboy hat that made him look like a kid waiting in line for the pony ride, Chico T-shirts for his girls, and Frank a poster. He borrowed Dwayne's Sharpie. They found their seats. When the teams came out for the game, they screamed, 'Bo!' until they caught his attention on the sideline. When he found them in the stands, Frank held up the poster on the back of which he had written BO CANTRELL IS A KILLER LINEBACKER. Bo stalked down the sideline.

'Boo! Boo!'

The fans booed Bo. He had missed an assignment; his man caught a short pass and ran for a touchdown. The Patriots were running over the Wranglers. Over Bo Cantrell in particular. He came to the sideline and kicked over the Gatorade table. Then he glanced up at them in the stands. Frank held up the sign again.

'Now this is what I call a haunting,' Dwayne said.

Bo's game went from bad to horrible. He missed assignments and tackles. The Patriots ran over him, around him, and through him. The coaches yelled at him, his teammates yelled at him, and the fans yelled at him. The Wranglers lost 48-7.

'Hey, Bo, sign my football!'

Bo had just exited the players' locker room at the stadium. A few fans had gathered in hopes of snagging an autograph. Chuck held his football out to Bo as he walked by.

'Bo! Come on, man!' Chuck yelled.

Bo gave Chuck a glare as if he wanted to deck him. He didn't. Sign his ball or deck him. He stormed past and to his truck in the parking lot. He drove directly to his favorite strip joint. He closed the place down at 2:00 A.M. They followed him home and parked on the street. He stumbled inside and apparently to bed as all the lights went out. They rolled the windows down and sat quietly for an hour. And another. They took turns napping. Chuck snored; Chico talked in his sleep. Frank couldn't sleep. He and Dwayne talked about the old days in Houston. Which seemed so long ago. A different life.

'The haunting didn't work,' Frank said. 'It's 4:30. Same time in Austin. William is set to plead at 9. What do we do now?'

'Get out of the fuckin' car.'

Bo Cantrell stood outside the car and pointed a big handgun inside the car.

Chapter 48

Frank, Dwayne, Chuck, and Chico sat on a couch in Bo
Cantrell's large living room facing a massive flat screen television on the opposite wall. A cable sports channel ran replays
from the football games the day before; the volume was muted.
Bo was not. He cursed each time his botched plays were
shown, and they were shown over and over again. He pointed
the gun at the screen.

'That fuckin' play, it wasn't my fuckin' fault. The fuckin'
strong safety, he's gotta help over the fuckin' top. But I fuckin'
got blamed.'

'Limited vocabulary,' Dwayne whispered.

'Linebacker,' Chuck whispered.

Cable sports ran 24/7 these days; problem was, there wasn't
enough sports action to fill all that airtime. So the highlight
and lowlight reels ran in loops. If you missed the recap of your
team's game, it would run again in ten minutes. The Wranglers' recap had run a dozen or more times over the two hours
since Bo Cantrell had abducted them at gunpoint. He paced
back and forth in front of the screen. He held the big gun in

one hand and a whiskey bottle in the other. Dwayne was thinking.

'Jack Daniels Tennessee Honey,' he whispered.

'We're gonna die,' Chuck whispered.

'Yep. Wouldn't mind a shot of JD before we do.'

'Why'd you say that?'

'It's good stuff.'

'No. That we're gonna die.'

'Oh. Just agreeing with you.'

'Well, don't.'

Bo shot the TV.

'Shit!' Chico said.

'Look, TV still works,' Chuck said. 'What brand is that, Bo?'

'Shut up!'

'Just asking. Say, Bo, would you sign my football?'

Chuck had brought the Wranglers souvenir football in with him.

'Shut the fuck up! I'm trying to think!'

'Do you have a hard time thinking, too? From concussions? I had ten concussions in college, one in peewee.'

'When you was a kid?'

'No. When I was a referee.'

Bo shot the ceiling.

'Shut up!'

'I gotta pee,' Chuck said.

'You gonna die!'

Bo paced again.

'You know,' Dwayne said, 'I'm never really gonna move to Panama or Ecuador or none of those places.'

'Why not?'

''Cause you guys are all I've got. I've never had a real family.'

Chuck leaned into him.

'Buddy hug.'

He gave Dwayne a hug. Dwayne whispered.

'We could attack Bo, maybe Frank and Chico could get away.'

'Or they could attack Bo and we could get away.'

'We're bigger than them.'

'They might be quicker.'

'We gotta man up, Chuck.'

'You sure?'

Dwayne sighed. 'Yeah, I'm sure.' He shrugged. 'Hell, we all gotta die sometime.'

'But do we gotta die tonight?'

'You goddamn right you gonna die,' Bo Cantrell said.

'You're going to kill us, too, Bo?' Frank said. 'Like you killed Dee Dee Dunston?'

Chapter 49

Dee Dee Dunston stood at the long bar in the Dizzy Rooster. She was pretty drunk. A meaty hand clamped down on her arm.

'Let's dance, Dee Dee.'

She turned and came face to face with Bo Cantrell. He had a dark face, dark eyes, and a dark mood. He was ugly, and he stunk. She recoiled from his body odor.

'Did you shower after the game, Bo? It is Saturday night.'

She yanked her arm free and turned her back on him. Bo expressed his displeasure in his typical vocabulary.

'Fuck you, Dee Dee.'

'In your dreams, asshole,' she said over her shoulder.

Dee Dee ordered another beer. A big hand grabbed her arm again; she whirled around to tell Bo Cantrell off, but she found herself staring into the bluest eyes she had ever seen.

Her knees felt wobbly.

She had grown up on a ranch, which offered little in the way of a social life. When she arrived in Lubbock, she found boys and girls gone wild. Most were from the country, the first time off the ranches and farms and ready to kick loose. Dance. Drink. Screw. God, everyone was screwing like rabbits! Dee Dee Dunston's virginity lasted exactly one week on the college campus. She loved sex. Private sex. Public sex. Wild sex. Sex. Anytime. Anywhere. But only with athletes. Star athletes. Like the one with the blue eyes standing before her.

'Hello, honey. I'm William Tucker.'

She gave him her sexiest look and said, 'I'm Dee Dee.'

But he turned to the bartender to order a drink. The tramp behind the bar was wearing a red silky corset and garter belt and black stockings; she gave him a come-hither look and cooed, 'Hi, William.' Dee Dee now felt the heat of jealously wash over her lithe body. She fought the urge to strangle the bitch. No one was taking William Tucker from her. She saw his cell phone in his shirt pocket; she took the phone and input her phone number. Then she went to camera mode and held the phone out and snapped a sexy selfie. He turned back to her. She slid his phone back into his pocket.

'I put my number and photo on your phone. So you don't forget me.'

He had a blank look on his face.

'What's your name again?'

The bartender bitch heard and giggled. Dee Dee gave her a look like she wanted to kill her. In fact, she did. But she smiled at William Tucker.

'Dee Dee.'

'Oh, yeah.'

'Here's your beer, William,' the bartender-bitch-whore said.

When William turned her way for the beer, she gave Dee Dee a snotty little look. Dee Dee's fists clenched; the bartender-bitch-whore didn't know that Dee Dee Dunston had castrated calves. She wasn't going to let some city slut steal her bull. So she grabbed William Tucker's shirt and yanked him back to her. She jumped up and wrapped her arms around his neck and her legs around his waist and gave him a long, wet kiss. He needed no further invitation. His hands cupped her firm butt, and she sat suspended in air. He smelled fresh and manly, and she wanted him desperately. Dee Dee opened one eye to check on the bitch behind the bar; she just smiled and shook her head and walked off.

'Jesus, get a room,' Cissy said from behind them.

Without unlocking his lips from hers, William carried her down a short hall past the restrooms and to a dark recess by the back door of the bar. He wedged her against the wall then slid his hand up under her Spandex shorts and around her bottom and between her legs. His fingers found her vagina; he slid one finger up inside her and she gasped and the heat now consumed her. She needed him inside her. She reached down to his waist and pushed her hand down inside his jeans until she found him. Oh, God, he was ready. He wanted her as much as she wanted him.

'Fuck me, William,' she whispered.

She heard drunken male voices and laughter behind them.

'Coeds in heat.'

'Man, get a video of this. That's William Tucker. We'll put this on YouTube, get a million hits.'

William obviously heard them too because he reached over and opened the back door, and she was suddenly hit by the cool night air. He lifted her with his other hand, but she still had one hand inside his jeans; she started to fall backwards so she grabbed his arm with her free hand. He jerked.

'Shit, my stitches.'

His left arm was bandaged. She hung on to his shirt as he stepped them outside. But either her grabbing his injured arm or the sudden change of temperature cooled his desire – and his erection. Must work like cold water. He lowered her to the ground. But she knew how to ramp up his desire again. She unzipped his jeans and released him and then squatted down and put him in her mouth. Guys went crazy when she did that.

'Hold on, honey,' William said. 'I left my beer inside. I'll be right back.'

He turned and zipped up and walked back inside the bar without so much as a 'Thank you, ma'am.' She started to get mad, but the heat was all over her.

'Hurry back,' she said.

She pushed her tight shorts down and stepped out of them. No sense making him fight his way through Spandex. Damn, where is he? She decided she'd better keep her body revving, so she leaned back against the brick wall of the building and slid her hand down between her legs. She knew how to please herself, something she often had to do with cowboys in Lubbock. She felt herself building to an orgasm when she heard footsteps coming close and saw his massive body in the shadows.

'You're just in time.'

Her words came out breathless, but who could talk at a time like this? She wanted to scream.

'Come on, William, fuck me.'

The next thing she knew, her face burned like fire from a big hand slapping her. She stumbled back and tasted her own blood, but she managed to stay on her feet.

'You fuckin' bitch! You want to get fucked, I'll fuck you.'

She knew that voice and that stink.

'Bo Cantrell!'

He stepped into the vague light, and she saw his angry, ugly face. He unzipped his pants and pulled himself out.

'Shit, I better use a rubber, way you're fuckin' every swinging dick in Texas. You might give me a disease.'

He tore open a condom packet and rolled the condom onto his erect penis. He had her boxed into a corner in the back alley. She couldn't run. But she could fight. Dee Dee Dunston had fought bulls and broncos and cowboys. She could sure as hell fight a coon-ass from the swamps. She spit blood and grabbed the nearest hard object – a small brick – and stepped toward Bo and swung the brick up and against his head as hard as she could. He groaned and stumbled back, and she bolted past him, but he grabbed her hair and yanked her back and flung her against the wall. He hit her again, this time a punch to her face, and her head slammed hard against the brick wall, and she felt her legs buckle. She fought to stay on her feet, and to think clearly, but her mind seemed hazy and his voice distant, and she felt his hand grasp her neck and his knee push her legs apart and then his stink suffocated her and pain enveloped her body as he rammed himself up inside her. He pushed his big body hard against her and her head pounded against the brick wall and she felt the air come out of her and now she gasped for air but his hand around her neck tightened with each thrust and she wanted to fight and she flung her arms at him but they seemed limp and had no effect and he thrust into her harder and harder and each time he drove her into the wall and he grunted like a feral hog rutting and Dee Dee Dunston closed her eyes to the pain and felt herself drifting off somewhere else and then she thought of her mom and dad and sister and she . . .

Chapter 50

'I didn't mean to kill her! She just fell to the ground. She was fuckin' dead!'

Bo Cantrell seemed utterly distraught. But he was also utterly drunk and heavily armed.

'Did you see William?' Frank asked.

'I saw them go outside, then he came back in for a beer but he puked, so some of his boys said they'd take him home. So I went out back.'

'You killed her, Bo. You've got to answer for that.'

'The hell I do! It was a fuckin' accident.'

'It was rape. And murder. You're going to prison, Bo.'

'Fuck you.'

He aimed his dark eyes and the big gun at Frank.

'I didn't mean to kill her!'

He really didn't. Things got out of hand, is all. He was still raging on the 'roids from the game. He always injected a big dose a few hours before a game, still did, so he'd be mean, real mean. He knew mean. He lived mean from birth. He sucked the teat of mean. Life in the backwoods of Louisiana is mean. It's a mean place inhabited by mean men. His daddy prided himself on being the meanest son of a bitch in Beauregard Parish and he sure as hell was, at least to his boys, drinking home brew and beating the hell out of Bo and his younger brothers damn near every day, to make them tougher, he said, otherwise they wouldn't amount to a hill of fucking beans and would end up in the state penitentiary just as he had on several occasions. So by the time Bo Cantrell left the swamps, he was damn mean.

But the 'roids took him to a new and exciting level of mean. Out of fucking body mean. Mean that took full control of his body. Mean that made him one of the best linebackers in the country. He played with a mean rage. On a football field, that was a real good thing; off the field, it often resulted in run-ins with the law. People think you can just flip a switch – 'mean' to 'not mean' – but it doesn't work that way. It's not on/off. It's more like one of those dimmer switches. It takes time for the mean to retreat. And the mean had made no retreat that night when he saw Dee Dee the stuck-up whore coming on to the UT players like a bitch in heat. The mean took control of his mind and body in that bar.

It was the mean that punched Dee Dee in the face. It was the mean that forced itself on her. It was the mean that choked her. When Bo had seen what the mean had done to her, he ran two blocks away and threw up. He went back to his hotel and cleaned up, sure the cops would bang on his door any moment. But they didn't. They never came. A week passed, then a month, then a year. No cops. No arrest. No prison. They said her murder was a cold case.

Bo was home free. And he meant to stay free. He couldn't give it all up now. He wouldn't give it up. The house, the vehicles, the stuff – he had amounted to something, sure as hell. He was a hero back in Beauregard Parish. How could he go home a murderer? How could he face the hometown folks and his drunk father? Course, he wouldn't go home. He would go to prison. How could he do that? How could he prove his daddy right after all these years? What if they gave him the death penalty? How could he let his drunk son of a bitch daddy sit on the other side of the glass when they stuck that needle in Bo and see him laugh and say, 'I told you, boy, ain't never gonna amount to a hill of fuckin' beans.'

He could not.

There was only one thing to do.

'Do it!' Frank said. 'Go ahead, Bo, kill us. But it won't be an accident like Dee Dee. Now you'll just be a killer. A mean son of a bitch. Like your daddy.'

Bo's face was clenched and red, his finger tight on the trigger . . . Frank waited for the gun to discharge and a bullet to slam into his chest . . . Bo's hand trembled, then shook as if the gun were too heavy to hold . . . and he took a step toward Frank.

'I'm not mean! I'm not like my daddy!'

Bo Cantrell swung the gun up, put the barrel to his own head, and pulled the trigger. He collapsed to the floor. They jumped up from the couch.

'Shit!' Chuck screamed. Then he smiled. 'Hey, we didn't die.'

He turned to Dwayne.

'Chest bump.'

'I don't think so.'

Dwayne stepped to Bo's body on the floor. One side of his head was gone, and blood oozed onto the carpet. Dwayne kicked the gun away just in case dead men could shoot.

'Three-fifty-seven Magnum,' he said. 'Makes a mess.'

Chico stood over the body and made the sign of the cross.

'For him?' Chuck said.

'He was still a child of God.'

'A mean, crazy, raping, and killing child of God.'

'True. And his soul will burn for eternity in hell for his sins.'

'That sucks. Least we're still alive.'

The four men stood over the body of Bo Cantrell, another victim in this tragedy called life.

'He confessed,' Dwayne said.

'But he can't testify,' Frank said.

'We can.'

'Our testimony won't save William,' Frank said. 'I'm his father and you're my friends.'

Chico held up William's cell phone. 'This'll save him.'

'His phone?' Frank said.

'I videotaped his confession.'

'You can videotape on a cell phone?' Frank said.

'Man, you've got to get off that beach more.'

Chico played the video. He had caught it all. Frank checked his watch.

'It's seven. He pleads at nine. How can we get that confession to the court?'

'Starbucks,' Chico said.

'We got no time for frappuccinos.'

'They got wireless. I can email this video to Billie Jean. She can take it to court, show the judge. Case closed.'

Chuck grunted. 'Not bad for four drunks.'

353

Chapter 51

They called 911. Dwayne waited for the cops at Bo's house. Chico found the nearest Starbucks on the phone, and at seven-thirty Frank pulled the rental car into the parking lot of the coffee shop. They got out and ran inside. Chico fiddled with the phone.

'I'm in. I'm connected to the Net. What's her email address?'

'How should I know?' Frank said.

'You're sleeping with her.'

'You know about that?'

'We're drunks, not blind. We need her email address.'

'Hand me the phone.'

He called Billie Jean's number.

Billie Jean Crawford sat in her candy apple red convertible Mustang on Interstate 35, the north-south thoroughfare that bisected Austin. She had been sitting right there for the last thirty minutes. Rush-hour traffic was always bumper-to-bumper, but seldom at a standstill. The radio said there was a multicar accident at Fifteenth Street. She was at Forty-sixth. She was driving to the courthouse to witness an American tragedy: an innocent man pleading guilty. Unless his father saved him. Her phone rang. She checked the caller ID: Frank. Last time he had called, he was flying to Omaha to find Bo Cantrell. She answered.

'Did you find Bo?'

'We did.'

'Did he confess?'

'He did. Then he killed himself.'

Frank filled her in on that morning's events.

'And Chico got it all on tape?'

'He did.'

'We've got to get that tape to the court.'

'We're in Omaha. You've got to get it to the court.'

'Email the video to me, I'll watch it on my iPad.'

'You can do that from your car?'

'Frank, you've got to get off that . . . yes, you can.'

She gave Frank her email address.

'Have Chico email it. I'll call you back after I watch it.'

Frank disconnected. She flipped the cover on the iPad and waited. Her heart pounded as if she had just run her five-mile loop around the lake.

William Tucker is innocent. And his father could prove it.

She was happy for William, perhaps happier for Frank. Now he could move forward with his life. Maybe with her.

The iPad pinged. An email had arrived. She opened the email and then the video file. She called Frank back.

Frank answered. 'Did you get it?'

'Got it. Watching it now.'

'Watch the traffic.'

'We're at a dead stop. Accident up ahead.'

355

She didn't speak for a few minutes, but Frank could hear Bo's voice and then a gunshot. Then he heard Billie Jean's voice.

'Ouch. That'll leave a mark.'

'Billie Jean, get that video to the court.'

Billie Jean disconnected and checked the clock on the dash. 8:07. She was sitting on I-35 at Forty-sixth Street. The court convened at nine on Eleventh Street. Not good. She pulled out her cell phone and called the jail. When the desk clerk answered, she identified herself and asked to speak to William.

'It's an emergency. I'm his lawyer.'

'No can do,' the clerk said.

'Why not?'

'A, according to our records, you're not his lawyer. Scotty Raines is. And B, they're transporting William Tucker to the Justice Center right now.'

The desk clerk hung up without saying goodbye.

'And C, you're an asshole!' Billie Jean screamed at the phone.

William Tucker waddled down the long underground corridor leading from the jail to the Justice Center. His hands and feet were shackled in chains. Two deputies escorted him, one on either side grasping his arms. He could not stop the tears rolling down his face.

'Dead man walking,' one deputy said.

They shared a laugh.

Travis County District Attorney Dick Dorkin gazed out the window of his first-floor office in the Justice Center. The media circus was setting up on the plaza outside. Soon all those cameras would be focused on him. Every cable sports channel in America, where the voters lived. He would take a big step that day to living in the Governor's Mansion.

356

He exited his office and walked to the elevator bank. He took an elevator to the third floor and walked down the corridor to Judge Rooney's courtroom. He entered as if he owned the place. He walked through the bar and shook hands with Scotty Raines standing there. The bailiff led them into the judge's chambers.

The numbers on the dash clock glowed red: 8:14. Billie Jean dialed the judge's office and got his court coordinator.

'This is Billie Jean Crawford. I need to talk to the judge.'

'He's with the district attorney and Mr. Raines.'

'Put me through.'

The coordinator laughed. 'You're a PD, and you want me to interrupt the judge? I don't think so.'

'I'm instructing you to tell the judge not to let William Tucker plead.'

'A, I don't work for you. B, you're not his lawyer. And C—'

'You're an idiot! William Tucker is innocent!'

'I thought he was pleading guilty today?'

'His father found the killer!'

'Where?'

'In Omaha.'

'Omaha? What's he doing in Omaha?'

'What? How the hell do I know?'

'Did the police arrest him?'

'He's dead.'

'Dead men can't testify.'

'We have it on tape.'

'Then his lawyer needs to bring that tape to the judge.'

'That's what I'm trying to do!'

'You're not his lawyer.'

She hung up on Billie Jean, and Billie Jean screamed.

'Everyone's an asshole!'

*

Chapter 52

The cops had arrived at Bo's house by the time Frank, Chico, and Chuck returned from the Starbucks. Frank dialed Billie Jean's number. She answered. It was 8:24.

'Are you at the court?'

'No. I'm still stuck in traffic.'

'Where?'

'Forty-sixth Street. Airport Boulevard is the next exit.'

'Exit.'

'The feeder road's backed up with traffic, too, everyone trying to get around the accident. Ten-car pileup.'

'Billie Jean, get off the highway.'

Billie Jean put her blinker on and motioned to the Mercedes Benz on her right that she needed to get over. The driver looked up from his texting and gave her the finger.

'Asshole!'

'Me?' Frank said.

'That driver.'

The car in front of Billie Jean abruptly cut in front of the car on the left, and the asshole on her right was texting again, so she turned the wheel hard and cut in front of him. He looked up and hit his horn, but his car cost ten times what hers cost, so he could do nothing except stick his middle finger in the air. She returned the favor and drove onto the shoulder of the highway.

'Frank, I'm off the highway.'

'You've got to get that video to the court.'

'The traffic is blocked in all directions. It's thirty-five blocks south and twelve blocks west on Eleventh. That's over three miles.'

'I'll call the court, try to stall the hearing.'

'What do you want me to do?'

'Run.'

They went inside and found Dwayne handcuffed.

'Hey, he's a cop,' Chuck said. 'Well, an ex-cop.'

'Who are you?'

'An ex-coach.'

The cop turned to Frank.

'And you?'

'Ex-lawyer.'

Now to Chico.

'Ex-con.'

'Any of you guys know my ex-wife?' The cop laughed. 'You guys look like the sequel to *Red*.'

'I love that show,' Chuck said. 'Can you believe Mary-Louise Parker is forty-eight?'

'You're shittin' me?'

'Nope.'

'I gotta watch that movie again.'

'Watch this movie,' Chico said.

He played the video for the cop.

'Son of a bitch! Bo Cantrell.'

At 8:32, Frank called the judge. His court coordinator answered.

'He's innocent. We have a videotaped confession. The killer shot himself.'

'Tell his lawyer.'

'I am his lawyer.'

'Scotty Raines is his lawyer. Call him.'

'What's his number?'

Scotty Raines was standing outside the courtroom with Warren the agent.

'You represent a lot of athletes in trouble with the law?'

'That's redundant.'

'What is?'

'To represent athletes means to represent athletes in trouble with the law.'

Warren's cell phone pinged. He checked his text message.

'Shit, one of my clients, Hernandez, the Patriots tight end, he got indicted for murder up in Boston. Well, hell, there goes the contract extension.'

'He need a lawyer?'

Scotty's cell phone rang. He checked the number and shook his head.

'Frank Tucker.'

He rejected the call.

Her running watch read: 8:38. Billie Jean reached up under her skirt and pulled her pantyhose down; fortunately, she also wore panties. The big rig driver next to her apparently had gotten an eyeful; he hit his air horn to show his appreciation.

She gave him the finger without looking his way. She unzipped her gym bag and removed her running socks and shoes and put them on. Three-plus miles to the court. She averaged eight-minute miles. Seven-point-five miles per hour. It was now 8:43. She had seventeen minutes to run over three miles. In a skirt. She put the phone in her purse and slung the purse over her shoulder. She grabbed the iPad, got out of the car, and shut the door. No sense in locking it; it was a convertible. She looked south and took a deep breath. She ran.

Chapter 53

At 8:45, the two deputies returned to the holding cell.

'Man, you ain't stopped crying yet?'

The deputy shook his head then turned to other deputy.

'We still got fifteen minutes. That's enough time for a donut.'

They left William Tucker alone again.

Interstate 35 veered east just north of downtown, so Billie Jean decided to cut the angle. She ran southwest, a direct route to downtown. She crossed the access road and cut between the stalled traffic at Airport Boulevard. She took a shortcut through the Hancock Center parking lot and hit Red River Street. She cut through the nine-hole Hancock Golf Course – 'Shit!' – and almost got hit by a golf ball. Golfers yelled at her. She gave them a finger. It was 8:47.

Becky Tucker entered the courtroom and sat in a pew near the back. Her father had taken her into courtrooms before, but this time was different. Her brother would soon confess to a crime

363

he did not commit. She needed to be there for him. So she had driven to Austin that morning.

Billie Jean understood now. This was her role in the case. She could run. And run she would. To save William Tucker. And Frank Tucker. Her client and his father.

At 8:50, Frank called Billie Jean. When she answered, he said, 'Where are you?'

'Crossing Thirty-eighth Street.'

'Run faster.'

She ran faster. She ran through the neighborhoods north of the university then entered the campus at the law school. She cut over to San Jacinto and ran south past the football stadium where William Tucker had achieved stardom.

The deputies returned at 8:55.

'Time to face justice, stud.'

They unlocked William's shackles and led him out of the cell and down a short hall to the door leading into the court-room. William wanted to wipe his eyes but couldn't reach up with the shackles. One deputy noticed.

'Will you wipe my eyes?'

He laughed. 'When the judge sentences your ass to death row, you're gonna need to wipe your butt.'

'Death row? But my lawyer made a deal.'

'You don't know Judge Rooney.'

The deputy pushed open the door, and they entered the courtroom. Camera lights flashed. The place was packed with television cameras and photographers. It looked more like a sporting event than a courtroom. The deputies walked William over to the defense table where Scotty Raines was waiting.

'Did my dad call?'

Scotty shook his head. 'Nope.'

William sat down. He felt alone. Abandoned. Now he knew how his dad felt. When William had abandoned him.

Billie Jean dodged oncoming traffic to cross Martin Luther King Boulevard. Her phone rang. She answered.

'Where are you?'

'Just north of the Capitol.'

'You've got two minutes.'

Frank disconnected. He faced the guys.

'She's not going to make it in time. What can we do to stop the plea?'

'Call in a bomb scare,' Chico said.

'A bomb scare? At the courthouse?'

'Yeah. I did it one time from my cell. Sentencing day, I asked to call my lawyer. Instead I called the courthouse, said there was a bomb. They evacuated the place. Course, it only delayed the sentencing for one day, and the judge tacked on another year for that stunt.'

Frank shrugged. 'It's worth a try.'

He dialed the court and waited for the call to ring through. He disconnected.

'Unbelievable.'

'What?'

'I got a recording.'

'What's the world coming to?' Chico said. 'You can't even get a real person to call in a bomb scare. Call back and leave a message.'

Judge Harold Rooney prided himself on his promptness. He ran his courtroom by the book and the clock. So at precisely 9:00 A.M., he entered the courtroom.

'All rise,' the bailiff said.

Harold stepped up to the bench and sat in his chair. He opened the case file sitting on the desktop. *The State of Texas v. William Tucker.* He sighed. He had actually thought the boy might be innocent. But he wasn't. He was guilty. Just as Bradley Todd had been guilty. He thumbed through the gruesome crime scene photos of a young girl whose life had been cut short. By William Tucker.

Dee Dee Dunston deserved justice.

'Mr. District Attorney, are you ready to prosecute this case?'

Of course, Harold was well aware that the D.A. and Scotty Raines had made a deal. Dick Dorkin stood.

'Your Honor, the state and the defendant have agreed to a plea bargain which we now present for the court's approval.'

He stepped to the bench and handed a document to Harold. He already knew the particulars. William Tucker would plead guilty to negligent manslaughter in exchange for a sentence of two to five years. Out in one. No rape charge so no lifetime sex-offender status. His face wouldn't be on the state's sex-offender registry. In one year, William Tucker would again live a normal life. But Dee Dee Dunston would never live her life. That didn't seem like justice to Harold Rooney.

'I understand that the defendant has decided to change his plea of not guilty to a plea of guilty, is that correct, Mr. Raines?'

'Yes, Your Honor.'

'Mr. Tucker, in order for this court to accept your guilty plea, I am required to ask you a series of questions to allow the court to make an independent determination of your guilt and that you are entering a guilty plea voluntarily and not under any duress or promises of leniency. You do understand that while you may have made an agreement as to sentencing with the district attorney, such agreement is not binding on this court. Sentencing is within the sole discretion of this court . . .'

*

Becky's phone vibrated. She pulled it out of her pocket and checked the ID: Dad. She went outside the courtroom and answered.

'Dad?'

'You're at the courthouse, aren't you?'

'Yes.'

'I knew you'd be there for your brother.'

'Where are you?'

'Omaha.'

He explained what had happened that morning. She cried. Her brother was innocent. And Billie Jean was on her way with proof.

'Where is she? The judge is already talking to William.'

'Becky, you've got to stop the hearing. You can't let William plead guilty.'

'How?'

'Make a commotion in the courtroom.'

'But, Dad, I'm scared to—'

'It'll make a great scene in the book.'

At 9:06, Billie Jean cut through the grounds at the State Capitol. She ran around the east side and south on the Great Walk past the Confederate War monuments. She exited the grounds through the front gates and turned west on the Eleventh Street sidewalk. Only four more blocks. She darted across Eleventh at the Governor's Mansion.

'—and this court may enter any sentence permitted by the statute, up to and including the death penalty. This court is not bound by agreements, only by the law. By justice. Do you understand, Mr. Tucker?'

William nodded.

'Please speak up, Mr. Tucker, so the court reporter can transcribe your answer.'

'Yes, sir.'

Harold couldn't believe that Frank Tucker's son had actually killed the girl. He felt sure there had to be some other explanation for his blood being on the girl. But there was only one explanation: he had killed her. Raped her and strangled her. Harold Rooney could not save Dee Dee Dunston's life, and he could not save William Tucker's life. Just as he could not save his own son's life. Apparently saving lives was not his role in life. His role was to get reelected.

'Mr. Tucker, the Supreme Court ruled that a court may not accept a guilty plea from a defendant who claims innocence. Therefore, this court must elicit your testimony under oath as to the acts that constitute the crimes charged against you and this court must confirm that you are making a knowing and intelligent waiver of your constitutional rights. William Tucker, do you swear to tell the truth, the whole truth, and nothing but the truth, so help you God?'

'Yes, sir.'

'William Tucker, do you understand that by pleading guilty, you are giving up your right to trial by jury?'

Scotty Raines nudged the boy.

'Yes, sir.'

'William Tucker, do you understand that you are giving up your right to cross-examine your accusers?'

Another nudge.

'Yes, sir.'

'William Tucker, do you understand that you are giving up your privilege against self-incrimination?'

No nudge necessary now.

'Yes, sir.'

'William Tucker, did anyone coerce you into making this plea?'

'No, sir.'

'William Tucker, are you entering your plea today voluntarily and of your own free will and not under any duress?'

'Yes, sir.'

'William Tucker, on or about midnight on November 12th, 2011, and continuing into the early morning hours of November 13th, 2011, did you forcibly rape and strangle Dee Dee Dunston until she was dead?'

Billie Jean ran past the old Travis County Courthouse and entered the plaza between the jail and the Justice Center. It was 9:11.

'Shit.'

The plaza was packed with the media. Cameras and reporters waiting for William Tucker's guilty plea. Protesters shouting 'Justice for Dee Dee!' and 'Abolish football!' and 'Abortion for all!' took advantage of the opportunity to be on television. They blocked her path.

'Move! Get out of my way!'

They didn't move. They didn't get out of her way. She fought her way through.

Three stories above her, tears rolled down William Tucker's face. He turned to his lawyer; Scotty Raines nodded at him, as if trying to pull the words from him. The D.A. nodded. He glanced back at his agent; Warren nodded. Reporters and cameramen and deputies – everyone nodded. Everyone wanted William Tucker to confess to a crime he did not commit. Only one man in the world wanted him to say no: his father.

'William Tucker,' the judge said, 'are you going to answer my question? Did you rape and kill Dee Dee Dunston?'

★

Becky Tucker had returned to the courtroom. Billie Jean still hadn't arrived. She would not make it in time. So Becky took a deep breath and stood. She shouted.

'No! He did not!'

Her brother turned to her. Everyone turned to her.

'Don't do it, William!'

The judge banged his gavel. 'Young lady, take your seat. You're out of order.'

She glared at the judge. The dialogue came to her.

'No! You're out of order!'

That prompted the guards into action. They headed her way. She pointed at the D.A.

'He's out of order!'

And then at Scotty Raines.

'And he's out of order! My brother didn't rape or kill anyone!'

The guards grabbed her and lifted her off her feet and carried her out of the pew and to the doors. She grabbed hold of the doorjamb. The scene was almost over. Only time for a few more lines of dialogue.

'William, believe in yourself! Believe in the truth! Believe in our father!'

The guards forced her fingers free and pulled her out of the courtroom. But she heard her brother's words.

'Becky . . . I'm sorry.'

Chapter 54

Billie Jean pushed her way to the front doors. The guard stopped her but then recognized her and let her pass. She ran to the metal detectors. She tossed her purse at the guard manning the detectors and ran through with the iPad.

'Don't you want your stuff?' the guard yelled from behind.

She ran to the stairs. Judge Rooney's courtroom was on the third floor.

'Mr. Tucker, please answer the question. Did you rape and kill Dee Dee Dunston?'

At that moment, William Tucker finally understood the justice system. Not the system in which he was a defendant standing in a court of law surrounded by lawyers – a defense lawyer who played with people's lives as if he were a football coach drawing up plays on a chalkboard, a district attorney concerned not about justice but ambition and jealousy, and a judge who had to show the voters he was tough on crime in order to win reelection – and spectators who viewed a criminal trial as a reality show and reporters who loved scandal and cameras that captured the moment for cable news. In that system he was innocent but about to plead guilty. There was no understanding that system.

He understood the other justice system, the one called life. That justice system had accused, tried, and convicted William Tucker. Because he was guilty as sin. He was an arrogant, egotistical, self-centered star jock. A jerk. A lousy human being. A lousy teammate, friend, brother, and son. Especially son. Life had given William Tucker what the gangbanger next door had wanted most in life: a father. Not a biological father, but a real father. A great father. A father who had always been there for him. A father who stood by him when the world had turned against William Tucker. A father who loved him more than life itself. But he had treated his father like a fan wanting an autographed football. He didn't have time for his own father.

Now life had come down hard on William Tucker. Life had rendered its verdict, and it was harsh. He had to be punished – how can life be just if the guilty are not punished? He was a bad son. He was guilty as sin, and he had to pay for his sins. He understood life now, so he accepted his punishment. It was his destiny. He stood tall and faced the judge.

'Yes, Your Honor, I am—'

'Innocent!'

William whirled around to see Billie Jean burst through the courtroom doors holding an iPad high.

Epilogue

It was Christmas Day on the beach. Lights were strung on the bungalow, and Dwayne, Chico, and Chuck wore red Santa caps. Dwayne smoked a cigar, Chico a joint, and Chuck a turkey. They played poker and drank eggnog. And Jack Daniels Tennessee Honey.

'Belize,' Dwayne said.

Chuck and Chico groaned. But they were happy. William Tucker had signed footballs for each of them. Chuck carried his with him always; Chico put his on eBay and made $10,000. But somehow it seemed less exciting when it was a lawful transaction.

Billie Jean Crawford, her daughter, Bobbie Jo, and Becky Tucker played with Rusty on the beach. Billie Jean had finally found her Prince Charming, a broken-down, recovering-drunk, beach-bum lawyer who didn't think he was a Prince Charming. Life had stomped all the bullshit out of him, and he was a better man for it. A good man. All the man she needed.

★

Becky Tucker flung the Frisbee down the beach for Rusty. She had finished her novel. It wasn't a tragedy after all. She gazed out to sea at the hero of her story.

Frank Tucker stood in knee-deep water in the Gulf of Mexico. He stared at the newspaper photo of Sarah Barnes, the photo he had carried with him always and the image that had haunted him for six years.

'I'm so sorry, Sarah. I pray you're in heaven. But I have to let you go now. I hope you can find a way to forgive me.'

He laid the photo on the water and watched the tide carry Sarah out to sea. He wiped tears from his face then cast his line. Only two kinds of men find their way to Rockport, Texas: fishermen and losers. As the sun set beyond the Gulf of Mexico, Frank Tucker stood in the surf and fished. With his family on the beach and his son next to him. His son stood six feet five inches tall and weighed two hundred thirty-five pounds, but to his father he would always be that twelve-year-old boy who thought his dad was—

'You're the best dad in the whole world.'

And he would be the best son in the whole world. Frank Tucker deserved such a son. William Tucker had been granted a last-minute reprieve by life. A second chance at life. Because of his father. His father had saved his life. He turned to his dad and held up an open hand.

They high-fived.